THE RAINBOW

REVOLUTION

*A Russian nuclear colossus, a corrupt state president
and a desperate struggle to save a failing country*

M L SMITH

KNIGHTS PUBLISHING
AUCKLAND

First paperback edition, Knights Publishing, 2020.
First online edition, Knights Publishing, 2020.

ISBN: 978-0-473-53992-4 (ePub)
ISBN: 978-0-473-53993-1 (Kindle)
ISBN: 978-0-473-53994-8 (iBook)

Designed by Michael Smith
Typeset in Aviner, Charter
Cover Design Jo Petzer

Website: ml-smith.com

Printed in New Zealand

Knights Publishing
27 Mariner Drive
Auckland, New Zealand

AUTHOR'S NOTE

I became a South African citizen immediately before the first democratic elections in 1994. Like many of the newly empowered nation I wanted to cast my ballot at this watershed moment that promised to send the country forward on a new and exciting path. After many years of Nationalist government the spectre of apartheid was finally banished.

Nelson Mandela, after 27 years of incarceration, was voted the first democratic president leading a powerfully enfranchised African National Congress: he seemed not to harbour any grudge for his imprisonment. These were heady times and many had high hopes of seeing Mandela's vision of a Rainbow Nation forged into existence with all races pulling together in true partnership. Alas he did not live to see his vision brought to fruition. Instead, over the years, a cancer of corruption crept into the party leadership finally reaching its zenith under President Jacob Zuma. The country seemed destined for eventual meltdown like so many of its peers on the continent.

A mood of quiet desperation grew amongst the thinkers of South African civil society. There was clearly no change that would be brought about through the ballot box and the rhetoric from far right elements could and would go nowhere. I started thinking about writing a novel woven into this fabric. I wanted to capture the politics of the time and reflect the desperate state that many believed the country had descended to. A broad-based military intervention to bring about the change I wanted to portray, was the vehicle I chose for the novel. The Rainbow Revolution had its genesis.

M L Smith
Cape Town
May 2018

PROLOGUE

NO. 1 MILITARY HOSPITAL PRETORIA

Intensive Care Unit

October 1987

Death stalked the ICU ward continuously seeking out those where the pulse of life beat weakly and too often claimed its prize.

One-Military hospital in Pretoria is a proud institution dedicated to healing the war-ravaged soldier. Such a war raged in Angola on the western flank of South Africa. In the neighbouring country the pick of South Africa's young men were heavily engaged in an attempt to stem the perceived spread of communism. The military hospital was overworked and the intensive care unit fought its own battles losing too many for comfort.

Colonel Stander followed the nurse in her starched uniform. He was sick to his stomach. One of his finest fought for his life in the ICU. He realised the irony of the cameo;

the nurse in front dedicated to saving men, he the career soldier, was trained to deny her the chance. War fed both sides of the equation impartially.

Her rubber-soled shoes screeched on the polished floor, his military heels clicked out a rhythm, the combination creating a hauntingly musical beat. They closed the distance to the private ward where Stander's man, the pick of his elite, hung onto life by a thread. A thread which could part at any moment — another skirmish would be lost to the enemy.

They approached the observation window where a sad tableau seemed frozen in time. A tall man clad in bush khakis had hands clamped to the handles of a wheelchair. He stared fixedly ahead as did the woman cocooned in the wheelchair.

The nurse smiled self-consciously and retreated sheep-like, glad to be away. Stander cleared his throat softly. The man before him turned deliberately, the motion laboured as if it hurt. The woman remained perfectly still.

He extended a hand. 'Colonel Stander, Reconnaissance. Pieter's commanding officer. You must be his father?'

'Armand Rossouw,' the man's voice was wooden; their handshake, the briefest gesture, barely satisfied the formality of greeting.

Stander, embarrassed by the failure, forced himself to look away and into the aseptic environment beyond the glass barrier. A motionless form lay in the tilted bed. Little more than a pupa encased in wrinkle-free sheets and endless gauze swaddling. A ventilator tube snaked away to its electronic brain; mechanical breathing came tenuous and shallow and polymer arteries fed medical cocktails from deflated plastic breasts at the bedside. Sentinel over all at the back of the room, an electrocardiograph flicked out its trace in pale neon.

'I'm going to ask in advance you forgive me for intruding on your vigil. I know your present anguish is beyond anything I can comprehend.' Stander retained his military bearing with increasing difficulty, unable to keep the quaver from his voice. Deep inside part of him agonised. He glanced once more at the inert figure.

'The man in there, your son, is the bravest heart I have ever known. It is an honour to serve with him, grieves me to see him this way. He is a man in a million. You have occasion to be very proud: showing no regard for his wellbeing he put himself in mortal danger, saved the lives of four of his comrades and went on to lead his troop and overrun an enemy position. He gained a victory the army had given up on. An action responsible for shifting the impetus of the conflict. It enabled squads of our finest fighting men to break out of badly compromised positions. Turned the tide of battle. He is a true hero: I will be putting him forward for a decoration worthy of his action.'

His voice finally faltered. He collected himself unsteadily.

'Please know I shall be praying for Pieter every day until he is fully recovered. May God be with you and your wife. And may God lift your son up in his hour of need.'

He turned on his heel and clicked away. The grieving couple continued to stare hypnotically into the room that entombed their flesh and blood.

Three Weeks Later

'How is he, doctor?'

The man fiddled with the stethoscope around his neck marshalling his thoughts.

'Out of danger on every front. Permanent brain damage at first seemed to be almost inevitable. Shrapnel lodged under the right temporal lobe usually guarantees that. However, there appears to be no structural injury. So his mental faculties seem unimpaired. We've done CT scans. No evidence of residual bruising or bleeding; he displays no spatial disorientation; no impairment to smell or taste; no memory loss. In short no evidence suggesting physiological damage or ability in cognitive function.'

'So we can anticipate a full recovery — he'll be back to normal?' Stander realised almost immediately that it sounded as if his only concern was the restoration of a military asset — 'given a fairly lengthy recuperation of course,' he finished awkwardly. An attempt to rescue the impression.

The medical man fidgeted. 'Well, we're on a bit of shaky ground there. We're not sure where normal is with Mr Rossouw.'

The Colonel regarded him under hooded brows. 'Please explain.'

'As I mentioned, there is no amnesia. Quite the reverse. Pieter can recall all the events during his encounter in remarkable detail. When he describes the demise of those he killed in the firefight, he displays absolutely no emotional connect whatsoever. It's as if he is describing a chess game; the number of his opponent's pieces taken. That's not normal, there should be trauma at some level.'

'He's a highly trained special forces soldier, doctor.'

'Oh, I'm aware of that. We get them through here all the time, Colonel.' He smiled indulgently. 'If I might expand?' He chewed his lip thoughtfully. 'Pieter, in his own eyes, kills with justification because he is trained to take the life of an enemy. I suspect however it would be the same if somebody shot his dog. If such an action transcended a set of rules he lived by, he could easily exact a response which might go way beyond what most of us would consider reasonable, or indeed lawful.'

'You mean like killing the perpetrator?'

'That's exactly what I mean.'

The Colonel reflected for a moment. 'You think then the shrapnel removed from his brain caused some impairment to his emotional capacity?'

'Far from it. If such were the case, we'd be seeing associated behavioural abnormalities.'

'I'm not sure I'm following.' Colonel Stander fidgeted irritably. 'He's showing some psychological abnormality after suffering trauma to the brain, but his condition is not related to the trauma?'

The doctor looked sheepish. 'That pretty much sums it up, Colonel. It's not my area of speciality however, so I'm referring him to a clinical psychologist for further evaluation.'

Eight Weeks Later

Colonel Stander sat at the other side of the psychologist's desk listening carefully.

'*Alexithymia* is a personality construct characterised by an inability to identify and relate to feelings in the self. The core marker is dysfunction in emotional awareness, social attachment, interpersonal relating... it's a disconnect. An inter-hemispheric transfer deficit affecting emotional information from the right hemisphere to the left hemisphere.'

'You'll have to forgive me, doctor. I'm having difficulty following this. Are we speaking about some form of mental disorder?'

'Strictly speaking, no. Statistically, the population at large has one in ten persons who could be diagnosed with some form of *Alexithymia*. Much more prevalent in men. Pieter Rossouw's is a very special type however, representing a further sub-division. Those with his condition would probably present one in half a million.'

'I'm still confused. Does this mean he doesn't have feelings like the rest of us?'

'Not at all. He certainly has feelings. Think about how some males have difficulty with a description of their feelings but no difficulty at all in identifying the fact they have them.'

'Let me understand. Are you saying in some way his condition is selective?'

'I am. That's what makes your soldier so different. When his brain identifies a threat contradicting his notion of what is right, his empathetic system is blanked out.'

'So he would experience no checks or balances in that moment?'

'Not for the person or persons he perceives as having violated his rigid code of right and wrong. For him, once such a point is reached, no transference of information passes to the part of the brain which would attach an emotional tag to it. Pieter has become judge, jury and executioner. And remember, at that point, he would feel fully justified. In his eyes the victim would deserve whatever punishment he saw fit to meet out. He would also have little personal regard for his wellbeing in exacting such retribution.'

'Do you think his condition played a significant role to produce his actions in the engagement?'

'There can be no doubt of it. As I say he would have no consideration for the lives he took nor for his own.'

'A born Manchurian candidate.'

The doctor laughed. 'From a military perspective, I suppose so. No brainwashing required to create a killing machine. Once his sense of right and wrong is triggered it's innate. There are likely to be other areas of his life where 'normal' will be compromised too.'

'Such as?'

'Because of the synaptic dissonance, it is quite possible he will have other gaps in the range of human emotion, somewhat like keys missing on a piano keyboard. My guess would be, his need for companionship, the desire to socialise could be one such area. From our sessions he appears to be lacking a pressing need to form attachments; he is not motivated by the risk-reward mechanism at play. Undoubtedly something of a loner not requiring the social connections most of us consider normal.'

'But he has strong relationships in the force. The men love him.'

'I'm not a gambling man, Colonel, but I'd be prepared to bet the men he has strong relationships with, who share the same values, have had those values tested in similar ways. If there are above one or two I'd be more than surprised.'

'Two actually.'

The doctor smiled.

Colonel Stander shook his head trying to come to grips with what he was hearing. 'Is he aware of his condition?'

'No, he's not. Which is where us medical men have a serious divide. Some believe the patient should be apprised of it, therapy embarked upon; the problem very often when that regimen is adopted is that it can lead to a deepening of the malaise, not infrequently full-blown psychosis.'

'Not a good outcome. Which camp do you fall into Doctor?'

'I think you can guess. As I've pointed out, his condition is classical *alexithymia* — more pronounced than usual. Unless it morphs into something sinister however, my view is to leave well alone. He could live a normal life without ever posing a threat to others. Of course for the military, it makes him a formidable weapon used in the appropriate situation.'

'Yes, quite.' This realisation hadn't escaped the Colonel. 'His military life aside however, you indicated his condition may predispose him to a lonelier existence than would otherwise be normal. He's still a young man. In the long term, what effect will the condition have on his overall development?'

'Probably, as I've mentioned, he will form few strong connective relationships. Those he does form will more than likely mirror himself. We've all seen individuals like Pieter. People who live on their own for much of the time crossing the bridge to society only when necessary.'

'And relationships with the opposite sex?'

'Much the same. He won't see the need to bond at an emotional level — unlike most of us. There's a correlate to the sex-drive too. He has all the chemical and physiological functioning in place but emotional attractors are rarely going to excite it.' He scratched his head. 'If I had to call it, I would say he'll stay a bachelor.'

The Colonel snorted. 'From the battlefield to the monastery.'

'Sorry to disappoint again, but unlikely too. Although his file shows him as Christian, from my observations, I would say that is a nominal tag only. He displays no belief system acknowledging a higher being, no religious commitment, no ties to a religious order.'

'You say you think he is never likely to marry?'

The doctor paused. 'For good reason. If I'm not missing the mark, sexual arousal will be infrequent, won't promote a swathe of relationships. Fewer attractors equate to diminished opportunity. I'd say the odds for a person like him entering into a life-partnership are slim. If he does, it will not be the same mechanisms at work which get most of us to the altar.'

The Colonel mulled this over. 'One last thing Doctor.'

'Yes, Colonel?'

'I don't want his condition recorded on the file.'

A frown ghosted onto the doctor's face. 'Not even in broad medical speak? Intelligible only to us professionals?'

'No mention at all,' the Colonel regarded him severely, 'and that's an order.'

Rank wasn't often pulled in the halls of the medico's.

CHAPTER 1

TO LURE A PRODIGAL

Stellenbosch September 2017

Armand Rossouw came in through the back door, bent to drop a kiss on his wife's forehead.

'How was your day, Sweetheart?' She knew he had gone to the city for a meeting tied to his political activities.

He rinsed his hands at the kitchen sink, chatting over his shoulder. 'Colin tells me the committee is worried. They think the bill just put before parliament is a Trojan horse. The increase to non-authorised expenditure a thinly veiled piece of legislation to facilitate further embezzlement. Formal accounting to the Auditor General not required. This time, however, they've gone too far. There's violent reaction on the streets. Municipal property in Port Elizabeth seized and barricaded in protest. Commercial buildings looted and burned as things got out of hand. Police went in heavy-handed, killed eleven. Similar situation in Durban; the highway blockaded and twenty trucks torched, millions up in smoke. Alarm bells are ringing. It could be the start of a meltdown.'

'These politicians think they can get away with anything,' she put the steaming dishes on the table, 'Zuma and his thugs believe they're above the law. Encouraging to see a reaction from the people at last. Sad it's so destructive. How does this affect what you're doing?'

'If the unrest escalates it would put South Africa under an international spotlight. Might even promote UN intervention. That would derail us completely. With the world looking over your shoulder, difficult to seize control of a country.'

She busied herself serving. 'So what will you do?'

'Accelerate the programme. A decision's been taken to intensify the recruiting tempo. Build numbers quickly, bring forward the launch date.'

'That will mean increased risk surely? You've often said you're amazed there hasn't been a leak as it is.'

'The risk was assessed — the planning committee believe accelerating the programme is the lesser of two evils.' He paused, a loaded fork halfway to his mouth. 'There's another consideration knocking squarely on the Rossouw door.' He looked uncomfortable.

She eyed him warily, a premonition forming.

'They're keen to recruit Pieter.'

A flicker of alarm registered. 'How would they manage that? He's thousands of miles away on his boat.'

'They want me to try to get him home.'

She regarded her husband coolly. 'Pieter won't come back to fight political corruption. It's why he left in the first place.'

'I know. But things have deteriorated considerably since. If I could sit one-on-one, could impress on him how bad it is, show him what we're doing to remedy matters...'

She cut him off. 'Well, your first challenge will be to get him home. That won't be easy. Then you'd be faced with the task of convincing him there's a chance to change things. You've bumped heads with him there before. And I'm not so sure it would be fair to him. He left because he'd grown tired of their self-serving ways.'

'I know, I know. If he could see there is a real possibility of the country failing, however, he may well want to get involved. It is his homeland after all.'

She was already running scenarios. 'What role would they want him in?' Once before they'd almost lost their eldest to military adventure. 'Non-combatant, please tell me? Pieter's not getting any younger. It's a long time since he's seen active service.'

'I said the same and asked the same question. Colin didn't commit. Just said it would be at a level way above that of the foot soldier.'

'I wonder what that means. No involvement on the ground?' Her mind steadfastly refused to visit the blood and gore of the battlefield.

'I'm not sure.' He fidgeted on his chair. 'A 'special mission' apparently. The Colonel believes Pieter has qualities which make him the perfect candidate for whatever that mission is. I tried to draw Colin on it. If he knew any more he wasn't saying.'

'I don't want our son in the firing-line again. We almost lost him once before. I should have thought you'd be like-minded.' She brushed a strand of hair from her forehead; a punctuation in the conversation. 'I don't like it at all. If he does come home, we must leave him to make his own decision without influence from either of us,' She gave him a knowing look. 'It must be his decision and his alone. If I know our son I wouldn't hold your breath — even supposing he agrees to come back to talk about it. Don't forget, he's a little miffed with you at present.'

'Just normal father-and-son stuff regarding the farm. I'll find a way past that. I've got an idea to get him here which could work. Provided always, I have your support to try.'

A passionate Afrikaner, she would sacrifice much for her land. She was also a fiercely protective mother. 'I'll sleep on it.'

CHAPTER 2

SURVIVAL AT SEA

Barbados September 2017

An encounter close and personal with a south Atlantic hurricane is not what most small-craft sailors welcome in their cruising itinerary. Piet Rossouw no exception. These phenomena further south are rare but just as deadly as their more commonplace northern cousins. What presented on the lap-top screen, filed itself somewhere in his brain under the tag 'danger — avoid'. The biggest hurricane he'd witnessed since being afloat. Its central vortex a vacant eye-socket staring at him malevolently from the screen. He wasn't happy it even chose to be in the same ocean that he sailed, notwithstanding his planned track would miss it by a fair margin. He shrugged off the uneasiness, snapped the laptop shut.

Normally he wouldn't have considered setting off across the Atlantic until the hurricane season was well and truly blown out, given unbridled choice. This time he hadn't been permitted that luxury. The phone call from home two days earlier tipped the scales: his father diagnosed with cancer, wanted him back pronto. The threat to his father's life brought a life-changing dynamic to Piet's existence. There would be no-one to run the wine estate as Rossouw senior weakened. In the Afrikaner culture that responsibility would fall squarely on the eldest son. That was Piet.

He had pressed his father to try to determine how advanced the condition was. He even offered to pull the boat onto a hardstand somewhere and fly home. The old man vacillated then, said it wasn't necessary — just urged him to get home as soon as he reasonably could. A couple of weeks extra wasn't crucial. A relief, because Piet would have had to scratch around for a marina with hardstand capacity which could haul the boat out at short notice. So it was he got busy. He managed to provision the boat quickly, purchase a couple of admiralty charts for the crossing and busy himself with taking on diesel at the fuel dock — his last action before kicking off.

He loaded the last of a dozen jerry-cans under the watchful eye of a dockside urchin clutching a makeshift fishing pole.

'You going long way, mister?' He had eyes like smoky mushrooms pushing out of leather-brown soil.

'We are,' Piet said, 'off to another place across the big sea.'

'You got missus with you?'

He laughed, realising his pronoun had misled the boy. 'No, it's just me and the boat. Us sailors always talk as if the boat is a lady.' He skirted around the youngster to untie the stern mooring, dug a note out of his shorts.

'Go buy yourself a real fishing rod,' Piet tucked the note into the lad's shirt pocket. His face lit like a beacon showing a set of teeth dazzling as bone china.

He eased into the current taking a last look back at the youngster. The picaninny hauled a small fish out of the water holding it flapping next to his face.

'We hope you have good trip mister.'

Piet laughed and gave him a farewell wave.

As he cleared the busy sea lanes and could relax a little, the true impact of going home began to register. A dying parent is a grim prospect. He'd had his differences with his father, but loved him as any good son loves a father. Yes, he'd abrogated his filial responsibility, but they were still blood. Strong Afrikaner blood. All sorts of things started going through his mind. How would his mother take her husband's eventual passing? Together forever, they were that rare couple carrying their love into the autumn of their lives. Piet had never considered the prospect of one surviving the other. Would her grief consume her once his father was gone? How would he deal with that? How would his brother, his sister take it? Was he going to be able to adjust to life ashore after having been a marine vagabond for so long? Take on the mantle of farmer again? The ocean slapped against the hulls, seemed to get in step with these thoughts. A rhythm pulsing in his skull.

On the first day out they made good progress, the boat on autopilot and looking after herself much of the time. It was easy helming. As daylight faded the sky darkened. A loom of light bloomed where Barbados slipped below the horizon. He watched it brighten as the day gradually lost its light, then wither to a death as they opened the distance into the dark ahead. An obsidian sky, a million stars jewelled on black velvet, opened up. Awed by the limitless dome, Piet experienced the familiar sense of insignificance his puny being represented; of how transient human life is. It made him think of his father. Would he fade slowly like the loom of Barbados? Or would there be a dramatic and agonising climax. A super-nova event? He gazed at the firmament. The timeless majesty put things into perspective, showed humans as motes of dust illuminated briefly in a shaft of light. The vastness also drew him, clutched him to itself somehow infused a sense of belonging as well as the one he felt of separation. He found himself a lone worshipper in a mighty cathedral. The sense of solitariness he embraced like an old friend.

His musings were nudged aside by the practical. A niggle teased the fringes of his mind. A hurricane churned out there. True, he shared a vast ocean with it but even in such vastness two was not company. He was normally fastidious when it came to meteorology on passage; always planning things in an attempt to stack the odds in his favour. Not possible this time. His misgiving wouldn't go away.

He had started monitoring the current system even before the call came from home. Barbados is right in the middle of the hurricane belt. Anything coming his way whilst he sailed there, he wanted to know all about it. This one was one of two systems that showed up on the weather application he used. The other fizzled to nothing: this one persisted. It began as a mere smudge, remaining that way for two days, a harmless cloud bank out in the deep. The third day it began to change. A circulatory trace crept in around a deepening core of low-pressure. The characteristic spiral no sailor wants to see soon formed. The die was cast by this time. He was well on his way, there could be no turning back.

Day four, the depression deepened further, core air pressure continued to plummet. It now classified as a moderate storm system. That worried him. It could go either way from there. For the first time he felt concern. Day five dawned, the US National Hurricane Centre finally took an interest. It fell to them to watch for and track, those dangerous weather systems. They gave it a Category One rating — winds to 150 kph.

Weather broadcasts over marine radio frequencies started to carry warnings for shipping in the area. How big would it get? Was he in the wrong place at the wrong time? Too late now. Only time would tell.

Two more days went by, the system continued to pull hundreds-of-thousands of tons of moist air into its maw. It still ranked as a tropical storm. Marine stations warned of extreme weather and broadcasts went out every hour now. The following day she earned herself a christening. *Matilda*. The NHC upgraded her to category four. She came of age. From tropical storm to fully fledged hurricane. She flexed her muscles generating wind speeds to 250kph. Beyond this only one ranking remained. *Matilda* was a lady with attitude. She would earn her place in the record books.

During this worrying development Piet hadn't been passive. He'd monitored her dramatic growth as she gorged her way to heavyweight, plotted a track on the chart with considerable course deviation. Naively, as it later proved, he sought to circumnavigate her rapidly expanding mass. On the new course, he threw as much sail on as he could cope with and made really good progress. *Magus* was a modern 12-metre catamaran — no slouch. She lifted her feet when he cracked the whip. Under a full press of sail, an exhilarating experience.

He rubbed his hands in childish glee picturing them skirting the edge of *Matilda*, giving her the finger as they raced away out of her evil path. A defiant escape. In his dreams!

Pushing *Magus* hard demanded a firm hand on the wheel. Thrilling for Piet to feel the vibration under his hands as pressure on the rudders surged through the linkage. A living thing he became part of, a composite with the boat ready to face all challenges. Resonating deep within himself, he even found the inherent danger exhilarating. Life capitalised itself for him in moments like this — he wouldn't have changed places with anyone on the planet.

Same with the wind. An adversary but at the same time, he became one with it. The odd powerful gust lifted spray off the ocean, hurled it in his face as *Magus* dug her nose in. That spindrift stung but the afterglow on his skin became a drug. A mariners masochism. The whole day he stayed topside keeping her under control, running down sea miles greedily. He could still visualise the narrow escape they would pull off.

Then the nature of the ocean changed. A steep chop built as the strengthening wind started to flex its muscles. They punched through the waves now as much as rode over them. On several occasions *Magus* shot off the top of one, slammed down hard on the other side and sent shocks through the hull into his legs. The boat could take it; the skipper much less comfortable. This new pattern he knew, could easily be the forerunner of something far more sinister.

Wind strength continued to build. He shortened sail progressively beginning to fear the worst. To see what this looked like on the weather plotter, he risked leaving the helm, kicked on the auto-pilot and went below. The satellite image did nothing to reassure. *Matilda* was a very different lady to the one he'd witnessed on that self-same screen early in the day. As well as being vicious she had grown into a really big girl, covering twice the ocean surface she'd occupied at his last viewing; her swirling mass, a very disturbing sight. She'd altered track too, as if sniffing out the change of course he'd made. She sat directly in their path. Far from avoiding her they were racing in for the fight.

To avoid her was now impossible — they were too close. All his smart manoeuvring came to nought. The wind continued to mount, the ocean fell in step. Some scary swells, down the face of which breaking waves danced gleefully, now lumbered in. The start of inevitably worsening conditions he knew; they were in for a tough time. The rigging wailed like a high-note on a violin string as he stripped more canvas off. A deafening maelstrom screamed at them, *Magus* down to bare poles. The anemometer registered a scary ninety knots with gusts well above that. And the worst not yet arrived. Shrieking in their face,

Matilda gave notice of what they could expect — a particularly violent blast carried the instrument off the masthead altogether. Their ability to measure wind strength now gone.

He ran both motors by that time to maintain headway. A matter of survival. He didn't have the option single-handed of trailing a sea anchor to run downwind. No-one else to launch the tackle. He seriously doubted in any event that they would survive if he left the helm on autopilot to throw the canvas cone and its coils of rope overboard himself. The strategy he questioned in any event. Running before the storm, even under bare poles with a sea anchor trailing, he doubted could slow the boat sufficiently and avoid the risk of her pitch-poling. Piet ran the image in his mind. Racing downwind with little steerage, one of the truly mountainous seas lifting the stern to send them head-over-heels to destruction. Not an option. They would take their chances with his alternate strategy.

And that was for him to keep her head-to-wind — ride the face of every massif that thundered down at them. None were smaller than an eight-storey building. Each time they climbed and, by degrees, lost momentum to a tortoise crawl near the crest. Just when it seemed they would plummet back to the depth they'd clawed out of, they struggled over, the wind banshee-like, in their face again. To ride that watery roller-coaster, canyons with bellies graveyard-still, took all his mettle. Time without number they prevailed. A truly terrifying experience every time. To face continuously, a nightmare. Any exhilaration he'd felt earlier had long since burned itself out. The struggle for survival imprinted itself on a canvas of dread, each desperate effort a brushstroke. He knew beyond doubt if he lost the helm, even for the briefest moment, they were done for. No quarter would be given. The Reaper would scythe his harvest should they slew beam-on to those malevolent seas.

An event which could occur if the steering linkage failed, or a rudder snapped off, or a motor gave in. If they finally lost forward momentum, *Magus* wouldn't steer going backwards. In an instant she would offer a hull to those ravening waves, flip like a page in a book. The deep would claim them. As it was, they barely maintained headway. The motors couldn't run indefinitely in the red zone; he fought the wheel against powerful lee-helm. *Magus* sought to defy him at every step; trying desperately to fall off the wind. A frenzied hound straining at the leash.

They balanced on a knife-edge, no margin for mishap, otherwise it was game over. Pounded to matchwood out there a million miles from everywhere. To say he never pictured death beneath thousands of tons of crushing water and amidst splintered fibreglass, would be a lie. He did. But he never let the image dwell for more than a nanosecond. He reasoned that in that mindset resides the start of real fear. Survival was the only game in town. He drew on reserves way beyond anything he believed possible.

The killer-storm raged a full twenty-four hours more. Close to his limits, he almost threw in the towel, equally certain *Magus'* Volvo Penta engines had long since passed the point where they should have given up the ghost. He waited for the axe to fall. They ran on a prayer.

Desperately tired, physically spent and losing concentration to the lure of sleep, a surge of adrenalin hit him — a lightning bolt jarring him to full awareness. The dirty-brown hulk of a capsized vessel wallowed directly ahead at the bottom of their cavernous trough. A foundered brother of the sea unfortunate like them to be caught out in that madness. He knew it was the end, braced himself for the jarring crash as they raced down on the overturned hull. And then — he couldn't believe his eyes — hallucinating he supposed, a set of massive flukes rose from the water higher than *Magus'* lower mast spreaders. It threatened to swat them dismissively like an irksome insect. In the next instant the juggernaut disappeared without a trace.

The encounter with the whale marked the turning point for them. They punched on for a while longer. The wind, almost imperceptibly at first, began to veer, lost some of its intensity. He knew then they'd make it. They were passing through one vector of the storm into another; more accurately, the storm tracked over them shouldering its way northwards. The epicentre was still far to the West. The wind shifted dramatically. Wave action began to lose its aggression, becoming a jumbled confusion. The blast dropped to a fresh gale. Swells retained their bulk for a few more hours, still demanded careful negotiating, but the chaos that had danced dangerously on their slopes was gone. He stayed at the helm for as long as he could resist falling asleep on his feet. He could eventually prevail no longer. He lashed the helm not trusting the autopilot, and staggered below, falling onto his bunk and passing out immediately.

A cloud formation appeared low on the skyline off the starboard bow five days later. It came as no surprise. Below the horizon he knew lay his destination. They skipped along under a brisk south-easter eating the sea-miles towards Cape Town harbour. The prospect of landfall, a haven on *terra firma*, sang its siren song. He gazed fondly at the familiar shoreline a while later as they closed the land. The bulk of Table Mountain wore her distinctive tablecloth. To him it seemed she disported herself in all her cloudy splendour to welcome home the prodigal.

CHAPTER 3

DMITRI IVASHCHENKOV

Ivashchenkov sat in his luxurious Sandton office suite feeling very pleased with himself. He stretched his legs, kicked off his Gucci loafers. The thick-pile carpet beneath his stockinged feet felt sensuous, adding to his sense of wellbeing. He put down the cellphone smiling to himself. The president's son, Duduzane Zuma had just confirmed the agreement between Gupta's Oakbay Resources and the Industrial Development Corporation, amended in a crucial area. The Gupta's had earlier borrowed money from the state financier to purchase its Shiva uranium mine. In the stroke of a pen, they wriggled out of repaying over two hundred and fifty-million rand in capital and interest to the IDC. The Gupta's would now be free to list the company on the Johannesburg stock exchange, satisfy the dodged liability by way of shares. A neat piece of refinancing by the miner which took the pressure off their overstretched cash flow.

Ivashchenkov had good reason to feel smug, it being his brainchild in the first place. When he suggested it to Jacob, the president immediately beamed. Zuma's son, as director and shareholder in Shiva Uranium alongside the Gupta's, would benefit handsomely when the mine started delivering raw uranium to Ivashchenkov's future enrichment facility. In a reciprocating move, the president invited Nuclatom's participation in the bid process to build six nuclear power stations for the state's energy provider, Eskom. Life was very sweet. He reached for the humidor on his desk, took out one of the cherry infused cheroots he favoured. Yes, things continued to progress very nicely. He lifted the phone. It would be sweet to get some well-deserved flattery from the beneficiary horse's mouth.

'Get me Ajay Gupta,' he instructed his secretary. He pulled deeply on the cigar and blew a smoke ring into the air. Presently the phone buzzed.

'Hello?'

'Jimmy, how are you?' The disembodied voice retained the sing-song modulation of north India.

He didn't enjoy the diminutive but let it go. 'I'm good, Ajay. Just had partner online.'

'Which one? There are many you know.'

'Dudu.'

'Aah, that partner. What has he been up to now? Not driving his Porsche over shopping mall pavements I hope.'

He chuckled at his humour. Dudu Zuma had earned his reputation as something of a spoiled playboy well known for his vehicular peccadillos.

'No. Not that. He told me about restructuring of loan with IDC.'

'Always trying to jump on the gravy boat for praise,' he misquoted. 'That young man's tongue is going to get him into trouble one of these days.'

'But good outcome. No?'

'Oh, extremely good. And all thanks to your splendid idea. I intended calling you later to tell you, but it seems my young partner has stolen my thunderclap,' he misquoted again.

'I'm sure is going to make president very happy.'

'It will. It will. He's coming for lunch tomorrow so I'll have a chance of chatting him then. And of course, it will do your cause much good.'

'If Jacob is true to word, it guarantees signature on agreement.'

'You can sleep assured your contract will now be ratified.'

'I'm happy to hear this from you, Ajay.' If this corpulent Indian businessman said Jacob Zuma would do something, it became almost a racing certainty he would do it. Ivashchenkov never ceased to be amazed at how much control the man seemed to have over the country's leader.

'I'm equally happy Jimmy,' Gupta said, 'you get your power stations, I get to sell you my uranium.'

'Perfect outcome. Looks as if are well on track.'

'What about the anti-nuclear lobbying? Not an insect in the ointment?'

'A couple of women waving placards outside parliament buildings? Is of no concern. To be on safe side my security people are looking into. Bigger worry is attention Standard and Poors show to South Africa.'

International credit rating agencies reviewed the country's credit risk continuously. Corruption in the country had become a major contributor to their ebbing confidence, resulting in two previous downgrades. The irony of his remark escaped Ivashchenkov entirely. Dubious activities such as the very one in which he starred as lead player, featured as prime considerations to the way the country's credit rating was viewed.

'Don't be worrying. Jacob will be able to put favourable spin on things, quieten down those fires. We will be fine. No danger of being downgraded to junk.'

'I hope you are right. Getting international loans for plants is going to be tough if country gets another downgrade.'

CHAPTER 4

RETURN TO VEREWIG

Piet spent two nights aboard *Magus,* moored on the visitors' berths of the Royal Cape Yacht Club on Cape Town's waterfront. Just enough time to clear Customs and Immigration, purchase an old banger from the first car dealership he came across. He paid the proprietor and gave him a healthy fee to deliver the car over the mountain. The much quieter sanctuary of Hout Bay would be home base. He would be more relaxed in a small backwater.

Next day he sailed the boat the short distance around the peninsula arriving early evening. He finally managed to locate the marina manager, secure an outer berth on one of the marina pontoons. The car was parked on the wharf. He pocketed the keys, happy in the knowledge he now had land transport.

He ate a late breakfast next morning then set off for his parent's home. A knot grew in his belly as he re-lived his desertion all those years ago, apprehensive knowing the return was occasioned only because of a dying parent. The intervening years had produced a strained relationship with his father. He had no reason to believe the forced return would do anything to loosen it. The black marks seemed to be mounting.

His journey meandered through extremes. The opulent homes of the super-wealthy eventually giving way to sprawling poverty of the shanties. Then out again into the countryside with a more rural flavour en-route to Stellenbosch. Here the softer landscapes of the wine-lands and their noble homesteads. These the vistas close to his heart. He grew up amongst them. Deep down they would always be home. Special places. He knew many of the estates first hand. Despite his misgivings, he began to experience the warm feeling of coming home.

Finally he swung the old Toyota off the tar onto the gravel road of the family farm. He almost took out a large male baboon ambling across the dirt in front of him. His scarlet rump flashed like a red traffic light as he scrambled aside. He looked reproachfully after Piet with those piercing eyes. Neither dog nor monkey.

'That won't please the Old Man..' he thought, as he dropped a gear to negotiate the slow ascent to the homestead, out of sight now from the lower reaches and nestling on upper terraces.

Baboons are commonplace in the Cape, a major curse to the wine farmers of the region. Legions of them have migrated to the lower mountain slopes, their natural habitat eroded by mans relentless urbanisation. The lure of a lush larder amongst the young fruit on the vines being the main attraction. Where one roved, not far away there would be a troop of fellow robbers.

Steadily climbing, he looked out over ranks of manicured steppes sweeping in and out of folds in the skirts of the mountain. Ancient knobbly vines studded these platforms; the lifeblood of Verewig, a sizeable wine estate by any definition. Vintage produce from these slopes had taken many prestigious awards. He rolled the name around in his mind. Verewig translated to English meant 'Forever'. He smiled sardonically. That may have seemed realistic when his antecedents carved the farm out of virgin bush amongst those foothills eight generations back, but it seemed very optimistic in today's massively changed political climate.

He thought about the Rossouw lineage. Among the oldest in the country. His family tree had its roots right back in the early days of the Cape colony. Back to the time when Jan Van Riebeeck made landfall after his epic voyage of 1652.

A rich history. Some of his forebears fought in native wars, others against the British in two so-called Boer Wars. They even sent a family member to soldier with the former 'enemy' fighting Germans in World War Two. The Rossouw's had served South African governments of every shade; the overtly paternal, the liberals, the conservatives, the oppressive — now the fully democratic.

Certainly, they had worn the mantle of colonists in the days when it wasn't a dirty word. He thought of the roots of colonisation in Africa — were it not for such pioneering spirit, the continent would today be a dark place indeed. He carried no sense of guilt for his family's part in all which had grown since. They'd experienced differences with opposing cultures along the way, but which emerging nation hadn't? The Afrikaner always endured. And helped build something to be proud of. Something to the benefit of all. Their country often drew awed admiration from first-time European visitors expecting to find an African dust-bowl. Not modern cities, infrastructure reminiscent of their own countries.

However, along the way their race made a rod for its back with the policy of apartheid. Almost the whole world turned against South Africa. Internal pressure from black African nationalism muscled its way to a voice which could no longer be denied or repressed. In South Africa a belated arrival of the winds of change Britain's Harold McMillan had spoken of many years earlier. Transformation became inevitable. Some whites resisted whilst others tried hard to embrace it. But all knew it must come. That change finally manifested in 1994. For the first time, fully democratic elections brought the African National Congress to power under the leadership of Nelson Mandela.

From a personal perspective, he could see this change of governance as his watershed. He thought everything happened far too quickly, the euphoria of the time as Mandela stepped to the plate would soon evaporate. It took some years but it did. It left a lot of people disgruntled as the fledgeling democracy started to lose direction. Being brutally honest with himself he could see it marked the birth of his nemesis. And led to his self-imposed exile eight years later. And the refuge to solitariness as an ocean nomad. A retreat into himself. An escape. Now with his return home, it seemed he would have to shoulder the yoke again, be tormented by the same old dynamics. It wasn't a comfortable fit, his stomach muscles tightened further as the demons got comfortable again.

He crested the last rise to confront the plateau on which the homestead nestled. His depressive state began to lift. An impressive panorama opened before him, the sort found on picture-postcards show-casing the fairest Cape and putting Cape Town firmly and deservedly on the travel itinerary of millions. Awesome in its majesty. He brought the car to a halt letting the engine idle to drink it all in.

In front of him stood a colonnade of Canary Island date-palms, soldiers at attention along each flank of a kilometre long driveway. At the end of the avenue a Dutch gable pushed its chest out proudly, defined the residence.

Brooding mountain sentinels towered behind framing the scene dramatically.

He glanced at the farm buildings off to one side. Recently painted an eye-searing white under contrasting slate roofs the colour of rhino-hide, the whole thing glittered like a jewel under the late morning sun. An achingly beautiful sight. Unbidden sadness washed through him. Was this noble estate eventually going to go the way of Africa, decay to a chaotic tangle of untamed vegetation?

He shrugged the thought aside, allowed the beauty to work its magic over him. Absorbed, he pictured vividly an earlier time when his brother and himself, youngsters at play, chased one another in and out of alleys between the vines. If the Old Man caught them there would be a cuffing, but this somehow heightened the sense of adventure. They revelled in it.

Another memory flashed to the fore. He could see the wooded slopes above the house as a towering wall of fiery orange leaping skyward, fanned by an eager breeze. Then, without warning turned by a capricious wind shift, the flames advanced on the homestead. These the dark chapters written into the annuls of Cape farms. Fire the constant and dreaded enemy. When it linked arms with the southerly Cape winds it became a terrifying foe. It could destroy in a day what had taken generations to build. Often the only real defence, the airborne fire service established to fight it. On that day those fearless warriors raced to Verewig to take on the enemy.

Huey helicopters underslung with massive monsoon buckets soon dumped tons of water on the conflagration. Those dare-devil pilots risked all. They flew their craft in and out of columns of thick smoke, no thought for their safety. Time and again, like bees to a hive, they dumped their liquid gold and disappeared to refill. The unsung heroes of the day, their involvement often meant the difference between devastation and salvation.

That day brought tragedy. A machine venturing too close to the blaze had its rotors seized in a fierce thermal roaring off the fire and spun out of control. The pilot was powerless, smashed into the fiery mountain and perished instantly.

Shrugging aside this dark shadow, he returned to the business at hand, began to steel himself for the meeting with his father. Would there be recriminations? How much would his illness already have withered his bulk? Assured of it being an emotional meeting, his stomach did its thing again and he barely suppressed nausea: the albatross of deserting son it seemed to him was a badge of cowardice hanging accusingly around his neck. The Rossouw estate he had abandoned is one of the largest viniculture operations in the Western Cape; running it a serious business. He had abrogated his responsibility. For him to step back to the plate was the counter he now played. His younger brother with little interest in farming, had majored in computer science at Stellenbosch University going on to pursue a career in the discipline. He did exceptionally well, eventually emigrating to Britain to accept a senior position with one of the major international players. Nowadays at the top of his game.

Piet's disillusionment had not reached full bloom at the time of his brother's going. Away with a clear conscience, and rightly so, he left Piet to mould to leadership under Afrikaner tradition. It seemed at the time things would pan out. Save for a thieving political elite muscled to power and busy on a systemic and destructive rape, things might have.

This became the bone of contention between his father and him. No died-in-the-wool Afrikaner in his heart of hearts welcomed black rule. Always present was the nagging fear it would go pear-shaped. However, a cavernous gulf existed between the attitude of the two extremes, *verkrampte and verligte*. Conservative and liberal. His father had sympathies towards the latter, he had a toe in the former. Both of them realised nonetheless, that in no way could a small white nation at the tip of Africa continue to frustrate the political aspirations of heavyweight black nationalism: in concert the rest of the world bayed at the door for change. His difference with his father — a disagreement over the right path towards change.

His father believed Mandela's Rainbow Nation, all races co-operating at every level of society, would be achieved.

Piet less sanguine. He couldn't help casting an eye northward to a basket of failed states which gave in to rampant black nationalism, to totalitarian rule. The scrap heap of Africa in his view.

He agreed to put his pessimism on the shelf for a while, stick around hoping against hope the Old Man's version would flower. He loved the land of his birth and desperately wanted to be proven wrong. But over time, he witnessed a land sliding further into the malaise he'd predicted. Corrupt leadership burgeoned. Blatantly disregarding its oaths of office it robbed the national coffers with disdain, no regard to the electorate.

Mandela's noble vision morphed into a ravening beast. A scavenger government intent on gorging. And a raft of unscrupulous corporates joined the unholy feeding frenzy ripping mercilessly at the carcass. The spectre of a gangster state had arrived.

To him, it seemed his bleak prophecy had matured, and then some. He decided the time had come to get out. He told his father he'd had enough. Rossouw senior tried reasoning with him, shaming him, finally threatening him. But nothing prevailed. Piet left under strained circumstances.

Shaking off the ghosts of history, he shifted the car back into gear, drove down the grand avenue. A major question still tormented him. Was the black sheep returning to-enter the fold? Or would he look for some sort of accommodation to satisfy the family need, leaving him free to run off again? He wasn't enjoying the dichotomy.

He parked the car and climbed the familiar steps under the colonnaded porch. As he reached the top the oak slab of the front door swung open. There stood his father. He grinned behind his neatly clipped Van Dyk beard, no hint of recrimination evident. Well over six feet, dressed as always in bush khakis, his father still cut an impressive figure. The stamp of good living showed in his ample girth. Not at all what Piet had expected considering the cancer.

'*Welkom, seun.*' Piet spread his arms. He allowed himself to be pulled into his hearty bear-hug.

'Hello, Pa.' he relaxed somewhat. They went through the usual male ritual of back-slapping and guffaws.

'Come in. Come in.' He stepped aside ushering Piet past.

Afrikaners almost universally favour dimly lighted and cool interiors. The Rossouw ancestral home fitted the mould. A lofty hallway boasted rich pleated drapes, heavy beneath a pressed-steel ceiling. It gave the interior an orthodox air. Gilt-framed portraits, in the best traditions of the *Volk*, showcased generations of Rossouws' standing sentinel around the walls. A richly hued Persian carpet covered an expanse of slate floor. Pieces of oak and yellowwood furniture appeared to have grown where they stood. Nothing had changed.

They went through to the lounge, his mother wheeling towards them. Victim to a horse-riding accident during Piet's early teenage years, she had remained confined to a wheelchair since. Despite the disability she beamed her joyous smile — always her hallmark. Too much for him, he choked with an emotion he rarely experienced. A stray tear she hadn't been able to suppress, slid down her cheek.

'What a day this is,' she rejoiced.

He bent to give her his home-coming hug. The familiar redolence of peach-blossom infused his nostrils. 'You're looking radiant, Ma,' he straightened to scrutinise her better.

If his father wore his years well, his mother shrugged hers aside with disdain. True, more grey stranded her hair than he remembered, but there was still ample evidence of fading chestnut. She wore it swept into a grip at the back of her head. The style took years off her. She had the sophisticated look most women would spend a small fortune at the hairdresser to attain.

'She still insists on a rigorous exercise routine come what may,' his father bragged on her behalf.

Ever solicitous of his mother after her accident, Piet's father spared no expense appointing the best surgeons and medical team to attend her: a desperate attempt to save her from the life of a paraplegic. But all to no avail. His mother's paralysis proved irreversible, a wheelchair became her legacy from that time on. Determined to keep her fully motivated and involved, his father moved into gear in his inimitable way. If she could no longer walk or ride she would have other activities to keep her engaged in life. He extended the house back from the lounge, the space becoming a compact gymnasium with a long and narrow exercise pool. In those days, as often as not, his mother needed to chase out three boisterous teenagers in order to give it the utility his father intended.

He dropped into one of the voluminous leather couches, resident in the family lounge for as long as he could remember. Initial greetings over, the unspoken spectre of his father's cancer hung over them. He decided to deal with it upfront. Left in the wings it would overshadow anything else they would be likely to discuss. Steeling himself he shifted awkwardly to face him.

'I must say, Pa, I thought you'd be looking gaunt or showing some signs of your condition'. A faltering start, but at least he now had it out in the open. He didn't know what reaction he could expect. It certainly wasn't the conspiratorial exchange which passed between his parents. His mother quickly regained composure, studiously busied herself with the ritual of pouring their tea.

Left to steer things, his father stepped into the breach. 'Let's have our tea, catch up on family news a bit before discussing that,' he passed the plate of *koeksisters* Piet's mother had fussed with. Unsure of what was going on, he indulged his parents anyway and took one of the sticky pastries.

'Ok, you first. How are Sarah and the kids?' he said.

His younger sister had married six years previously and moved to Pretoria, her husband a doctor in a large state hospital — not far from the military establishment where Piet had slowly regained his health. The couple had two children neither of whom he'd met. A slight whiff of the abrogating brother tainted their sibling relationship but fortunately hadn't reduced it to a point of putrefaction. Although still close enough to exchange emails, they hadn't seen one another since her wedding when he flew in on his whistle-stop visit. She often peppered her missives to him with references to 'home', by which she meant South Africa in general. Often oblique hints at the prospect of his returning. He was sure she missed him as he missed her.

They kicked about the family football for another hour or so until his mother made her excuses, said she wanted to catch the TV news in the television lounge. It left the playing field clear for his father and him to get down to the topic they'd skirted awkwardly around. Rossouw senior's illness, Piet's return. This time he didn't rush in. His father spoke first.

'*Seun*, I haven't been entirely straightforward with you.' He coughed in a contrived manner attempting to mask his awkwardness.

Oh my God, Piet thought. It's far worse than he's given me to understand.

'How bad, Pa?' he dreaded what he might hear.

His Old Man fidgeted with his beard in what Piet recognised as a reflex action he had when uncomfortable or embarrassed. 'I don't have cancer son.'

He couldn't believe his ears. One minute a dying parent, the future looks uncertain seun, the next… what? Yes, what? His mind churned in a frenzy. At a loss, the ground shifted under his feet.

'What do you mean, Pa?' he stammered, the words sounding ridiculous, inadequate even in his ears.

'I'm not sick at all son' he pressed on. 'In fact, I've rarely felt better'.

He was sure his mouth worked stupidly like a feeding goldfish. He couldn't frame any cogent response, his head spinning, his brain letting him down badly. He could make no sense of the bombshell.

'It was disingenuous of me I know,' his father limped on, 'but we didn't think anything else would bring you home.'

He shook his head in disbelief. The adrenaline coursing through his system caused his heart to hammer uncomfortably, his diaphragm to shut down not giving the slightest assistance to his respiration. Duped into coming home — for God knows what — he wasn't enjoying it.

'So I'm not back here to help Mom nurse you through a terminal illness?'

'No, nothing like it I'm happy to say.' he seemed to recognise the irony in the last part of his statement. He grinned sheepishly at his son and rushed on. 'Again son, I do apologise for the deception. If it wasn't something really important you wouldn't have been subjected to it.'

Piet looked pole-axed. His father finished trying for some middle ground. 'No, it's something far more important than my wellbeing.'

By this time the thumping in his chest had slowed to jack-hammer tempo, the screaming in his ears down to jet engine pitch. His brain also gathered the pieces, started to function again.

'Let me get this straight, Pa. You phoned me delivering an outright lie. You as much as said the doctors diagnosed cancer. Using your own words, the future looks uncertain. You allowed me to believe you'd fallen victim to a dread disease.' Piet fixed him with what he hoped radiated as a very hostile stare, but if so, he just held it, saying nothing.

He raced on. 'You gave no thought to my emotional wellbeing nor to what I went through to get back here at the drop of a hat.' Now he hammed it up without shame. 'No thought for me sailing a hostile ocean; for the inherent personal danger which almost cost me my life; for the roots I'd put down for God sakes!'

This last an outright lie, but what the hell? He'd been cruising in the Caribbean when he received the news. A backwater anchorage in Barbados had taken his fancy, he'd planned on spending a few months there before moving on. No intention of permanence, but he did look forward to exploring the island, relaxing for a while. What wasn't a lie; the fact he left before the end of the hurricane season, tempting fate and receiving his comeuppance mid-Atlantic.

'And all this for what?' he now asked himself as the deception hammered home again.

Needing a temporary respite he reached for the water jug on the table, managing to get half of what he poured into the glass.

'We needed you home, thought nothing less would get you here,' his father continued lamely.

'Why couldn't you have just told me the real reason — left the decision to me?' His father could see it really bugged Piet to be on the receiving end of an outright lie.

'Because as I've said, you wouldn't have come if I'd done so.'

'So what am I here for?' he got a grip on himself, began to calm a little, intrigued as well as annoyed. He knew it must be important to his father, no matter how pissed-off he might feel.

Piet could see the gears change as his father grabbed the welcome opening his calmer mood presented. Rossouw senior leaned forward clasping his hands between his knees, his stance purposeful.

'This country needs men such as you *seun*. It needs them now…before it's too late.'

This was a facet to his character Piet hadn't seen before. He carried the frenetic urgency of the zealot. He felt misgivings as to where this would lead. His anger just about under control, he resisted the cheap shot of asking what the hell the country's welfare had to do with him. He had distanced himself long ago. Now someone else's problem. Leave him out of it.

'Go on.' He resolved to remain calm.

Again his father shifted awkwardly finding himself blocked temporarily behind the eight-ball, but as a seasoned campaigner, he was quick to gather himself; to organise his delivery so that when he presented it it would achieve maximum impact. His problem was that he had a hostile as well as an unreceptive audience of one.

'It's about the very existence of whites in this country, son,' he started, knowing these words would be brickbats to his son's ears.

'Not that old chestnut again' he groaned inwardly as the older man pushed on.

'I'm sure you've been following our politics since you left.'

Although Piet didn't bust a gut doing so, he did keep a weather eye on mainstream news regarding South Africa.

More often than not he found it depressing, so didn't overdo it. But he still had family there. He felt it his duty to keep abreast of developments which might affect them. Even painted a picture in his mind that if the crap hit the fan resulting in a scrambled exodus, he could sail *Magus* to those troubled shores, uplift them all to safety. He supposed it was romanticism.

Now the victim of deception, he wasn't going to make this any easier for his father. The Old Man's trickery had kicked into gear his 'fight or flight' responses. On the rare occasions when he got very upset or needed to fight his way out of a corner, his body overdid the adrenalin rush. When he was in this window motor actions were initially clumsy but rapidly gave way to exaggerated calm. In that zone his mind enjoyed crystal clarity; he was able to view things with a perspective rarely experienced otherwise. It brought with it a sense of absolute control. And sometimes a ruthlessness foreign to his default state. When it presented there was no compromise. Like now.

'The whites in this country, especially the Afrikaner, are going to have to get used to the mantle of second class citizen. That's if they haven't got the smarts or the wherewithal to get out.'

He looked at Piet almost pityingly but Piet didn't care.

'Go on,' he said.

'This sense of national guilt you all seem to be suffering from isn't going to cut it. You're not somehow going to get a second bite at the cherry. You can beat your flesh with a cruelly thonged discipline to assuage all your past sins if you like. But it's not going to help you. The black man wants what you've got; all the privilege, all the status, all the power, all the land, all the money. Mortifying your flesh to show penance for apartheid means absolutely nothing to him. These rabid black nationalists had good role models in the Afrikaner nationalists who ruled this country for so long. We gave them the blueprint from which to build. A privileged class enjoying all the fruits of prosperity, an underprivileged class wanting the same things. And we gave them the country more or less on their terms. Now it's their turn.' he paused, wanted to reinforce what he said years ago.

'We had these conversations before — I told you then we would reap the harvest of what we'd sown.'

He made to interject, but with an imperious wave of the hand Piet cut him off at the pass.

'Mandela shone wherever he went — you hopefuls desperate enough to be dazzled. You believed he represented black moderation, could implement his Rainbow Nation setting the mould for those to follow. But Mandela was one in a million. Already too old, out of touch after his long internment to bring real political muscle to the leadership. The radicals beneath him had long been plotting for succession after his tenure. That's where your focus should have been. If you'd been looking there, you'd have seen some nasties from the armed struggle rising with only greed driving them.'

'We weren't blind to the radicals,' his father countered, 'but what are you suggesting? That we could have somehow sued for a better deal?'

'The way I see it the Nationalist party had run out of both steam and ideas by then, nothing to offer. De Klerk a disaster herding the faithful into a cattle-crush to get a deal at any price. We needed a tougher statesman to shepherd this country into a stronger black-white alliance. A Churchill for our time, or a Smith.'

His father didn't see it this way. Here they represented two very different points of view. A microcosm of the Afrikaner nation which still remained divided. Those who thought De Klerk a sellout versus those who felt he and his government were in an almost untenable position, that he'd made the best of a poor situation. Piet wasn't a racist but his sympathies lay firmly in the former camp.

'You mean along the lines of what Ian Smith tried to do in Rhodesia?' his father responded.

'Something like it. That's the sort of statesman we needed here. I'll grant you it didn't work for the Rhodesians in the long run, but they fought hard for years hammering out scenarios which could have worked. Could have worked if they hadn't a duplicitous Britain selling them out quietly in the background. The great betrayal which scuppered them in the end'

Piet took a moment to reflect.

Their northern neighbour and former ally had had a tiny economy compared to South Africa's. At its peak, the white population numbered a paltry quarter million, whilst their black citizens numbered four and a half million. The politics very liberal by comparison to apartheid. Black's enjoyed many more privileges than their brothers to the south. Smith worked hard for an equitable solution as the black nationalists took the cudgels to secure self-determination. He met repeatedly with their leaders when an intensifying bush war failed to give either side the spoils it sought. With foreign observers mediating, he went to great lengths conferencing in unlikely, even exotic locations. Perched in a railway carriage atop the Zambezi gorge; aboard two British warships, Tiger and Fearless. Wherever called, he went. Britain could have brokered a gradual handing over but the international hounds were baying at the door. Harold Wilson became the architect to coerce Smith, give the black nationalists what they wanted. Ultimately it forced rapid transition. In the final analysis, 'the solution' worked out disastrously for all concerned. Black and white. But Britain had long moved on by then leaving Zimbabwe a burned-out shell with a worthless currency.

South Africa's whites numbered twenty-five times that of Zimbabwe. The black population of some forty million dwarfed theirs. Couple this to the mightiest economy on the continent, a strategic coastline, deep-water seaports, and the matter of scale and resource became apparent. A sprat compared to a mackerel. But the fundamental issues starkly similar. It seemed modern history was shifting inexorably to repeat itself on a far grander scale.

Piet's father countered with his argument.

'Precisely to prevent ourselves following the kind of situation Rhodesia found itself embroiled in, is why we went the way we did. They ended with a full-blooded terror war fought on home soil, every able-bodied man in and out of the bush on a six week cycle. We couldn't afford for it to happen here. We needed a solution based on universal franchise. Otherwise, we'd have gone the same way. We couldn't continue to suppress black aspiration for self-rule. You know as much. You fought in a war here.'

He let that go. 'Where has appeasement, rapid accommodation got us Pa? A state more indebted to the World Bank than ever before; black politicians continuing to steal taxpayer money despite riots protesting lack of delivery on basic services from the people; unemployment running close to fifty per cent; huge SOE's on the brink of collapse;

unchecked illegal immigration. For the first time, our international credit rating downgraded to junk status. And a steadily devaluing currency which will eventually leave us all poor in our land.'

Indeed a damning list.

'Sadly all true,' his father conceded. 'It's those very dynamics we have to change. Allowed to slide much further, we'll end up just like Zimbabwe. We can't allow that to happen, son. We need to make sure the incumbents are removed and a responsible moderate black government installed to work for all its citizens.'

'Obviously your memory's not serving you well, Pa.' his irritation setting in again. 'Let me remind you — back in the day I hung around here for your sake when I wanted to get out. You counselled I should give them a chance as Zuma took the leadership. I told you then these politicians set their stall to plunder. You said they needed to "settle to governance." But they couldn't keep their fingers out of the cookie jar just as I'd predicted. And that did it for me. You may further recall just before leaving, I forecast it would continue to slide; they would press on with their smokescreen communist ideology, whilst craving the spoils like slavering dogs. You put your head in the sand not willing to see the obvious. You said the democratic process would be the mechanism that would bring the politicians into line, make them accountable.'

He paused, then kicked the man whilst down. 'Who was proved right, Pa, you or me?' Not a rhetorical question. He wanted his pound of flesh.

His father, seasoned with a steely core, didn't buckle so easily. He countered with some sage logic of his own.

'It's not smart to crow from a position of righteousness when your birthright is at stake,' he warned simply.

Piet was however, a chip off this same old block — not a pushover either.

'My birthright got given away all those years ago when De Klerk washed his hands of any responsibility to his electorate, disappeared into the political sunset.'

'There's been major political movement since you've been away, son.'

'I've noticed, Pa.' He was not above heavy sarcasm either. 'Julius Malema now leads the third largest political party in South Africa.'

This firmly put the boot in. Malema, a racially motivated firebrand, led the far-left Economic Freedom Fighters party. They came from nowhere gaining, in a short time, a not insignificant following. Now occupying twenty-five seats in the four-hundred seat National Assembly. Their rhetoric targeted mainly uneducated black youth; openly anti-white despite a constitution outlawing racism. Rabble rousers stirring racial sentiment. Potentially very dangerous. Malema, the archetypal bogeyman for most whites as well as for more politically conservative blacks. Again his father had found himself wrong-footed here. Back in the day, he predicted Malema's party wouldn't get off the ground. Now he shifted uncomfortably allowing an edge to creep into his voice.

'This isn't going to get us anywhere son. Reel in your righteousness and grow up.'

That did it. A fresh surge of anger rushed into Piet like a flooding tide. 'You're dead right Pa,' he said, getting indignantly to his feet and knocking more spillage from the water jug. Again he gave what he hoped passed as a withering look.

'You just don't get it, do you? You've given the country away, now you're crying over spilt milk arriving at God knows what nonsense to try to salvage something.' he pushed past the coffee table in high dudgeon. 'Say goodbye to Ma for me.' The next minute he strode through the door, battling to control his anger. He climbed clumsily into the old Toyota, crashed it into gear and roared away.

CHAPTER 5

REUNION

Piet settled into a routine on the boat. Roused at daybreak by the cacophony of an awakening seal colony, more effective than any alarm clock, he made his way to the galley. First chore of the day, a strong coffee taken topside to greet the morning.

His companions basking on the adjacent breakwater were noisy neighbours indeed. Their booming calls passably resembled anything from a braying mule to a bovine bellow; this last almost impossible to distinguish from the real thing — not unlike living next to a waking farm.

Vapour from his 'one's company — two's a crowd' mug curling into the air, he let the beverage and the early-morning bite stir his cells, get him properly awake. His near neighbours were bonus entertainment as they got their day started. He had a ringside seat. Fabulously evolved to their habitat, their oily black bodies slid there as if poured like motor oil. Once immersed they became hydrodynamic missiles hunting for grey mullet amongst the leathery blades of the kelp forest. Woe betides any unsuspecting fish busy nibbling breakfast in this rich larder should one of these torpedoes part the protective veil. Highly impressive in the water they morphed to comic blobs when out of it. It was a marvel they weren't paper-shredded hauling themselves over razor-sharp rocks.

With coffee done he got back to the galley to take care of his breakfast. In port, invariably a generous serving of bacon and egg not often practical on passage. Shipboard for many years now, he prided himself on being a passable chef albeit of simpler dishes. *Magus'* small galley no longer resembled a bomb-site after he'd finished in there. He could rustle up most meals on his menu in under an hour; breakfast a twenty-minute affair start to finish including pans washed and stowed. Then down to the business of the day. Currently that meant a trip to the starboard engine compartment where he had the motor stripped prior to installing a new bearing on the main shaft.

Work which was occasioned by their brush with the South Atlantic hurricane. Punching into those monster waves hour after hour at maximum revolutions had taken its toll. The starboard motor made an awful din when started. He'd ordered spares to be shipped in by air freight and expected them any day now. So the hat he wore currently was that of ships engineer. Tiring work in the paucity of space in the compact engine compartment.

The morning slithered to mid-afternoon. He'd had enough for one day, his body crying out for temperature extremes. A hot shower. A cold beer. He backed out of the cramped space and stretched full length hearing crackles and pops that wouldn't have sounded ten years earlier. He made for his cabin, threw a change of clothes into a sports bag and headed for the yacht club ashore.

Half an hour later, showered and feeling human again, he grabbed a quick beer at a bar which he shared with a couple of old-timers nursing drinks then started for the nearby village.

Woodcutters Arms is an unexceptional bar-cum-eatery, a favoured watering hole, styled in the tired but ubiquitous Irish pub mould. The decor is corny but the draught beer first-rate, food passable and the prices not piratical. He was meeting the two closest friends he had on the planet. They didn't get to see one another often enough, but a gulf never existed no matter how long the separation. Both were so much more than friends. Kinship forged in the crucible of war in Angola where they'd served as combatants together.

He grabbed a beer, slid into one of the faux-leather, non-Gaelic booths, the better to avoid the crush of happy-hour minutes away. No sooner did the hands of the clock inch past five than the stalwarts began arriving in number, summoned it seemed by a bugle blast heralding cut-price pints.

Already on his second, he spotted the unmistakable form of Rusty Roberts squeezing through the inadequate pub door. Brother Rusty cut an imposing figure in any setting. Towering just short of two metres, with the build of a rugby front-row forward to boot, this was a man you wanted in your corner if things got rough. You didn't want him facing you with a grievance from the other side.

'You old pirate' he rumbled in a voice like an idling v-eight as Piet rose to greet him. He returned the bear hug with as much upper body strength as he could muster. Not to do so with Rusty invited a cracked rib or two.

'How's the Jack Sparrow of Gansbaai?'

'Still robbing the purses of the rich and famous but keeping out of trouble for the most part,' he grinned his usual disarming smile showing a flash of gold capping on an incisor and squeezed into the booth opposite Piet. 'You haven't got any prettier since you've been away — showing a bit of mileage I see.' He tapped the dusting of grey at Piet's temples.

Piet could easily have done without the reminder. 'That's for sure,' he took an appraising look at his friend. 'I hate to admit it, but I think you're doing better than me old mate.' Since their last meeting at Piet's sister's wedding it seemed Rusty had hardly aged. He could easily pass for mid-thirties, whereas he was pushing fifty.

'I bet you say that to all the girls,' Rusty ordered their beers from a roving waiter. They fell to easy patter, pulling contentedly on their pints.

'What is that terrible bloody smell in here?' a derisive cry above the background hubbub. Almost to a man, heads swivelled. Bustling towards them through the throng was the figure of George Taft. A full head shorter than Rusty, he also carried plenty of beam in his upper body. One jarring feature robbed him of a debonair suaveness — George was prematurely bald. Each point of light he passed under, bounced off like a lobbed tennis ball. He sported a passé Freddie Mercury moustache in defiance of complete hairlessness. It gave him a comedic look which fitted his personality like paint on canvass. The quintessential clown showered greetings on all as he squeezed by. George bloomed in front of an audience.

He slid in beside Rusty delivering a none too playful thump to a massive bicep.

'Not been eaten by a hungry fish yet, big man?' he teased, settling in.

Rusty, a veteran diver, ran a shark cage-diving operation. To build capital for the venture he knuckled down to six years supplying muscle for a guarding firm dispensing protection to senior corporates as well as dodgy politicians. The hard nine yards as Rusty put it. His savings launched his business which was a success from the start, becoming the premier operator in the Cape. Tourists eager for a surge of adrenalin parted with hefty sums of money to get into Rusty's dive cages. It seemed coming face to face with lethal predators on the other side of minimal protection rounded out the vacation for some.

'Gotta be in the water to tempt them,' initially Rusty was in the cage half the time with the clients but as management functions from busier schedules demanded, he found himself topsides almost permanently. 'I keep my feet dry, brother George, but if you're looking for a vocational change, we can always fit you in as chum-bait.'

'You won't get me in one of your lobster pots, my mate,' George shuddered theatrically, looking about for a waiter. 'Some catching up to do I see.'

The friends horsed around enjoying the get-together. When Rusty raised the topic of his father's illness, Piet wondered how they would take the news. Both knew and liked Rossouw senior and had stayed at Verewig on occasion.

'You two aren't going to believe this,' he prepared to drop his bombshell. 'He doesn't have cancer at all. He's not even sick. He tells me he's rarely felt better in his life.'

They exchanged bewildered glances. George got in first with his customary sardonic humour. 'So it's dementia then? Better than the Big C though.'

Rusty shushed him with the wave of a hefty paw. 'That doesn't make sense, Piet. There's got to be a good reason. He wouldn't bring you home pretending sickness unless he felt justification. Your Old Man's not stupid by a long shot. What do you think's behind it then?'

Piet raised an eyebrow. 'He believes he has good reason. He regaled me with a mini-political profile of the country. How bleak things look. You both know how pissed off I got with that scenario before I took the gap. Anyway, he went on to tell me things had gone from bad to worse. That government is now out of control, something has to be done if the whites have any chance here, etc, etc. All stuff I forecast years ago. Told me to grow up when I reminded him of it. That really pissed me off.'

Piet gave them the situation as he believed it to be. 'He appears to be associated with some organisation which will try to change the status quo — bringing me back, an attempt to get me involved. I got a bit excited at being duped. Stormed out.' He was a little ashamed at his reaction for the first time since the event.

'So he knew well enough you wouldn't come if you got wind of that,' Rusty summarised nicely. 'Can't blame him for trying — see how successful he's been.' He shot Piet a mocking grin before getting serious again. 'Look, it's no secret plenty guys like us who put their lives on the line in the Border War got pissed off. We all thought what we'd been fighting for had gone out the window in '94 when the ANC came to power. But admit it, things looked promising when Mandela painted a picture of his rainbow nation. Even you thought it had a chance at the time. But after he stepped down it started to go to custard. The exodus began. You were part of it. No shame in that. The guys like George and me — even your father, admittedly a financial prisoner because of the wine estate, hung around hoping Thabo Mbeki would deliver.'

'Then out of the weeds popped Uncle Jacob and the Gupta Republic,' George made no effort to hide his scorn, 'and that's not to mention other notables like the Russian Mafia scurrying in to rape and pillage.'

Piet remembered that bit of history clearly. Jacob Zuma defeated Mbeki at the polls becoming the country's third democratically appointed president. Soon to become the puppet of the corporate gangsters; notably the Guptas, an insignificant migrant family from the Indian province of Uttar Pradesh arriving just before the fall of the old government. In a little over twenty years the three brothers built a business empire that spanned continents. They now ranked high on the list of the wealthiest men in South Africa.

'All good and well' some would say. Smart businessmen working hard to build successful enterprises in their adopted land. But they were crooks from the start. Their whole game-plan turned on a hub of massive graft and corruption. A web of influence so telling they were able to dictate ministerial appointments, in turn manipulate the President. No quarter was given as their companies robbed the fiscus of billions through over-priced as well as under-delivered state tenders. Gradually but significantly they weakened the country, discrediting it internationally, became a significant factor in its devaluing currency. The Russians as malefactors ran a close second.

These shady dealings eventually brought Zuma under scrutiny, resulting in a formal public enquiry. Ducking and diving a judicial system many believed riddled with nepotism and corruption, he managed to sidestep seven hundred corruption-related charges. Rumour held that his illicit gain ran to billions of rand. The prosecutorial process as yet yielded nothing.

'Yeah, until the Guptas and Zuma,' Rusty echoed. 'The worse things got, the more I thought you'd made the right decision, Piet.'

'Funny thing though,' George leaned in keeping his voice low. 'Thinking about your Old Man and whatever he's involved in, there's a sniff of something in the air. I've been going to the Recce old-boy get-togethers recently. Got chatting to Buster Clark; bent his ear a bit about how these monkeys were breaking everything it's taken centuries to build. Told him it could tip my hand to leave, that I saw no future here for us whiteys. He said something then which has troubled me ever since,'

George gave them a measured look. 'Buster said I should hang in here. That I might get a big surprise. I didn't give it much thought at the time 'cos things had become a bit festive by then. But it bugged me later. I tried to get hold of him a couple of times to see what he meant. Two weeks ago now. The voice message on his cell said he was unavailable, to leave a message. Still saying it.'

'Call a couple of the other guys. See if they know where he is,' Piet suggested.

"Already done.' George shook his head. 'Same result. Not contactable.'

'So what do you read into it *boet*?' Rusty's frown summed up what they were all feeling.

'Maybe something — maybe nothing,' George knew Buster better than Rusty or Piet. 'I thought he may have gone overseas, perhaps wasn't on voice roaming but was text enabled so I flicked him a few — all showed the same result. Undelivered.'

'He could be out of range, or his phone's switched off,' Rusty said.

'This long? And the others?' George voiced the sentiment they were all arriving at. It didn't fit.

Rusty gave up.

Piet began to feel the tug of the cloak-and-dagger stuff. Ghostly shadows of secret strategy meetings all those years ago deep in the Angolan bush drifted to the fore.

'Military secrecy you think?'

'Could be. Mobile phones are trackable. On or off.'

'Within the range of a network,' George qualified.

'Sure.'

'If he's on manoeuvres he's not going to have his phone with him. Trust me on that.' George said.

Rusty offered one last thought. 'What about the Karoo? There are areas there not covered by cellular networks. He might just be camping out of range.'

The Karoo is a vast desert region in the central part of South Africa with a skeletal spiderweb of gravel roads. Away from the few small towns, it is sparsely populated. In the main by sheep farmers. A challenging alternative holiday destination for a few rugged South Africans, it remains a hostile environment for most. Temperatures often climb to mid-forties, surface water is patchy, as is cell phone coverage. The region has snared victims from the unprepared, those failing to give it the respect it deserves.

'Not without telling his mates.' George chirped.

'Okay, guys. Intel 101. Consider what you know, eliminate unlikely possibilities, then you're left with a probability.' Piet wet a finger in the condensate that pooled under his glass.

'Number one.' He traced the numeral on the table. 'An ex-military mate of ours has gone walkabout without telling anyone where. Number two. No voice-note on his cellphone to explain his absence. Number three.' He kept tracing the numerals. 'Other ex-military mates of ours are also uncontactable. Number four. The country is in a mess, a backlash movement in the wings wouldn't surprise us.'

'And don't forget your Old Man is involved in something too.' Rusty raised the possibility that Buster and Piet's father could be on the same team.

'Which gives us Number five,' Piet acknowledged.

'For Buster we think a vacation is out?' They all agreed.

'What about a business trip?' Piet asked. It seemed a possibility.

'He's a rep for a west coast canning operation, so a sales trip is a consideration. But long odds.' George was weighing up other snippets. 'He usually has a bit of a bash at the club the night before he leaves. It didn't happen — wouldn't explain his dead cellphone either.'

'Fair enough. What about the other two guys; any likely scenarios for them?'

'One is a self-employed electrician, serves the greater Cape Town area. His cell is the lifeline to his customers. Where would he go without it? The other is the owner/operator of a small gym in Muizenberg. Virtually married to his business. I phoned to see if it still operated.'

'And does it?' Rusty jumped in ahead of Piet.

'It does. And guess what? He's away; his girlfriend is babysitting the gym. He told her he was off on a road trip with a couple of his Harley Davidson biker chums. Headed for Namibia. No fixed itinerary. Just following their noses going wherever the fancy takes them. I asked if he'd called her, she said he hadn't. Wasn't expecting him to — cell phone coverage would be 'iffy' he'd said.'

'Nice cover.' Piet thought it sounded too pat to be the real explanation.

'Did she say when he'd be back?' Rusty asked.

'Yeah, she did — back by Monday.'

'Going to be interesting to see if Buster is back by then too,' Piet was getting a sense of something 'out there'. 'Doesn't look as if any of the three are either on vacation, business trips or anxious to flag their movements. All special forces ex-military men. Prime targets for recruitment if you were raising a fighting force.'

'No disputing that,' George agreed.

'Time I buried the hatchet with the Old Man, had another meeting. See what he's up to.'

CHAPTER 6

HARBOUR ON FIRE

The night air was crisply bracing. He turned down their offer of a ride to the boat, left Rusty and George and decided to walk back to the marina.

He stepped it out, the better to work his muscles as well as his lungs. A pungent fish odour from the nearby processing factory wafted on the breeze. Seaward, the ocean chewed lazily at the shoreline sending sand-slapping pulses his way. He hadn't gone far when the distant wail of sirens shattered the idyll. Coming off the ribbon of road which climbed over the mountain descending the lower slopes into the village; a decidedly intrusive clarion-cry. He pushed it aside, trying to reabsorb.

He emerged from the wind shadow under the shoulders of the dunes; a new odour wove itself into the rankness of fish. Fire. Combustible stuff burning. The attractor for which the sirens wailed? He strained upwind trying to get a fix on the source. A new sound now. Muted but easily recognisable. A restive crowd. Something was afoot. His curiosity got the better of him; he followed his nose heading towards the old part of the harbour, the dockland. As he drew closer, an orange glow, like the halo around a bonfire, began to silhouette the skyline ahead.

The wailing sirens swelled to banshee pitch as a brace of police cars raced past. They were followed by a lumbering armoured personnel carrier, the police service letters SAPS emblazoned boldly along its white flanks. Could something serious be going down? Last in the convoy, a heavyweight fire-engine shouldered by and splashed its eerie blue-light dramatically over buildings.

The old harbour, first commercialised by early fishing enterprise, was a hotchpotch of dated structures hastily erected to handle a piscatorial gold-rush. This was in the days before town planning departments. The resulting jumble could not be described as aesthetically pleasing. A scraggy spine of deserted buildings threatened to fall to dereliction after a slump in fishing hauls left a bankrupt industry. Fortunately, a new tourism industry eased in to fill the void. Structures got remodelled. Chiller rooms morphed to waterside restaurants; a weekend craft market sprang out of a large packing shed; a microbrewery, at pains to preserve the steam pipes of a former canning facility, gained popularity as much from its steampunk decor as the quality of its brews. The quarter now a mix of downsized marine activities, funky gift-shops, trendy eateries, took on a lopsided charm all its own. The area's resurgence could not be described in terms of boomtown dynamics, but the village economy gratefully accepted what was on offer.

Weekends were the busy time, but today was Tuesday. Things were quiet. Restaurants would have closed early, few folks were abroad as Piet wound his way into the locale. He played mind games to see if he could guess the cause of the fire. Perhaps a fish-fryer carelessly tended in the kitchen of one of the fish and chip outlets? A coastal trawler ablaze? A car having burst into flames? He rounded the last corner and wouldn't have won any prizes. The weekend craft market was well and truly ablaze at its one extremity.

A minor crowd, mainly coloured folk, milled around the fire drawn like moths to a lamp. Police officers newly arrived kept order, their hands full. As he got close, a shot unexpectedly rang out. He ducked reflexively. Almost immediately a salvo of retorts followed. The whole tenor of the scene changed in an instant. The former press of bodies fanned out like oil dropped on water. He got his back against a nearby wall, happy to be swallowed by deep shadow, comforted by the solid barrier behind him. The crowd erupted to full panic. Desperate to escape the danger behind the shots, individuals stampeded past him like spooked horses. A terrified crowd isn't a pretty thing. People jostled, stumbled and leapt over one another, trampled the less fortunate underfoot. He saw a woman favouring a wasted leg hobble as best she could to escape. She was knocked unceremoniously to the ground, quickly steamrollered. Before he could react she was back on her feet, galvanised by her fear and scooting away athletically, all the while screaming at the top of her lungs.

The place cleared in no time. In the wake of the fleeing crowd, he could see quite clearly two prostrate forms on the tarmac; one clothed in police blues, a peaked hat lying incongruously on the ground nearby. He glanced toward the firemen; a frozen tableau in the wake of the shots. The police contingent seemed just as bewildered, lacking leadership, wandering around with sidearms drawn.

Deep within the conflagration, a gas cylinder went off like a bomb. The explosion galvanised the fire-fighters to action, the shooting forgotten — someone else's problem, combatting the fire theirs. In no time streams of high-pressure water arced into the blaze, already greedily consuming greater reaches of the building as the fire fed off the energy it generated. They faced a challenge.

He watched for another fifteen minutes as they gradually got on top of things, damping hot spots, putting down minor flare-ups. Slowly the blaze lost its intensity. But the old building had been tested beyond its limits and gave an agonised groan: in a clatter of corrugated sheets and crashing roof timbers it collapsed sending a welter of sparks heavenward into the night sky — a veritable Roman candle.

Off to one side, an ambulance crew laboured to load the two downed forms into their vehicle. From where he stood, impossible to determine whether they were fatalities or not. He decided either way bed called, time to set off for home and turned to leave. A black police constable stood in front of him. He presented a suspicious character skulking in the shadows.

'Excuse me sir, what is your business in the area?'

'Rubbernecker,' Piet felt he should offer. Instead he explained his walk from the pub back to the boat, curiosity dictating his deviation. It didn't satisfy the officer. Piet realised with growing uneasiness that he should have left much earlier. Better still not to have been there at all.

'If you don't mind sir, I'm going to have to ask you to come along to the station to make a statement.'

At first he protested, said he had nothing to offer. The more Piet remonstrated the more resolute the man became. He cursed under his breath for having been stupid enough to let his base curiosity get the better of him. Now it looked as if a bracing walk home would extend to an irksome session at the local police station. And so it turned out.

The good constable proved to be civil enough, but his writing skills and sentence construction left a lot to be desired. Two false starts to his literary effort resulted in scrunched paper balls tossed to his wastepaper basket. A third document, forty-five minutes later, made it to completion. Piet breathed a sigh of relief and signed it.

He had the good grace to offer Piet a lift back to the marina, which he accepted. He made no small talk in the patrol car, neither did the policeman. He dropped Piet off and watched as he fiddled with his key at the palisade gate locking off the path leading to the yacht berths. Only when safely on the other side, making his way along the catwalk, did Piet see him leave. Solicitous consideration for his wellbeing he wondered? Or mistrust with the part of his statement saying he lived on a boat? Good policing or the innocent concern of a good Samaritan?

He unlocked *Magus'* hatch, flicked the light switch as he dropped into the main saloon. His watch showed one thirty in the morning. Long past his intended bedtime.

Curled under the covers, unanswered questions buzzed, preventing him from sleep. What started the fire? Why the shooting? Who were the downed victims? His perception of the sleepy little backwater was undergoing serious re-evaluation. How could an insignificant coastal village generate the sort of violence he'd just witnessed? Had things changed so radically?

He would live to rue the day his curiosity drew him to a fire clearly none of his business.

CHAPTER 7

IVASHCHENKOV'S DILEMMA

Dmitri Ivashchenkov pulled his Mercedes into the gate of Dainfern residential estate in Johannesburg's northern suburbs and swiped his card across the electronic sensor. The boom lifted and he drove through.

Inside the estate, tranquility reigned, jockeying-traffic-madness left outside. The up-market estate was home to mansions set in luxuriant gardens. He crossed a stream feeding a mirror-still lake, thick reed-beds softening its banks. Red-billed coots darted in and out playing hide-and-seek whilst Egyptian geese honked imperiously as they strutted on the upper slopes or teased the water.

He entered a cul-de-sac leading to his driveway. The garage door ratcheted aloft and packed itself away in the roof space as he triggered the remote. He came from the garage through the space-planned kitchen greeting his wife in their native Russian. A beautiful dark haired woman with milky skin busy at the sink preparing vegetables, she was considerably younger than Ivashchenkov. She puckered her lips for a kiss from her husband as he passed by her on his way to the lounge and the drinks cabinet. A crystal tumbler half full of scotch and rattling ice cubes in hand, he dropped into the lounger and kicked off his shoes. His furrowed brow gave the clue to his state of mind.

Anti-nuclear activists were giving him more trouble than he'd bargained for. From being irksome niggles, two factions had consolidated and now formed a serious lobby group which could badly upset his plans. At first he'd ridiculed their activity. Two women, one black one white, seemed like busybody nonentities. United, they became his nemesis. Despite assurances from Jacob Zuma that their activities would come to nought, they gained traction. He put one of his surveillance teams into action to watch them; if it became necessary, had dark plans to deal with them.

He checked his cellphone opening the messages application, and scrolled to an image received earlier. A heavy-framed black woman in a shift emblazoned with tribal patterns stared out of the phone defiantly. Alongside her, a colleague brandished a placard. 'No Nuclear Deals.'

His wife dropped onto the arm of his chair.

'New girlfriend?' she teased glimpsing the image over his shoulder whilst running her fingers through his hair.

'Worse,' he said. 'A *balamut* in Cape Town. Another troublemaker like her in Johannesburg. White woman this time. They give me grey hairs.'

'They are powerful women then?'

'Separately no power at all. Lead small anti-nuclear NGO's. Joined together, press begins giving them prominence. Big donations coming from sympathisers. Enough to fund appointment of legal team and lodge court action attacking our deal with Zuma.'

'Can they do that? I mean, can't Jacob help you there?'

'Zuma is bloody blowhard. Says has everyone in the pocket. But this thing now is getting serious. Gaining momentum. Zuma powerless despite all chest-beating. I have meeting with bitch from press tomorrow. Am going to have to lie through my back teeth to keep deal on rails.'

'What will you tell the media?'

'That no deal is signed. Only we have given letters of intent for technical support to government.'

'Is it true?'

'No, is not true. We have bloody full-blown agreement in place, not arrived at by due process. That gets out, we're in deep shit.'

CHAPTER 8

PROPOSITION

Piet phoned the Old Man suggesting lunch somewhere quiet. They settled on the Stellenbosch Flying Club, close for his father and suitably off the beaten track. The facility got used pretty much only by members and their friends. Undiscovered by tourists. A great place to sip a drink, unwind, chat.

He got there early taking a table under the canopy of trees protectively shrouding the bar and restaurant buildings. The day was one of those glorious interludes, the air crystal clear. The mountain range in the middle distance invited you to reach out and touch it. A good day to be alive.

As Piet settled, a single-engined Piper dropped gracefully from the sky, an alighting insect to the runway. It taxied along for about a hundred metres before the engine pitch rose again, the pilot applying more power, clearly not intending to complete the landing. His speed increased until he lifted off, the ground falling away effortlessly beneath him.

The airfield sat atop a gentle dome, a perfect training ground for student pilots intent on becoming seasoned aviators. Almost a certainty he watched one now busy doing his early 'circuits and bumps', repetitive approach, touch-down and take-offs which would form the backbone of his training. Piet remembered the time he had completed this same exercise. In another life. He failed however to complete his training, the love affair with ocean sailing proving a more seductive mistress.

His day-dreaming got interrupted by the arrival of his father. 'Hello *seun*,' he dropped onto the bench at the other side of the table.

Piet drained the last of his pint. 'What will you be having, Pa?' he got to his feet.

'Same as you, son.'

He went off to the bar, coming back with the drinks.

'How're you finding the return to the old country?' His father lowered his glass eyeing his son with interest.

He'd been back ten days, feeling as if he'd never been away. South Africa is that kind of place. A climate practically unrivalled anywhere on the globe, everything on the surface running along smoothly. Locals appearing by-and-large, content, at peace. The veneer only ran surface deep. Scratch beneath it, a different picture presented. If you followed TV news, read a newspaper or eavesdropped on situational conversations in crowded bars, you soon got the impression of a country in trouble: corruption endemic, a population growing ever angrier. For one thing, money misappropriated meant an electricity utility increasingly unable to deliver its services. Rolling electricity blackouts were the norm as the organisation reeled under a budget wrecked by pay-offs and mismanagement. Xenophobic outbreaks were another serious problem: lost job opportunity for locals spawned violent attacks on gainfully employed foreign nationals. Add to these woes aggressive civil upwellings against a government not delivering on promises, and the extent of the country's malaise started to show. A river of anger surging under the veneer.

That wasn't the response his father sought. 'You know how it is Pa,' Piet answered, 'if it flies, swims and quacks like a duck... then it's a duck.'

He laughed good-naturedly. 'Feeling at home in the old pond again then?'

A good invitation to get down to bedrock. 'Yes and no. Great to see you and Ma again, meet with the old mates. I'm enjoying that. And of course, there's the beautiful Cape scenery. But we both know all this is a bit like enjoying the party in the ballroom of the Titanic. It's great if you choose to forget you're steaming in an ocean peppered with icebergs. The band's giving it stick, everybody drinking and dancing, but just ahead, something massive is going to put a stop to all that. Survival then the only issue.'

Piet hadn't intended pouring cold water on their get-together, but his earlier euphoria evaporated as these sobering thoughts took hold.

'Sadly it could be a very apt analogy, Piet,' he gave one of those level stares Piet knew to be his marker for getting down to business. 'But there is a chance we can slow the ship down. Put in a course correction, avoid colliding with that iceberg.'

He took a swallow of his beer. 'Nice use of the collective pronoun, Pa.'

He smiled good-naturedly. 'Not lassoing you with it, son. My 'we' means the country at large, all those who want a return to sane leadership.' He eyed him again. 'Let's not be silly, however. I would like you to be a part of that 'we', the reason for my deviousness in getting you back here. However, we've had our spat over that so let's move beyond it.'

Piet shrugged non-committally, well over his angst by now.

His father got back to his topic. 'All I ask is you give it a fair hearing. If you still think it's not for you by the time you've got the facts, I'll respect your decision. Then you can sail off into the blue again or do whatever else you decide upon.' He tried to put him at ease. 'And with our blessing.'

A reasonable negotiating position.

'Okay. Fair enough. I'm prepared to listen. I've also been doing a bit of digging off my own bat since last we met. It begs some questions. Okay if I fire them at you before you try to evangelise the prodigal?'

He laughed again. 'I hope I don't come across as the proselytising zealot.'

Strange, Piet thought, how sometimes people don't see themselves in exactly the role other's cannot but see them in.

He let it go however, getting straight down to cases. 'You're going to have to educate me a bit. This commission of enquiry Zuma faces, the thing everybody seems to be talking about. What is it? Seven hundred and twenty-odd corruption charges? What chance do you give the process of reaching a just conclusion? A sentence being handed down, prosecuted?'

He considered that. 'Will it end in jail time for Zuma you mean? Justice prevailing?' He scratched at his beard. 'A bookmaker would probably only give you even money. It is a tough one. Some say the judiciary at large is above political influence, can act in terms of its mandate without fear of political influence. Those in that grouping believe justice will be served. The other camp thinks the judiciary is badly compromised — our scarlet robed gentlemen influenced by ANC party politics. It largely depends on who will be hearing the case, whether they are clean or not.'

'What's your take on it, Pa?'

He paused. 'I'd have to say I'm something of a sceptic. Whilst there must be some straight judges with no agenda, there are certainly others tainted. Appointees through political manipulation. Zuma is street smart. If he can manoeuvre his case to come before one of the latter, I believe a judgement going against him is unlikely in the extreme. And it's hard to see who's who in the hallowed halls these days. How will we know? So it's going to be a bit of a lottery. It could go either way.' He smiled apologetically. 'I'm afraid it probably doesn't help you very much.'

Right enough — it didn't. 'Okay, as I see it then, If he gets away with his nonsense, doesn't serve prison time, it sends a message to the country. The fix is in. It's dirty business as usual?'

He nodded.

'On the other hand, if he does get sentenced, it should be an encouraging sign surely? Show the country corruption is being rooted out, set a course for a new direction?'

'It could be. But even then, not necessarily. We know, within the party, there are other aspirants for the top job. Many as unsavoury as him. Also Zuma is too cavalier. Something of an embarrassment to the party's executive, corrupt or not. It might just be clever politics to sacrifice him for the greater good. A case of throwing a brother, even the top dog, to the wolves to appease a clamouring public. That could work well for them. The embarrassment gone and more discrete continuance of the malfeasance. We just don't know.'

'I assume there's no chance of unseating the ANC at the polls when the time comes?'

'None. On that everybody is agreed. And don't forget we are at midterm now, a couple of years to new elections.'

'Who would be the front runners vying for the top job if Zuma got the boot?'

'Front runners? Two heavyweights. Cyril Ramaphosa and Nkosazana Dhlamini Zuma. Both look like pitting themselves against him at the upcoming pre-elective party conference.'

'That's Zuma's ex-wife?'

'Correct. Very wily, well educated. Currently chairperson of the Africa Union executive. Doesn't have a good image with the press. The word is she hasn't enough of a following to clinch the party's top job. But she will have a go for it.'

'And Ramaphosa?'

'The big challenge I'd say.'

'How clean is he?'

His father gave a mirthless grin. 'Sorry to sound like a stuck record, son. There are two camps there as well. Smarter than Zuma — no clear indication of how straight he is. Some think he could be the country's salvation. Others say he's out to feather his own nest, will be no better than

Zuma. Remember, he was deputy under the President all the time that notable has been playing his games.'

'If Ramaphosa won the vote, got the top job in the ANC, what would it mean?'

'Most importantly, as head of the ruling party he would automatically become acting President of the country. All the way to the next elections.'

'Which would reduce Zuma to a simple card-carrying member. His title gone, his premiership lost?'

'It would.'

'You said 'acting'. Does that mean it would be temporary?'

'Not temporary, even though acting. De facto all the way to the next elections in 2019. Then subject to the party continuing to back him, he'll become President-elect for the following term. So we'd have him for six years. If he is dirty it would be too long for the country as we know it, to survive. At this juncture, a chance most of us are not prepared to take. Other worrying things are being bandied about quietly amongst the party elite.'

'And they are?'

'Well, the first is wanting to tamper with the constitution.'

'I thought they needed a two-thirds majority to do that? What do they have presently, sixty per cent or something?'

'Sixty two.'

'So they're let's say, five per cent shy?

'They are. A coalition with a minnow could give them the required margin though.'

Piet hadn't been down the path to that scenario. 'Do you see it as a possibility?'

'It's a major concern. The other worrying thing they're talking about — compulsory land appropriation without compensation. Another way of impoverishing the whites, token for appeasing the electorate. It would require a constitutional amendment. Believe me, a very hot potato. If they ever get that passed to law, you can expect blood in the streets. Our Afrikaner folk will never stand for it.'

'Supposing the ANC did need to form a coalition, who would they align with?'

'A party with extremist views almost for sure. Probably the Economic Freedom Fighters.'

'Julius Malema?'

'I'm afraid so.'

'That wouldn't be good.'

'No, it wouldn't. Apart from his politics, he's also under scrutiny for financial crime. He's managed to duck prosecution by the skin of his teeth. If his party joined a coalition, corruption could only worsen.'

'I see your point. An expanded covey of thieves?'

'Exactly.'

'Okay. And your political party, the one you now belong to. How strong are they — what's the plan? How could my involvement have any impact?'

'We're not a political party, son. That isn't to say we don't have political friends. Our solution is not via parliamentary process. Naive to believe we could effect rapid enough change that way.'

So here it was; the animal emerging. Piet's recent conversation with Rusty and George resonated. It seemed certain now that his father was involved in something more extreme than peaceful change. He recalled the secretive nature of Buster Clark's absence as well as that of their other friends. A military beast eased out of the thicket.

'So we're saying your movement is seeking a solution by force?' Piet put it bluntly, 'a direct challenge on government? A coup d'etat?'

'With sophisticated civil and political structures behind it. Yes.'

There it was. The buffalo out of the bush. His father involved in a movement intent on wresting political control through military means.

'How much are you in a position to tell me?'

He knew from his army days that sensitive planning such as this was shrouded in secrecy. There would be vast areas of information administered on a need-to-know basis. He might be Piet's father but if privy to covert information, he would certainly be sworn to secrecy. He would never betray that trust. Even to his son, an outsider to the cause at that point.

'I can give you broad-brush stuff, not the detail.'

'Alright. That I understand. Can I assume then I'm here because of my special forces history? You've always overvalued the decoration beyond its merits, Pa: a long time ago now. I hope you haven't been over-selling my value to your colleagues. If I agreed to get involved...' he brightened perceptibly, '... and I'm not saying it's more than a remote possibility right now — then I'm not sure I would be an asset.'

'Believe me son, I had nothing to do with targeting you for recruitment. That directive came from way above my head. My task, simply to attempt to get you back here. At first, I resisted, thinking it better to leave you wherever you were. Let you live out your life the way you'd chosen. If you didn't want to join this fight, then it was your decision. I would respect it. Then I got to thinking about it. Of how much you loved this country. How you cherished the farm. It slowly dawned on me you were the archetypical white African. A lot invested, a lot still to give therefore a lot to lose. My viewpoint changed. It didn't seem fair you were driven from the land of your birth by a bunch of scheming politicians, in it only for personal gain.'

I discussed it at length with your mother. She knows what I'm striving for, supports me fully. But she doesn't pry. You know how she is. Anyway, we chatted for hours about whether or not to try to put the proposition before you. I didn't attempt to influence her, wouldn't have been fair. In the end, she pointed out you had already laid your life on the line more than once for this country, came close to losing it. She believes you should be presented with all the facts and you will make your own decision from there. We agreed neither of us would try to influence you. As far as possible I would make sure you got all the facts to enable you to make an informed decision. It just left the matter of getting you home to do so. The dishonesty there all mine, nothing to do with your mother... or anybody else for that matter.'

The lights were coming on for Piet — illuminating on two fronts. First, he had judged his father too harshly. His parents had agonised about even approaching him. Humbling in itself. Crass of him to have been indignant he realised. Second, the meeting with Buster Clark once he'd returned from his mysterious absence. Buster had been tight-lipped. Revealing in itself. All he would say; that he was part of a para-military outfit sworn to secrecy. A sure sign to the friends that he involved himself in a revolutionary force. Now Piet's father confirmed its existence.

In the current light of what family and friends were doing, his decision to get out all those years earlier no longer sat comfortably with him. Here they were, mobilising to right serious wrongs in their country — he had done a runner. A deserter? He squirmed uncomfortably under that one.

'So how much can you tell me about the military preparations? How strong is the organisational structure? What is the tactical philosophy? What sort of ordnance is in place? Things like that.'

'I'm going to have to pass you along for all of that. I simply don't know. It's beyond my ambit. What I can tell you is the entire structure is years in the building, extremely well funded, multi-faceted, and involves a lot of important people.'

They chatted on and worked their way through lunch. Piet fired questions, his father gave him answers where he could. The more he learned, the more he could see a sophisticated structure emerging. Perhaps a long-odds chance to pull the irons out of the fire after all?

Did he have the appetite for it? Realistically what were the chances of success? Equally, what were the consequences of failure? He knew he teased the bait; now much more than an interested party certainly. But he recognised there was a barb on the hook. Once he took that bait he wouldn't wriggle free easily. Too early to rise to it. He needed time in the swim. Time to test the waters.

His father had pressing issues at the farm and excused himself. He tossed a couple of notes on the table and disappeared. Piet paid the waiter as the small Piper swooped in again on its relentless circuits. The pilot, after executing a near-perfect touch down, brought the machine to a standstill in front of where he sat. The cockpit door opened, a figure jumped out, took pains to secure the door firmly. He stood back, gave a thumbs up. Clearly the instructor. His student about to embark on his first solo flight. The engine revs built and the little craft strained eagerly against the brakes. A moment later it surged forward impatient to be away. Piet relived the day he was that student. Heart in the mouth, choking with unbridled anticipation. Then came momentary panic that something was amiss as the aircraft lifted off much earlier now, unburdened by the other body. Eyes big as saucers as he realised for the first time he was the sole agency commanding that heavier than air machine. The one to cock a snook at gravity. Mind-blowing, spiritually uplifting. How different the burden he now considered taking upon his shoulders. Life was a far simpler affair back then.

CHAPTER 9

SIMON ZONDO

Piet's father brokered a meeting for his son with his organisation's lawyer. The man knew all there was to know about the client that retained him, would give whatever information was needed.

Five days later Piet took an Uber to Cape Town's International airport and climbed aboard a Mango Airlines Boeing, its bright orange fuselage glowing like the skin of the fruit from which the airline took its name. The banter from cabin crew once aboard, quirky and fresh. It put him in a good mood for his two hour trip to Johannesburg. The company's approach to the market together with its sharp price-point was paying dividends — there wasn't a vacant seat.

Soon climbing and banking in the turn over the magnificent Cape mountains, they pointed at their destination 1400 kilometres to the north. He watched the ocean drop away, closed his eyes to reflect on the man he would see in Johannesburg, the key to his immediate future;

the cog at the centre of all his father's people did. A conduit through which the leadership worked to organise. The strategy had merit. In effect the lawyer acted as the 'dead drop'. The buffer separating a policy-planning executive from its operations people in the field. A clever device; the attorney/client privilege an effective shield should there ever be unwanted enquiry.

He dozed off. The next thing he knew the thump of the landing gear roused him as they prepared for their landing. Fifteen minutes later he walked out into the busy arrivals hall, the semi-circle of expectant faces scrutinising the new arrivals. He didn't have to look very far before spotting his name on a raised placard. He eased his way to the smartly uniformed chauffeur and announced himself. Soon on their way towards the Sandton business hub, he basked on leather-clad luxury in the back of an impressive top-of-the-range Mercedes. Diplomatic treatment indeed, excepting for the absence of a fluttering pennant. Impossible not to be impressed.

He settled comfortably, kicking off his shoes the better to enjoy the thick carpeting underfoot. A stark contrast to the utility aboard the aircraft. Air-conditioning sent riffs softly across his face. Beyond the tinted windows traffic crawled along miserably in step with them. The pace something they all shared, luxury limo or beaten-up banger, it mattered little. A shimmering heat-haze wafted off a sea of tortuously overheated metal. He gave silent thanks for the aircon.

Welcome to Johannesburg, he mused! The sprawling metropolis boasted a respectable road infrastructure, but like most major cities it is home to an over-supply of vehicles, the resulting gridlock the inevitability they now endured. Five lanes of freeway in both directions did little to assuage the slow crawl. It took almost as long to traverse the fifty kilometres to his appointment as the fourteen hundred by air.

Finally they turned into Fifth Street approaching the most expensive real estate on the continent. Perched atop a rise were iconic skyscrapers thrusting heavenward in a bid to outdo one another for dominance of the skyline.

They climbed the hill to a marble-clad edifice announcing its occupants to the business world: ARCHER ZONDO ran vertically almost the full height of the building. A bronze Apollo perched above the name, busy firing off an arrow into the heavens. They cruised under a boom which sensed the approach of the car and were quickly engulfed by the building.

The chauffeur dropped him to make his way to the lift-well and up to a central lobby. Photographed and voice recorded at reception, he was given an electronic pass which gave access through glass bat-wing doors. A high speed lift whisked him gut-wrenchingly to the top of the building. He stepped out into a lavish reception foyer, one wall floor-to-ceiling glass, the view beyond spectacular. He felt somehow disembodied, suspended. Like riding a hot-air balloon. Far below, modest commercial buildings popped their heads through a forest of greenery. He had heard somewhere Johannesburg laid claim as home to the largest man-made forest on the planet. Confronted with this view, he could easily believe it.

He accepted the offer of tea from a secretary before being ushered to a boardroom. The silence of a library ruled. On the rear wall away from direct sunlight hung two large oils. They depicted the sort of bucolic Cape landscapes he grew up in. They were classics. He identified the artist immediately. Tinus De Jongs' work wasn't easy to miss if you were interested in local masters. He wasn't current enough to guess at their combined value, but it could easily run to seven figures. Probably enough to buy a yacht like *Magus*. He thought how much his father would appreciate them.

'Are you an art lover, Mr. Rossouw?' The voice carried a deep basso.

Piet hadn't heard him enter the room. He was dressed expensively in a pearl-grey city suit, and closed the door quietly behind him.

'Very much so. It's the Western Cape. Home soil. I know how much my father would like them. He has a couple of the son's works.'

'Ah yes, Gabriel. A fine painter. But for me he doesn't capture the same mood in his work his father so often achieved.' He came over to shake hands. 'Simon Zondo.'

Close to Piet's age, somewhere around fifty, a couple of centimetres taller, he clearly kept himself in shape. There wasn't an ounce of fat on his frame. His features were finely chiselled in mahogany, remarkably European save for the three short tribal scars high on each cheekbone. He took to the man instantly.

He drew out one of the leather-upholstered chairs for Piet, taking his place at the head of the boardroom table. 'Welcome to Archer Zondo, Mr. Rossouw.'

'Please call me Piet, I'm not big on formality.'

'Piet it is. And Simon from this side.'

Piet paid careful attention to his speech. There was a hint of something slightly foreign. He took a stab at it. 'Do I detect a legacy of the US?'

He laughed. 'Your file notes said you were perceptive.' He patted the thin manilla folder in front of him. 'Starting out, I spent ten years in Cambridge Massachusetts. I thought the accent long since gone.'

'So that would have been Harvard?'

He raised an eyebrow in silent salute. 'Impressive. Knowledgeable as well as perceptive. I wrote my masters at the law school there.'

'Perhaps the most prestigious of them all,' Piet was showing off a bit now, 'it seems to have stood you in good stead.'

'Ah yes,' he followed Piet's gaze. 'Little more than a marketing extravaganza. The trappings of our fine profession; I'm afraid we have to keep up with the Jones'. Our esteemed clients wouldn't cross our threshold if we didn't bedazzle them with opulence. They see it as a barometer of our success — which links straight back to innate competence.'

A tentative knock at the door interrupted him as the tea-lady brought in their tray. He busied himself pouring two cups. Novel for Piet to be handling fine bone china. A far cry from the rugged mugs aboard *Magus*.

'I trust you had a good flight?'

'No turbulence, so yes thanks. Managed to sleep through most of it. Cat-naps are one of the vestiges from the old army days.'

'You're fortunate. I'm not the best air traveller myself. A little too much anxiety regarding the competency of the pilot, I'm afraid.' He smiled sheepishly from behind his teacup. 'But you're not here to listen to the peccadilloes of an air-scared lawyer. I'm sure there is lots you're keen to address. Perhaps we should get down to cases. I have my instructions to answer everything you might care to raise. In so far as they do not compromise my client of course.'

'Am I allowed to ask the identity of such client?' Had to start somewhere Piet reasoned, pretty sure of the response he would get.

'Corporate in nature, but for the time being, as I'm sure you will appreciate, identity has to remain confidential.'

Piet decided to play open cards. 'Perhaps I should briefly explain my position. I'm here in two minds. And perhaps to a degree I'm here out of respect for my father. I've only recently returned to the country. Upped sticks a number of years ago, disillusioned with the politics back then. That was years on from 'the transformation' as I believe it's now termed. In my eyes things slid from a very brief window of hope under Mandela, to hopelessness under Zuma. I hadn't the stomach for the self-serving politicians who gained control. The corruption the electorate tolerated without a whimper. SOE's already in trouble under graft and incompetence. I didn't take to the policy of Black Economic Empowerment either — the way it prejudiced the white minority in the job market regardless of skill-sets.' This last remark he threw in as a tester. He sat on a different side of the colour fence, curious to see if it would rankle with Zondo. His expression didn't change. If any racial sensitivity existed he didn't show it. Either he faced an exceptional lawyer or the man's personal politics were above race. Or both.

'The ANC were mandated to bring balance to the economy,' Piet went on, 'to right previous wrongs, take us into a democracy where benefits would accrue to all. What happened was the political elite treated the fiscus as their private cashbox. They didn't give a damn about the man in the street. I decided then South Africa was going the same way as most other failed African countries, had moved beyond the tipping point, things could only get worse from there. For me it signalled the white man's days were numbered here, reached a point unacceptable to me. I got out.'

'Strong views. Not altogether an unjust picture, I'll concede. Your argument is well made politically. Where I would differ however, is on the matter of having gone beyond the tipping point. We have certainly allowed ourselves to be taken over by opportunists. Gangsters if you like. However there is a very solid core of the population who will not tolerate it anymore.' He regarded Piet steadily. He felt the lawyer was about to bat the ball back across the net. 'Your father is among that number.'

He'd never asked his father if he'd met Simon Zondo.

'You've met my father?'

'On numerous occasions. A fine man. Salt of the earth, an asset to South Africa. You have every reason to be proud.'

In his culture, as in Piet's, elders were revered. Family counted for something. Another brownie point for Mr.

Zondo. And as it now began to dawn on him, a strike against himself for not toughing it out in the country of his birth, as so many others had.

'I'm beginning to feel a bit ashamed for having deserted a listing ship.'

'Deserting with justifiable cause it seems to me. You'd fought for what you considered right, saw no fruits manifesting for your efforts. The reverse in fact.'

'I thought I was done with South Africa, would never live here again. My dear old Pa had other ideas however, luring me back with a bit of deception.'

'I am aware of the subterfuge,' he looked abashed for a moment. 'As I recall you were cruising the Caribbean at the time.'

That came as a minor shock on both fronts. He'd done his homework.

Barbados,' Piet said, 'my father knew the right button to press to get me home. Only once back, did he hint at what he was involved in. I thought at first he'd lost his marbles.'

Piet half expected a mild repudiation. The lawyer kept his peace. He pressed on.

'All this prior to him filling me in on some of the detail. The more he told me the less crazy I thought him. I've got a broad picture of the organisation now. It's a far cry from the mad-cap scheme I first suspected. But I confess I'm not yet convinced it has real prospects for success. I'm here to see if I may be wrong.'

Simon took a few moments. 'I hope I can show you a compelling sketch which may tip those scales. Development is at an advanced stage. The organisation's sophistication reaches levels which may surprise you. There are no power-hungry generals charging onto the field to seize power. If the plan reaches maturity it has every chance of achieving success. Perhaps the biggest risk is of being exposed before implementation. Being compromised by a leak.'

'Speaking of security, how tight is that?'

'Many people are involved so a breach is always possible. However, the organisation is built on a cellular construct. Sensitive information is only shared on a need-to-know basis. Identities are protected as far as possible in much the same way. If one cell is compromised it doesn't bring down the rest. That event could spell a hiccup in the timeline but not overall collapse.'

'Where would I fit into this structure, supposing it's me not my father who has lost his marbles?'

He smiled. 'Clearly your military background is what has brought you to our attention.' Reaching for the file on the table he flicked it open leafing through. 'Allow me a little history.' He scanned a particular page. 'You sailed through your induction training with honours. You were top of a group of only five who managed to cut the mustard for the elite Reconnaissance unit on your induction year. It's the toughest screening process for the entire armed forces. In itself a remarkable achievement. You entered your second year embarking on specialist skills training. Your parachute instructor couldn't believe you'd had no previous experience. Your attack-diving course earned you a citation for bravery even at that early stage. A fellow trainee severely savaged by a shark. Showing no regard for personal safety, you entered the water to rescue him. He lost a leg. You came under attack, were yourself bitten. However, you succeeded in repulsing the animal to get your colleague to safety.'

He selected another page. 'You saw service with your unit in the Angolan Border War. Leading one of the most successful missions ever. Operation Mebos. The unit you led penetrated deep into enemy territory totally destroying SWAPO headquarters. Again, your selfless actions came to the fore when you risked your life to save comrades who otherwise would have perished. For the deed you were awarded the Castle of Good Hope medal. South Africa's highest military decoration — you the only man ever to receive it. 'For most conspicuous bravery' the citation reads.' He looked from the file regarding Piet closely. 'You're an incredible human being, Mr. Rossouw.'

Always uncomfortable talking about the medal, he wanted to move past it. 'You make it sound very glamorous. However little more than a case of 'kill or be killed'. Scant heroics. When a man's life is on the line he finds resources deep within himself which even he is unaware of. It's a reactionary thing. And the brotherhood of comrades under fire is universal. I owe my life to the action of others too.' Piet rubbed the wound on his thigh reflexively — a trigger action he was trying to break himself of. Whenever those memories were stirred it itched annoyingly.

'It's an outstanding profile, Piet. There's more too. But we needn't go there. In a word, even to people like me without armed forces experience, it's exceptional. And it is your outstanding leadership, your military strategy skills, which has brought you to the attention of my client.'

'It's a long time ago now. I'm no longer that young soldier. And very rusty. Unlike others I haven't taken a career in, lets say security, which might have kept me in physical as well as mental readiness. I'm not sure I would have any value or be of relevance today.'

'The attributes you displayed at the time are never lost. They may need polishing, but always there. With the sort of training you've had, that's especially true. Let's not forget your strategic plan turned operation Mebos into such a success. The chiefs of staff had despaired, thinking the objective beyond reach even with the deployment of a larger force. Your small unit did what the army considered unattainable. Your show — you pulled it off. That's the sort of thinking and strategising which would be very very valuable to our present cause.'

He wasn't used to that sort of eulogising and brushed quickly past it. 'What would be my specific role in your organisation if I decided to come on board?'

'My client's organisation,' he corrected.

'Okay. Your client's organisation.'

'I can't give you detail. That will fall to others. What I can tell you is you would be tasked with high level planning. Military objectives critical to the endeavour would fall under your ambit.'

Piet paused for thought. 'We are talking about a coup here are we not?'

'Coup, by definition, is inflammatory, sensitive,' he countered, 'we prefer not to use the term. Shall we say my client seeks political change to redress an untenable situation in this country. Hopefully it will be the catalyst which removes the rot at the top.'

'Nicely put. But it's legal-speak.' Piet regarded him quietly for a moment. 'Let me ask a direct question. Would this very conversation we are currently having be seen in itself as a treasonable act?'

'It's an interesting question. The law on treason in most jurisdictions is usually defined by statute as a specific crime having corresponding statutory provisions for prosecution. In other words where a country's penal code clearly defines an act of treason, it sets out and lists those acts. That certainly applies to most of our neighbours. But here in South Africa there is no statutory provision, treason is prosecutable under common law. It's a crime which requires the individual to be a citizen or owe allegiance to the country against which the act is alleged to have been perpetrated.' He paused. 'I assume you are a citizen of South Africa, haven't sworn allegiance to another country?'

Piet nodded.

'Which identifies you unequivocally as a party owing allegiance to this country.' He went on. 'But it doesn't end there. Another provision of our criminal code states you have to be guilty of conduct unlawfully committed with the intention of overthrowing the government. Or alternatively of coercing the government to use violence in an action or inaction which would compromise their mandate. There are other provisions but those are the two best fitting your question.'

'So this conversation would be a treasonable act?' Piet pressed. But it wasn't so easy with Simon Zondo. He got neatly side-stepped once again.

'The state would clearly have a case. However the onus of proof which they would need to bring would be difficult against an informed and vigorous defence.'

'And in such an eventuality, that defence would be you?'

'Provided I wasn't indicted as a co-accused for the same alleged offence.' He grinned boyishly. 'But yes, it would be me. Or more precisely, this firm. We're talking hypothetically of course. Don't forget our conversation is between attorney and client. You're asking questions of your lawyer concerning treasonable acts. If our consultation were exposed for any reason, we would argue the consult concerned you obtaining legal opinion on mechanisms which could bring about a change of government. You were not planning treasonable acts. We would be seen to clearly advise you against that. You were asking us if there existed a route to remove government legally without relying on a democratic process. You have every right to do that. I could then claim attorney-client privilege. Withhold transcripts or file notes.'

'So you would need to perjure yourself?'

'Aaah Piet, you have a habit of finding these harsh terms. Let's just say we would present a version of the interview which best suited the interests of this country. We find ourselves in very troubled waters in South Africa today. Mostly brought about by major illegal activity. We need to trim our sails accordingly, not be troubled too much by niceties.'

'And what if you did happen to get indicted? What would happen then. Where would it leave me?'

'The Archer of Archer Zondo would carry your defence.'

'He's not involved in your movement?'

'Absolutely not. He may not even be aware of it. If the necessity for a defended action were to come about, a very comprehensive file kept in a secure location away from these offices, would be brought into play. It would admirably equip him to run your defence.' He smiled at Piet reassuringly. 'I realise you haven't received the sort of replies you might have hoped for. A 'yes' or a 'no'. That in itself might strike you as legal obfuscation, but it really isn't. Prosecuting a treasonable act here is fraught with difficulty. In the unlikely event of it coming about, the way the law is framed would work in our favour.'

'And if you were in the dock too, wouldn't your partner need to recuse himself because of the association?'

'Impressive. We'll make a lawyer out of you yet,' he gave a generous smile. 'You're right of course. My partner could not act for me in the event of me ever being charged. It would be a conflict of interest. I would need to get representation elsewhere or carry my own defence. But he would still be able to act for you.'

'So I would have representation if the proverbial hit the fan?' Piet recognised wryly, his use of tense suggested he'd already made his decision. 'Do you think this coup is going to happen?' Time to get direct.

Piet had forgotten he didn't like the word. He winced at its use. 'I'm going to ask for your indulgence, Piet. From the legal perspective I want to eliminate the word 'coup' from all dialogue. Placed under oath in a courtroom I would want to be able to answer without perjuring myself... any further than necessary.' They both smiled at the irony. 'To be able to say that no coup was ever discussed in these offices. Please call it the Endeavour.'

'Fair enough.' It seemed a valid point. Get into the mental habit of avoiding the word, psychologically it became much easier to convincingly deny the reality behind it. As the meeting progressed Piet's respect for this man grew. 'So to reiterate. Is the Endeavour a reality which will eventuate?'

'As I mentioned previously the biggest risk is a leak, even a slip of that nature would probably not prove fatal. So yes, I do believe it is going to happen.'

In Piet's mind the project ramped to 'probable' rather than 'possible.' A very clever man central to all planning was telling him so. He knew then he had been guilty of gross injustice to his father in suspecting him to have aligned with some hair-brained loonies.

'Okay,' he carried on. 'Assuming the military targets can be achieved. What happens afterwards? You would still have a country to run.'

'Indeed we would. Which is perhaps what will differentiate this Endeavour from many others consigned to an ignominious history on this continent. We have extremely solid structures already in place for governance, for running the civil service. Think of it as a shadow government in waiting. It is equipped to perform all facets of civil administration. Running the central bank. Managing the bourses. Keeping the seaports, the airports operating. Exports flowing. Paying out social grants. Administering health and education. Seeing to it the courts and the prisons function normally. Ensuring a responsible press corps disseminates real, not fake news. Maintaining consular services with open channels to international organisations.' He paused. 'Years in the building, Piet. As I mentioned, some very influential people are involved. People who can think. People who have international connections, under-the-table support from forums like the World Economic Forum at Davos and the United Nations. People who can count on securing national credit lines once it is shown there are responsible hands at the helm in South Africa. Just like you and I, these men and women are tired of the greed and corruption which has brought this country to the brink.'

An informed delivery, Piet couldn't help but be impressed. A compelling man who had deservedly earned his respect. If there were others like him, success seemed a very real possibility. That earlier sense he'd experienced of something 'being out there' fleshed out now as a hard reality. His sense of national pride well and truly re-awoken. The runaway was in his death-throes. A citizen again, he had a decision to make. He felt once more a bond of connection to his country. A right to belong. A right to build a life in it. A right a bunch of greedy opportunists would steal if honest men did nothing.

'I'm sure I don't need to ask this, but here goes anyway. Are all racial groups represented in your shadow government?'

'They are. Not jobs for the boys you understand. We've seen too much of that already. There are real people from all races who have something to contribute, genuinely care about the welfare of this country. It's as it should be. Very prominent business as well as political names feature amongst them. Some you would recognise instantly, may surprise you. We couldn't aim for acceptance from the international community without a representative, not to say, inclusive following. And such acceptance is something we are banking on. Unachieved, it could be a long road indeed. We have to show this is an endeavour to right many wrongs. From a historic as well as a contemporary perspective. We need to be seen to be squeaky clean. No partisan politics. No hidden agendas. A clear road to democracy with responsible government. As I mentioned earlier, an elaborate structure built over years.'

'And eventually when people start voting for elected leadership again what prevents a return to the same corruption we have now?'

'Largely the removal of the perpetrators, careful preparation of a level playing field on which all parties can play. It is a cornerstone of the plan to bring the current abusers to justice. To make an example of them with the sort of extensive prison time they deserve. Believe me there's a raft of evidence already collected to put them there. Extended prison terms will send a message to future politicians; that together with the removal of skewed legislation.'

'Such as?'

He smiled. 'Black Economic Empowerment.'

Piet's earlier barb about selective job opportunity seemingly had registered.

'Something unappealing to you I seem to recall,' he said.

'Mostly because it doesn't work. All it's done is to drive excellence and expertise from the country, entrench the gangsters we are now governed by.'

'Point taken. And of course in addition to forcing a skills exodus, it contributes in a big way to the breakdown of State Owned Enterprises. Entrenching incompetents in the resulting vacuum, purely because they are party card-carriers, is truly a recipe for meltdown."

'So there'll be a period of military rule? Then you see it reverting to a democratic process. How do you plan to win over the electorate? Not everyone is going to support your goal. You cannot hold a country in check militarily for an indefinite period. What will you offer them? How do you secure their vote when you finally prepare the stage for elections? The majority don't understand the complexities we are discussing.'

'Very true. But to answer the questions you raise. What the people do understand, is that under the present administration there is a lack of delivery on the promises they received. Homes and amenities for example. Funding in place but mostly misappropriated. We have a dynamic plan to deliver on such expectations. And we will be careful to show how we are doing it. Not everybody is going to be helped immediately. But they have to understand why that is. We will take pains to have public programmes spell out the plan, legislation passed to limit salaries and fringe benefits for public servants. Our judicial system overhauled to ensure serious financial fraud can be prosecuted expeditiously. The educational system substantially re-engineered, greatly strengthened. No more of the abject failure to deliver text books and learning aids so widespread recently. A meaningful public works programme will provide jobs as a buffer until the economy begins to recover from the woeful state it now finds itself in. We need to show the people their tax rand is working for them. Hopefully they will see democracy is at last delivering for them. There will be a means test for political parties wishing to register for elections. In this way we will show the electorate their vote is meaningful — should be cast wisely. Essentially it is a drive for transparency in all facets of governance.'

'That's an ambitious plan. Can you deliver on it?'

'We're not naive. It will be a process. There are some major structural reforms to implement. A trimming of the burgeoning bureaucracy we see today. It will be a streamlined administration, leaner, meaner. Wherever possible jobs lost in one department will be channeled into the public works programme. The gross inefficiency in regional government will be aggressively tackled. In many disciplines we currently suffer from a skills shortage. We will embark on an extensive campaign to encourage skilled South Africans living abroad, to return home. But to answer your question, yes, we have great confidence we will achieve success to turn this country around, harness its great potential.'

'You're going to need administrative manpower to govern after the military takeover. If you have a hostile civil service it could prove difficult.'

'Surprisingly, the two most heavily politicised branches of the civil service, numerically form a small minority. And those branches are law enforcement and foreign services. These are areas which will also see substantial thinning of manpower. Once done we anticipate smooth running.'

'What about the rest of the civil service?'

'Happily, not heavily partisan. Content for the most part to draw a salary, do their jobs. Presently the service represents close to twenty percent of the country's work force. Unionised they are a resource which needs to be handled tactfully.'

'Clearly something you've considered.'

'More than that. We have insiders in all the trade unions. We've been amassing data for years. Happily, the mood is for change. We've modelled many scenarios. Our team of specialists, labour lawyers and others have a strategy which we believe the unions will embrace; it doesn't displace their members or their executive. We think they will buy-in, but of course the acid test will be when we get to the table with them.'

'And your programme to the process of implementing free elections?'

'Difficult to give a calendar date. Certainly years rather than months. Naive to think otherwise. We need to demonstrate the delivery I mentioned earlier. That will take time, but will be a marked difference to what has gone before. Votes won't be easily won by political parties failing to offer meaningful policies they can implement in their own manifesto's. The state growing beyond there, will hopefully continue to reflect the ideals we will have put in place.'

'And you think you can install the right political party to power?'

'That's not in the plan. It will be a true democracy. The people will elect who they wish to lead them. We would definitely send the wrong message if we tried to impose a ruling party. We see our job as interim caretakers to clear the playing field, prepare an environment for free and fair elections. After which it's over to the people.' He paused for a moment. 'I hope I haven't painted a picture of some Utopian dream. What we are driving for is pragmatism with corruption out of the way. A return to the vision Mandela painted for this country.'

'Are you sure, once your military council have the reins in their hands, they will relinquish them to a democratic process? Lord Acton I believe said, "power corrupts — absolute power corrupts absolutely". Hard to relinquish once you have it.'

He threw his head back laughing. 'We're not renegades attempting to substitute one corrupt administration for another. The plan needs substantial funding. In principle we've secured large packages already via protracted off-the-record negotiation with international agencies. Believe me, bankers are very skittish creatures. They require lots of checks and balances before they lend their money. We'll need to pass muster there too.'

'Sounds like you've covered all your bases.'

'I hope so.'

'So where do we go from here, Simon?'

'Where would you like to go, Piet?'

'I would like to meet my new bosses. The big men planning the military strategy.' The fish was hooked it seemed.

CHAPTER 10

COLONEL STANDER

Despite him being in civilian clothes, Piet saluted smartly as his old commanding officer entered the room. The man beamed beneath his shock of silver hair.

'No need for that these days, Lieutenant,' he took Piet's hand in both his shaking it warmly.

'It's been a long time, Sir.'

'Indeed it has. Indeed it has.' The old soldier regarded him steadily. 'You seem in fine shape. Not as lean as the old days. The extra bulk fits you well.'

He patted his midriff theatrically. 'Bit too much of the good life I'm afraid.' The beers had begun to show — he'd taken out a gym membership the previous week.

'If you're unhappy there I know you'll set about doing something about it.'

'Already work in progress, Sir.'

'That's the spirit,' he said, 'what about your personal life, Pieter? Never married I understand?'

'Bit too much of a rolling stone, I'm afraid.'

'Still lots of time. I don't know if you are aware — I married very late myself. No frivolous motives or romantic illusions. Tends to make for solid relationships.'

A relationship was not something he gave much thought to. The Colonel continued to regard him quietly, nodding almost imperceptibly; perhaps reliving memories of shared combat experiences long ago.

'Unfortunate that you were tugged back here by such trying circumstances, Pieter. I know you left for similar reasons. Many of us who remained thought it would work out better than it has. Sadly disillusioned these days, I'm afraid. Things here have gone dreadfully adrift. Not what we anticipated at all.'

He couldn't think of an appropriate response, so held his peace.

'It seems artless for me to beat around the bush. Our people believe the scales have tipped out of balance. Without dramatic intervention we are convinced this country will be bankrupted; its currency reduced to toilet paper. Tens of thousands will starve. Maybe more.'

'Seems incredible considering the fact we are still the continents largest economy.' He didn't know how else to respond.

The Colonel became pensive. 'No matter how incredible it may seem, it's a sad reality. Because many of this country's population have had it so good for so long, they will not, or cannot, see the looming spectre. That's what has taken us so close to the edge. Anything but prosperity is anathema to them. A scenario of complete breakdown if this regime continues with its nonsense, just doesn't seem possible to most. They're burying their heads in the sand, refusing to believe this economy can actually fail.'

'Can it?'

A shadow passed across his face. Piet wondered if he was envisaging some future apocalypse. Something which chilled him. He collected himself quickly.

'Pieter, we have in our number men who understand far more about economics than I could ever hope to. To a man they are of the opinion that unless drastic corrective measures are taken, this country will hit the wall in under two years. Civil unrest at an unprecedented level will run rampant.'

Piet let that digest for a moment. Was it possible an advanced country over three hundred and sixty years in the making could fail so completely in as little as two? The jewel of the continent shattered? He got a chill at his very core — an image of death and destruction flashed into his mind. Mobs running in the streets burning and looting. Whites targeted for their relative affluence. Wholesale butchering and murder. Another Belgian Congo. The spectre of a failing South Africa.

It boomeranged him back to his days of specialist training in the army; scenarios enacted then. Emergency care-taking amidst urban unrest situations. The role: to secure a strategic city stronghold whilst repulsing an attacking force; fighting at the fringe to progressively enlarge the occupied territory until the entire urban population it was their job to protect was within the cordon. Sobering to think exercises then could be tomorrow's reality.

'I'm just amazed the rot has got as far as it has, Sir.'

'Disturbing isn't it? Seems greed still drives the actions of the politically powerful wherever one looks on this globe. A further problem here is that it has a domino effect. Once one dips his fingers in the till the rest quickly climb aboard, fearful of missing the gravy train.'

'How deeply involved is this Gupta family everyone is talking about?' Piet still marvelled at the influence they appeared to have. 'Seems they're public enemy number one.'

His lips compressed. 'Without our very corrupt politicians it wouldn't have been possible. But as a catalyst, the Guptas are without peer. It is truly astonishing how far into the fabric of the country's civil and commercial structure they've penetrated. And all this, by three brothers who arrived in the country only twenty five years ago. It's no exaggeration to say the Guptas have become a rotten shadow cabinet.'

'Can't they be brought to book?'

'Investigation into their activities is ongoing. However they've been fiendishly clever. They have the Public Prosecutor in their pocket. Very difficult for the state to get anywhere when that office is in itself compromised.'

'I had no idea it went that far.' The fact was, he'd given little thought to the term 'state capture' —somehow an abstraction in his mind. It took on new meaning now.

'It gets worse. We have it on reliable authority the government have aspirations to nationalise the Reserve Bank. Lobbying right now. Once they get enough tacit support you can rest assured they will put a bill before parliament.'

'Wow, that's scary.'

The central bank vested in private hands, served as a bastion of the country's financial stability. It set the interest rate at which commercial banks borrowed or lent to one another which in turn determined the rate at which the banks could lend to the public. The Reserve Bank, as it was labelled, also traded internationally in the country's currency, acting as a regulator to prevent wild fluctuations in the value of the rand. In this way it protected against opportunistic traders who scavenged amongst unstable currencies, making fortunes on the arbitrage between buy and sell rates. To lose control of the central bank to the machinations of a corrupt cabal would be dynamite. Piet could picture hyper-inflation running unchecked, bringing down an already shaky house of cards.

Colonel Stander echoed his thoughts. 'I'm afraid it would signpost the end for us. We would slide from a robust economy, albeit ailing, to a banana republic with worthless currency. Like Zimbabwe.'

'That's disturbing. I'm beginning to see why there's such widespread concern. Can these people be stopped in time — your movement bring change?'

He regarded Piet carefully. 'With respect, Pieter it is already much more than just a movement. We have enough covert structure in place to run this country efficiently as it should be run. Top expertise operating in commercial and civil structures. But all of this — the many years it has taken to build and to nurture, will come to nought if we cannot wrest control from the incumbents.'

The necessity for military intervention; the reason Piet was there. A flight of butterflies flapped their way into his stomach. He knew he would shortly be on centre stage, would have to deliver his lines. Except he didn't have any. What could he offer? Did he have anything to give from his platform of middle age? The young combat soldier of yesteryear was not the same person who sat there today. Could he still perform under fire? Still lead a troop and not place them in jeopardy? To himself his worth was questionable but his decision to commit, inviolate. He would willingly undertake rigorous training if that's what it took to get him battle fit. Nervy territory after having been so long away from combat. The man in front of him, once before an overarching force in his life, would command it again. And soon. Becoming a liability was not an option.

He felt it necessary to be brutally honest. 'I'm not battle fit, Sir. Haven't done any soldiering since I served under you; to be frank I'm battling to understand why I'm even a target for recruitment. The addition of one man from afar can't make much difference surely?'

'You were the finest soldier who ever served under me, Pieter. Not just because of the heroism you display when the chips are down. But because of your astonishing ability to read the situation on the ground, rapidly adapt in ways others wouldn't see. It truly is a rare soldiering gift. And one I believe the Endeavour can benefit from greatly.'

'A long time ago now. Overstated in my opinion, Sir.'

'But not in mine. A leopard doesn't change his spots. Your leadership under fire in Angola was no less than astonishing. Even with all the fire power at our disposal, the chiefs of staff all but gave up. Yet you persevered with a brilliant piece of strategy, your small force winning the day. Had politics gone differently at the time, there's no telling where your action at the Lomba river might have taken us. Your medal wasn't awarded lightly, believe me.'

Keen to move past this, he pressed on. 'Respectfully, Sir this is a very different situation. I'm way past my prime for serious field activity. What role could I possibly play?'

He considered Piet carefully for a moment. 'We would like you at the very top. On the planning panel. One of our Chiefs Of Staff, if you like.'

Thunderstruck. That would be the best way to describe Piet's reaction. He had visualised a probable role as platoon leader. Perhaps even company commander. Or maybe spearheading a guerrilla group. Being propositioned for a leadership role at the very top, way beyond anything he'd thought about. It seemed incredible. Scant weeks previously he cruised carefree aboard *Magus* in the Caribbean. Now here he was, invited to help steer a revolution in Africa's largest economy.

'I don't know what to say, Sir. I'm truly flabbergasted. Still not sure that I have anything worthwhile to bring to the table.'

'We believe you have. I realise this must be somewhat overwhelming. Let me make a suggestion. Don't come to a decision here and now. Attend the next couple of planning sessions. Meet the other members of the team. Give me your answer then.'

CHAPTER 11

UNWELCOME VISITORS

Piet's neighbour at the Hout Bay marina was a quiet New Zealander whose speech was always going to betray his origins. In his early sixties and a maritime junky like Piet, he had designed and built his boat from scratch. A beast falling somewhere between a fishing trawler and an oil tanker. He planned to do some serious-ocean sailing in it. For Piet the last thing he would want to be caught in if the weather turned nasty. However, the man seemed happy with it, so to each his own.

Unlocking the main hatchway in *Magus*, after his return trip from Johannesburg, he heard Jeff call.

'Aaah, Piet,' starting nervously as he always did. 'Couple of fellas came looking for you whilst you were away.'

'Not with handcuffs I hope Jeff,' he joked.

'Aaah... funny thing, they were policemen,' he looked embarrassed at having to tell Piet that and bobbed his head like a parakeet.

His disclosure wiped the grin off Piet's face. Why was the law visiting him?

'I've got the kettle on for a cuppa. Pop over, I'll give you the calling card they left.'

Back aboard after tea, he looked at the card again. It announced a Detective Inspector Khumalo. Why had he been looking for him? Very discomfiting to have a visit from the authorities so soon after casting his lot in the role of enemy of the state. But surely it could have nothing to do with that? There was no way intelligence could work at such speed. Then he remembered the fire, the shooting at the old harbour the night he walked home from drinks with Rusty and George. That must be it. Nothing sinister then. He relaxed straight away, would phone Khumalo in the morning to see what he wanted.

He did. As he'd suspected it was to question him further on the harbour incident. He agreed to pop down to the station in the afternoon.

He parked the car in their yard, reported to the charge office and got shown to an interview room at the back of the building. The furniture — typical government issue, utilitarian, uncomfortable and well worn into the bargain. He took a seat settling to wait. After ten minutes his irritation was taking root when the door opened and an overweight individual wallowed into the room followed by a taller colleague. Laurel and Hardy.

'Detective Inspector Khumalo,' he announced without offering his hand. 'This is Mr Patel.' He shook Patel's hand as they moved to their seats around the interview table. As Khumalo fidgeted like a fat broody hen fussing at the nest to get his ample girth moulded to the tub-type office chair, a concealed firearm squelched to view from under his shirt. Unperturbed he made the adjustment and resettled himself.

'We would like to ask some questions about the incident at the harbour two Fridays ago,' he opened the file in front of him. Piet recognised the constable's carefully crafted document — the statement he'd given.

'Fire away,' he hadn't intended the pun.

He regarded Piet without humour. 'You say in your statement you were drinking with friends at the Woodcutters Arms. You decided to walk home from there.'

'That's right.'

'You also say you live aboard your boat. What is its name?'

'*Magus*. It's in my statement.'

Unnecessarily, he repeated the name, flattening the first vowel so it sounded like an 'e'. 'Meegus.'

Piet held his peace.

'Why is it you didn't go straight to your boat? It adds more distance to your journey to go via the old harbour.'

Piet realised he was testing his statement. Looking to see if he made any factual errors on the retelling. Interrogation

101. He played along for a further twenty minutes not permitting his irritation to get the better of him. Finally Khumalo appeared satisfied. Patel had not uttered a word during this time. Piet wondered what role he played, whether he outranked Khumalo. He raised the question.

'Why is it necessary to have two officers corroborating my statement?'

Patel broke his silence. 'I'm not a police officer, Mr Rossouw. I'm with the Department of Home Affairs, Immigration Inspectorate to be exact.'

That came as a surprise as well as something of a shock. He worked hard at not letting it show.

'Am I suspected of an immigration offence?' he felt he had nothing to lose by being direct.

'No, not at all. My department got the request to confirm your date of entry into the country. The one you gave in your statement.'

'Did I get it wrong?'

He smiled. 'No, you didn't. Simply routine to check on recent entrants once they show up on a police report. Monitoring for undesirables.'

Now he had reason to kick himself, for his dumb stupidity being at the scene of the fire that night. It had served to get him onto some sort of government inter-departmental watch list. Something he could well do without at that particularly sensitive time.

'A senior police officer was killed the night of the fire,' Khumalo broke in. 'You were at the scene having recently re-entered the country. And you're an ex-army man trained in the use of firearms."

They'd been busy. He would need to be on his guard.

'Am I a suspect for involvement in the shooting?' Might as well have it out in the open he reasoned, if this was what it was all about.

'No. But you were there. With no good reason we can see.'

'As my statement reflects, simply raw curiosity. A walk home after a night with my friends. I saw the fire, the police vehicles and the fire engine rushing by. I decided to take a look.'

'You do not identify your friends in your statement. Why is that?'

Piet didn't like the way this was going at all.

'It wasn't relevant to the incident.'

'I think we should be the ones to decide that.' He took a pen from his pocket flipping Piet's statement over to expose the blank space at the bottom of the reverse page. 'Their names please.'

This posed a problem. They'd already investigated him to a level where they'd uncovered his military history. If he lied or tried to cover for Rusty and George, it could result in a police visit for them too. They would soon see all three of them served together. Better to steal his thunder, volunteer information before he dug for it.

'Two of my old army chums, we've been mates ever since Angola. We get together occasionally to chew over old times.'

'Their names please.'

Piet gave the names, cursing himself under his breath. Innocent of any criminality, none of this would matter; but involved in subversive activities… he could afford none of this scrutiny. He had managed spectacularly to scupper any anonymity he may have hoped for. Additionally, George and Rusty were on his radar for later recruitment to the Endeavour. Now the possibility existed they would also find themselves on a watch list. Before Khumalo could ask him for their addresses, he took out his cell phone volunteering their numbers. Maybe making it easy for them would deter a personal visit. Certainly more preferable than the rigours of a face-to-face interrogation.

Khumalo put his pen away, closed the file. Piet made to stand, when Patel slid another question across his bow.

'What brings you back to South Africa at this time, Mr Rossouw?'

'I have family here.'

'Yes. Your mother and father, a sister in Pretoria, I believe?'

His sense of unease deepened. Why did they have this much interest in him? Had he been singled out for exhaustive investigation for reasons he could not fathom? Or did this relate purely to the incident he'd witnessed? In either event South Africa's organs of government had earned renewed if grudging respect from him. They weren't bankrupt to the level of banana-republic institutions he previously suspected.

Patel hadn't finished.

'Our records indicate you also have a younger brother in Britain.' Showing off now, but he began to get the sense the interview was carefully structured. If indeed he had something to hide, they were at pains to show him Big Brother knew about it. He realised he could not give him the lie that a sick parent brought him back. He had allowed himself to be deceived by that lie, but they would not be.

'Just a visit home after a prolonged absence.'

'Over eight years now isn't it?

'That's right.'

'Will you be staying, or are you planning to be off again soon?'

'Probably going to stay,' he thought he'd better round this out a tad. 'My father is getting on now. We own a large wine estate which takes quite a bit of management. He's not going to be able to stay at the helm for very much longer. There is nobody else.'

'Well let me wish you all the best with your endeavour.' The choice of noun — the code word for their planned revolution — was jarring considering its recent inclusion in his personal lexicon. He looked to Khumalo who was regarding him intimidatingly and seemed in no hurry to end the interview. Finally, the policeman checked his watch and began the task of hauling his bulk out of the chair. It seemed the interview was over.

On his feet Khumalo faced Piet. 'We appreciate your time. I'll be in touch if there is anything else.'

He left the charge office and emerged to the car park. A boiler-suited mechanic passed him hefting a toolbox and disappeared into the building.

He cursed angrily under his breath as he got to his car. 'Shit.' he'd called down dangerous attention on himself. 'Shit! Shit! Shit!'

CHAPTER 12

THE MILITARY PANEL

Colonel Stander lived in the northern suburbs of Cape Town, his home close to the airport. So he turned down Piet's offer to pick him up, electing to make his way there himself. They were to travel north for Piet's introduction to the planning team.

During the flight they studiously avoided talking about the serious issues occupying their minds. Instead, they chatted around lighter topics. The state of South African rugby, its preparedness to contest the world cup in 2019. Piet wasn't a dyed-in-the wool rugby buff, but the game approached institutional status in the country; the Colonel an avid fan. To have no interest at all, tantamount to a treasonable act. Piet smiled at the irony; treason was after all, his new stock-in-trade.

The skies turned to drizzle as they landed. Transit terminals are dry havens of warmth in wet weather yet always seemed subdued to him. The prospect he guessed of having to leave them to face those same elements they protect you from.

They were soon out of the buildings and aboard a taxi taking them towards the outskirts of Pretoria. As they got closer to where they were going they passed through the suburbs on the the slick ribbon of highway, finally leaving it to get into larger sub-divisions and small-holdings further out. This was the 'mink and manure' belt much favoured by the horsey crowd. It seemed every property was home to at least one equine peering over a paddock fence.

Their destination was a sprawling ranch-style home set in park-like surroundings. Behind the house, a rolling meadow ran down to a brook struggling to stay viable and avoid being a series of isolated pools. Green trunks of 'fever' trees shone like soft neon along the watercourse. Just north of here the land transitioned to proper bushveldt with this flora in profusion.

Their arrival didn't go unnoticed. Two curious mares interrupted their cropping to give them the once over. Puffing out his feathers imperiously not to be outdone, a large male ostrich stamped along the multi-strand electric fence. On guard and not to be lightly messed with, this bird could eviscerate with a single kick of his powerful legs and was stark testimony to the state of lawlessness prevailing in the country.

Once inside, their host, a lizard-lean individual in his early sixties, welcomed them from the shelter of an umbrella.

'Good morning, Ronnie. Trust you had a good flight?'

'Minor turbulence on the way in. With this weather, nothing to complain about. Legroom getting a bit cramped as my knees stiffen with the years,' he turned to Piet. 'I'd like you to meet Pieter Rossouw.'

He introduced himself. 'Colin Farrell. Good to finally meet you. Ronnie's told us a lot about you.' They shook and he turned into the house with the new arrivals following. A wide passage led to a room in the middle of the house. Their meeting room. He breathed deeply, steadying himself to confront men who would orchestrate a revolution. Men who could be responsible for writing history. Names that would then carry to future generations. Might his be amongst them? The thought did nothing to calm seriously jangling nerves.

Murmurings carried from the room. Three men rose as they entered. After the introductions Piet stole a look at the Colonel. He was beaming as if his prize bull had just received the winners rosette at an agricultural show. Feeling very much out of his depth, he wondered how much the Colonel had made of his military history; the medal he felt he hadn't earned.

'Thank you all for your attendance today,' the Colonel began, 'I realise I called this meeting at short notice, I'm grateful to you all for shuffling your diaries. From my past disclosures, each of you is aware of who Pieter Rossouw is. And why I've brought him here today.'

Piet smiled feeling as exposed as a baby in an incubator tank. Colonel Stander continued to talk him up.

'I believe Pieter will prove to be a major asset in all we are trying to achieve.' He again regarded Piet with that same laudatory look. 'I've had the honour, during the Border War, of being his commanding officer. You all know how highly I regard his soldiering, his leadership skills. Pieter undervalues those, questions their currency. I do not.' He knew it was important for his war cabinet to buy in. 'He will sit in on one or two of our meetings to get a feel for what we are about, better understand what his role would be should he elect to help us in our task.'

Piet sensed the bond binding that fellowship. The unity of purpose. He became aware of the stirrings of a metamorphosis taking place within himself. He had been a deserter. He felt that now. Knew then that a deep sense of patriotism had been fanned to flame — felt he was hugely privileged to find himself in a position where he could play a pivotal role. The choice would be his. These men were trusting him at the level of their very lives. Would be equipping him to make that decision on an informed basis.

He underwent an epiphany. An illumination that brought purpose to a life of escapism. Suddenly he needed to belong. Nothing less would fulfil him.

'Alright, without further ado, let's get down to cases,' the Colonel cast around the room. 'Archie, starting with you. Tell us for Pieter's benefit, where we are to date with our recruiting, our troop strength. I'd like you to be expansive. Explain our strategy in these areas. He needs to get a handle on our philosophy here.'

The thickset man he'd addressed shifted slightly in his chair. Steady eyes which would miss little glittered behind rimless spectacles. The bearing of a regimental sergeant major.

'Assembling a fighting force and remaining undetectable on the radar, comes with its own set of challenges,' he said. 'The approach to each candidate, carries risk; circumspection vital in each and every case. The candidate could be attractive to us but negative facets of his character may be a limiting factor. Not to put too fine a point on it, a loose mouthed individual could cause us severe embarrassment.' He removed his glasses and polished them vigorously. 'Wherever possible we target men with previous armed-forces experience. Not always possible, but for obvious reasons desirable. In the assessment process we run various checks; criminal, military, credit and the like.' He noticed Piet's raised eyebrow. 'You're no doubt wondering why on earth we conduct a credit check. To assess a man's military capability it seems unrelated I'm sure — but it goes towards establishing character. Credit irresponsibility in civilian life is hardly a marker towards a leadership role. A person unable to manage his accounts could not be expected to manage men. May be suitable to serve as a foot soldier though.'

'Okay,' Piet could see the sense in prioritising candidate canvassing, 'being able to target men who've served would suggest access to military records?'

'Unfettered access. We've taken pains to ensure we have people strategically placed. Records offices are gold mines. Helps enormously as you can imagine.' His glasses wandered down the bridge of his nose, he pushed them back. 'If the profile is acceptable we conduct a 'feeling out.' Generally done through a member already on strength. If possible someone known personally to the candidate.'

'And the approach would encompass all races?'

'Important observation. We canvas roughly twice as many black candidates as whites. The ratio goes someway to the demographics in the country at large. Our final mix needs to be somewhere in the two-to-one range. A white biased weighting would come under critical scrutiny in the international forum. Can't afford to get that wrong. Too much power in white hands could be seen as a thinly veiled attempt to put control back where it cannot belong.'

'Are you successful in maintaining the ratio?'

'Lagging a bit in black combatants. We're continuously reviewing, tweaking the recruiting drive as the situation demands. It's a sensitive issue. Supportive power blocs off-shore keep a weather eye over our shoulder to make sure we get it right. It will also go a long way in encouraging a sympathetic press when our takeover is analysed. A hostile media could be the kiss of death. We need them on our side to gain international recognition, negative perceptions being the invitation to the party for a United Nations force here.'

The Colonel interceded. 'You've got the numbers Archie; perhaps you'd run them out for Pieter?'

'Certainly. We have just under twelve hundred men on strength currently. Target is to build to eighteen companies grouped across three battalions. That's an optimum force of slightly less than double the present number.'

'And the candidate flow? Can't be an easy matter to build numbers given the need for secrecy.'

'Fortunately, there's an exponential kicker there. As the force grows, it opens up more possibilities by association, broadens opportunities. Flows currently are healthy. Of course, the associated risk profile is exponential too. We can't afford complacency.'

'Can I come in there Archie?' The man, ruddy complexioned beneath a monkish band of white hair and wearing a black eyepatch, raised a hand from the table. He had about him an almost theatrical air and kept unwavering eye-contact from his good eye, the colour of tempered steel. 'Security is a major concern. To date luck has favoured us. But as Archie points out, the more men in the mix the more the risk grows. Same for the programme. The longer we wait the greater the danger. The men know they're involved in a movement for change, part of a fighting force to achieve it. Beyond there they are not privy to detail — standard army protocol. In training we keep them grouped in small cells. Little contact with other groups. Until of course we bring them together for major field exercises. That's the real finger-nail-biting area when they go home afterwards.'

Piet had given thought to the field exercises that had been mentioned. They were a non-negotiable to prepare a fighting force. An inescapable necessity for live combat missions to follow. He understood the concerns. Mental discipline in all aspects would be as challenging to achieve as military fitness, in fact, would be part of it. Now that the topic was on the table, he wanted to know more.

'How is the mens' conditioning overall? Fitness? Psychological preparation?'

'Much the same as the regular military. Psychological conditioning is as important a part of modern warfare as physical preparation. The same way competitive sportsmen get coached, so too the men. We aim to instil a mindset all about winning — emphasise it, reinforce it with strategies which dovetail, show them the correlation. As a final caveat they are reminded of the criminal risk they run if discovered in their activity. A long prison sentence is a deterrent in itself.'

He began to see the bigger picture of a deeply structured initiative. His mind wandered back to field exercises. Hard to hide. Intriguing to find out where they were taking place. Certain to be a location where discovery would be all-but ruled out. He was pretty sure he knew where it was. Even in a vast country like South Africa, there weren't many places would tick all the boxes.

He ventured a guess. 'Field exercises wouldn't be in the Karoo would they?'

Colonel Stander looked at the other commanders smiling. 'I did warn you, gentlemen.'

Carl laughed freely. 'If it came from anybody else, I would be genuinely concerned.' He chuckled again. 'You're right of course. We have a farm in the north-west Karoo. A very large farm. It's a bona fide sheep ranching operation a long way from anywhere. We've got all the bells and whistles there. Barracks, armoury, indoor rifle range, transport depot, workshops. Everything. It is remote, hardly anybody comes past or visits. From a casual glance, there is nothing extraordinary to give it away. We're so far from other habitation even the sound of small-arms fire doesn't reach inquisitive ears. It's an ideal location — we've turned it into a sophisticated facility.'

Bingo! Mentally he patted Rusty, George and himself on the back. They had worried to death the topic of Buster Clark's absence, what he might have been up to. Given all the pointers, convinced he was training, believing it must be in the Karoo. Vast and arid, the perfect location. Buster was almost certainly on strength with the Endeavour. He wondered how many of their old friends might be too.

Colonel Stander spoke again. 'We also created a very visible public front behind which we hide. Have you come across an organisation called the South African Emergency Evacuation Initiative?'

'I think I've heard mention of it on a news broadcast.'

'Quite likely. Well, it's us. Officially a civil defence organisation constituted lawfully in terms of the Geneva Convention. Generally referred to under the acronym SAEEI but we chose the expanded name deliberately. We wanted it to convey rather obviously what it is we are supposed to be doing. Wearing this hat, we portray a strong intentional bias towards the Afrikaner farmer and his well-being — God knows his need is real enough. From officialdom, we don't get treated very seriously at all. A right-wing anachronism in the new South Africa. But it gives a thin layer of cover if cell activities ever get uncovered. From time to time our media friends are encouraged to keep SAEEI in the public eye.

We're almost a laughing stock in the population at large. Happily our real members don't have that view. But outside of them, the more we rattle our gourd the less gravitas we seem to command. As I say, it's a bit on the thin side but may serve a purpose one of these days.'

Piet recalled the occasion he'd heard the organisation mentioned — a radio jockey interviewing a very passionate *boer* from a remote area, his neighbour killed during one of the country's ubiquitous farm attacks. The man openly berated the police, claiming them to be woefully inefficient to the point of disinterest. He went on to add how he was contacted within hours of the incident by SAEEI who quickly visited, helped him strengthen his defences, got him on their radio network. He couldn't speak highly enough of the organisation. The empathy displayed; the level of professionalism under which the organisation operated. A stark contrast to the police approach he ranted. He called for solidarity urging fellow farmers to join for their own wellbeing.

He related the incident. 'I'm impressed, Sir. Seems to me it's a clever cover. I would never have guessed it masked a deeper initiative.'

'Well, that's gratifying. We have genuine members as the incident illustrates. They're catered to by a management hierarchy looking after their concerns. That's the civil defence aspect, but back to our military activities.' He turned to the individual seated next to him. 'Leonard, perhaps you'd like to sketch your side of things?'

'Certainly, Ronnie.' A softly spoken man but once again carrying the assurance of authority. 'It falls to me to manage all our logistical needs. That's everything from off-road motorbikes to troop carriers, minibuses, artillery pieces. I make sure we have the right vehicles in place in preparation for manoeuvres, for instance. A lot of the fleet we keep dotted around the country. SAEEI locations. Perfect cover for parking vehicles of a more obvious military nature. Armoured units particularly. Under article four of the Geneva Convention, all very legal for SAEEI to own. Provided of course they are not employed in an aggressive role. The protection of civilian populations in times of conflict, satisfies that part of the charter; enough farmers have been lost for it to go unchallenged.'

'And what about the ordnance, how does that look?' In South Africa it would never be easy equipping a small army with firearms outside of government.

'Work in progress. There are still some gaps in the inventory of course; we're busy taking steps to fill those.'

'Probably a good point at which to sketch out our position there,' the Colonel said.

Leonard took a sip of water. 'Of course. We've our challenges accessing sufficient weapons. Most of what we do have we'd like to replace. It's old and tired, acceptable at a push. We can't use SAEEI as a cover to equip. Quantities are too great. We made application through official channels via SAEEI for a licence to obtain a quantity of new rifles. Turned down unceremoniously. We suspected it would be of course but had to try.' He glanced at his writing pad. His absent doodling sketched an umbrella, the overarching protection of SAEEI, fending off raindrops that looked like bullets. 'Getting what we need will have to come through the black-market. No other way. And of course that has to be handled very carefully. If we get caught at it, then the balloon would certainly go up.'

To say the least. 'Where are the shortages?'

'Assault rifles.' He was emphatic. 'We've been accumulating locally wherever an opportunity presents, but as I say it leaves us with a pretty mixed bag. We're currently looking further afield — the black market.'

Piet wanted to know about other ordnance. 'What of field pieces? Artillery play a part in the plan?'

'Not so much, one or two pieces for specific actions. The offensive will be mostly infantry operations. Largely conducted with smaller manpower units. In terms of overall success objectives have to be overrun quickly. If we're forced to dig in anywhere, it's more than likely the harbinger of failure. Give the national troops time to regroup, they'll swamp us with numbers.'

That brought a sombre mood to the room. He looked at the faces around the table. Jawlines were set, he doubted any one of them so much as considered the spectre of failure. They were knights joined in a noble cause.

Colonel Stander broke the silence. 'Gentlemen, it's not going to happen. We will achieve our objectives — and with speed. We are not going to allow ourselves to get bogged down in trench warfare.' He turned to Piet. 'Are there any more questions you would like to raise at this time, Pieter?'

He shook his head.

The Colonel looked at his watch. 'Well then I think this is as good a time as any to break for lunch. Colin tells me he's laid on a bit of a spread. As always of course gentlemen, only conversational topics at the table.'

They flew back to Cape Town in the afternoon. He reconfirmed his commitment to Colonel Stander — he was irreversibly on board. Whatever there was for him to do he would do to the best of his ability. The Colonel was delighted with Piet's passion. 'I'm thrilled, Pieter. I knew I hadn't misjudged you. Now that's out of the way, I'd like you to come around to the house tomorrow. Mustn't waste any time. There's a crucial mission I'd like you to undertake straight away.'

CHAPTER 13

ANTI NUCLEAR LOBBYISTS

The Russian approached the small group parading with placards outside Cape Town's parliament buildings. He greeted them warmly, his English east-coast America accented — legacy of the six years he'd spent there. 'You guys getting anywhere against this nuclear programme?' he asked a bearded muslim in a *kameez*. The man held aloft a placard with 'No Nuclear Deals' smeared across it.

'From America?' He asked the newcomer and beamed when he received confirmation. A lie on the part of the Russian but it suited his purpose.

'I think we are,' the protester gushed, 'we've lodged an application at court to challenge government's signing with the Russians. Their deal did not go through required procurement procedures. No advertising in the government gazette. No open tender process. Nothing of that was done. We're sure there are pay-offs to politicians.' He looked self-satisfied. 'Are you anti nuclear yourself?'

'I sure am,' he lied again, 'ever since the Three Mile Island affair in '79 and of course the Chernobyl meltdown since then. Nuclear power is dangerous.'

The man agreed enthusiastically. 'It is. But not why I'm here. I am against the loss of South African jobs it will mean if these power stations go ahead. There's enough unemployment without creating more. We don't need that in this country.'

'How so the loss of jobs?' the Russian still played the game, 'I would have thought new power stations would create them.'

'Aah, only at first — in the construction phase.' Proud to air his knowledge. 'And even then, short lived, very limited. Perhaps only the civil structures would give temporary work. These nuclear reactors would be built in Russia, shipped to South Africa as sub-assemblies. They would be put together here with specialised personnel. Russian engineers. And when they have been commissioned they run on a handful of staff. That's not job creation.'

'Sounds fair enough,' his questioner seemed to show genuine interest, 'so what's the alternative? I mean there are lot's of power outages every day, so there's obviously a capacity problem.'

'Our power utility is close to completing two large plants up country. When they come on line it will boost the present electricity supply, satisfy the shortage. And create a lot more jobs to run them as well. Those coal-fired stations support local mining activity. We need that. What we don't need is fat off-shore conglomerates generating work in their own countries and lining the pockets of their pet politicians here. These nuclear plants are simply surplus to requirements only in prospect to give the dirty politicians an opportunity of taking massive bribes.'

'It's a convincing picture but what's the basis for the court action?'

'A challenge to the procurement process itself. If we can stop the current deal, they'll have to start again. That's a delay of years, it will give us time to lobby for more public support against nuclear. But you'll have to speak to Makoma Lekalakala if you want more detail there. She's the head of our organisation, knows the ins and outs. That's her over there.'

The woman stood a little way off chatting with another group of protestors; a robust black lady wearing a loose fitting *boubous* printed in colourful geometric patterns. She would always stand out in a crowd.

The Russian watched her for a few seconds. 'I'll chat to her now.' He turned back to the man. 'What is it you call yourselves?'

'Izimpilo Africa. We're a non governmental organisation fighting for safe, sustainable power generation.'

'Can I snap a picture to show the folks back home?'

'With pleasure.' He puffed out his chest and oriented his placard so it would be captured in the image.

The Russian moved back, positioned himself to take the shot. He adjusted the angle to his subject until the lady in the colourful *boubous* sat squarely in the frame. He loosed off a number of shots, then pocketed his cellphone waving a friendly farewell to his conversationist.

CHAPTER 14

UNDER SURVEILLANCE

Ivashchenkov put the phone down leaning back in his chair. He massaged his temple, frowning. The information he'd just received puzzled him. There might be nothing to it, but then again his sources were paid to keep their noses to the ground. Feed him anything which could threaten Zuma — threaten the premiership. He reached across his desk for his cell phone. He keyed a number getting an answer almost at once.

'Meet me at coffee shop in half-hour.' He pocketed the phone, took his jacket from the hatstand and went through to the outer office.

'Out for one hour. Not more. Anything urgent you can get me on my cell. Other than urgent — no calls.' His secretary nodded, checked the clock on the wall.

He took a table under one of the awnings, positioning himself to enjoy the view of the pedestrian square in front of him. A favourite place. Bordered by restaurants with just the right density of patronage, it reminded him of a European piazza and invoked nostalgia. The floor-level water feature centre-square, sent soothing ripples over marbled flagstones. Sentinel at one end was a six metre bronze of Nelson Mandela keeping vigil over the square which bore his name. A reminder of a country in transition.

Ivashchenkov's coffee came as his colleague arrived. He doubled the order as the man settled himself.

'Do we still have lobbyists watched?' he wasted no time. Not a man for small talk.

'*Da*. But think maybe we should pull resource off. Is only a handful of protesters every day. Nothing changes. Unless of course, you want us to take care of women?'

'Too late. Battlefield has changed. Is now in courtroom. People you watch have secured funding to fight government on procurement policy — have applied to court to challenge deal have with Zuma. Need to change tactics. I will give instruction.'

The man nodded. 'Have photographs. Will be easy to arrange accident.'

'Not for now. But is something else. Source at police headquarters passes new information today. A man, Armand Rossouw in Cape Town, is person of interest to police. For couple years now. Is wine farmer. Anti-government sympathies.'

His colleague scoffed. 'Radical? Old type *boer* waving flag?'

'No. Not racist. Is liberal. Pays workers over industry rates, gives houses they never have without him.'

The man looked puzzled. Ivashchenkov allowed himself a rare chuckle. 'Is still Afrikaner. Has problem with way business is done in new South Africa. Is descendant of old Cape family. Belongs to civil defence organisation — South Africa Emergency Evacuation Initiative. Not taken as threat by authorities, but watched anyway. Not why alert came. Son has just returned to country. Is also now person of interest. Special services soldier in Angola war. They watch because of history.'

'Sounds like they waste their time.'

'Maybe. Maybe not. They alert us, so good to watch until we are sure. Son left country eight years ago. Could not take new politics — ANC rule. Is eldest child in line for inheritance. Family farm worth big money, is leading wine producer in Cape. Abandoned it — because became pissed of with black government.'

'And now is back. Maybe to line up for inheritance. Change of heart, can be. A good soldier?' As a past career soldier, he was always keen to know the mettle of another.

'Good. Very good. Big distinction in special-forces unit. Only soldier ever to receive country's highest military award. Equivalent to Hero of The Russian Federation.'

The man whistled softly despite himself. 'How earned?'

'Angola. Border war — us on other side, saving useless Cubans' arses.'

The man remembered the war which escalated to an international hot spot dragging in the super-powers. 'This Rossouw, they think becomes involved with father's activity?'

'They scratch their balls. But will lose interest quickly. You know how are.'

'You think may be something to it?'

'Is early to say. But I want watched. If works against government — works against us. Is already difficult keeping Zuma at top. The fool now on shaky ground. Upsetting wrong people in own party; people who want him gone. We spend more money to buy loyalty. If Rossouw is another threat — must know. Put people on it.'

'Can count on support from authorities?'

Ivashchenkov pulled down the corners of his mouth in an act of dismissal. 'Much talk little action — will mess up. Rossouw will be too clever for them. Use our resource, but stay close to local police for information they may get. Make friend of Detective Inspector Khumalo at Hout Bay station. Smarter than others, has political connections linked to ours. Was first to open file on Rossouw. Tell Khumalo we mount surveillance on Rossouw, no need for his manpower. Say we will report progress. Keep happy, throw some money his way.'

'How many men?'

'As many as it takes. Rotate surveillance. Rossouw will be smart, will see quickly if same faces always around. I leave detail to you. But I want information on everyone he meets. Pictures, backgrounds, jobs, addresses. Everything. We need to build picture. If he travels follow him. See where is going, who is meeting.'

At that very moment thirty kilometres south of where they sipped coffee, their quarry was aboard a taxi in downtown Johannesburg.

CHAPTER 15

SOPHIE BIRMAN

Back in Johannesburg, he was on his way to an appointment arranged by Simon Zondo. The lunchtime crowd was frenetic. As the taxi dropped him, he had his work cut out not to be swept along by the busy throng. He navigated his way through a river of humanity aiming for the red-brick tower — his destination. This older quarter of the city showed signs of decay. Encrusted grime and broken pavements were testament to hard use and little care. Even his target building looked as if a thorough pressure wash would perk it up no end. The restaurants and coffee shops pumped doing a brisk trade, however. If patrons noticed the signs of dilapidation they didn't show it. He eased out of the stream and entered the lobby.

The cool interior and open space brought welcome relief from the masses outside. Johannesburg's business population is an eclectic mix. Locals rub shoulders with coal-black Nigerians, lighter-skinned Ghanaians, cousins from the Ivory Coast, the Zimbabwe diaspora, Malawi's gentlefolk, cheerful Mozambicans — just about every sub-Saharan nationality you could point a stick at. Scattered amongst these, perhaps more thinly these days at least to his jaundiced eye, were the white South Africans; grains of salt scattered amongst a bed of ground pepper — the condiment of transformation to be sure.

He approached reception; a dated marble barrier behind which sat a black lady bulging out of a grey business suit. She was making a good job of defying the laws of physics to remain balanced atop the rickety swivel chair of her perch. Wary custodian, she eyed him speculatively and offered no greeting. At her back, set high up on the rear wall, a larger-than-life bronze raptor clamped possessively a world globe in its talons. iGoli — the city of gold, wasn't shy in setting out to impress. The bird looked just about as friendly as the receptionist. Beneath the talons an ornate scroll proclaimed he too guarded the home of Phoenix Press Agency.

He announced himself and who he was there to see. She managed grudging acknowledgement, fiddled with the dated phone system of her protectorate. Moments later the lift trundled him shakily to the ninth floor.

Sophie Birman greeted him as the doors opened. She came forward offering an outstretched hand and a welcoming smile. He guessed her to be in her late thirties. Attractive with chestnut hair cut simply in page-boy style. It suited her but he suspected the cut to be dated by today's fashion standards. But what did he know? Her eyes were wide-set, the colour of tigers-eye. She put him in mind of an elegant temple-cat.

They exchanged names and pleasantries to set off toward her office. He was not up on the trappings of corporate hierarchy, but knew an office such as hers to be a badge of rank. She motioned to black leather furniture around a chrome-and-glass coffee table. As he sat she called her outer office giving instruction to hold calls. He studied the black-and-white mural filling the wall behind her. A massive board-mounted image, it captured the moment the Berlin wall started coming down.

'Heady days,' he gestured at the graphic.

She glanced over her shoulder. 'A little before my time in terms of journalism. However, when I first saw the picture it resonated immediately. Symbolic of the advent of a new world you might say. I commissioned a studio to enlarge it for my office when I received my promotion.'

'Not to be rude,' he said, 'but what is your position?'

'I'm assistant to the editor.'

'Sounds very demanding.'

'It can be. Lots of competition in our industry. The trick with a news agency is to be relevant, to be early. Our clients pay good money for the service we provide. They want content which touches their readers, their viewers, and they want to get it first. It's part of my job to make sure what they receive meets that criteria as closely as possible. As I say it can be tricky.'

'I can't profess to understand much about press agencies. Except I do know you don't sell newspapers.'

She smiled. 'No, but we do sell news. Our customers are those newspapers, those magazines. And of course electronic media — TV and radio stations.'

She regarded him quietly for a moment.

'My turn to risk being rude,' she batted the ball back, 'I understand you've recently come back to South Africa? Simon mentioned you're unhappy with the way things are here, may get involved with his organisation. His military wing if you like. He wants me to give you an indication of where Phoenix positions itself regarding all he is doing. What is it I can help you with?'

She certainly didn't waste any time getting down to cases. 'I'm a bit out of my depth,' he confessed, 'never been in a situation vaguely similar. I rather expected...'

He didn't know how to finish. What did he expect? Cloak and dagger stuff? Fifth column coded incomprehensible dialogue? Whispered furtive conversation? He certainly hadn't been ready for this level of transparency.

'It's a very delicate subject I'm sure you'll agree,' he tried for composure so as not to appear a complete idiot. 'Forgive me if I seem naive, but isn't there a risk associated with being this candid?'

She chuckled. 'Apologies. I must appear blasé from your point of view. Perhaps even reckless. I think I must give you some explanatory background. This organisation, Phoenix Media,' she swept an arm in an expansive gesture, 'belongs to very wealthy, not to mention commercially influential owners. They're disillusioned with what's happening in the country, knowing unless it is stopped their business interests will end in the gutter. So they are determined to bring change. As well as the role you met him in — orchestrating the Endeavour, Simon Zondo is the firm's corporate attorney. If he sends you to me then I am above one hundred per cent sure I can safely share anything with you.'

Security indoctrination is ingrained. To the trained soldier, life at risk if he allows a lapse in awareness, it becomes second nature. She noticed him scrutinising the room for obvious security weak points and pre-empted his next question.

'You're wondering about the walls having ears. Or perhaps eyes for that matter. You can see that none of the windows has line-of-sight to other buildings — double glazed so electronic eavesdropping isn't possible. The plaster screed on the walls contains a fine metallic powder making it impassable to electronic snooping too. A leaden sheet is embedded in the door. The office gets electronically swept every week. Believe me Mr Rossouw, anything said in this room, stays in this room.'

He felt more than a little sheepish. 'Forgive me. Ingrained military training coming to the fore.'

'No apology necessary. These are delicate times. Wise to be cautious.'

That put him a little more at ease. He had been a cat on a hot tin roof a lot of the time since having made his decision to join the Endeavour. Still a bit skittish. Something which would pass with time.

'The truth is I'm already on strength. It's taking a bit of getting used to. This is a fact-finding mission to help me understand the bigger picture — get a feel for the plan.' Time for his explanatory background. 'Simon may have mentioned I'm involved on the military side.'

She laughed. 'From what he told me you're going to be one of the big cheeses. None of my business. Happy to help if I can impart any information. Fire away, I'll give you what I can.'

'Great. The macro-environment to begin with. First, the Gupta brothers; they seem to have earned themselves quite a reputation. How much influence do they have at government level?'

'With this current administration, It's truly staggering. Phoenix first coined the phrase 'state capture,' — which just about sums it up. We hammered the phrase until it became embedded in the lingua franca, got the reality well-and-truly into public consciousness. That in turn brought huge heat onto the Gupta family. But to expand on your answer; they've managed to entrench political puppets into key ministerial positions, SOEs; also to manipulate state supply contracts to their own companies. Particularly coal for Eskom's generation plants. It's brought the electricity utility close to collapse. Sub-standard product delivered — when the product is delivered at all. Mind-blowing how much damage it is doing. No analyst can say how the corporation is going to survive. Their debt is already over four hundred billion rand, climbing all the time.'

'How was it ever allowed to get so bad?'

'Lot's of us have asked the same question. But there's a simple answer. The Guptas were clever enough to get their appointees into the Public Prosecutors' Office.'

'What I know as the National Prosecuting Authority?'

'Exactly. With a seat on every high court bench in the country. Brings the judiciary into question at all levels.'

'I've heard so. What about these looming nuclear power plant contracts? Are the Guptas angling to work those into their fold?'

'Not directly. But they're very chummy with Ivashchenkov of Nuclatom. He's the golden boy on that front. Has some sort of a deal already signed with government although no-one has seen the document yet. They're keeping it very close to their chest. Rumour has it Ivashchenkov involved himself with helping the Guptas buy the Canadians' mothballed

Dominion uranium mine near Klerksdorp. Canadians closed the mine in 2010, wrote off a reported R1,8billion. The Guptas paid R37million for the asset in 2014, renamed it Shiva Uranium. Many will tell you the seed capital came directly from the government's Industrial Development Corporation. It doesn't take a rocket scientist to work out where the nuclear plants will source their uranium feedstock if the plants get built.'

'And Zuma will get a kickback from the Russians once the contracts are implemented?'

'Probably nothing as crude. But Zuma's son is on the board of directors with the Guptas at Shiva. Pricing for raw uranium between them and Nuclatom will be almost impossible to strip for hidden commissions. It's a money printing press should the power stations get the green light.'

'A wicked web indeed.'

'With some unwholesome spiders spinning it. Nuclatom's deal might even eclipse the Gupta's malfeasance. It's super-league stuff. Those contracts are worth over one and a half trillion rand, likely to go way beyond by the end of the day.'

'Have you met this Ivasch...?'

'Ivashchenkov? I've been trying for an interview for a long time but getting the hand-off. Of late however, we've started putting a very negative bias on our reporting where Nuclatom is concerned, they don't like it. Coincidentally I've shamed him into a meeting tomorrow morning.'

'Well, that should be interesting.'

'It'll be a scoop for us, so yes.'

'Is the nuclear agreement a done-deal then?'

'No it's not. Nuclear isn't popular with the electorate. There's a powerful anti-nuclear lobby. An opposition which may put a spanner in the works.'

'But let's say it did go ahead. What are the implications if the Russians secure those contracts?'

'Many believe it would be the final nail in the coffin for this country. As I've mentioned, the scope is for an initial six plants costing one-and-a-half trillion rand. We simply cannot afford such sophistication and the additional debt in our energy supply sector, conservatively taking the national debt over three trillion rand. And that's without capital cost over-runs, which are virtually guaranteed at the hands of crooks. Nuclatom itself has a chequered history in its native Russia.'

He pondered what she'd told him. The murky spectre of corruption presented wherever he looked. He could hardly believe his country so badly compromised. Far worse than he'd imagined. He began to understand why the underground movement was such a magnet for honest endeavour.

'You're certainly painting a bleak picture,' he felt dispirited even saying it. 'If the move to unseat government goes ahead, I'd like to understand what that would mean in the international arena. Simon was at pains to underscore the importance of winning acceptance there. In your opinion how important?'

'Vital. Simon is right. If we don't get broad acceptance we would almost certainly face a hostile United Nations. That would virtually guarantee intervention from them, leading to more bloodshed and eventual reinstating of the present junta.'

'What are the chances of the takeover being viewed negatively?'

'It's a question of how it's arrived at. Not every country is going to be supportive. There'll be cries of 'foul' from the minnows. But the real power at the UN is with the five permanent-member countries comprising the Security Council. And more specifically their power of veto. China as well as Russia would probably be hostile. However, remember 'veto' is latin for 'I forbid'. If only one of the big five uses it, then a resolution for military intervention would indeed be forbidden.'

'So there's China, there's Russia. Who are the other three?'

'The USA, Britain and France.'

'You think we could count on support from any of them?'

'We don't need support. Just a single vote against a resolution to intervene. As long as our motives are seen to be for the good of the country, my opinion is, that the veto would be exercised.'

'Comforting.'

'But remember, below the surface politics are churning in that august forum too. Trade deals, inter-governmental loans, technology transfer arrangements between member states. A whole raft of other considerations. It's a constantly twisting river. A country might not always vote for what is right. It could be swayed by a trading partner, pressured to protect its self-interest.'

He was learning a lot. He thought back to his military adventures in Angola. To where the politics eventually took it. Win the battle but lose the war. In the modern world, things rarely seemed to go the way they should.

'If you were a betting girl, who would be your front runner to exercise a power of veto if there was pressure for intervention?'

'With Donald Trump in the White House, the United States for sure.'

'And in the event of him exercising his veto, it would scotch any chance for a peacekeeping force in South Africa, you say?'

'It would. With one caveat which I cannot overemphasise. If we are not seen to be doing the right thing, we could face all sorts of economic and trade sanctions. That would be as devastating as military intervention. We couldn't survive that. No, we need to be seen to be doing the right thing, get support once the deed is done.'

'I'm beginning to get the picture.'

'And we will need supportive media, at least in part. A hostile press will seek to discredit no matter what the real motives. We must avoid that at all costs.'

'Do you think it's a possibility?'

She cocked her head. 'A hostile press? Yes, it's possible. But the news on the ground here at home will set the trend. Media outlets are sheep who flock together these days. No one wants to be the maverick when it comes to reporting. The risk is too great. If you're wrong as an individual media provider you can be slaughtered. If everybody's wrong, nobody gets sacrificed. Press agencies such as this one have become collectors, repositories of raw news. So it's the same news for everyone with individual editorial spin put on it from our clients downstream. For us of course, reputation is everything. We can't afford to get it wrong. We're a relatively small agency but we have voracious news gatherers. We've earned respect. My board of directors are zealous South Africans. Editorial policy is fiercely defended. I represent such policy. My board have my back. Simon knows it. He knows as well, that to a man, we are supportive of the effort to rid this country of its corrupt leadership.'

She became a very passionate lady when aroused. The lights in her eyes flashed like sparks.

'I hope you're right; hope we can pull it off.'

'If we don't try, nobody else will. The wealthier nations don't want another failed economy, a prospect of millions of refugees with the begging bowl out. But they're not going to step into the breach either. This country will continue to slide if no-one here takes the initiative. It has to come from people like us.'

He felt the tug of the collective pronoun.

'How much are your hands tied when reporting on the antics of the politicians?'

'Do you mean specifically from this office?'

He nodded.

'I'm not sure I'm with you. Tied in respect of what?'

'To discredit Zuma and his cronies.'

'As I've been at pains to point out, a great deal of reliance is placed on our copy. It has to be real, it has to be true. If we fabricate, we lose customers, lose credibility. We can't sell a crock of you-know-what. That's where creative writing comes to the fore. A fact can be written many ways. It will read differently under differing editorial policy. That's my back yard. I make sure what gets written here does not lionise heavyweight politicos' because of the power they wield. Quite the reverse — not always good for the bottom line as you can imagine. It loses us access to certain customers, especially government agencies. We cast ourselves in the mould of a force for change in our own right. As we see it we have a responsibility to play a part in bringing down this corrupt administration. Helping to return the country to responsible, to honest governance. So our copy will always expose malfeasance wherever we find it.'

'Does it get you any pressure from the incumbents?'

'More than that. I've received direct death threats, as have a number of my staff.'

He raised his eyebrows. 'Scary stuff.'

She laughed. 'All in a days work.'

'Not for the faint-hearted then.'

'I suppose not.'

'Do you think it likely Zuma and his ilk will ever see the inside of a prison?'

'I sincerely hope so. Simon has done heaps of work in that regard. He's amassed a mountain of evidence against many at the top. If it goes the way he sees it, there will be a day of reckoning for sure. They'll find themselves behind those prison bars you speak of.'

'Is any of the evidence Simon has, already in the public domain?'

'Some.'

'But more to come you think?'

'Simon has the low down on most who are corrupt within the judiciary. He has taken it upon himself to lead that particular crusade.'

'And you think it will eventuate in prosecutions, to sentencing?'

'I do.'

'I must say I'm encouraged.'

'We just need to pull off the military side, establish an administration. Then I think Simon will have his day. Heads will roll.'

'It sounds like a given when you put it like that.'

'Not going to be a walk in the park. Not everyone wants to see a fair administration, either here at home, or internationally. The world these days is a breeding ground for unscrupulous corporates and crime syndicates. Look at Oakbay and Nuclatom for instance. It suits them to have corrupt governments where they ply their trade. Without a bought Zuma, Nuclatom would be nowhere.'

'I can see that. So the bad apples need to be removed. But as you keep reminding me, it's not going to be so easy. We're not talking about a stock-standard takeover, where state military challenges a ruling political party. In our case we will be taking on the establishment complete with its military muscle. Lock stock and barrel. A very different proposition. This will be a David and Goliath contest.' Suddenly he didn't feel comfortable putting the negative spin to her. He rescued the mood with what he hoped was a reassuring smile. 'But when good men do nothing…' he let the well-worn cliche hang. 'As you say we have to try.'

She studied him a long time, those hazel eyes never wavering.

'Yes, Pieter I believe we do.' There it was again, that collective pronoun. If ever he harboured a vestigial trace of backing out, it evaporated there and then.

CHAPTER 16

PRESS INTERVIEW

'Won't you follow me, Miss Birman?' Sophie had been kept waiting in the reception area for fifteen minutes. She was unimpressed by the wait and the over-the-top furnishings; silk flowers cradled in obvious expensive ceramics and a photographic gallery of Nuclatom installations all over the world.

She fell in behind the secretary as they passed glass-panelled meeting rooms on the way to the executive suite. The woman knocked discreetly and eased the door for Sophie.

'Welcome, Miss Birman,' Ivashchenkov rose behind his desk and pushed out a hand in greeting. 'Lovely to meet at last.'

Sophie thought, *thee of the forked tongue*. 'Good morning Mr Ivashchenkov. Thank you for agreeing to see me.'

He gestured her to the seat at the other side of his desk. It hadn't gone unnoticed to Sophie that he chose not to use the less formal coffee table and its seating.

He's not comfortable, wants to keep this meeting as brief as possible, she thought, smiling disarmingly and placing her leather folder on his desk.

'Permit me compliment,' he leaned back, 'I did not expect fourth estate to be represented by such attractive person.'

She held the smile still running the internal dialogue; *uncomfortable for sure, working me with unction. Trying to impress with his idiomatic English. 'Fourth estate' indeed.*

'Could I offer drink? Tea, coffee, water perhaps?'

That won't work either — she was amused at how il-at-ease he seemed. She tightened the smile and declined. It wasn't her that was nervous.

He pushed with thumb and forefinger at the corners of his mouth. A nervous gesture, trying to sum her up. 'Well, perhaps should start. I'm sure you have questions about Nuclatom to fire.'

She scoffed inwardly. *Not 'fire,' Mr Super-exec, rather roll out carefully.* Set the trap.

'Would you mind if I recorded the interview? Notepads went out with the Ark.'

He shrugged indifference.

'Perhaps we could start by taking a look at the company. In terms of nuclear reactor manufacture, I believe Nuclatom is ranked globally as one of the top five?'

'Third.' He looked pleased to get the brag aired and expanded on it. 'But we go much further. Not only reactor manufacture. We give full nuclear package. Design, manufacture, installation, commissioning as well as fuel supply cycle. From enrichment to waste management, even disposal.'

'I wasn't aware of that,' she lied, keen to stroke his ego, keep the information flow going. 'You have an enviable international footprint. I understand you are in more than forty countries?'

'Forty-six to be exact.'

'Impressive.'

'We have growth philosophy — will challenge front runners over time. Place Nuclatom at top.'

'Those front runners would be Westinghouse of the United States. France's Areva?'

A nod of affirmation. 'You are well informed, Miss Birman.'

'It's what I get paid for Mr Ivashchenkov. But let's get back to your aspirations here in South Africa. As I understand it you are competing for the contract to supply six plants to Eskom? Is that correct?'

'Is first phase of national upgrade. Ministry of Energy's wish list. Six plants — total generation capacity 9600Mw. To be followed by more plants as country's electricity generation gets in step with twenty-first-century technology. We engage with Ministry in advisory role for first phase.'

'There is considerable public sentiment to nuclear power here in South Africa. What is your view on that?'

'Always there is opposition against change at beginning, Miss Birman. Is human condition.'

'And your view on the safety issues surrounding nuclear plants? There have been some notable scares in Japan and Russia for instance.'

'Faulty management issues, which have led to new protocols on plant management worldwide. Electricity generation by nuclear reactors is safest, most eco-friendly, of all power generation. This includes renewables. Nuclear has lowest carbon footprint, no polluting sulphides, no ash or greenhouse gases. Is smart option.'

'Those are valid points. What about the initial very high capital cost? Many would argue South Africa simply cannot afford nuclear on this scale.'

'Capital costs come down with time. Technology continues to advance, brings economies of scale.'

'Even so, figures of between one-point-two and one-point-five trillion rand are being bandied about freely as the cost of this first phase. Our power utility is already in serious trouble. Can it afford to take on a level of debt which would triple its current liability?'

He steepled his fingers, regarding her over them — an act of condescension.

'Maybe better to take pain now; no sense to build big coal-fired plants today; also expensive — doomed for short life span as Kyoto protocol grows teeth, forces closure of big polluters.' He was educating an uninformed outsider. Sophie could see he was in his comfort zone. Time to start casting bait on hooks with barbs.

'Do we have sufficient raw uranium locally to be able to feed nuclear enrichment plants or will we need to import?'

He gave her a complacent smile. 'More than enough. Local interests have bought mothballed Dominion mine from Canada's Uranium One. Will be prolific producer. Good for nuclear industry, good for country.'

She paused for a half-beat. 'And good for our president, clearly.'

She held his gaze without flinching.

'Why would that be?' He hadn't allowed his poise to slip but a guarded note had sharpened his words.

'His son Duduzane, is a director with the Guptas at Shiva Uranium — the renamed Dominion.' The sparks flashed in her eyes. 'Those are the local interests you speak of.'

He shrugged as if it didn't matter to him either way.

'You don't know them?' She prepared to spring the trap she'd planned.

'Have read about them; not met personally.'

'Not even Ajay Gupta?' she pressed.

'No.' His voice, flinty, had an icy edge now.

She leaned forward, flicked open her leather wallet at the edge of his desk and pushed a colour photograph across to him. It showed him with an arm thrown companionably around the shoulder of Ajay Gupta, his free hand brandishing a slender cheroot. Both men were laughing as if sharing a joke, patently enjoying one another's company.

His eyes dropped fleetingly to the image. He fixed her with a cool stare. 'It appears have met gentleman at some stage — meet lot of people in my work. Cannot recall occasion.'

'Fair enough. So you don't have any business interests with the Guptas?'

'None.'

'No draft contracts for their supply of U238 to an enrichment facility you intend building?'

'Of course not.' The irritation started to show.

'Please bear with me Mr Ivashchenkov. These are questions raised by the public at large. A readership looking to be informed. It's my job to pose these questions, deliver the truth. Unsubstantiated rumours gaining traction would do nothing to further Nuclatom's cause. It is in your interest to answer truthfully.'

A thin veneer; she harboured no doubt he hadn't bought it. She was out to get him — he knew it.

She pressed on. 'Have you ever met Jacob Zuma?'

He flicked a glance at her recorder still doing its work on the far side of his desk.

'Not personally. Have attended public events where he speaks of course.'

'You've never been a dinner guest at the Gupta Saxonwold compound with Mr Zuma also a guest?'

'You forget, Miss Birman, have said no meetings with Gupta's... aside from occasion in photograph. So, no, have no meeting with Jacob Zuma at Guptas' home or anywhere else; have never been to Gupta's home.'

'Well, you couldn't be more emphatic.'

He maintained his level stare, the steepled fingers replaced by a firm grip on the arms of his chair — a fighting pose.

'You are aware, Mr Ivashchenkov certain elements are suggesting you already have a signed agreement with the government for the supply of those first six reactors. How would you respond to that?'

'Is pure fantasy. You know as I do, government contracts need passage through due process. Publication in government gazette; issue of tender documents; invitation to tenderers. Bidding procedures. Is a competitive platform.'

'So that would be a no?'

He paused, his approach measured, cautious. 'We do have letter of intent signed with Energy Ministry. We supply technical assistance. I have said this. Is a long way from hardware contract of any description.'

'That seems to clear up everything then.' She widened her eyes a little. 'There is one final thing,' she paused for effect, 'you are aware our president as well as certain top ministers are in the spotlight facing substantial corruption charges?'

'I do read tabloids, Miss Birman.'

'Of course you do. And some of what you read will be originating out of our offices.' It could do no harm to remind him they were muscle within 'the fourth estate'. 'I have to ask this Mr Ivashchenkov. Are you in any way party to that corruption?'

'Nuclatom is global company. Has powerful reputation. We would not risk getting hands dirty.'

'That's a wind-up then.' She leaned forward, switched off the recorder. His demeanour changed immediately, hands returning to the steepled power pose.

'Off record, Miss Birman. Nuclatom is determined to secure country's nuclear power generation business. We generally get what we are after. We are not in South Africa for our health. For your health, it would be far better if you worked with us. Not against. We never forget friends. Or enemies,' he added darkly.

She cocked her head allowing a quizzical expression. 'To my journalistic ear that sounded like a threat and a bribe in one.'

'Then hearing is deceiving you.'

'Good. Because I don't respond to threats or bribes.'

She closed her desk wallet and rose to leave.

'You have forgotten photograph, Miss Birman.'

'Compliments of Phoenix Press, Mr Ivashchenkov. She turned on her heel heading out. At the door she faced back momentarily. 'By the way, the photograph was taken on May 1st 2013 at Sun City — Vega Gupta's wedding. You were a guest of honour seated at the head table with the entire family.'

CHAPTER 17

KOSMO FOTAKIS

He peered out of the aircraft window as they started their descent into Lanseria international airport sixty kilometres north of Johannesburg. He was beginning to feel like a corporate animal. It was his second visit after only a six-day absence.

Rolling hills slipping by below were carpeted a rich olive green after good early-summer rains. The highveldt landscape swelled as it burst from beneath the seared browns and faded khakis of winter's mantle.

Lanseria proudly proclaiming itself 'international', still served mainly in its historic role as a regional domestic facility. It took overflow from the larger and stretched OR Tambo — Johannesburg's principal portal to the international crowd. At Lanseria a recent upgrade to the terminal buildings had raised the bar making it a pleasure to fly into these days. Less obvious but an enabling vital statistic was a main runway three kilometres long which could handle the big and the buxom. This, together with a far more relaxed customs and immigration environment to that of its big cousin, attracted the 'less formal' freight operators working into sub-Saharan Africa. A euphemism which had obliquely brought Piet to its doorstep.

He was there to meet a 'less formal' operator, a certain Kosmo Fotakis, Greek Cypriot by birth: a man who spent much of his life in the murky central Africa region, his air-freight service available to all prepared to pay his premium rates. The other hat he wore was that of arms dealer. He danced both sides of the thin blue line, frequently supplying all elements engaged in bloody African conflicts. Headquartered in Kiev, Ukraine, his company operated three huge Russian Antonovs crewed by surly Slavs which added to his outfits shady reputation. Fotakis did little to dispel this image. In his eyes it attracted the right sort of clientele, often those wanting to stay below the radar. Enter centre-stage Pieter Rossouw.

He was on his first official duty tasked by Colonel Stander. There to purchase combat rifles. Specifically Kalashnikov assault rifles coming from the same city where Fotakis headquartered. Absolute secrecy a non-negotiable. They did not have a licence to buy arms, a requirement in South Africa, so the black-market was the default setting for them.

Any shipment would need to enter the country way below the radar, Fotakis the only operator who seemed to have the ability to achieve that. There would be a premium but they would pay it.

At the first floor of the terminal building, an open-air terrace shared by two fast-food restaurants overlooks the apron. Patrons killing time get the bonus of a ringside seat from which to watch the planes come and go. It was here he chose to be — highly visible for easy identification. The Wiesenhof brewed a passable coffee. He sipped it looking down on the passengers climbing aboard the 'plane he had flown in on, ready for their quick hop to Cape Town.

Into his second cup, the chair at the other side of his table scraped back — Kosmo Fotakis dropped into it. Small and wiry, somewhere embedded in middle age, he sported police-style sunglasses pressed to his face like lens-caps on binoculars. Hair severely slicked-back from a deeply furrowed brow — the look of a Douglas Fairbanks Junior for those old enough to remember the early movies heart-throb. A pencil-line moustache completed the mimicry, studiously worked at Piet was sure. With his olive complexion he could be nothing but the progeny of Mediterranean forebears: all round an apt caricature of the boss of the shady operation Piet was there to parley with.

'Kosmo Fotakis,' he extended a hand. A heavy gold ring set with a glittering diamond, at least two carats, glinted in the sunshine. He shook the expensive extremity and introduced himself.

His earlier resolve to act normally strangely evaporated; he found himself glancing around to see if anyone was taking a special interest in them. Surely they must leap to centre-stage yelling 'crooks-and-spooks'. An individual with his nose stuck in a newspaper was the only other customer sharing their part of the deck. It had to be his paranoia then. Other patrons busy about their lives were oblivious to them. Fotakis noticed his body language and laughed.

'First time at the table with a notorious arms dealer, Piet?'

'Lots of firsts in my life right about now,' he made a conscious effort to relax and signalled a waiter to order Fotakis a coffee.

The Greek remained completely relaxed. 'My apologies for dragging you out of Cape Town. At short notice I couldn't do any better. I only have a couple of hours here today en-route to Lubumbashi.' The Congo was central Africa's festering hotbed, armed conflict between rival factions the order of the day there. You didn't need to be a clairvoyant to guess the nature of Fotakis' business in the region. It wouldn't be much different to Piet's.

Fotakis looked at a gold Rolex as if to underscore his tight schedule. 'We have enough time at our disposal in which to conduct our business I hope?'

'Probably.' he did want to move things along, even finalise at this first meeting if possible. He launched in without preamble. 'I assume the manufacturer alerted you to our needs?' The steering committee at the Endeavour had made direct contact to Kiev only to be politely rebuffed — the facility conducted its business exclusively through accredited agents. Fotakis was one such — a referral made.

'They have,' he confirmed.

'We're looking for a full-service package; supply to delivery. All elements in fact; certificates of origin, bills of lading, import documentation. The whole nine yards. You'll need to tell me if it will involve multiple shipments.'

He laughed again. 'We will swallow your shipment on one of my ladies like carry-on luggage. Hardly notice it's aboard.'

Piet wasn't sure how much of a brag it constituted, but was impressed nonetheless. He thought two thousand Kalashnikov automatic rifles, a payload of ammunition, would be a small mountain as far as logistics was concerned.

'And documentation? That won't be a problem?'

'Not at all. Ukraine is the preferred source for most sub-Saharan customers, paperwork these days is often creative. Especially where the client is an antagonist to a de facto government.' He paused significantly, but Piet couldn't read his eyes behind the dark lenses. No way to tell if the reference was a barb for them specifically or used as a generalisation for the kind of client he was used to dealing with.

'My supplier isn't squeamish,' he looked every inch the dodgy dealer, 'if you've got the money, then they've got the weapons.'

'What about import documentation?'

'We'll have to finesse those a little. Unless you can furnish me with an arms permit?' He cocked his head.

Piet shook his.

'Understood. So we're left with the need for window-dressing, bringing in your goods under a friendly customs tariff. Let's say agricultural spares. We have our friends in customs at this airport. They won't look too closely. Of course, it comes at a cost.' Of course. 'You'll also need short term warehousing. Fortunately I have a bonded facility here. We can keep the goods under lock and key. Only for a very short time mind you. You will appreciate the risk we run. The consignment will need to be moved quickly.'

Piet gave him his assurance that they would be just as anxious to get the shipment into their facility. He didn't identify it as an armoury in the Karoo.

'I am going to need one thing from you however. In terms of the paperwork.'

'Which is?'

'An official order on company headed documentation.'

'That won't be a problem.'

'I'll mail you a draft, exactly how it needs to read.'

'I'm keen to get this done. How long for delivery into your warehouse?'

'Send me your official order, I'll mail you a pro-forma invoice. It will call for a seventy per cent payment upfront. Once you confirm the document is acceptable, I'll courier the commercial invoice. You can take it to your bank to effect the payment. Once money lands in my account, you can expect your 'spares' within three weeks.' He grinned, Piet's new co-conspirator.

'And we can count on this happening? How sure are you SA Customs are squared away?'

He smiled. 'In Africa Piet, if you throw the right amount of money in the right direction, everything can happen — all a question of greasing the right palms.'

Piet winced at the irony; becoming party to a class of crime he now campaigned, risked his liberty to stamp out at a national level. For just a fleeting second, he questioned the very nature of their crusade. Was Africa beyond redemption when it came to eradicating graft? A bribe-free environment impossible on the continent — a quaint nicety which simply didn't work there? He shrugged the thought aside. Down that path lay insanity.

'I don't suppose there's much more to discuss. I'll wait for your draft.'

'You'll have it within forty-eight hours.' He looked again at his watch. 'We still have some time left. Light lunch on me, Piet? I can recommend the chicken-mayo tramezzini.'

Dealing with the devil, he might as well sup with him.

They kicked around some detail over their sandwich, just finishing when the air thrummed to the beat of powerful turbines, louder by orders of magnitude than those of domestic jets. As he looked to the far end a monstrous aircraft alighted to the runway barrelling towards them.

He turned to Fotakis. 'One of yours I'm guessing?'

'Antonov 124, more than likely the aircraft which will bring your stuff in. That's Olga, the oldest of my three ladies. Bit long in the tooth I'll grant you, but she can out-lift almost any cargo aircraft operating in Africa.'

'She certainly likes plenty of runway.' The plane overshot the terminal buildings becoming a toy in the distance.

'She's carrying a big payload today, a hundred-and-forty tons. At highveldt altitude, she needs lots of room when she's this heavy.'

'All bound for the Congo?'

'Not today. A shipment of Turkish high-spec steel pipes, high-pressure valves for one of your thermal power stations. Small balance goes to Congo.' he wondered if the 'small balance' would be ordnance, but retained the good sense to curb his curiosity.

'And I'm guessing your taxi to Lubumbashi?'

'Right again. She'll off-load the local stuff and refuel, then we're on our way.'

The Antonov's engine note built as she taxied towards the adjacent cargo warehouses. With her drooping wings she looked predatory — a stooping hawk.

Kosmo took money from his wallet pushing it into the billfold to pay for lunch.

'Until we meet again my friend.' They shook hands and he disappeared down the stairs. Piet checked his watch, still a couple of hours to kill before his return flight. He ordered a beer. The tables had pretty much emptied save for the guy with his newspaper who he figured to be a financial services type, his attention now riveted in the financial section.

The beer arrived as he settled down to reflect on things. Events were moving at a pace. Within a month they would have their ordnance. The training tempo would intensify. After that there would be nothing to stop them pushing the button to make their bid for the country. A very heady thought indeed.

CHAPTER 18

THE FARM

Back in Cape Town following his trip to rendezvous with Fotakis, it seemed he hardly got his bearings before being on the move again. This time on his way to the all-important training facility deep in the Karoo. Fotakis, good to his word had sent his pro-forma invoice, they approved it and made payment. The arms were on order — the clock ticking.

He was on his way well before dawn to beat the early morning rush and assure he arrived at his destination in daylight. The old Toyota rode smoothly enough on the tarmac, but when they reached the gravel roads of the desert, it wasn't so comfortable. Her worn steering joints began to protest at the corrugations which deepened the further into the desert they pushed. The steering wheel became a living thing in his hands. He tried both increasing and decreasing speed to dampen out the oscillations, finally settling for eighty kilometres an hour — the least punishing to both driver and car. Even then he had to stop every hour to shake pins-and-needles out of his hands, flex his arms and shoulders. It wasn't exactly a joy ride or a high-speed transit either.

Due one of his breaks, he checked the rearview mirror for any following traffic, forgetting the only thing visible would be the pall of mustard-yellow dust they trailed. That obscured everything else. In any event there hadn't been another vehicle for well over two hours. He scanned the road ahead searching for a gap in the powdery drifts flanking on both sides. Finally he spotted a place where he felt he could pull over without getting bogged down. He slowed, getting as far to the side as he could without risking a slide into the ditch — a ditch that looked as if it wouldn't give up its prey easily. His careful manoeuvre was insurance against a repeat of an earlier encounter with one of the huge multi-level livestock transporters thundering down those roads. The behemoth narrowly missed taking him out even as he squeezed as far to the side as he dared; it still didn't save his wing mirror which disappeared with a frightening bang. A close call, not one he wanted to repeat. He nursed the car to a halt, waiting as their dusty wake rolled past before climbing out.

The countryside breathed a palpable calm, the only sound the car's metallic clicking as the engine cooled. He ambled a few paces putting in some stretching exercises to dispel the numbness hammered into his body. Along the sandy ribbon only mean barbed-wire fences slavishly followed the gravel as it stretched to infinity in both directions. A shadow ghosted over the ground. Skyward a hunting jackal-buzzard, his white wing bands flashing in the harsh light, banked into a thermal kicking off the parched terrain. He floated effortlessly on the air column then tightened his turn as he locked onto something below. He held the turn for a full revolution before stooping earthward in what looked like a suicide dive, impacting the ground in a welter of dust alongside a tussock of *Karoo feinbos*. Job only half done, he stomped around energetically in the scrub. Whatever had attracted his attention was having a very hard time of it. Piet took a few paces to get a better look, but the bird spotted his movement and took to the air. Not without his prize however: trailing from his talons a still writhing, very unfortunate snake. That would be Mister Buzzard's work for the day done — reminding him his wasn't, the sun relentlessly arcing towards the horizon. Several more hours of gruelling Karoo to traverse before he could close his day.

The cascade of warm water over his body came as a balm. For a few minutes, he luxuriated in it soaping off the dust of the journey. He felt like a new man as he climbed into fresh clothes and left the rondavel to walk to the main house. His host was Glen Fergusson, a wiry Celt who could trace his Gaelic ancestry right back to David II in the fourteenth century: a third-generation South African who continued the farming of his father dead some thirteen years.

Like many of his antecedents, the Scot favoured a solitary lifestyle. Sometimes taciturn but rarely antisocial. He had a wife whom he met in Scotland on a vacationing visit. Theirs an unusual marriage. She lived in the village of Kintyre, both the place of her birth as well as the seat of the Fergusson clan. Having tried an unsuccessful stint with Glen on the farm for two years, she now refused ever to move from her native Scotland. As Glen averred to Piet conversationally, she was like a sprig of heather which battled to survive in the desert. He convinced himself she would wilt if persuaded to stay. The couple worked out the compromise. Glen bought a crofters cottage in the Ayrshire town, spent a small fortune extending it whilst going to great pains to preserve the original character — a town planning requirement. In true Scots fashion, he wasn't above bemoaning the fact he spent another small fortune equipping it with the finest fittings and appliances money could buy. It apparently satisfied the good lady but the couple remained childless, a consequence perhaps of their long spells apart. Overall the arrangement seemed to work, Fergie, as he liked to be called, visited twice or three times a year.

'Care for a wee dram, Pieter?' Save for the flat South African accent he was in all other aspects the quintessential Scot.

'I'd love one. What are you having?'

'Bit of a purist. Only keep single malt. I can offer you a Glenmorangie or a Glen Grant.'

'Pearls before swine, Fergie. I'll go with whatever you're having.'

He brought the drinks over.

'To health and happiness,' he toasted.

Piet settled back into the comfort of the lounger.

Sipping the expensive spirit in those convivial surroundings, easy for him to forget the country was going to hell in a handcart. He buried the thought, allowed the moment to take him. Fergie, eyes shut head resting on the back of his chair lapsed into silence deepening the companionable stillness. Happy to let the whisky work its magic, Piet let go. The day's fatigue seeped out of him. A carriage clock on the mantle ticked rhythmically underscoring the peace. His mind teased the issues bringing him there. Could a small force such as theirs realistically expect to prevail, overcome the national military might? Could the political landscape be changed to steer the country away from ruination? Would a lasting solution be birthed from that? And finally, did they have the right to try? The same thought that cropped up whilst he was with

Fotakis. Was European culture a poor fit on the continent? Perhaps the default setting of graft and corruption belonged there? His soldiering days floated back. Had he been justified in accepting dictates from his superiors without question? Were they trying to impose their value standards on a much simpler race who they would never change?

'Don't go there, Piet.'

He shook his head. 'Sorry, Fergie?'

He paused. 'You're wondering if our enterprise is worthy.'

He couldn't believe it. How was it possible Fergie had tuned in to his thoughts? He collected himself. 'It's uncanny you've picked that up,'

'Good choice of words.' He took a sip of his Glenmorangie. 'As a youngster in the family home my dear old Mum tagged me as being fey — canny as we Scots term it.' He laughed at the recollection, 'she often said she was uncomfortable thinking freely in my presence.'

Piet asked how it was possible, still trying to compose himself.

Fergie took a moment. 'I suppose it's got something to do with spending a lot of time alone. Us Scots can be solitary animals at times. Even as a child I spent an inordinate amount of time by myself. I've always been very comfortable in my own company. My senses have become honed accordingly I guess.'

'To the point of mind reading,' it still seemed incredible. 'Well you were spot on this time. You caught me asking myself whether we have the moral right to be interfering in Africa at all?'

'I presume you mean as the dominant force? The colonising white man?' Asked rhetorically. 'Believe me there's no mileage in that sort of soul searching, Piet. If the good Lord engineered mankind differently we might all still be running around in animal skins. But we're not. Some of us are hugely inquisitive. And the more inquisitive we are as a species the more we advance. That's just the way it is. Enquiry brings invention in its wake. And invention brings change. Mostly for the better.'

'I keep telling myself that. I mean where would the black man be if we hadn't arrived on this continent? Probably still time-locked in a hunter-gatherer existence. I still have a vestige of guilt somehow though. Yes, we've brought change, we've brought innovation. But at a cost perhaps. Have we disturbed some delicate mechanism in nature? Are peoples indigenous to Africa ready for the level of sophistication we're striving at? Every time we take our hand off the tiller they appear to revert.'

'Entropy. The second law of thermodynamics. All systems left entirely to nature will wind down to their simplest states. Without man's active management that is. Try running a sheep ranch without supervision, without husbandry. You'd soon see the consequence — an animal returned to its most primitive form.'

'So you're saying you think these people need management?'

'I'll answer that with a question.' He raised an eyebrow. 'Do you think the modern continental European is better off today than his counterpart in medieval times?'

'I'd have to say, yes, I'm sure he is. Don't know much about the period mind you.'

'The average life expectancy then, a little over thirty years. Wholesale infant mortality the norm. If he survived through infancy our serf might have lived to his twenties. Statistically, once he made it to a little over thirty he would join the majority and perish. Few made it to fifty and beyond. Today the same individual could reasonably expect to get to his eighties.'

'And you think it's mostly down to enquiring minds, innovation, managed systems and the like?'

'Think about it. If we weren't managed at school we'd learn nothing. Without structure in the armed forces, no battle could ever be won. If corporations didn't have hierarchies, there'd be no growth. So the sense of management I'm referring to, is management through an organised system. After the collapse of the Roman Empire Europe did exactly what you see so often in Africa. It backslid into chaos for many centuries. Only the advent of the feudal system much later started to turn things around again. Without it, we could still be primitives ourselves.'

'Feudalism doesn't have a good profile in the history books, as far as my schoolboy memory serves,' Piet ventured.

'I'm not saying it constituted the perfect system. Far from it. There were harsh aspects certainly. Just like more recent colonialism with its strata of entitlement. But both were agencies for change. And the changes wrought were for the greater part, beneficial to mankind. We're looking at baby and bathwater stuff here. Throw the dirty water out certainly, but hold on to the infant.'

'So you believe the native African should be embracing the best of introduced technology, reap some cultural benefits, but still retain his roots?'

Fergie nodded encouraging him to press on.

'Seems to me they're more interested in confronting past ills, exacting retribution,' he still wrestled himself over that one. 'Rather than adapting to the times, reaping those benefits — they don't seem to mind the baby getting tossed with the bathwater.'

Fergie took it up again. 'And the lack of understanding is fanned to flame by a self-serving elite. As they stir the masses, they skim off billions to their own pockets. No concern for what happens to this country. Slavishly pursuing all the nice things the colonist has brought. Wanting more.

As long as they can rip enough off for themselves, their families, the people at large can go to hell. The broken shell left behind will be somebody else's problem.'

'On the face of it that doesn't make sense. They're shooting themselves in the foot. Their assets here would be devalued too in a collapsed economy?'

Fergie laughed derisively. 'Take some time to do a bit of research. You'll see ninety per cent of their ill-gotten gains are in assets held off-shore.'

That gave Piet food for thought.

'You think we have justification then? A right to be here?'

'Consider it. A handful of gangsters is stealing their people blind. Wrecking the very potential for change full democracy should be delivering. Mandela's rainbow nation kicked to oblivion. His vision of a country where eventually colour would not be the defining characteristic, torn asunder, the system to deliver the promise shattered. Somebody has to put it right.'

'So why don't the electorate see that?'

'They're a lot like the serf I sketched in the feudal system of medieval Europe. Members of a lower social class. Largely uneducated, a sharp contrast to the lords and royals enjoying the strata above them. For the African it's almost inevitable he sees his past masters and captains of industry as oppressors. Especially when encouraged by his leadership. That's your voter easily persuaded by empty promises. And he's slow to realise he's being duped. His big men have unseated the oppressor. The better life of the promised dream is just around the corner. The big men have pulled it off — let them feast first — they've earned the right. The poor peasant thinks it will be his turn next. But as he begins to see the hollow promise, as it dawns, he becomes disillusioned, angry. That's the flashpoint when the lid starts to come off. We're already seeing early signs with the outbreaks of civil unrest everywhere.'

'Which puts pressure on what we're doing.'

'It does. A riotous situation on the streets won't help.'

Piet could understand that. But he wanted to know how Fergie envisaged the post-military period; the new democratic environment Simon Zondo had spelled out to him. 'This new political beginning, you don't think it will be 'more of the same', greedy politicians rushing in to secure positions of self-interest?'

'Not going to be allowed to happen. That's a prime construct during the interim military administration. Office bearers will need to satisfy a means-test for eligibility. The political parties they represent will be subject to intense scrutiny. Hopefully, the lessons learned from watching this administration will be enough. No jobs for the boys, no more nepotism.'

'That's certainly Simon Zondo's vision. He's gone through it with me at some depth.'

'It's more than a vision. It's a shared ideal with no racial bias. The very hub on which the wheel of change will turn.'

A very noble ideal. Behind which Piet had thrown his weight — pray to God it delivered.

'Believe me, Piet you need have no misgivings about the crusade you're involved in. It ticks all the right boxes as far as the welfare of this country is concerned.' He drained his glass, reached for Piet's. 'We'll have another. This time the Glen Grant. A birdie cannot fly on one wing.'

Up before dawn the next day, he looked forward to the familiarisation tour. He stepped it out briskly on his way to the main house as an orange glow suffused the eastern horizon. The air carried a sharp edge. Fergie met him at the door throwing him a bush jacket.

'You're going to need that till the sun gets up a bit; the Landy's got an open cab.'

Twenty minutes later they approached a low range of hills, Fergie telling him it marked the border on the north-western extremity of the farm. As they drew closer a fence line materialised out of the gloom. They came to a gate and slowed. 'Breeding Research — No unauthorised Entry' was boldly displayed on a board wired to it. A guard in army fatigues stepped out of his sentry box, smartly saluted Fergie. They filled in a security register and drove through towards the base of the hills. Light spilled from a row of dormer windows betraying the existence of a building — a half-cylindrical metal structure squatting like a hen on eggs — the old Nissen huts of World War 2. Other camouflaged and sandbagged structures tucked themselves into the hills. It required close scrutiny. They pulled up at the one bleeding light.

Contrasting the chill outside, the warmth within came as a welcome relief. A buzz of conversation issued from a hundred or so men busy with breakfast. Army fatigues the dress code, it took him back to his service days.

'Deja vous, hey?' Fergie being canny again. They approached a group near the entrance, the equivalent of NCO's in a regular army. Fergie made the introductions.

'Piet is here to take a good look at us. He's one of the big wigs so watch your p's and q's.' Smiles all round. 'Shift along, make room for us while we go get our food.'

Back at the table, Fergie expanded on the exact nature of Piet's visit. To everyone's credit, no politics or awkward questions. Focus stayed on field strategy and the like. Upcoming exercises took centre stage. To Piet it felt as it should. Military men discussing military matters; no surprise to learn that to a man, all his breakfast companions had held rank in the country's armed services at some time. A good start.

'How did you find the food?' Fergie jumped aboard the Land Rover and Piet scrambled up beside him.

'Big improvement on my service days.'

He laughed. 'All part of the plan. The chefs are top-notch. Rank and file must have no cause for complaint. They have to be aboard heart, soul and stomach. No place for shoddiness anywhere.'

'They seem pumped I must say.'

'You'd know better than most; a fighting force is more effective when morale is high. These guys are conditioned from the beginning.'

They drove towards another building, its hanger type doors firmly closed. A sentry came to attention as they approached then wrestled one of the large sliders open to allow them entry.

Along both flanks of the building an impressive array of vehicles stretched away. Fifty or more. Minibuses rubbed shoulders with SUV's. Armoured personnel carriers, the letters SAEEI stencilled along their flanks, out-muscled twin-cab utilities.

'Impressive,' they strolled the length of the building, 'quite an investment clearly.' They were passing a clutch of expensive Toyota Land Cruisers.

'This isn't the half of it,' Fergie looked over the fleet. 'The rest is scattered all round the country. Mostly on other farms. We rotate them, bring them through here for regular servicing.'

'Any particular reason for brand selection?' he patted one of the Cruisers.

'Several.' Fergie opened the car door. 'Try closing that now. See if you notice anything.'

Piet took the handle, moved the door. Many times heavier than it should have been. He looked at Fergie questioningly.

'Armour plate. Concealed in the panel. All our vehicles get modified for combat roles, including the minibuses.' Fergie turned to one, used both hands to slide the access door back.

'Try it.'

He did. Hardly possible with one hand.

'As you can feel, a lot of additional weight,' Fergie said, 'which means we have to stiffen all the suspensions too.' He heaved the panel closed. 'But going back to your earlier question: we wanted vehicles which lent themselves to modification but were also commonplace in everyday traffic blending towards anonymity. I'm sure you wouldn't pick these out in commuter traffic.' He glanced at the personnel carriers. 'Except for those of course. They are what they are — and as you can see from the lettering we advertise the fact. Shuffle them around freely, under the banner of the Emergency Evacuation Initiative. Achieve public awareness that way — gain a level of acceptance.'

'How resistant is the armour?'

'Good enough to take a hit from an RPG.'

A rocket-propelled grenade was a serious piece of infantry firepower.

'We're hoping to avoid anything heavier,' Fergie went on. 'The whole military enterprise relies on surprise. If we're not in command within forty-eight hours, we've failed. We're not equipped to take on the heavy ordnance. How much have they told you of the planning?'

'To date broad brush stuff. I'm just getting familiar with things, hence this trip.'

'Well stop me if I go over items you are already privy to, but here's the general idea. Key strategy is to hit hard, to hit fast, co-ordinate major actions so everything happens at once. The army's heavy units are based in Pretoria and Bloemfontein. We don't see a big threat from them. You can't fight small highly mobile units in urban concentrations with tanks and heavy artillery.'

'Understood. That particular element we've been through in detail.'

'Good, I needn't dwell there then. The units we are going to have to neutralise quickly are the special forces and crack police units. Most of what you see here is for those objectives.'

'That I know too.'

'Okay. You're pretty much up with the play as far as I can see.'

They'd reached the far end of the building. Two vehicles sat atop hydraulic hoists, mechanics working at their underbellies.

'Routine maintenance, running repairs. We can handle anything a commercial workshop tackles, right down to engine and gearbox swap-outs.'

'What about installing the armour-plate?'

'That all happens next door. We'll go there next.'

A full fabrication shop was busy about its business. An overhead gantry-crane grumbled its way down the length of the shop: swaying at the end of the hoist, a heavy steel plate.

'On the way to laser cutting,' Fergie shouted above the din. 'State of the art equipment; cuts like a knife through butter, additional dressing after the laser unnecessary. Panels go straight onto the vehicles from there.'

Everywhere he looked there was activity; a chassis on trestles having new suspension fitted; an enclosed spray booth, panel van within getting its final coat of paint; stuttering arcs photo-flash brilliant, signposted the welding bays.

'Inert-gas wands.' Conventional welding can't hold a torch to it — excuse the pun.' Fergie looked pleased with his quip.

'Are all these tradesmen part of the fighting force?' Piet had to shout above grinders and percussion hammering.

'Absolutely. Fully combat trained, part of the fighting force. They'll have their part to play on the day.'

'Must've been a challenge to find tradesmen who are fighting men or vice versa.'

'Not as difficult as you might think. A question really of scratching in the right place. We quietly canvassed the army's engineer corps. Recruits from there soon multiplied in a knock-on effect. We had our own engineer corps in no time. Some of the older hands have been on strength for over four years. A few are full time, live on the farm. Permanent force you might say.' The dour Scot wasn't above a touch of dry humour.

Next stop the armoury. They drove along a paddock fence en route. A flock of sheep sporting colourful ear tags grazed contentedly within.

'So you have real animals on this farm, Fergie,' Piet bantered.

He scoffed. 'You're in a restricted experimental breeding area. Inside the outer fence there are six camps like this one. It's a very real component of the farming operation, also an effective blind to mask the military activity. Nobody's going to penetrate this far overland without being stopped and questioned. That's a function of on-the-ground security. It's another matter entirely if a nosy parker flies overhead.'

'How serious a sheep ranch are we talking?'

He gave Piet a pitying look. 'About as serious as it gets. We run over twenty thousand units on this farm. It's been in my family for three generations. There are rams bred here which sell for as much as a small family car. You've probably sat down to a Sunday lunch, put mint sauce on lamb raised here.'

Impressive indeed. Fergie might be a revolutionary, but clearly that took nothing from the gravitas he brought to his farming operation.

They pulled up in front of an earthen berm tucked into the very base of the ridge-line. A shallow stairwell at one end descended to a heavy steel door. Piet may have been ignorant when it came to animal husbandry, but drop him in front of that type of structure, its function was immediately apparent to him. All but invisible even close to, he knew he stood before an ammunition bunker.

Fergie fiddled with a bunch of keys, soon had the heavy door open. Beyond, a small ante-chamber gave off a musty odour. He opened a panel on the wall, flicked a switch. Piet heard the distant mechanical clatter as a diesel generator kicked into life. Fergie hit another switch. A bulkhead light flickered to life casting a weak yellow halo.

'Too far to run a cable from the main generator so there's a small jenny around the side,' he opened a second metal door in front of them. The familiar odour of cordite wafted out, swamping the musk.

'Evokes more memories,' Piet was thinking back to Angola days as they passed into the gloom and Fergie hit another switch.

He moved ahead of Piet, 'not your standard ammo dump though. 'We've combined it with the armoury. Saved us having to put up another building.'

He peered as bulkhead lights warmed. Down the length of the building gun racks ran out to both sides like skeletal ribs.

He hefted a weapon from its slot. R5 assault rifle. He weighed the piece in his hands.

'Regrettably not too many of those,' Fergie caressed it like a mother patting a baby's cheek. 'What we do have are thanks to a raid on the police armoury last year. At the time the theft was put down to criminal elements, but it was us nevertheless.'

'Massive stopping power,' Piet remembered the statistics from the manual, '5,56mm jacketed hollow-point rounds, fragmenting on impact. Very damaging in soft tissue. Leaves a huge exit wound almost always fatal.'

'I can see you haven't forgotten your stuff,' he sounded impressed. 'Incredibly the weapon is still used by our police force, not with hollow-points I'll grant you, but has invoked public outcry nonetheless. There's pressure to replace them with a less-lethal alternative. Hardly suitable for crowd control as you know. We had an incident in 2012 — you wouldn't have been here — thirty-four deaths at the hands of the police controlling a strike crowd at one of Lonmin's platinum mines near Rustenberg. The R5 got itself a very negative public image from that — gained the incident the same sort of notoriety as Sharpeville. Indelibly imprinted in the history books now.'

'Highly unsuitable as a police weapon,' Piet re-racked it, 'must rate as one of the ultimate assault rifles. Designed to put the enemy down, keep him down. I'm not surprised there's been a public outcry.'

'The fact they are still police issue is something we'd do well to remember. We're going to be confronting SAP units in the field,' Fergie finished soberly.

Their last port of call was the shooting range. Like the armoury, a subterranean structure sandbagged extensively and practically invisible against the foothills.

'I'm more than impressed, Fergie. These structures are undetectable at a glance.'

'Aye. Well they were years in the building. Not without considerable expenditure,' he added passing into an ante-chamber staffed by a sergeant. 'Fortunately not much of it mine.'

For the first time the muted popping of small arms fire became noticeable from beyond another steel door.

'Care to try your hand?' Fergie had the confident air of a fairground shooting range proprietor.

'Why not? A man has to start somewhere.'

He requisitioned two pistols and the storeman issued them. They donned earmuffs entering the range. Even so the racket was a continuous niggle.

Fergie shepherded them to a couple of unoccupied booths. 'Handgun section this side,' he raised his voice to penetrate the earmuffs and background noise. 'Rifle range next door.'

They got busy setting up. In adjacent booths a couple of instructors were giving direction. Fergie waved a greeting. He turned to Piet. 'A wee wager just to spice things a smidgin?'

'Why do I have the feeling you only make bets you know you can win?'

'I'm not so sure. From what I hear you were quite the marksman in your day. What say a bottle of Glenmorangie? Three targets, ten shots per target, best target to win.'

'Visitors, to have the first choice of weapon?' They had drawn 9mm pistols. A Beretta 92 and a South African manufactured Vektor SP1. The local gun, a crib on the higher pedigreed Beretta but modified by way of a counterweight on the discharge end. It also came with a couple of other subtle variants. It had been Piet's service weapon in army days. He had a kinship with it.

'Fair enough,' Fergie passed the Beretta.

'I'll take the SP1 if you don't mind?'

Fergie looked surprised. 'Why do I have the feeling I just lost the first round?' He passed Piet the Vektor.

They went through the ritual of checking slide actions, hefting for balance, sighting to targets. The latter were standard issue, dun-coloured outer rings closing to a black bullseye at centre and its adjacent circle. Ten and nine points respectively, diminishing incrementally to six at the outer edge. Beyond the outer ring a scoreless desert.

'May the best man win,' Piet hoped he wasn't as rusty as he feared.

'That's what I'm afraid of now,' Fergie looked like a punter at the races wondering if he'd backed the right horse. They took their stations.

Piet palmed home one of the magazines, pulled the slide back cocking the weapon. The precision of the mechanism brought a deeply satisfying feeling... and created an evocative moment. For an instant he rocketed back to Angola; to wild bush country, tracking a deadly enemy with a stomach uncontrollably knotted, expecting any moment the maniacal chatter of an automatic weapon. Explosive oblivion. His adrenalin pumped reactively, a slight tremor working its way into his hand. He breathed deeply, the trained response for steadying nerves. Composure returning, he locked onto the target thirty metres distant. He focussed everything on the black circle at the centre. Bringing the weapon to bear and deliberately aligning the sights, he took careful aim. The Vektor kicked in his hand at the steady squeeze of the single-action trigger. A black spot opened on the target in the no-score zone. He repeated the sequence lowering the weapon fractionally. This his chosen method of shooting. It taught accuracy, initially at the cost of speed, but eventually delivered both. By his fifth shot, the hits were inside the outer circle all scoring. By his tenth shot, he could feel muscle memory returning. Except for one hit high out to the right, all others were in the nine to twelve o'clock quadrant, creeping closer to the bull. Getting there. He glanced over at Fergie's target as he wound it back. It looked better than his.

He stepped around the partition holding it aloft. Nothing in the bullseye but two snugly in the nine circle outside of it. The remainder spread over the rest of the target in no particular pattern with only a couple non-scoring. Good shooting but it wasn't marksmanship.

'Forty-three for me,' Fergie beamed.

Piet took his target out of its clip examining it. An encouraging grouping of four, but they were towards the outer circle so didn't score highly.

'First blood to you,' he conceded defeat. 'Thirty-three.'

'Round two coming,' Fergie disappeared to prepare. Piet slotted his new target to the frame winding it to the back of the range. He sucked a couple of deep breaths taking careful aim. This time compensating for the previous bias to the top left quadrant. He squeezed the trigger but saw no tell-tale appear. Compensating too much. He adjusted, loosing off another round. This time a black dot jumped into existence at the extreme lower right of the paper square. Two gone. He adjusted again, a hole appeared just outside the outer circle. Three gone. Still no score but the hits now in the area where he expected to see them. He was getting used to the slight mis-alignment of the weapon. He tweaked his aim, firing again. Same place. A slight tremor from him he was sure. Keeping the sites aligned exactly as they were he fired again. A satisfying dot appeared in the six ring. He held the line, firing again. The previous hole opened wider. Getting better. He adjusted, loosed off again. This time the hole appeared in the eight ring. He kept the sights where they were, inhaled deeply then slowly out. Almost at the end of the exhalation, he fired again. He saw no evidence of the shot, knew it must be in the centre black rings. He repeated the sequence with his last two shots getting the same satisfying result.

Fergie reappeared around the partition looking very pleased with himself.

'Nine scoring shots. Sixty-four points,' he gloated.

'Can't compete with that Fergie,' he would need to improve, 'better than last time but no cigar. 'Forty-eight scored.'

Fergie laid his winning target down. Piet discarded his.

'I can taste single malt already,' Fergie crowed.

They got ready for the final round. Piet took a moment to relax sure now that he had the measure of the Vektor. The only variable now... himself. He regulated his breathing once again, slowly raising the pistol. Next to him, he could hear Fergie, encouraged by his earlier performance, getting through his rounds quickly. Piet let off his first shot. No evidence of a hit. He went again. Still nothing showing. By the fourth shot some light appeared at the centre ring. Daylight. As he progressed the hole grew increasingly visible. He finished off and wound the target back. Fergie had taken station behind him, by this time shaking his head slowly.

'Unbelievable. I thought I had you with that second target.' Piet unclipped his. A ragged hole, hanging flap, all that remained of the centre.

'Unbelievable,' Fergie looked as if he was just waking from sleep. 'I would have to allow that as a maximum. The best grouping I've ever witnessed.'

Piet grinned at him. 'Nice to know I haven't lost my touch altogether.'

'Bloody ringer.' He slapped Piet's shoulder affectionately as they headed off to the cleaning station.

He spent four more days on the farm, taking the opportunity of joining some of the training exercises. Impressed with both the way they were organised and with the quality of the recruits; those with previous service history particularly. It made a difference. Fergie showed him a grading system which evaluated every man. This would be used in allocation of manpower to specific missions closer to launch.

On his last day, he breakfasted with Fergie, going afterwards to the transport section where his old banger was garaged. Inside, Fergie walked to a buff-coloured Land Cruiser, took a clipboard off the driver's seat.

'Sign here,' he said, pushing it under Piet's nose.

'For what?' he had no idea what the form represented.

'You don't think we're going to let you take half-a-bar off the farm without a signature?' He kept a poker face.

Dumbstruck, Piet stammered. 'What about my old Toyota?'

'You won't recognise it when you get back.'

CHAPTER 19

FEEDBACK

The trendy restaurant buzzed. Busy, clamorous — Sandton's rush-hour-cheating commuters making the most of their earlier sacrifice. Heading off for work at dawn, the noble effort. A bacon and egg breakfast washed down with steaming coffee amongst fellow martyrs, the palliative.

Ivashchenkov was one of the throng. He liked to keep ahead of his staff. It created pressure among them to know the boss was at the office first. He loaded his fork and shovelled it to his mouth. His security man sat morosely across the table contenting himself with the dregs of his coffee.

Ivashchenkov communicated in their language. 'You're telling me Rossouw flew into Lanseria, spent few hours, went back to Cape Town? What was doing here?'

'Meeting shady business person.'

'And we know who this is?'

'Now, yes. I send two top men to airport as soon as Cape Town team say Rossouw is coming. Lanseria is not busy —

no problem to find him.' He chuckled. 'Igor was two tables away in same restaurant. Very easy.'

Ivashchenkov let his irritation show. 'Get to point. Who is contact?'

'Air-jockey name of Kosmo Fotakis. We followed after he left Rossouw — boarded Antonov freighter flying to Democratic Republic of Congo. Is aircraft owner — runs cargo business out of Kiev. Busy man in central Africa.'

'Working out of Ukraine? What freight does he ship?'

'Moves anything. But here is gold nugget. Is arms dealer; does not hide it.'

Ivashchenkov knew where this was going. 'Our friend arrives Johannesburg, meets shady gun runner, flies back same day?'

The security man warmed to the theme. 'Is obvious, no?'

'Rossouw is buying arms?'

'Almost — how do they say — racing certainty. And Fotakis headquartered at Kiev is not coincidence I think. Is large arms factory there. You can remember it?'

'Of course.' Ivashchenkov snapped his fingers. 'Avtomat Kalashnikova in Vinnytsia.'

'Yes. That one. Is big producer of AK47. Sell to anybody. No prizes to guess who is key account with them.'

'This Fotakis?'

'Da. Fotakis.'

Ivashchenkov tugged at an earlobe. 'This is good work. Find out for sure if Rossouw is buying.'

The other man beamed. 'Already busy, have comrade — worker at plant. We have made contact.'

'You think will be able to get information?'

'Maybe take short while, but we get it.'

'Use all resources — make things happen fast. I want to know soon if Rossouw is buying.'

'Then what?'

'Take measures to cut balls off dog.' He wiped away the breakfast grease with his napkin and called for the bill.

CHAPTER 20

RECRUITING

He'd been busy running all over the country so hadn't met with Rusty or George for a while. They'd stayed in touch via text however, now getting together for Saturday lunch in Gordons Bay. Berties Landing, a waterside restaurant-cum-bar they chose for its convenience. Midway between Gansbaai where Rusty's business operated, and Hout Bay where *Magus* was moored, it offered a midway compromise. George would agree to anywhere as long as a good brew was in prospect.

On the day the elements were being kind to them. Gordons Bay has a well-deserved reputation as the windy corner of the globe. It is home to the Cape south-easter; when it blows in this back-yard, it blows. But today there wasn't a breath of air as he strolled along the deck, picking his way past diners to where he spotted Rusty and George.

'Hey brothers,' he dropped onto a barstool. 'How goes it?'

'Must be a tour bus outside,' George chirped.

'Don't joke, I've been running my backside off all over this country.'

'Pray tell,' Rusty had that cynical look on his face. 'Normally a lady involved when a man's on the move like that.'

'Nothing of the sort.' An image of Sophie Birman flashed into his mind.

'Well don't mess around. Get a pint, fill us in on all that's been happening.'

Piet did both. They listened intently making the odd interjection to get clarity on some small point here and there. Fifteen minutes later they had the story to date. He'd made sure they understood the extent of his involvement in the Endeavour. In some way, it seemed to assuage his guilt, a show of how committed he now was. If there were two men on the planet he could trust with his life, trust with sensitive information, they were seated with him at the table.

'Unbelievable.' An uncharacteristically brief interlocution for George.

Rusty made it easy for Piet and gave him the opening to broach what came next.

'We're in. Right?'

'That's what I'd hoped.'

'To avoid an explosive device blasting a hole the size of a beer keg in that paddleboat of yours, you better not think otherwise.' George, back to form.

'You guys have no idea what a relief that is,' he was genuinely relieved. 'I thought maybe you might not be so keen considering I gapped it all those years ago. After all you had the backbone to stick it out, I didn't. If it's any consolation to you both, I don't feel good about that today. But trust me when I tell you, I've gone through my epiphany. The people I've met these past weeks have humbled me. I'm behind this thing a hundred and ten per cent.'

'The prodigal home to roost,' George chirped, 'not only home but perched on the top rung. One of the planners *nogal*. And for my money the old Colonel couldn't have made a better choice.'

'I'll go with that,' Rusty was running stuff in his mind Piet could see. 'What's the next step for George and me?'

'You'll join my squad. It's been tasked with a pivotal mission. Battle experience in the unit will be gold-dust. No timeline yet but things will happen at a pace. Once the new ordnance arrives, training intensifies. It's a short push from there to launch date.' he glanced at them both. 'What it means is there's not going to be much time for you to organise your lives. The call to action is likely to be at the drop of a hat.'

'Not a problem for me,' Rusty relaxed a notch, 'my second-in-charge is very capable. He'll cope with the operation in my absence, no trouble. I'll be ready.'

'Ditto,' George beamed. 'Showtime brothers.'

After lunch they split to go their ways. He walked to the carpark and climbed into the Cruiser. Fastening his seat belt he looked up and happened to make eye-contact with a swarthy individual halfway across the carpark. The man quickly dropped his eyes and busied himself with keys at the door of a black Mercedes. Piet felt vaguely troubled. Had he seen him before? He waited, checking as the car pulled out and disappeared. He let a couple of minutes pass then drove off, his senses on full alert. He checked the rearview mirror every few seconds. No black Mercedes all the way back to Hout Bay. Maybe I'm getting paranoid he thought. But then again it wasn't every day he got involved in a revolution. Smart to have the senses honed. That way he might make it to the finishing post. No prizes in that game for coming second.

Back aboard *Magus*, he poured a scotch then went topsides to watch the sun go down. Early evening undoubtedly his favourite time of the day. The hustle and bustle seeped slowly away as the sun slid beneath the rim of the ocean. In its place, a quiet peace. He let himself flow to it at a lower vibrational pitch.

That didn't last long. His cell buzzed as a message came in. From Fergie. He would be in town the following day, needed to meet urgently. Could Piet rendezvous with him in the village? He confirmed, gave Fergie a coffee shop easy to find. More than puzzled, a little perplexed, he wondered what brought Fergie out of the desert to his little fishing hamlet? Should he be concerned? Or was he being paranoid again? In the event it turned out he had every reason to be worried.

The following day he left the marina early afternoon. He hadn't slept well and decided to walk to the rendezvous to get some air in his lungs. He badly needed to relax. A brisk walk always helped. Getting in the spirit he detoured along the beach. A champagne day. The sun high in the heavens glittering like tinsel on the rippled surface of an ocean lapping rhythmically at the shoreline. He passed Mariners Wharf. The famous restaurant had a double-decker tour-bus disgorging tourists in front of it. The car park was crammed to capacity. A vehicle in the front rank caught his attention. A black Mercedes. Common enough perhaps, but after yesterday's sighting in Gordons Bay his senses were on high alert. He crossed the beach to check the number plate arguing internally the for and against of the action and then reminding himself it was smart to be alert. He got a nasty shock. The same car he'd spotted in Gordons Bay was here in Hout Bay, sixty kilometres distant. It stretched the bounds of credibility way beyond coincidence. He had picked up a tail. But who? The police? Not likely — they didn't run to Mercedes' for surveillance. Who did that leave? Customs and Immigration? Even more unlikely... he drew a blank. Suddenly he could feel eyes on him.

Keeping his composure he scanned all around without making a show of it. The usual beach strollers — dog walkers, sun-bathers, day-trippers. Nobody out of context first off. Perhaps his jangled nerves were giving him grief? It still didn't explain the Mercedes. He ambled slower; anyone tailing him would have to do the same. Easier to spot when they did. He took off his sandals and paddled out into the water. A recreational stroller with not a care in the world. Or so he hoped it appeared.

A red setter splashed past him intent on retrieving the stick his owner had thrown. He watched as the animal paddled out, grabbed his prize, turned for the shore. Reaching solid ground he ran straight to Piet, dropping the driftwood at his feet then backed off barking excitedly. Piet joined in the game, swivelling his body for the throw. It gave him a panoramic view along the beach. He spotted his man immediately, watching him, posing too as a casual paddler. Thirty metres distant, he shuffled in and out of the shallows. Squat and barrel-chested, a mat of dark hair sprouting from a half unbuttoned shirt, his trousers rolled to mid-calf, he carried his trainers in his hand.

Piet hoped he made a better actor than his tail did. If the man had ever visited the ocean before it didn't show. Wave dynamics were something new. He ventured too deep and one caught him properly, drenching his trousers. That should have had him wading ashore but didn't, so a second added insult to injury. He looked as if he would be happier guarding the portals of a seedy nightclub than sloshing about in the ocean. He simply didn't fit. At all. His skin was pallid enough to have taken on the first blush of sunburn. Not an outdoors type. Eastern European Piet guessed — but not the man he'd seen climbing into the Mercedes yesterday. Which meant there were at least two of them. Someone was going to great lengths to keep him shadowed.

The dog scampered back for a second run. Obligingly he threw the stick once more, sauntering off as the dog raced into the waves. He needed to lose his shadow. But by the same token had to know who they were; he didn't want to alert him, couldn't discover their identity if they became spooked and pulled off. He had to shake the man in a way which appeared natural. Piet glanced across at the Dunes pub and dismissed it as quickly; its single entrance too restricting. It would have to be somewhere he could enter one way, leave by another. Woolworths — it came to him in a flash. The retailer in the village had two storefronts, both with access doors. His tail wouldn't know that. Perfect for his ruse. When he popped in, his shadow would certainly post himself outside to watch the door he'd gone in by, allowing Piet to disappear out of the other.

He reached the store and went in. Weaving in and out of a couple of aisles to leave him unsighted, Piet made for the other exit. Once outside he checked behind him. No sign of him. From there, easy as you like. Making his way to the main road, he crossed and turned down a side street. Two more corners gave him the separation he felt happy with. The man would kick himself when he tired of waiting and went into the store to find Piet. It still left him with the thorny problem of identifying his followers.

Fifteen minutes later he arrived at the coffee shop. Chosen deliberately, it occupied a corner position with plate-glass windows on two sides making observation easy — unobserved approach all but impossible. No more taking chances.

Fergie arrived shortly after him.

'Sorry for the cloak and dagger stuff, Piet, but in the circumstances quite necessary.'

'Sounds serious.' he wasn't looking forward to whatever was to come.

'Could be. We're facing an unexpected precedent so it's difficult to say.'

'What's happened?'

'We began refurbing your old banger last week. Stripped it right down. Anything clipped, bolted or fastened came off.

We had it down to a bare shell. The guys were pressure washing, prepping for the spray booth, when one of the lads found a device high under the wheel arch.'

'A device. What sort of device?' A sinking feeling lurched in his gut.

'A GPS tracker.'

What was happening to him? The nightmare kept getting worse. He fumbled for words. 'Is it something that could have been there when I bought the car?'

'We considered that. Until that is, we found out it's the latest generation technology. The same being issued to our boys in blue.'

'The SAP?'

'Very same. Used primarily to track the movements of possible subversives, other characters of special interest, drug dealers for example.'

'So what the hell is it doing on my car?' The words were those of an innocent, hardly out of his mouth before he realised their idiocy. He had become a person of interest to the authorities as well as to an unknown party, had attracted tracking devices and surveillance teams. But how the hell could anyone suspect his involvement in the Endeavour? So soon?

Fergie broke into his deliberations. 'To answer your question, we believe it's linked to your recent interview with them.'

Piet had told Fergie and the planning committee about his session with the Hout Bay police following the fire. No-one, including himself, attached much significance to it at the time. That all seemed to be changing. He tried to make sense out of this latest disclosure; suddenly an image flashed. The man hefting a toolbox as he came out of the police station; had he planted the bug on his car? Certainly a possibility.

'Why do you think they're taking such an interest in me?'

'Again it's speculative. We think your military history makes you irresistible for a spot of high drama. With your decoration you must appear quite exotic. Something to brighten their lives so to speak.'

Dreading having to heap coals on the fire, Piet told him about that day's tail.

Fergie didn't bat an eyelid. 'You see, it's just as I say. They simply can't resist a colourful animal like you. But we're going to have to be doubly careful from hereon in.'

'I'm almost certain it isn't the police, Fergie.' Piet gave him chapter and verse.

'That most surely doesn't sound like the flatfoots. You're quite sure you threw off today's bloodhound?'

'Certain of it. I don't believe he even suspects I'm on to them.'

'And you say you have no idea who these people could be?'

'Not a clue. I got the Mercedes registration though. Possible to run a check, see what we can find?'

'Piece of old *tekkie*.' Fergie made a note on his cellphone. 'We'll have the results within a day or two. I'm guessing it'll turn out to be a hire car though. Not likely to get us very far.'

Fergie finished his sandwich and summarised. 'It's a given the police are interested in you. If not just to spice their lives a little, then why? I'm sure the GPS is theirs. Which means they're able to put you at the farm. That is if they've got the energy to check. It's going to be interesting to see if they come out for a sniff around.'

'That could be devastating, a search warrant might spell game over.'

'Maybe,' he mused, 'but at least now we're forewarned. I'll get in touch with the Colonel. I think we shut down operations at the farm for a short time. At least until we can fathom what's going on. Intriguing me more right now, is the identity of the outfit tailing you. Hope the licence plate yields something, although I'm not holding my breath.'

'Failing getting something, what else is there we can do?'

'Not much I can think of right now. Except to state the obvious. You're going to have to be extremely careful. Be at pains not to lead the hounds to the fox.'

'Rest assured there.' He resolved not to be such a liability in future.

'One last thing, Piet.' He looked at him almost apologetically. 'The Land Cruiser. They may have stuck a bug on it too. If so, we'll leave it there. Don't alert them to the fact we're onto them. Which means you have to be circumspect about where you go in it, and who you visit. Sorry, it's turned out to be a bit of a Greek gifting.'

'I'm the one who should be apologising,' he knew his discomfiture must be showing. 'How long have I been aboard? A matter of weeks — in which time I've become a real Jonah.'

'Not your fault. Could have happened to any of us.'

'If only I'd kept my nose out of the harbour the night of the fire. None of this would be happening.'

'Can't live your life on 'ifs'. If your father hadn't winked at your mother, you wouldn't be here. Events in isolation are of minor importance. It's the sum of their parts we have to concern ourselves with. Are these incidents part of a bigger picture or unrelated, of little significance? We'll work it out. When we do, we'll have a strategy for it.' Fergie's sangfroid in adversity was heartening. 'In the meantime, need to get the Cruiser swept electronically — a tracker onboard, we need to know it's there.'

'Who should I take it to?'

He grinned mischievously. 'Ironically, you'll have to arrange that through your father. He handles the nuts and bolts here in the Cape. I'm sure he'll be able to set something up at short notice.'

CHAPTER 21

DAMAGE CONTROL

The following morning Piet drove past Constantia wine estates then the village shopping mall on his way to a vehicle workshop in nearby Wynberg. Rush-hour traffic, over volumes were light. He kept one eye in his rearview mirror, vigilance the new order of the day. He couldn't afford to be compromised again.

His father had supplied the workshop address when he'd phoned the previous evening. To give credit, he didn't press for details when Piet told him what he needed. Within half an hour of the call his father rang back with the information.

He found the place with some difficulty tucked away in a low-rent back-street location — shared with a minibus tour-operator-cum-paragliding adventure outfit. He parked outside and entered through a pedestrian access in a battered roller shutter door. The interior brooded outside a cone of yellow cast by an ancient halogen lamp. In the 'spotlight' a late-model Jaguar. The car gave the appearance of devouring a mechanic half into the engine bay. He surfaced flicking grey shoulder-length hair as Piet entered. A ragged goatee and eyes that had seen too much lent him the air of a sixties-era biker. It wasn't until he flopped back from the engine bay, Piet realised he was a paraplegic. He wheeled around to meet him.

'You'd be Pieter Rossouw — come for the service on the Cruiser?' A vice-like grip, hallmark of the long term paraplegic, would have given Rusty a run for his money.

'Percy,' the mechanic raised his voice to attract his assistant, 'bring the Land Cruiser in, get it on the hoist.' The man dropped his task and went out to the car wiping his hands on cotton-waste.

'Make sure you put plastic covers on the seat, or you'll be looking for a *klap*.' Piet was sure it was said in jest. Almost.

'Give us half an hour, we'll be done. There's a little coffee shop just around the corner.'

The last of his coffee cooled beneath a milky film. His cell buzzed. A text from Fergie. A meeting with Colonel Stander in the city the following morning. Something he'd been anticipating — an urgent need to discuss damage control he felt sure, still a source of embarrassment to him. He had tossed and turned through the night struggling for a solution and felt he might have arrived at a strategy if they agreed to go with it.

He got back to the workshop expecting bad news to add to his woes. The Cruiser was back on the driveway. Inside the biker mechanic was again buried in the innards of the Jaguar.

'All done,' he waved a meaty hand.

'And you located the problem?'

'Clean bill of health.'

'You found nothing?' He could feel his relief bubble up.

'All clear.'

'You're sure?'

'Stake my life on it.' He offered it with a certitude that put Piet at ease. 'Percy, get the boss's keys.'

On the drive back he almost floated on the elation. Had he been losing sleep for nothing? Were the authorities not so interested in him after all? If they'd wanted to place a bug God knows they'd ample opportunity. Why they'd put one on the old Toyota remained a mystery. Perhaps at last they'd lost interest, no real damage done. That still left the identity of the other snooping party to fathom.

In the galley back aboard *Magus* he rustled up a sandwich. His phone buzzed. A message from Sophie Birman. The last thing he'd expected. He felt a rare tingle. *In Cape Town on business Wednesday and Thursday. Care to buy a girl dinner?* His heart skipped a little faster. This was an invitation to date; he hadn't had one of those in living memory. He wasn't good at this sort of thing and wrestled with a response finally managing, *With great pleasure. Wednesday?* The best he could do. Pathetic really. Embarrassment hit the second he'd sent it. He wished he could call it back, manage something better. But within seconds her reply bounced back. *Pick me up 1930 Commodore Hotel?* Relieved, he quickly confirmed. Then he just stared at his phone stupidly — hoping for more messages. Infantile he knew, but it's what he did. What was happening to him?

The following morning he left very early for his rendezvous with Fergie and the Colonel. Still on the lookout for spooks. And not without reward. As he left Hout Bay a silver-grey Audi eased into the traffic several cars behind him. He had half expected something, had a plan worked out. He drove to a yacht chandlery in the city, bought a small piece of gear and got back on the road to the Bay. He saw the Audi in the mirrors again, made it easy for the guy to stay latched on keeping several vehicles between them. That played to his plan. They approached a traffic light on the climb to Signal Hill. He had often cursed it. A seriously abbreviated green phase had caught him out on many occasions, changing before he could get through. He timed it so he would be the last vehicle to pass as the green phase ended. Four cars back, no ways the trailing vehicle would make it through now. He got trapped in the queue as Piet accelerated away climbing the hill. The man would lose touch now, but second-guess Piet to be on his way back to the marina. He turned down a side street making his way through Gardens suburb weaving back to the city centre.

At the Rockwell Hotel, confident he wasn't followed, he parked in the hotel basement and made his way to the lobby. The lounge served coffee and snacks. An open plan layout allowed line-of-sight to the entrance. No one was going to catch them unawares.

He took a seat settling down to wait. First on the scene was Fergie. He slapped him on the shoulder dropping into a lounger beside him.

'Anything sticking to your shoe?' he knew Piet would catch on straight away.

'Shaken off about an hour ago.'

Fergie looked relieved.

'Anything on the Merc?' The question he'd been burning to ask.

'There is,' Fergie looked smug. 'I got that wrong. Not a hire-car at all.'

Piet was all ears.

'Registered to a private company. Corporate Cover by name.'

'Sounds like an insurance outfit. Does it take us anywhere?'

'Patience, tiger, patience,' he milked the moment. 'Corporate Cover is not an insurance company. Well, not in the traditional sense anyway. It does, however, offer executive protection — body-guarding in other words, as one of its services. But here's the thing,' he looked suitably conspiratorial. 'It's a wholly-owned subsidiary of Nuclatom.'

'Ivashchenkov's Nuclatom?' Piet was astonished.

'The very same. Interesting isn't it?'

His mind raced. 'What possible interest could they have in me?'

'We've been pondering the same thing. We know, like the Guptas, Nuclatom are invested heavily in Zuma. They badly want those nuclear power station contracts, will do anything to close all opposition out. There's huge money at stake — a massive opportunity to be the number one nuclear player in Africa. Other countries will flock to them if they secure South Africa as a client.'

'So why would they be looking at me?'

Before he could answer Colonel Stander arrived.

'Gentlemen,' he greeted them.

'Just bringing Pieter up to speed on the identity of the outfit responsible for trailing him.'

The Colonel glanced at him. 'Fascinating isn't it?'

'I just said to Fergie, Sir, I can't make sense of it.'

'Neither can we at this point. But the fact remains they seem to have you in their cross-hairs as a threat of some sort.'

'Surely it can't be connected to my involvement with the Endeavour? I haven't been on board for long enough for them to get onto that.'

'Hard to say. But if it is linked they can't know much regarding yourself, as there isn't much to know yet. Should Nuclatom be working in concert with the police however, they may be appraised of the farm's location.' He glanced across at Fergie. 'I think we are agreed, it's sensible to shut farm activity down until we have a better handle on this?'

'Confirmed. No way we can hide everything if they do get a warrant to come snooping. There's only so much we could explain away under the guise of SAEEI. Better if we can avoid it.'

The Colonel nodded. 'Agreed. So, two items. Pieter and the farm remain our biggest worry out of all this.'

'I think I may have a solution, Sir — at least in part.' The plan he'd lain awake birthing.

Both looked sceptical.

'I'd like to propose we make a public announcement. Get a press release out stating the South African Emergency Evacuation Initiative is, more than ever, convinced this country is on the brink of civil war. Really make a big play of it. Say it has prompted a change of policy; the organisation now believes it needs strong military-style leadership. A seasoned ex-army man at the helm. Suggest I got lured back to interview for the role. Put lots of spin on my history as a war veteran, ham up my decoration, infer the salary package is substantial. Say I was the obvious choice.'

He looked from one to the other. The Colonel shook his head almost imperceptibly.

'Brilliant,' he breathed.

'Outstanding, Piet,' Fergie echoed.

Initially apprehensive they wouldn't go for it, it came as a relief to get the buy-in from these two men. Piet enlarged on the theme.

'As I see it, the boxes get ticked nicely. It's a reason for my being back. An organisation like SAEEI would be a perfect fit for a disgruntled Afrikaner ex-soldier intent on looking out for the wellbeing of his tribe. Good strategy to make oblique reference to a 'secret' training facility. If they are indeed on to the farm, it would at least give a reason for its existence, hopefully forestall a visit if one is intended. Plus it gives cover for me trooping around in a fancy Land Cruiser instead of the old banger.'

'It's excellent, Pieter,' Colonel Stander said. 'We'll get Sophie Birman to write it for us. No one better. She'll get us the widest possible coverage.'

He shifted a little at the mention of Sophie. 'Sir, she's going to be in town on business this Wednesday. I could run it past her then.'

This time only one of the Colonel's eyebrows twitched slightly.

CHAPTER 22

SOPHIE'S VISIT

Wednesday came. Piet found himself fussing about on the boat in preparation for his date with Sophie. He still dared call it a date: he'd anguished about that though. It could be that whilst in Cape Town on business, she was taking the opportunity to give him more in-feed about what he was involved in. His romantic exposure to the fairer sex could, at best, be described as limited — no real history by which to bench mark. The fruits Piet supposed of living alone on a boat, solitude the default state for a long time now.

The 'date' brought rare pressure to his wardrobe; scant would best describe the range there. In the end he had to content himself with a pair of jeans that selected themselves because they hadn't seen the rigours of hard sailing. A linen shirt kept for special occasions was the above belt accoutrement and deck loafers, an obvious footwear choice over trainers, completed his outfit.

He set off early for The Commodore on Cape Town's famous Victoria and Albert waterfront and arrived with half an hour to spare. Killing time had never posed a problem for him since army days, when quiet concealment in ambush could last for days. An attribute he took to sea, where it became a boon when becalmed for long periods going nowhere.

Just before seven-thirty, he climbed out of the Cruiser and made his way to the hotel lobby. The receptionist rang Sophie's room. Five minutes later she glided into the foyer looking stunning: ivory hued trouser suit simple in its elegance set off her russet hair. Vibrantly alive, her eyes glowed like burnished amber.

'You look fabulous,' he managed, 'whereas I feel like a yobbo.'

She took half a pace back, gave him the once over. 'You'll do for me,' she took his arm. 'Now, this girl is hungry. Where are you taking me?'

She wanted somewhere fun and noisy, but not at the cost of good food. Not easy to find, but he knew just the place. Dias Tavern, near the city's old castle, a Portuguese restaurant which has been around forever. For his money it boasted the best food on the continent. And at prices that weren't crippling. They made their way there, soon to be buried in a menu which made choice difficult. Eventually, wanting the best of both worlds and jibing one another at the inability to decide, they agreed to share from the other's plate. A spatchcock peri-peri chicken and a beef trinchado. Squid heads to start.

Dias' is always busy. It ticked the other box on Sophie's wish list; buzzing, everyone having fun. Cape Town's eclectic mix knowing how to enjoy itself.

'Just what I had in mind,' she grabbed his hand and squeezed it. 'Tell me what you've been up to since last we met, Mr Rossouw?'

He swallowed hard, more excited by the hand-hold than he cared to admit. He gave her a run down, leaving out sensitive elements and glancing around occasionally to make certain he wasn't overheard.

'You mustn't give a lady reporter juicy material like that,' she chided when he'd finished, 'there's one hell of a story there.'

'Well it's funny you should mention the subject of a story; there's something I want to talk to you about.' Piet recalled her professional ethics — would she be prepared to air a piece fulfilling their objectives, or see it as the distribution of misinformation? He could well find himself on shaky ground.

'We need to try to diffuse all this interest which I seem to have generated. The Endeavour wants to go public with an announcement of my appointment to the top job at SAEEI. Hoping it will mask my real purpose in being here. A red herring to confound whoever is on my case.'

'Oooh,' she cooed theatrically, 'disseminate fake news you mean?' The smart temple cat had nothing on this lady. He thought his misgivings may have come home to roost.

'Well, in effect it is a half-truth' he ventured, 'what I'll be doing will bring a better country for farmers, so the membership of SAEEI will be benefitted.' A thin subterfuge, they both knew it. He waited for her rebuttal.

She laughed then. A rich melodious sound that resonated deep inside him.

'Tell you what,' in a heartbeat she was the journalist, 'if I get a free hand with the copy, writing it as I like — no censorship from your chiefs of staff — then you've got a deal.'

'Well, I'm sure that there won't be a problem with that, I'll need to get clearance of course, but I think everyone knows where your heart is.'

'Oh, they do do they?' she looked coquettish, 'and where is my heart, Mr.Rossouw?'

Caught off-guard, he coloured, stammering for a response. 'In terms of what you believe in, what you stand for, what you want for the country — feelings regarding those things.'

There came that wonderful sound of her laughter again. 'Nobody forecasting on my personal emotions then?' The flash of her teasing was gone as soon as it appeared. She was all business again. 'We'll need to go through a few things you people may find sensitive. I don't want to scuttle the ship unintentionally,' she allowed a serious look, 'no time like the present, so tell me what you want. I'll put it into journalese adding my own riders; you can present that to the war cabinet before we go to press, providing they don't choke on it. Agreed?'

Relieved, he relaxed and launched into it. He must have passed muster: when he'd finished, she regarded him as a senior staffer might look at a cub-reporter. 'Very good, Mr Rossouw. You'd have made a creditable journo.'

High praise coming from this lady. 'Undeserved acclaim. Remember it's my tardiness which made this necessary. Given my background, unforgivable. I should never have attracted so much attention.'

'Do you think you were followed tonight?'

'Maybe initially. I've become an expert at giving them the slip when I need to. Sometimes coming into town, I run them down the highway. Other times over the Nek; there's a coffee shop in Gardens I've kept them outside for hours. Then again, maybe take the coast road through Seapoint. Hard for them to second guess me. So tonight I used the highway, probably got a speeding fine gunning it to see if they were there, then did a bit of a detour through Woodstock to be sure. No tail was going to survive that.'

'Comforting. With Ivashchenkov's outfit shadowing you, it might be wise not to advertise our social engagements.

Important he sees Phoenix Press without me having an agenda. That way I can still stick a pin in him when I need to.'

She made a good point. Piet hadn't considered matters from her perspective — a relationship with him could compromise her and be dangerous. Rushing his fences by the proverbial country mile he suddenly realised — relationship indeed — barely two hours into a first date. He'd do well to slow down; this could be a first and last.

'And you say you have no idea why he's taking such an interest in you?'

'Unless it's somehow linked to the police activity, no idea at all.'

'Well, that's a possibility. It's not unknown for government agencies to work with private organisations when it suits. Especially in the interests of national security. Don't forget we know Ivashchenkov to be a dirty buddy of the Guptas, who are in turn in bed with the president. Ivashchenkov could be putting his resources at Zuma's disposal. My sources tell me that for Nuclatom's interests to be realised, it's important Zuma remains at the helm until their shady deal gets ratified by government. One hand washing the other. Let's assume you are somehow seen as a threat. We need to work out how. Could he have wind of your involvement in an overthrow attempt? You say you don't believe that is possible?'

'We don't think so; I've been in the mix for too short a time. We're mystified and it's worrying the hell out of me.'

'Justifiably so, I'd say. If Ivashchenkov is onto you, it would suggest he knows far more than is healthy for you or the Endeavour. Very dangerous.'

'I know.'

A sobering note stealing some of the fun. Sophie it was who shrugged it off. She suggested they finish the meal with a Portuguese brandy. They did. Capped that with a simply sublime espresso. He settled the bill and they made their way to the street below. A beautiful evening. It wouldn't stay that way for long. A south-easter was filling in. Before long it would flex its muscles blowing hard enough to worry the trees and dislodge roof tiles. Sophie pulled a silk scarf from her pocket and tied her hair back as they strolled to the car.

'I don't want to go back to the hotel yet,' she reached for his hand. 'I'm enjoying myself — having fun. Show me this gin-palace of yours.'

He looked across at her, hesitated. She laughed.

'I've shocked you? The liberated woman making improper suggestions?'

'Not that, although it did give me a jolt. Just thinking there's sure to be eyes on the boat — a visit could expose you.'

'I can wrap the scarf around my head... unless you've got a beanie or something?' She reached for the glove compartment. 'Whoa. No beanie, no cigar… but what do we have here?' She pulled out a bottle of scotch. Glenmorangie single malt. 'Do you always carry hard liquor on first dates — slug of the old Dutch courage?' She was teasing him again.

His turn to chuckle. 'Ill-gotten gains from a bet — won fair and square over drawn pistols.' He had forgotten the wager with Fergie, thinking Fergie had simply overlooked giving the scotch. He should have known better: honour would allow no such slip. He told Sophie the story of their wager.

'Good old Fergie then — our benefactor providing the perfect nightcap. Let's go, the night is but a pup, I will not be deterred because of a bunch of Russian hoods. We'll fox them somehow. This is my first chance to go aboard a proper yacht, they're not going to rob me of it.'

He loved her grit. Something he could readily identify with. He had showed the same fervour when he walked in a younger man's shoes. God, it seemed so long ago. Easy to see she would be immovable once set. A bonus that she shared the same taste in whisky.

They got aboard *Magus* without incident. The lighting around the marina would barely shame a colony of glow-worms. No way of seeing who accompanied him, even supposing there was observation running.

In the main saloon, he closed the curtains and flicked on the cabin light. *Magus'* soft illumination a deliberate choice so as not to interfere with his night vision when on passage. The soft glow set the right mood tonight. He gave Sophie the guided tour. She oohed and aahed appreciatively.

'I'm impressed, Mr Rossouw. Not at all what I expected.' She told him she'd pictured a spartan interior, functional with no frills. 'This is almost as luxurious as my apartment.'

'Been home for the best part of a decade now. I'm not into sacrificing creature comfort just because my house happens to float,' he dug in the freezer for ice for their drinks.

She seemed to be weighing something as he came back. 'So which is it at core being — old tar or gentleman farmer?'

'Hard to pin a tail on the donkey right now. Torn I guess. I'll wait, see what comes out of all this. If we can wrest this country back, it'll more than likely be the latter. Meanwhile, I'm still a maritime junky.' he raised his glass. 'Saluté.'

She sipped and sighed contentedly. 'When there's this on offer why would you drink anything else?'

'The price might have something to do with it,' he teased.

'Not something us ladies have to worry about too often.'

'Spoken like a true ambassador for the pampered sex.'

She pulled a tongue at him, took another sip. 'Do you realise in the time you've lived aboard, I've called three apartments home?'

'Begs the question of who the real gypsy is.' His turn to tease.

They settled to easy conversation. A rare opportunity, he guessed for both to be themselves. She had a high-pressure job demanding a flinty exterior. He was preparing for battle. He re-filled their glasses, the ambrosia beginning to work its magic. A companionable silence enveloped them.

Eventually, she stirred. 'Does the kitchen run to coffee? she languished like the cat he often compared her to.

'When afloat that kitchen is a galley,' he said, 'and this galley runs to a passable cappuccino. Served in something a long way from bone china.' He remembered the dainty ceramics at the restaurant. 'After the Lord Mayor's show…' he said.

'…comes the donkey cart,' she finished out the cliché for him.

'Poor ending after Glenmorangie supped from crystal, I'm afraid.'

'You're in luck. This girl got raised on instant coffee in mugs — doesn't mind it a bit.'

They chatted on for half an hour lazily learning more about each other. Her schooling in Johannesburg; the desire to become a journalist with her as long as she could remember. Her first rookie job, a gofer on a small-town rag in the mining town of Vereeniging. Immersed deep in the Afrikaaner culture she was immediately tagged 'English' even though fully fluent in Afrikaans. That made the journey tougher she said. Forced to jump through hoops. Far from breaking her spirit, it stiffened her resolve and got her grit noticed. She got her first promotion to cub reporter under the wing of one of the old hands.

Vereeniging had its beginnings atop the great gold reef which runs a hundred kilometres from Benoni to Randfontein. The town grew with the gold-boom, other industry burgeoned to support the mining activity. Her assignments covered hum-drum events such as ladies teas as well as more weighty mining disputes involving a black, often volatile workforce. These were the days of serious labour unrest in South Africa. She chortled as she recalled the time she presented a story written from the viewpoint of the aggrieved black mineworker who'd had the gall to stand his ground, and pursue his rights.

'What happened?' he enjoyed peeping into her earlier life.

'They refused to publish, found my slant 'inflammatory'. Told me it would cost the paper readership, ignite racial tension if it went to print.' He could see she still found it galling. 'No denying racial issues were very sensitive at the time. White management nervous and gun-shy of black aspirations. For my part as a young highly principled journalist, I wanted to say it as it was. The employer had blatantly abused labour law, even the watered-down labour law of the time. I wanted to expose it. I might as well have whistled in the wind. The story never got to print.'

'What did you do?'

'Quietly started looking around for another job.'

'With success I'm guessing.'

'It wasn't easy. As I say things were delicate at the time. There were pockets where change was taking place, but they were few and far between. A principled cub reporter wasn't the hottest goods in town. I banged on a lot of doors. Eventually a sub-editor on The Citizen liked my grittiness, gave me a start. Right at the bottom, but I didn't mind. I knew I could work my way up, do what it took. It wasn't a big paper with massive circulation, but I'd learned patience and perseverance in Vereeniging. I stuck it out. The Citizen taught me real journalism. I loved it.'

'How long were you there?'

'Five years. Until head-hunted by The Star.'

'Into the big league?'

'I suppose so. But things in the printed media were changing too. On-line publishing and television news coverage were gaining momentum, adversely affecting circulation of print-newspapers. The accountants were brought in. Broadsheets and tabloids soon found bean-counters at the helm. It was the start of a new era. Profitability was the watchword: first to suffer, the reporter pools — more often than not surgically slashed down to a single reporter. I began to see the growing role the news agencies were playing. That altered my focus. Raw news became a commodity. I wasn't going to get left behind so started to look around. That's when the opportunity at Phoenix presented. After that, it's all history as they say.'

'You clearly enjoy it.'

'It's my life. Just as sailing seems to be yours.' She regarded him steadily, the amber flecks in her eyes sparkling as they reflected the lighting. He swallowed hard, trying to hide the fact his mind had gone elsewhere.

They held each other's gaze for what seemed a long time. Gently she leaned into him, her hand going to the back of his neck, pulling him into the kiss. He had never experienced anything remotely like it. It was as if an explosion took place in his chest. His heartbeat seemed to rock him at every pulse. His inexperience perhaps magnified the quality of that kiss. He had read of kisses described as 'sweet' in pulp fiction and dismissed it as author's licence. But here, he could swear, he tasted a hint of very delicate wine in which there were honey tones. Not the pungency of fine Scotch whisky. They hung in the kiss for what seemed an eternity, the pleasure intense. Then her tongue probed sensuously into his mouth. He thought he would explode.

She drew back slowly eyes glowing like coals. 'What do they call a bedroom on board ship?' she breathed.

'They call it a cabin,' he managed in a hoarse whisper.

CHAPTER 23

EXPLOSIVE INFORMATION

Ivashchenkov sat at his office desk reading a press release his people had crafted. It would go to the newspapers after receiving his sign-off. The piece painted Nuclatom in the image of African benefactor bringing its nuclear technology to the continent. It was raw spin. He was happy with it after making minor amendments. He tossed the approved document into his out tray as his cell phone buzzed.

'I have information. Need to meet,' the security man sounded excited.

'Coffee shop. Half hour.'

His man was already at the table when he arrived. He waved away the offer of a beverage.

'What do you have?'

'Dynamite from our man in Kiev. A shipment currently processing for South Africa.'

'How many weapons?'

The man paused. 'Is hard to believe.'

'How many?'

'Two thousand.'

Ivashchenkov repeated the number slowly. 'Two thousand?'

'*Da.* Two thousand.'

'And we are sure of this information?'

'We are sure. Our comrade is very thorough — still SVR agent undercover. Does not make mistakes.'

SVR is Russia's external intelligence agency penetrating deep into the fabric of civil society throughout the former Soviet bloc.

Ivashchenkov's mind raced. 'This arms contract, it is placed through Fotakis?'

The man nodded.

'To be shipped aboard his aircraft?'

Again a nod of affirmation.

'When?'

'Less than two weeks.'

'Our SVR comrade — he will help us?'

'Likes money — for enough will do anything.'

'Listen carefully. Is what I want you to do.'

CHAPTER 24

DEADLY SUBSTITUTION

The conveyor belt uttered its rhythmic clatter as crates swept around a turn on their way to the transfer station. Two workers manhandled the boxes from there for a final run to the inspection table. A work-study engineer would have torn his hair out at the obvious inefficiency. But it worked in Ukraine. Two men's wages were ratshit compared to the capital cost of an upgrade.

Each box contained four Kalashnikov assault rifles. The inspector checked them as they came to rest in front of him. He entered serial numbers on the quality assurance certificate and dated it before scanning with an electronic reader capturing data to the company's computer. He stapled the certificate to the underside of the lid prior to a mechanical grab snatching the box away for another run to the pneumatic nailing station. An asthmatic hiss from air pistons there drove the fasteners deep into the wood. A final run took it to despatch.

Halfway through dealing with his next crate, the factory klaxon sounded lunchbreak. He dropped the task immediately, put his hands to the small of his back and stretched expansively. Throughout the plant men deserted work stations for the welcome break of the canteen.

'Come Boris" he shouted to the man adjacent, 'time for smoke. And today is your turn. Bring packet — been smoking mine whole week.'

'Bullshit. Maybe I bummed couple yesterday — one or two day before. Not whole week.' He dug in his overall pocket pulling out a carton. 'Here,' he tossed them to his friend. 'Leave couple for me. I join you at canteen, but first I make phone call.' He watched as his friend caught the pack, ambled off, then made his way at a pace to the locker room. With the exception of a solitary figure busy at the far end, he had it to himself. Fishing out his keys he fiddled with the padlock until a satisfying thunk separated the staple from the brass body. A travel-scarred rucksack took up all the space in the bottom of his locker. He lifted it out and shucked it gently onto his shoulder. A final check of the room and he hurried back the way he came.

The shop floor on the return journey was quiet save for the background hum of idling electric motors. No one roamed abroad. He made his way to the inspection station where he hefted his rucksack onto the conveyor. Making certain there was no-one observing, he opened his bag and carefully removed slabs of plastic explosive bound tightly together. He fiddled intently with a pressure sensor attached to a detonating device. The mechanism now primed, he laid it carefully at his feet.

'Hey Leonard, what you up to?' The man had approached unnoticed on the far side of the conveyor.

He almost jumped out of his shoes, heart thumping in his chest. It became clear it was a greeting and not detection but it rattled him. He managed with difficulty not to show it.

'Comrade Aleksandr. Goddam roller jammed — screaming like baby all morning. Annoying shit out of me so I fix it now plant stopped.'

'You want hand?' the man offered.

'Is not necessary — almost done — thanks anyway.'

The man waved, continued on his way.

He took several steadying breaths before continuing. Two AK47's came out of the crate; he laid them at his feet then nursing the explosive device like bone-china he placed it carefully in the void left by the weapons. A snug fit — crafted to be. He taped the bundle to the adjacent rifles eliminating any chance of movement. Finally he checked the QA paper stapled to the inner surface of the lid — the consignee — Sunbird Agricultural Machinery, South Africa. Finished, he re-positioned the lid and pressed a button on a panel below the level of the rollers. The crate got hauled along to the nailing station. Pneumatics kicked in — fastenings drove deep into the wood.

Almost done he dragged the next case to the inspection table, filled out a new QA paper and stapled it to the lid. His friend would not know the box upstream was now a deadly Trojan horse. One final task. He stripped the stocks from the two loose rifles. Broken down they fitted comfortably into his rucksack. He shucked it to his shoulder, set off for the locker room checking his watch. Still twenty minutes of lunch break remaining. He smiled wickedly to himself. Time for a smoke to calm his jangling nerves.

CHAPTER 25

FATAL FLIGHT

Hostomel airport borrows its name from the neighbourhood in which it lies. It is situated in the north-west of Kiev. The facility, a major international cargo hub, is home to owners Antonov aircraft company. The famous manufacturer use it as a test and service facility. Kosmo Fotakis' employing good Greek horse-sense, kept his ageing fleet of Antonov freighters there.

In hangar D one of his 'ladies' yawned, her aft cargo hatch gaping as she took on her cargo. Last load aboard was an illicit arms shipment destined for South Africa and on the manifest as agricultural spares. The loadmaster checked his calculations. A weighty diesel-electric locomotive shipped earlier from China and destined for Nigeria, was snugged deep in the belly of the aircraft and comprised the bulk of the load. The loadmaster's responsibility was to make sure everything distributed correctly so the aircraft would trim safely for flight.

'Those in bay number eight towards tail,' he motioned the busy forklift driver to one side of the aircraft.

'How it goes with loading?' The pilot approached peering past his loadmaster at the Antonov.

'We go heavy once all South African stuff on board. Nothing new. She will trim good.'

'And fuel load?'

'Good for leg to Cairo. There will be margin.'

'Nice to miss Cairo. Is shithole.'

The loadmaster chuckled. 'Is big shithole. But no choice. If not Cairo then two refuelling stops. Big burn off for extra take-off.'

'*Tak*. I know. Would take smile off boss's face when fuel bill lands on desk.'

They both laughed. 'Could kiss year-end bonus goodbye for sure.'

'How long before finish here?'

'One hour. Not more.'

The pilot consulted his watch. 'Good. In one hour and half I want crew aboard. Have her pulled from hangar not later, then we start pre-checks. Take off seventeen thirty.'

Two-and-a-half hours later the giant Antonov rumbled down the Hostomel runway, her four D 18T turbofans roaring out over two hundred thousand pounds of thrust. An impressive machine she gained momentum to lift the thick end of two hundred tons into the air. Add this to her weight, it represented over four hundred tons defying gravity.

From the flight-deck, towering as high as a six storey building, the pilot continued to ease the throttles forward. The power units whined at a higher pitch. Slowly she began to reach for the sky as the seventy linear metres of aerofoil bit into the evening air. He coaxed the controls, gently enticing the nose ever higher. She held for a while, seemingly reluctant to be aloft, then slowly broke free of her earthly shackles. Unashamedly oversized, all her movements were measured and deliberate. She possessed the dignity of an elephant, even if she lacked the grace of a gazelle. The pilot held her steady in the climb as they cleared the airport perimeter, passing over the abutting suburb shrinking beneath them. He eased thrust ten per cent in a token gesture to lessen the roar of jet-wash rolling over the houses below. Even with the reduction, the blast would be powerful enough to rattle glass panes in window frames, shake any ill-fitting door.

They held the climb clawing their way to altitude like a mountaineer inching up a rock face. Once clear of the city the pilot gave the old lady her head, pushing the throttles fully home. His headset crackled as the air traffic controller gave him a course adjustment from the tower. Banking the lumbering giant into a shallow turn he locked onto the new heading. They would be ascending for some time.

Passing through twenty-thousand feet, an atmospheric pressure-sensor deep in the cargo hold sniffed the pressure differential and switched on its circuitry. A digital counter began to ratchet in tiny increments towards a pair of electrical contacts. Due to a fault in the device, it had activated five thousand feet higher in the stratum than it should have. The freighter would remain safe through the additional margin. It left them a prayer of hope.

Arriving at their first cruising level on the flight plan the captain had filed, the altimeter showed twenty-eight thousand feet. The pilot checked his heading, satisfied he locked the aircraft onto auto-pilot. He passed the con to his co-pilot. It would be a little while before they were out over the ocean, could go to a higher level. The flight plan requested thirty-one thousand feet for the remainder of the leg to Cairo. He rose from his seat heading for the washroom passing the flight engineer and loadmaster crammed in the rear of the noisy flight-deck. He gave them the thumbs up, they smiled as one, returning the gesture.

Once back he donned the headset again. The altimeter showed them happily cruising at twenty-eight thousand feet — airspeed seven hundred and fifty kilometres per hour. It could be coaxed quite easily to eight hundred once they got to thinner air, but for now they were conserving fuel to give them a comfortable margin to the refuelling stop. Crossing the coast of Ukraine they headed out over the Black Sea. He pulled the microphone closer to his mouth speaking to his co-pilot.

'Ask ATC if we can go to higher altitude early. We burn more fuel down here — higher we save.'

'Have already requested. Controller has much traffic going north. He holds us here for time being. He says request again in twenty minutes.'

'Bloody traffic wardens.' There was no love lost between air-cargo crew and air traffic controllers, the former believing they always got the raw end of the deal in routing and flight level allocations: second fiddle to the more glamorous passenger airline pilots. They were however bound to obey instructions.

Fifteen minutes later they called again and this time were cleared to thirty-one thousand feet. The pilot increased power, eased the yoke back. He watched the altimeter inch its way from twenty-eight thousand clawing towards twenty-nine thousand. The electronic device in the cargo hold ratcheted another notch towards its deadly end point.

They passed through twenty-nine thousand without incident, continuing the climb, striving for the thinner air above. Through thirty-thousand they remained viable, disaster free. Finally they plateaued at the new flight datum and levelled out, airspeed now up fifty knots. The pilot smiled contentedly unaware a man-made electronic device had malfunctioned and that a higher authority, for now at least, shepherded them safely along their path.

In due course the Ukraine controller gave a new radio frequency and passed them on to Turkish ATC. They checked in confirming Cairo as their destination and were cleared to continue at the same flight level. Forty minutes later a weather alert came through. A strong front rapidly developing along their route. They were cautioned to keep an eye on it although it was not yet visible on the aircraft radar.

The system crept onto their scanner an hour later. At first a broken line at the top of the screen. As they pushed further south it ripened to a bunch of neon grapes, before long growing to a vine spanning the entire screen. Somewhere over central Syria its nascency stretched out and reached the Mediterranean as far west as Cyprus. A serious weather front.

'Pushing through will be rough I think,' the co-pilot traced the image on the scope with a finger.

'Have no choice. It blocks us. We will punch through. Old lady easily can handle it.' He patted the instrument panel in front of him affectionately.

By the time night fully engulfed them the weather front had grown to a towering impenetrable wall. Still some way off, but at their cruising speed, they would be there soon enough. Their altitude remained rock-solid at thirty-one thousand feet.

Presently the black curtain out in front began to flicker as electrical activity showed itself.

'Strap in,' the captain instructed his three-man crew. The command superfluous, all were tightly cinched in ready for the turbulence they knew lay before them. The distance closed and the night sky became spectacular, blooming to a pyrotechnic display as far left, as far right as the eye could see. The flight-deck flared in stobe-like flashes. On their radar, the system now dominated, leaving an eerie afterglow as the radial rhythmically swept the screen.

The first minor bumps came ten minutes later: the wall of cloud a boiling mass, spasmodically lit by high voltage electrical discharge. Like entering a fairground tunnel-of-horror, the next instant they were into it. Beyond the cockpit's toughened glass the world became a buffeting hostility. A smoke-like confusion in which a thousand arc welders pulsed maniacally. Rain came suddenly in a deluge that hammered the hull viciously. Even the note of their powerful turbines muted to a hum in the ear-shattering roar. Conditions deteriorated rapidly as the rain morphed to hail the size of golf balls. The clatter achieved a level of intensity difficult to comprehend. A racket like a legion of riveters attacking the aircraft's thin aluminium skin. Despite her bulk, she bucked and jolted — a plastic duck on a storm-lashed pond.

A sudden violent updraft scooped them effortlessly, tossing them hundreds of metres higher in seconds. The altimeter needle jerked crazily. His face frozen in rictus, the captain wrestled frantically with the controls, a desperate contest to cope with the updrafts and keep the craft flying straight and level. They got sucked ever higher.

In the cargo hold, a faulty sensor which should have already triggered blowing them to oblivion, continued to inch towards its critical limit. As the plane passed through thirty-three thousand feet, still locked into violent updrafts, the circuitry closed. Four kilograms of high explosive ignited in a blinding flash tearing a hole the size of a small car in the fuselage and mangling control cables passing to the tail section of the plane.

On the flight deck, all four men felt the pressure wave. The pilot and co-pilot exchanged frightened glances as the plane began to yaw sickeningly to starboard.

'Lightening strike,' a frantic spasm into his headset as he wrestled to correct the yaw. 'Check cargo hold,' he screamed over his shoulder.

The loadmaster unclipped. A paroxysm of fear gripped him. He grappled for handholds on the wildly bucking flight-deck inching his way aft. The pressurised pod housing the flight crew held for the moment. He pressed his face to the observation panel peering into the cargo hold. A searing lightning flash briefly illuminated the scene. He could hardly believe his eyes. A massive rent opened the fuselage. His bowels turned liquid. Flaps of metal slapped like washing pegged on a clothesline, debris scattered everywhere; firearms littered the floor and lay amongst splintered crates. Lightning continued to stutter through the aperture. He felt the bile rise in his throat. Their main payload, dislodged from the anchoring floor rails, wobbled menacingly. His fear blossomed to full terror.

At that instant, the Antonov got savagely wrenched into a powerful downdraft. She plummeted nose-down slewing further out of control, entirely at the mercy of natural forces. Had it not been for the downdraft snaring them, there may have been a vestige of hope. Now there was none. She staggered in her final death throes, the scene set for the closing act. The loadmaster, hurled to the floor managed to claw his way to his feet just as the plane entered a sickening spiral dive. An ominous rumble came from deep in the planes' guts — a violent shuddering shaking her floor panels. He peered through the inspection port as yet another flash lit the interior. It was his last living moment. Thundering towards him at breakneck speed freed of its restraints, came one hundred-and-fifty tons of runaway locomotive. It smashed through the bulkhead killing him instantly, tore its way into the flight deck and punched the aircraft's entire nose off. A shattered mausoleum began falling to the ocean far below.

CHAPTER 26

DISASTER

He scrubbed the deck energetically enjoying the work-out, even though sweating freely in the mid-morning heat. His cellphone rang in the saloon below. Sophie. They were in the habit of calling each other every couple of days, compensating for the distance separating them.

'Hi, Sweetheart.'

'Have you seen the news?' she started in breathlessly. He could sense something gone badly wrong.

'I haven't. What's up?'

'Last night a transport plane went down in a storm over the eastern Mediterranean. An Antonov out of Kiev bound for South Africa.'

His heart lurched. He posed the next question with dread, feeling he already knew the answer.

'Was it one of Fotakis'?'

'We don't know yet. No mention in the first releases. But it has to be doesn't it? Who else flies Antonovs on that route?'

Struck dumb, his head became a jumble of confused thoughts. Please God let it not be a Fotakis aircraft carrying their shipment. But suppose it was — as seemed likely? Where was the crash site? Was the cargo lying scattered about waiting for discovery? Were there survivors? Would the authorities be coming for him?

'How much more do you have?' he finally managed to croak.

'Right now that's everything. I'm trying to get more from our foreign associates. I'll keep you posted if anything comes in. Stay positive.'

And with that she was gone. He sat looking hypnotically at his cell for fully half a minute. Refusing to allow the full impact of the nightmare to hit home.

Snapping out of it, he tried Kosmo's number but got no response. He phoned the Colonel telling him a cargo freighter had gone down in the eastern Mediterranean. The Colonel suggested a meeting but he deferred. No point right then. He would call later as more information came in.

Sophie called back late afternoon confirming the worst. Fotakis' aircraft had crashed over the ocean. Nothing further yet. A maritime search launched, little hope of finding survivors. He relayed the news to Colonel Stander saying he would keep him updated.

The local TV channels carried nothing. BBC World ran a short piece showing generically, an Antonov and making mention of its impressive load capacity, the craft's ability to perform as an airborne freight train. Ironic — the very load she'd carried. Al Jazeera also ran the clip. They made much of the storm, speculating that it had led to the undoing of the flight.

That night he climbed into his bunk feeling worse than he could ever remember. He slept fitfully dreaming weirdly of an adversary — seeing an unknown hand raise a rifle at him, take aim and fire. A locomotive surged from the barrel racing towards him. He woke in the morning his jaw muscles sore from clamping.

Mid-morning he tried calling Kosmo Fotakis again, his cell still going to voice message. Piet could well imagine the turmoil in his life right then. Next, rather than call, he texted Rusty suspecting he would be running clients on the boat. He left a message for him to make contact as soon as he found a gap. Then, at a loose end, he made a cup of coffee, sat topsides looking dejectedly seaward. His phone startled him. Kosmo Fotakis.

'I'm flying to Cape Town in forty minutes,' there was the briefest of pauses. 'Urgent you meet me.'

Piet would drive to the airport, Kosmo would fly in spend two hours then immediately return to Johannesburg. He checked the time. Four hours to kill.

Impatience got the better of him. He arrived early, passed through the concourse heading for the coffee shop. A slack period, he had the pick of the seating. Sliding into a booth at the window where they would have privacy, he settled to wait. Kosmo arrived an hour later, his skin the colour of dirty ivory — a gaunt caricature of his usual buccaneering persona. Trademark teardrop sunglasses were absent, in their place owl-like rings stamped to dog-tired eyes.

'Sorry for your loss, Kosmo.' Weak and fatuous, but the best he had.

'It is a catastrophe my friend,' his voice lacked its normal flippancy, mono-tonal now. 'Let us hope it does not turn to a Greek tragedy.' He flashed Piet his owlish scrutiny. 'You and I could become stars in a sensational show.'

He chose not to dwell on that or let a picture take hold. 'Any chance of survivors?'

'Little hope. A search has begun but it is a big area. Olga was out of range of any air-traffic radar so even position is at best a guess. Fifty kilometres off the coast probably, long odds against finding survivors or wreckage.'

Piet hoped it didn't show but relief flooded in. A loss at sea. 'How many crew aboard?'

'Four. All good men including the captain, my chief pilot. Very hard to replace.'

'What do you suppose happened?'

'For me, it is a mystery. Igor is a very experienced pilot. He has flown every weather condition including violent storms. The aircraft could handle extreme weather. So could the rest of the crew. My loadmaster was as good as you get. We have flown battle tanks through turbulence without batting an eyelid. So I can't see a load shift causing the aircraft to trim disasterously.'

'A lightning strike?'

'No chance. Somewhere on the globe an aircraft is hit by lightning every day. The charge travels through the aluminium skin, more often than not exits at the tail causing little if any damage. It's a myth aircraft get knocked out of the sky by lightning strikes.'

'Okay, but maybe exceptionally violent turbulence...' he let the suggestion trail.

'I already have people checking meteorological data to see if it was the perfect storm. We will see.'

'With the accident, I'm guessing we have other problems?'

'That is why I'm here. The loss assessors are calling for the cargo manifest. Normal routine. They will get it tomorrow morning. Sunbird Agricultural Equipment will be on those waybills. From the supposed Ukrainian supplier side, I have people in place. They will produce copies of ghost invoices to show goods on the manifest were shipped. That will not be a problem. Your people at the client end will also be contacted. You need to demonstrate convincingly you are actually in the business of supplying farming equipment. They will want to visit a facility, get your copy of the order for the consignment and a copy of my invoice.'

'That won't be a problem.' Sunbird was a sizeable agricultural enterprise, the CEO deeply committed to the Endeavour.

'Do you think there will be any wreckage found?' he couldn't help wondering what the upshot would be if any trace of an arms shipment came to light.

'I can't see it. It's a big ocean. Guns, even in wooden crates do not float. I have in any event, already put into action a plan — teams visiting the coastal fishing villages. A substantial reward offered for any debris confirmed to be from my aircraft. There are many such villages, it will take a little time. You can appreciate if anything washes ashore I need to be the first to hear about it.'

Silently Piet saluted Fotakis. The man may often position himself on the wrong side of the law, but he remained the consummate professional.

'You think there is little chance of the true mission of the aircraft being discovered?

'You must remember your cargo comprised a small part of the payload. The insurance assessors will readily confirm the locomotive was aboard. No problem there. As long as your people play their part, there is no danger of them discovering the existence of contraband cargo. We are a legitimate freight delivery service into Africa. Any damaging evidence to the contrary is sitting at the bottom of the ocean.'

'We'll play our part. Will your insurers honour the claim?'

He grunted derisively. 'Bloodsucker's have been taking my premiums for years without a single claim. They'll pay. Imagine how much freight insurance they'd sell if word got out they voided a claim for no good reason.'

'Provided they don't find good reason.'

'They won't. We just have to get our cover stories watertight, then there is no danger. Make sure your people are up to it.' He regarded Piet grimly for a moment. 'And of course, you will get your money back. Less a fifteen per cent administration fee.'

Piet was relieved it had been Fotakis who raised the topic. He'd steeled myself to do it but, in the face of his loss, hadn't felt comfortable about it. Fotakis could as easily have shrugged his shoulders and walked away. It wasn't as if they could access official channels. Him agreeing then, just a formality.

Fotakis wasn't done. 'It leaves your arms requirement in a vacuum of course.'

'That's for sure.'

'Let me think about it and get back to you.'

Mr Fotakis was nothing if not an enigma. Piet hadn't expected him to be concerned with their needs in the light of all he faced. Honour amongst thieves: the cliché popped into Piet's head not causing as much disquietude as it should have.

CHAPTER 27

RE-SUPPLY

As soon as Kosmo left, Piet called Colonel Stander suggesting a meet. He made his way from the airport to Century City Mall, the venue the Colonel had chosen. Large and busy enough to ensure anonymity.

'A sad episode for all involved,' their misfortune had rattled the Colonel.

Piet stated the obvious. 'A very serious blow for the Endeavour, Sir.'

'It is. We can't go to war without weapons. It's going to set us back months maybe longer… unless we can re-arm quickly.'

Piet told him about Fotakis' cryptic comment at the end of their meeting. It seemed to lift him a little.

'You think there may be a possibility he can offer re-supply without delay?'

'I'm hoping so. Otherwise we have to start again — find another supplier. That would be a massive knock. I'm holding thumbs he can conjure something.'

'I suppose it's all we can do for the moment. We need assault weapons, and we need them sooner rather than later. Give him a few days, Pieter, if he doesn't make contact, initiate it — let's at least try to get the ball rolling again.'

Their fortunes had ebbed to a low point. The challenge was for them to rise from it.

'I'll do that, Sir. In the meantime we'll be getting a visit from Fotakis' loss assessors.' Piet told the Colonel what would be expected of them.

'That won't pose a problem. John is a commanding and dynamic person. Built Sunbird from nothing. Loss assessors won't phase him in the least. I'll meet with him this evening, give him the necessary briefing.'

'What would you like me to do at this time?'

'Just keep those fingers crossed. I'll start to cast around for alternative supply sources in the meantime — just in case Fotakis can't, or no longer has the appetite, to help us. From our previous experience its not going to be so easy.'

Fotakis' doubts in regard to the cause of the aircraft loss occurred to him. He mentioned it to the Colonel.

'Strange that he suspects it to be anything other than natural causes. From the media reports, it seems emphatic the pilot flew into a violent storm — his undoing. Why would Fotakis think otherwise?'

'He believes his aircraft, his crew, were equal to the conditions. They've been through as bad before — highly experienced — he had absolute faith in them. He's finding it hard to accept they got it wrong this time, set himself the task of collecting data on the weather system to determine if it could have produced the perfect storm.'

'What's he saying? That there may be something sinister at work here? Sabotage?'

'He didn't go so far. But the current explanation doesn't satisfy him.'

The Colonel began to harbour the same niggle gnawing at Piet since Fotakis aired his doubts. He watched the thought take root in the Colonel.

'Could it be our shipment became known to a third party, somebody brought the plane down because of it?'

'It has to be a strong possibility, but it doesn't sit well. It would mean someone knows a lot more about us than we've ever dreamed of.'

He looked worried. 'I'm sure you're asking yourself, Pieter, whether Nuclatom's surveillance of you is directly linked?'

'It's the last thing I want to believe, Sir. It would mean the Endeavour is blown wide open. But how could he possibly have learned of the shipment if in fact he is responsible?'

'It could mean only one thing. Nuclatom was shadowing you even before we became aware of them. Perhaps you were being watched even on your first mission to Fotakis.'

He'd considered this scenario too. It sat very uncomfortably. 'Long odds don't you think, Sir? Even if I missed any surveillance early on, how could he have sabotaged the flight? Could another aircraft have shot it down? A fighter jet? It seems too incredible to merit consideration.'

'I agree — more likely to have been the storm. But if Fotakis' radar is pinging, we'd do well to be alert too. Nuclatom is a truly global outfit. They're playing for really huge stakes here in Africa. And they have an unhealthy interest in you. It's not beyond the pale to imagine a sophisticated fifth column. Until we know better we must regard Nuclatom as the enemy. I'll have our intel chaps dig around a bit, see what they can find.'

It was good council. Ivashchenkov was beginning to loom large in Piet's personal rogues gallery. Plenty to lose if Zuma was unseated. And his corporation with anything but a clean track record. Could Nuclatom be their nemesis? They would see another piece of the jigsaw drop into place within a week.

CHAPTER 28

SOURCE

Two days later he received a text from Fotakis, *Come to my warehouse asap. Advise arrival date/time.*

He booked his flight to Lanseria, confirmed it to him. It looked as if things might be starting to move. An exciting prospect. To him Fotakis' text could only mean one thing. The arms-dealer had something to offer.

Losing tails shadowing him was now easy. They had become sloppy by this time, not seeming as committed as at first. For the most part he let them tag along on innocent journeys. Other times he didn't have to do much to give them the slip.

The day dawned for his trip. He started for the village as the sun climbed its way into the sky. He dropped into a coffee shop as they were opening and dawdled over a light breakfast. His shadow tagged along. He spotted him beyond the shop front trying to look casual on a public bench. Lots of time to play him — his flight was booked only for early afternoon.

He paid the bill and meandered through the line shops to the metro-bus stop outside the post office. Carrying no bag, his tail wouldn't have him pegged for a trip out of the city. The man's guard would be down.

The bus arrived. As he swiped his card he glanced up. He spotted the guy climbing into a silver Audi just along the street. He knew the car. One of two they used. The man got in the passenger side, so, a two-man team. Maybe they were more committed this day. The bus driver ground his gears as they rumbled away. The Audi pulled out to follow.

In the city he jumped off scurrying to the rail station. Maintaining contact would now be getting difficult even for a two-man team. Piet bought a ticket for the line he would travel. As the train pulled out, he worked his way through the carriages to the one he wanted. He was sure he'd already shaken them but, was taking no chances. The train slowed for the first stop. He moved to the doors. When he jumped off he would be opposite the station exit, could pass effortlessly into the street beyond.

Once out he quickly absorbed to the busy throng and weaved his way down a side-street, re-circling to the main road. He called an Uber, boarding it outside MacDonalds. Within minutes his cab had him on his way. An hour later they pulled into the airport. Two more — he was in the air flying up-country to Lanseria airport.

He located the freight area readily enough. Kosmocar — the name of Fotakis' operation — was emblazoned in paint faded by years of ultra-violet exposure, across a gable-end in a row of hangars. A security guard gave him access only after he showed his identity document and had been cleared via intercom. He crossed the concrete apron; aircraft of all shapes and sizes were littered over it, a couple of forklifts nudging cargo around like truffling hogs.

He entered the warehouse, mildly surprised by the absence of further security. In front of him a wall of green shade-cloth, cable-tied to a chain-link fence, offered a visual barrier. He found the office crammed under the eaves at the end of it.

Kosmo sat behind a workaday desk chatting with an individual at the other side. A staff member Piet guessed. The man got to his feet excusing himself as he entered. Kosmo beamed a welcome. He had his colour back, the dark rings under his eyes faded to smudges.

'Apologies for dragging you all this way,' he motioned to the chair.

'Not a problem,' he got comfortable, 'you must have your hands full in the aftermath of the crash.' A shadow crossed Fotakis' face.

'It is very difficult. Igor was with me at the beginning. I miss him already. The others too. They were very loyal. It is difficult feeling the pain, dealing with the families.'

He expressed his sympathies.

'How is it going with the assessors?' Piet changed the subject.

His spirits rose. 'Excellent. They are happy with all the documentation — the aircraft's service log. They've sent someone to Abuja to interview the Nigerian locomotive client. They foresee no difficulties with my claim, even suggesting I start looking for a replacement aircraft. How did it go with their visit to your people?'

Piet told him things went off smoothly. No hiccups.

'Did you learn any more about the storm?' Piet thought it likely Fotakis' doubts would have been washed away with any statistics he managed to unearth.

'Meteorological data suggests shear stresses in the storm of about four-hundred kilometres per hour.'

'That's enough to tear a plane apart, surely?'

'Not my planes. I've personally been through worse storms aboard Olga. Rough sure, but Antonovs are built to withstand such forces. Only explanation seems to be that the load shifted — but with my guys I find that hard to get my head around too.'

Piet decided it could do no good to tell him of the interest being shown in him by Nuclatom, the niggle beginning to creep into their minds.

'But I didn't bring you here to share my woes. I have good news for you.' He looked suitably smug.

'I'm all ears.'

'I've located some replacement equipment.'

He had Piet's attention.

'The pedigree?'

'Kalashnikovs too — of Chinese manufacture.'

This was getting interesting.

'How many?'

'Slightly less than you were looking for. Four hundred cases. Sixteen hundred weapons in total. Plus a generous amount of ammunition.'

'The weapons are new?'

'Still in their packing crates. Straight from the factory.'

'Immediately available?'

'Ready to ship. The consignment was in transit when it got stolen. An act of piracy on the East China Sea whilst enroute from Shenzhen to Pyongyang in North Korea. The Chinese are not amused. They've put a price on the weapons. Which incidentally, means on the heads of any party dealing in them. The North Koreans still want them, won't pay a second time, suspecting a scam. Puts the pirates in a quandary — no access to an easy market, very hot goods threatening to burn them if the Chinese ever catch them at it. So they want to move fast, a positive for us. Hot goods always carry a discount. The price is very attractive.'

Piet couldn't believe this swing in their fortunes. 'How did you get to hear about them?'

He scoffed derisively. 'The nature of my business, Piet. I'm not a bit-player. if the market didn't seek me out as an opportunity presents, I would be offended.'

'Where are they now?'

'Indonesia.'

'And logistics?'

'As before it's my baby. They come in through the same customs port here. I'll cover all of that.'

'What do you need from me?'

'You're not worried about the bounty placed on the goods by the Chinese? If they ever discover you have taken possession of them they could come after you.'

'The same goes for you — they find you dealing in them, I'm sure they'll be after your tail too.'

He laughed. 'I'm just a logistics company moving a shipment for a client. Your identity will be all over my waybills.'

Piet knew he should have realised Fotakis was far too smart not to have considered that aspect. He would more than cover himself if the deal went ahead.

'To answer your question Kosmo, I'm not even vaguely concerned. We'll cross that bridge if we come to it. How much money are we going to have to stump up?'

He gave the figure. It amounted to less than half of what they'd paid for the previous shipment.

'Count me in. Let's get this going. It might take a day or two to raise the money. But I don't want to miss out on the parcel. Can you secure in a hurry?'

Fotakis opened his desk drawer, slid a document across the desk. 'Sign this,' he instructed Piet.

'What is it?'

"It's a lien on your insurance claim for the loss of your agricultural equipment. You can have it back when your money hits my bank account.'

Lost for words Piet looked at him dumbly.

'Oh, one more thing. Have your truck here by Tuesday next week. I don't want those Chinese crates sitting in my warehouse overnight.'

CHAPTER 29

NUCLEAR HICCUP

Dmitri Ivashchenkov sat in the comfort of his lounge sipping a drink. A golden Labrador lay at the side of his chair; he stroked its head distractedly. A warm spring evening, the lounge sliders thrown wide welcoming evening bird song. The air stirred, a soothing zephyr after the heat of the day.

Local news ran on television. He watched with scant attention — until the announcer began reading a piece about a court ruling handed down in the Cape Town High Court that day. He stiffened. Two minutes later his worst fears were realised. The court had overturned his contract with Zuma. He slammed his fist down hard on the table. His whisky glass jumped, rattling heavily on the glass surface. The dog got to its feet quietly and slunk away.

'*Zhizn' ebet meyer.*' His anger burst forth.

His wife appeared at the kitchen doorway trying not to drip water off yellow latex gloves onto the carpet.

'Who is fucking you, darling?'

'Those mother-fuckers have trashed our contract with Zuma.'

'What does that mean?'

'It means we have to start again.' He hit the table a second time with renewed force. It was too much for the delicately bevelled glass. Cracks like fork lightning shot out across the polished surface.

The newscaster ended the piece informing viewers the verdict paid tribute to the efforts of two independent anti-nuclear agencies headed by fiercely motivated women. Getting the analogy wrong, she said it was a true David and Goliath victory. It painted Nuclatom as a corporate bully.

Ivashchenkov hit the table forcibly a third time. This time the master-crafted piece exploded, shards of glass raining onto the thick-pile carpet.

CHAPTER 30

DAMNING EVIDENCE

Back from his Lanseria visit, he briefed the Colonel on the latest developments. He could hardly believe their good fortune. Replacing their lost shipment so quickly came as a godsend. They discussed the mechanics of payment which would be effected post-haste. For the importation they would use a similar cover to the original, except this time the importer would be a mining supplies outfit. Their arms would enter the country as a used conveyor system, sourced from a defunct Indonesian mine.

They chewed their fingernails as the days ticked by. In the event they needn't have worried. The consignment arrived in the country without a hitch. Their truck loaded it at Fotakis' warehouse and got on its way within hours en-route to Fergie's farm in the distant Karoo.

It seemed they'd entered a purple patch. The heat was off in terms of Piet's surveillance. He hadn't seen either the Mercedes or the Audi for a couple of days, equally sure nobody tailed him on foot. Could it be Ivashchenkov was after all the enemy responsible for the air freighter's loss? And if so, did the Russian believe their wings clipped, a force no longer to be reckoned with? It seemed likely. Or were they constructing a Machiavellian plot where none existed?

Second-guessing themselves was, however, soon to be taken off the table. Kosmo Fotakis made contact yet again advising he was once more coming to see Piet. Something serious to discuss, he wanted to do it face to face.

The meeting took place in the same coffee shop at Cape Town International. 'We have a serious enemy my friend,' Fotakis opened without preamble.

Piet's innards tightened. 'Go on.'

'You remember I told you my people would work the fishing villages in case any debris came to light?'

Piet nodded.

'Well it's paid dividends. The captain of a coastal trawler claimed the reward offered. He hauled something aboard in his nets.'

'What was it?'

'A cheap piece of timber. The sort used in packing crates.'

'And you think it may be from the Antonov?'

'I know it is.'

'How can you be sure?'

'The first thing the captain noticed was a length of cargo strapping still attached to the wood. The sort of strapping used in cargo aircraft — fused to the wood by intense heat.'

'Well it's indicative I'll admit. Hardly conclusive. I'm sure the same sort of strapping gets used in marine logistics too.'

He gave Piet his hawk look. 'There is more.'

'Go on.'

'Cyrillic lettering on the wood. The last half of a manufacturer's name. It is the name of the armaments factory in Kiev.'

'Where we sourced the Kalashnikovs?'

'Yes.'

That rocked him. 'Certainly sounds conclusive.' he pondered a moment. 'And the scorching suggests a fire on board — could explain a lot surely?' It gave a credible reason for the loss of his aircraft and would satisfy his earlier doubts.

He gave Piet a penetrating look. 'Not a fire my friend. An explosion.'

'An explosion?' That was harder to digest. 'You think some of the ammunition may have detonated?'

'No. The ammunition did not detonate.'

'How can you be sure?'

'The scorch marks are on the wrong side of the timber. The reverse face to the printed lettering. And it's from a rifle packing case, not an ammunition box.'

'You're saying there was an explosive charge inside one of the crates.'

'That's exactly what I'm saying.'

Piet's mind raced. It seemed more likely than ever now, that Ivashchenkov had indeed discovered their business with Fotakis, taken steps to thwart them. Deadly steps.

Fotakis waited for a response but Piet kept quiet hoping he wasn't going where Piet thought he might.

'The only thing on my aircraft anybody could have an unhealthy interest in, was the arms shipment. The rest of the cargo was kosher. Who would benefit most from making sure those weapons never arrived in South Africa?' He studied Piet carefully. 'It is time for straight talk my friend. We have never spoken of this, but clearly your organisation is engaged in preparation for a coup. That has little to do with me. Other than the fact your needs are good for my business. Without people like you — no arms supply operation.'

He continued to regard Piet. The way a mongoose might take an interest in a snake.

'It cannot be the government. There would be no need for such measures. They would simply seize the consignment at the port of entry, lock away for a very long time everybody even vaguely connected with it. So who does it leave, Pieter?' His stare never wavered.

Piet shifted uncomfortably. 'There is something you need to know.' he steeled himself for the disclosure and told him about his surveillance, their suspicions regarding Nuclatom.

'Why didn't you inform me of this before?' His mood shifted.

'We were second-guessing ourselves much of the time, Kosmo. At best speculating. We felt we may be jumping at shadows.'

'But you were being followed by these people.' He was staying on top of his anger. 'Very bad mistake not to have alerted me to the fact.'

'At that point we had no idea they were aware we did business with you. Until your aircraft went down we thought they merely showed interest in me personally — someone involved in activities possibly detrimental to their objectives. They have Zuma in their pocket, a lot to lose if he is unseated.'

He battled to move past it. 'I wish you'd alerted me. If they will bring down a foreign aircraft to further their ends, these are very dangerous people.'

'We're beginning to see that.'

'How badly is your organisation compromised?' He wasn't done yet.

Piet told him they weren't sure but were going to press on regardless.

'What I still can't understand,' he struggled to make sense of the way things had played out, 'is why they didn't have the authorities just move in and stop you.'

'We don't think they told Zuma — so the authorities wouldn't have been aware. Alerted, we think Zuma might've put the nuclear deal on a back burner, thrown all his energies into a witch hunt. He treads on thinner ice in terms of the leadership every day. Spooked, he could even have declared a state of emergency. That wouldn't get their nuclear deal bedded down, could scotch it properly.'

'Big chips in a big game,' he was thinking hard.

'Yes indeed. And Nuclatom is a major-league player. They've got entrenched networks globally. We never saw this coming.'

'As didn't I.' He had a set to his jaw. The inference wasn't lost on Piet.

They sat in silence for a short time. Piet turned to him as a thought occurred. 'How will this new evidence you've found affect the insurance claim?'

'It will have no effect,' he remained grim, 'they are never going to know about it. My insurance policy doesn't cover me for loss from acts of war or terrorism.'

If ever Piet had witnessed irony, that was it.

CHAPTER 31

POLITICAL MUSCLING

In October 2017 Jacob Zuma chose to reshuffle his cabinet for the second time in seven months. It was his way of manipulating the organs of government to suit his nefarious ends. This time some minister's lost their jobs, others were shunted into portfolios where he could either influence them or simply roll over them.

His motives were twofold.

Firstly, there was growing opposition to his premiership within the ruling party. This at a critical time leading to the party elective conference, the run-up to general election in 2019. It would not harm to reward those supportive, slap down those opposing. Chief among his detractors was his Minister of Higher Education. A vocal dissident calling for him to step down.

It cost 'Blade' Nzimande his portfolio. He remains, however, a powerful figure in the post of General Secretary of the South African Communist Party, a key partner in the tripartite alliance with the ANC led government. His removal from his ministerial post prompted speculation the SACP may leave the alliance.

Further, the presidency announced moving David Mahlobo, former minister of state security and a longtime Zuma ally, to the energy portfolio.

This was seen as Zuma's most significant appointment in the reshuffle. It came as the third change in the energy portfolio during the year. Mahlobo had earlier accompanied Zuma on an official visit to Russia. They met with Putin; the press hinted Russia may now have a sympathetic platform within the South African government.

Most analysts believe the second reason for the reshuffle is a desperate effort by Zuma to resurrect his nuclear deal with Nuclatom allowing him to skim off millions when it matured.

Meanwhile, on another flank, Zuma continues to frustrate the judicial process attempting to prosecute the re-instated eighteen charges against him. Woven into these are more than seven hundred counts of fraud, corruption and money laundering. His premiership staggers becoming more fragile by the day.

CHAPTER 32

CLOSE ENCOUNTER

Sophie took a couple of days leave, tacked these onto a long weekend to give her a five-day break. They would spend them together aboard *Magus*, do some sailing. Piet told Rusty they'd sail to Gaans Bay where Rusty operated.

He cleared it with the Colonel, telling him he would be off-shore sailing for a couple of days. He told Piet not to worry, to go enjoy himself; they would be getting into some serious strategy work once he returned.

He collected her from the airport late afternoon and they drove back to the boat. The weather forecast looked good for the period so he'd scheduled to leave the marina early next day.

Sophie was curled into him, her head resting on his shoulder as he awoke pre-dawn. He felt a sense of peace, listening to the slapping of water against the hull close to his head, and luxuriated in the cocoon of warmth enfolding them. A magical feeling. Insulation from the world outside. But tucked in there too, was a discordant note. Something which didn't belong. He worked at it for a while trying to isolate it. And then he had it. Anxiety. Unbidden. Unwelcome. An intruder, a serpent in the garden. Part of his military training had been conditioning to recognise this shadowy sense of unease, and having recognised it, work out a strategy for dealing with it. Yes, he'd recognised it, but where was it coming from?

Try as he might he couldn't get it. It wasn't the Endeavour and its life-threatening risks. He'd, come to terms with those. It wasn't the spectre of Ivashchenkov's people hanging over him either. He had a strategy to counter Nuclatom he intended putting to the planning committee next week so, that enervated him. Where was this niggle coming from then? Sophie stirred languorously in his arms — in that moment the realisation dawned.

A realisation that for the first time, he now shared his life with someone who reflected the values he cared about, someone who brought real meaning to his life, meant more to him than his solitary existence.

They had known each other for the briefest while, but he already felt they could take on the world. And overcome it. That sense of joining, coming together to make a whole greater than the sum of its parts. A truly humbling experience. He realised the wellspring of his fear was his sub-conscious taunting him with the prospect he would only have it for a short time. He wanted it for life; for a long life at that. The odds against that seemed extreme with what lay ahead. A ticket in a lottery.

Sophie woke then. She looked at him, her temple-cat eyes glittering in the half-light creeping into the cabin.

"morning sailor,' she croaked in her awakening voice.

He gave her a peck on the nose. She traced his lips with her finger then let her hand trail down his throat to his chest. She found his nipple teasing it to prominence before straying slowly to his abdomen. Already fully erect, he found it difficult to breathe properly, kissed her hungrily, chewed softly at the nape of her neck. She moaned sensuously and thrust her pelvis into his thigh. He could feel her heat — the hunger took them both. They made love passionately — both quickly spent. It seemed only minutes before arousal stirred them again. This time they made love slowly, keying to each other's rhythm.

He cooked breakfast as Sophie showered. Within an hour they were headed out of the bay not much behind schedule. A light north-wester teased the skin of the ocean: he soon had *Magus* on a beam reach eager for the open reaches. Sophie was enthralled, the conditions ideal for her maiden sail. The morning retained a crispness from the night which would burn off as the sun got up and baked the air like a giant griller. Later when evening came it would cool again bringing a sultry cloak to wrap them in.

As they got out from under the lee of the land, true Atlantic swells rolled under them like watery hills. He stole a glance at Sophie. First time out, he thought she might succumb to seasickness, but he needn't have worried. She was into it like an old tar.

On their port side the land shrank as they gradually opened the sea miles. He kept *Magus* trimmed on the same tack skimming along nicely. The wind slowly backed to the west. He eased the boat off it half-a-point, steering a heading almost due south. They sailed on a beam-reach, a point-of-sail at which *Magus* showed off her pedigree. If the wind held they would sail the same tack right the way down to Cape Point, the southern extremity of the peninsula.

'So the Cape of Good Hope is the southernmost tip of the continent?' Sophie peered off into the distance. She had the helm, quickly getting the hang of things.

'One of them. But not the furthest south. That distinction goes to Cape Agulhas a hundred-and-seventy odd kilometres south-east of here.'

'Which of them is the most dangerous to sail around?'

He could see she was getting a buzz out of handling the boat knowing there was latent danger out there.

'Any true cape needs to be treated with respect,' He looked out over the ocean, 'but Agulhas is the big brother, potentially far more dangerous. It's the true dividing promontory between two oceans. The Atlantic, a mass of cold water meeting the warm Indian Ocean. The fast-moving Agulhas current pushes those warm waters down to collide with the chilly Atlantic. A recipe for turbulent weather. When Bartholomew Dias first rounded Agulhas in the fifteenth century, he named it the Cape of Storms for good reason.'

'How would *Magus* fare in a really big storm?'

Piet laughed. 'She's been through a few believe me. But it's how the skipper and the boat interact which is the defining factor. A well-found boat sailed by a bad skipper making sloppy decisions, is far more likely to founder than, say, a leaky boat with a good man at the helm.'

She glanced at him over her shoulder appraising him and missing nothing. 'You love this boat don't you?'

Caught flat-footed for a moment Piet thought about that. He'd been a part of *Magus* ever since owning her, realising only then, she'd been the lady in his life for all that time. He'd never considered the symbiosis in terms of a strong emotional bond. Suddenly he realised it was.

'Now you put it that way, I suppose I do.'

'Well at least I know who my competition is,' she tossed her hair theatrically in the breeze.

He laughed again. 'You'll never have competition.'

She spun quickly giving him one of those enigmatic looks only a woman can manage. It carried a full spectrum of emotion; incredulity, scorn, dismissiveness, warning, pleading, adoration.

He wilted under it, meant to he was sure, and grinned clownishly; for all the world a chastised puppy. Glad to find distraction, he busied himself with the chart plotter.

Piet had planned the trip to sail through the night arriving at their destination early next morning. He explained all his route charting decisions to her — Sophie asked some intelligent questions. As she cockily averred, she was quickly getting the hang of 'this sailing thing'. The weather was holding as forecast; nothing sinister presenting.

They rounded the Cape as the sun dipped close to the horizon. It was idyllic. The ocean behaved itself, they had it all to themselves. *Magus* practically sailed unassisted. The lofty heights of the Cape through the binoculars, still towering even at that distance, were pastelled in subtle shades of amber and rose. The backdrop of a movie set.

'I can see why this is such a part of you,' she studied him as if she was learning a deep secret.

He thought about that. 'It gets into your blood after a while.'

'And you seem tailored to it. You're hardly a socialite after all. The solitary life fits you well.'

'It has until now,' he gave her a meaningful look.

She smiled, quick with an answer. 'I'll take that as a compliment. And just for the record, this lady can see herself in the role too... ' she teased the idea. '... freelance correspondent aboard a roving yacht.'

He chortled. 'Ever the hard-nosed journalist.'

Twilight arrived, lingered. They went through procedures for the night's sailing ahead, the chart plotter their electronic navigator. But Piet still had one foot in the old school. If technology failed he wanted to be able to find his way using admiralty paper charts. He'd pencilled a progressive plot using old-fashioned pencil and parallel rules since they left Hout Bay. He showed Sophie how all that worked. Then he took out the Admiralty List of Lights for their sector, told her how to decipher the information. Finally putting it all together, he pointed out on the chart the same lights they would be navigating by. As darkness finally fell he went below to rustle up a sailors dinner.

They'd discussed sitting four-hour watches, one helming the other sleeping. He wasn't at all tired so on Sophies first watch stayed topsides with her. They nattered about everything from journalism to UFOs. With an hour to go, he did snatch a cat-nap before his watch at midnight. They made steady progress; by sunrise a low bank of cloud hugged the horizon off their port bow. Just where it should be — their navigation spot-on.

Three hours later they sailed into tiny Kleinbaai harbour at Gansbaai. He found the berth Rusty earlier told him to make for, coming alongside just as Rusty strode along the jetty.

'You old sea dog you,' he boomed, taking the painter Piet threw ashore and securing it to a bollard. Piet tethered the stern, gave Sophie a hand ashore. Back on terra firma she wobbled a bit, Rusty steadied her.

'Whoa,' she laughed, 'what's happening?'

'That'll be your sea legs for a little while. Your gyroscope has got used to the ocean — takes a while to re-adjust. Not that we're going to allow that to happen. Back to sea in *Chumbucket* soon. I'm Rusty by the way,' he proffered a giant paw.

Chumbucket was Rusty's dive boat. A state of the art power catamaran constructed in aluminium. Just about the same length as *Magus*. Powered by four 250hp outboards, she was fast and could cater for thirty-five tourists in addition to her crew. The business end of the operation was a shark diving cage which lowered to sit just below the waterline. Six thrill-seekers at a time could fit in there at a push.

They climbed aboard and soon sat alongside Rusty at the controls high on the flying bridge. From there a commanding view of the ocean could be had in every direction. Rusty gave Piet a conspiratorial wink.

Sophie picked it up. 'Why do I get the impression I'm not privy to all you boys have organised?' she eyed them with suspicion as Rusty's crew busied themselves casting off.

Rusty grinned. 'Can't come all this way to the great-white capital of the world without seeing one of our planet's most fabled predators,' he had that master-of-the-ship assurance.

Sophie shot Piet a thrilled look. 'Will we get to see one do you think?'

Rusty hooted.

'That's a given. With a bit of luck we could have half a dozen around the boat.'

Her excitement was infectious. She grabbed Piet's upper arm squeezing it. 'This is so awesome.'

He'd thrown their swimming togs into a bag knowing what was in store before getting off *Magus*. Sophie, not privy to the planned surprise, would go in the cage with Piet if comfortable with the idea.

'Where are the rest of the punters, Rusty?' Piet had assumed there would be paying clients aboard.

'You're it, buddy. I didn't take bookings for this run. Don't get to spend enough time with family as it is. Don't fret. I'm going out again this afternoon with a full boat of fat-wallets.'

Rusty's allusion to family was reserved for George and Piet. The three of them behaved like biological siblings, their relationship that strong. The current excursion would cost him a small fortune to lost revenue. It wasn't peanuts.

They glided out of the harbour, Rusty gunning the motors. Sophie grabbed a rail as the power came on, her hair kicking out like a bobbed mare's tail as they picked up speed. It was good for Piet to see her having so much fun. In the city she had an exacting job, rarely taking time for herself. For his part, momentum was building within the Endeavour, stress levels ratcheting up. The time for setting a date closing. Piet was part of all that. Responsible for mens' lives. That in itself carried huge accountability. He shrugged it off. Time spent with Sophie, a jewel — he rescued the moment.

'How far do we have to go?' she shouted above the wind rush.

'Almost there,' Rusty started to ease the throttles. He pointed ahead. 'See the island coming up. That's Dyer Island. The smaller outcrop is Geyser Rock. Between them is Shark Alley. The great-white capital of the world.'

He cut the motors shouting a command to his crew. A couple of anchors went over the side.

'The boys will chum a bit now, toss out tuna baits — there on the end of those lines. When we get our visitors, they'll be coming in for a look at those. The guys then trawl the baits towards the boat to draw them in. 'Hey-presto' —

we'll be surrounded by man-eating predators. Shouldn't be long before we see our first.'

And sure enough, it wasn't. Within ten minutes a shark was circling the boat investigating the activity.

'Juvenile,' Rusty had his brows knit, 'but Mamma won't be far away.'

The words were no sooner out of his mouth than a much larger specimen glided into view. This animal fully four metres, an awe-inspiring specimen.

'Wow,' Sophie was clearly becoming absorbed. Then an even bigger beast appeared. She got stuck for words.

Rusty brought out binoculars. 'You're honoured today, ladies and gentlemen,' he focussed on the latest arrival. 'This is Slashfin, a local celebrity,' he passed the glasses to Sophie, 'you see those deep grooves on his dorsal fin? It's what remains of his injuries after what must have been a very fierce battle with one of his kind. When first spotted his fin was literally in tatters. He's healed remarkably well.'

Sophie was rapt as she studied him. 'How long has he been coming here?'

'Six years since the first sighting. Probably much longer.'

'He looks heavier than Mamma,' she was getting the hang of this too. 'A big boy indeed.'

'Want to have a look at him close and personal?' Rusty threw the remark out innocently.

Her excitement was palpable. 'In the cage you mean?'

'Sure, why not? Ever done any scuba diving or snorkelling?'

'No scuba. But some snorkelling.'

'As long as you're comfortable with a mouthpiece between your teeth, not phased having a face-mask glued to you, you'll be fine.'

She didn't miss a beat. 'Count me in.'

'We use a hookah system,' Rusty explained, 'the oxygen supply tanks stay on the boat so you don't have to carry about all that weight on your back. The only extra's you'll be hefting — a weight belt to counteract your natural buoyancy. It's easy. All you have to do is breathe at the end of a long tube. We'll have a dry run before you go in the water. If you're comfortable then, away you go.'

They donned wet suits. Piet could see the excitement in her eyes. She was loving it. The sharks still circled, occasionally came closer to investigate the baits.

Rusty shouted down to his deck cameraman. 'Make sure you get it all, Sam. These folk probably won't get to do this ever again.' He suddenly realised the irony of his words and burst out laughing. 'What I meant is, it's a once-in-a-lifetime experience. And I'm talking about a long, as well as healthy life.'

The cage, already in the water, ran along the port side for six metres. A hinged flap on top gave diver access via a short ladder. Toting an underwater camera Piet entered first,

Sophie following. In minutes she adjusted and gave him the okay sign. Outside, gliding in the gloom at the limit of their vision, several sharks cruised. As they got used to them being in the water they became bolder, powering by just outside the cage. Flinty fathomless eyes regarded them without emotion. He looked at Sophie. Behind the face-mask, in contrast, her eyes were orbs of wonder. Enthralled she shook her head slowly.

They stayed submerged for another twenty minutes then got out. Sophie tore off the mask. 'Unbelievable,' she gushed, 'so much raw killing power close enough to touch. Don't they ever try to get at the divers?'

'Occasionally bump the cage,' Rusty, down to join them, took her breathing apparatus, 'and that's more out of curiosity than anything else.'

'And they can't get in?' It was little-girl wonder. At once amusing and endearing.

'Highly unlikely,' Rusty gestured to somewhere beneath the surface, 'only one access down there — just wide enough for production film crews to go outside and shoot footage.'

'In our wet suits we must look a lot like the seals they're here to hunt.' She entered the spirit of the moment, her mind talking up the danger.

'You'll be pleased to hear, there has never been an attack on any diver in a cage worldwide.'

'But imagine what could happen if one did get in?' She still milked the moment deliciously.

Rusty and Piet looked at one another and burst out laughing.

She huffed theatrically. 'Well, it could happen. Then you wouldn't laugh.'

They drank some very welcome coffee from Rusty's thermos, chatting amiably. Piet had peeled his wet suit off but Sophie still wore hers.

'Aren't you getting hot in that?' The neoprene heated quickly out in the sun.

'I'm going in for a second dive.' She looked questioningly at Rusty.

'With pleasure. The boat's here for you guys.'

She left for the dive deck again. 'Keep the camera rolling,' Rusty shouted to the cameraman.

They watched as Sophie dropped into the cage. The attendant closed the grill over her head.

'Very spirited lady; beautiful into the bargain,' Rusty was keeping an eye on her exhaust bubbles, 'you're a lucky man.'

'Don't I know it,' Piet watched the bubbles lazily frothing the surface whilst the crew continued baiting. It wasn't long before the sharks were back, close in.

'What's the programme looking like on our little adventure?' Rusty raised the topic of the Endeavour. Piet made it policy to keep him and George abreast of developments. Both had been to the farm for refresher weapons training.

'Big strategy meeting next week. Close to setting a date.'

'I'm ready,' he gave Piet one of those steely combatant looks. 'And very willing.' Rusty was always honed to a knife edge when an operation approached.

They chatted on about the military side of things for a while then Rusty, like a hound scenting the air, lifted his head scanning the water around the boat.

'Somethings changed,' he had the cage-dive skipper's sixth sense.

'I don't see anything?'

'That's the point. They've all pulled back. See how they're standing off?' he pointed to the sharks circling, now much further out.

It was then they saw it. A dorsal fin slicing through the water at speed harassing the other fish.

'I don't like that,' concern crept into Rusty's voice. Next instant the animal veered sharply, racing at the boat and closing the distance in seconds. It hit the cage hard, violently rocking the boat. A wild thrashing followed — excited yells from the crew. Piet made the dive deck in leaps and bounds as the cage assistant tugged open the access gate.

'He's in the cage,' the man's agitation accentuated all his movements making them jerky.

Piet leapt through the opening. His feet impacted something solid as he plunged into the water. Rough sandpaper, but gone in an instant. He opened his eyes to a welter of foaming energy, a very large fish frantically trying to escape. He turned to where Sophie was wedged sensibly into a corner. In two strokes he got to her. Her eyes were wide behind the face-mask — a child's face when a coveted present materialised under folds of wrapping paper.

Piet looked over his shoulder, the shark throwing his head from side to side impacting the restraining metal aggressively; more intent escaping his jail than devouring its contents. For a sickening moment, he thought he might have got that wrong as the beast rolled and went hard at them. He balled a fist preparing to go for his gill or eye as the shark impacted. He didn't get the opportunity. In a flash a mighty scythe-like tail thrashed next to them and the animal exited through the trapdoor. He smacked hard on top a couple of times and was gone.

Loud cheers greeted them as they climbed out. The cameraman grinned inanely. 'I've got it all on film,' he waved his camera victoriously.

'That's a first,' Rusty sounded quietly impressed as they all sipped coffee later on the upper deck. Sophie's hands shook from the adrenalin still rushing through her bloodstream.

'Oh, please can I have the footage?' She gave Rusty little-girl eyes.

'It's yours. All part of the package. Video belongs to the client.'

She grinned at Piet — mission accomplished.

'For more than posterity, I'm guessing,' a wry smile from him.

'You're too smart for your own good, Mr Rossouw. Imagine the scoop this is going to make?'

CHAPTER 33

PASSING MUSTER

Day five — docking after the return run from Gansbaai. Piet showed Sophie how to use the motors to nudge the boat in snugly alongside the pontoon. Like everything else, she got it instantly. It no longer surprised him. She had helmed most of the night on their return leg, hadn't put a foot wrong, displaying abilities way beyond her experience. Difficult to believe she was brand new to it. She had the touch, the innate savvy of an old sea-dog.

Early in the afternoon they drove to Buitenverwachting wine estate. Aside from Verewig it was Piet's favourite. Nestling at the back of Constantia hills at the end of a quiet backroad, a hidden gem. They sat on a shady terrace overlooking the lawns. A two hundred-and-fifty year old Norfolk Pine took pride of place at the centre its top high enough to be out of sight from where they sat.

Neither of them relished the thought of Sophie returning to Johannesburg. 'I don't want to go home,' she doodled amongst the cheese and charcuterie board they picked off.

He poured another glass of their prize-winning Chenin Blanc. 'Hand in your resignation come live on the boat,' he only half-joked.

'Don't tempt me,' she waved her glass losing a splash over the rim.

It seemed they didn't dare take his suggestion further, holding one another's gaze for a long time. The reality was he would soon be in the front line of a military push for power; she back to garnering news footage to keep a nation informed. Both challenging environments. But such are the moments dreams are made of, they teased a fleeting glimpse at Nirvana — each of them too much the realist to let it take root. The moment passed, an idyll evaporating as they came down to earth.

'Stupid suggestion. Let's live in the now,' all too conscious it was all he had to offer. Tomorrow wasn't a given in his new life. He popped an olive into her mouth. 'I've never felt more alive than I do right now. Why spoil this?'

'Me too,' she was coming out of it. 'No will-o-the-wisp can take that away. Let's finish the bottle, go back to the boat and make love.'

Her candour no longer shocked. 'Do we have to finish the wine?'

She balled her serviette and threw it at him.

'I'm dreading this,' she wrung her hands in a very un-Sophie like gesture as they drove onto the Verewig grand avenue approaching the house. Arriving for afternoon tea and for her to meet his parents. Sophie had been working up nervous tension for hours.

'Can't be any worse than being in the cage with the great-white yesterday,' he joked.

She punched his leg playfully. 'Says you.'

His father greeted them on the steps taking Sophie's hand in both his, refusing to let go. He beamed at her — no time for Piet. Finally he ushered them through to the lounge where Piet's mother waited. In a way men find hard to comprehend, the two women meshed instantly. His father and he were left to look on like dumb beasts. For a full five minutes they chatted animatedly. His father nor he retained any recall of that conversation to this present day.

His father went to the drinks cabinet and returned with decanter and glasses. 'A sherry before tea?'

They sipped their drinks, he could see Sophie was now completely at ease. They chatted about her work, the wine estate, politics in the country. His father handled the last very diplomatically — no mention of his role or Piet's for that matter.

Afternoon tea soon became exposed as a mini-buffet. His mother, in true Afrikaner fashion, over catered by a country mile. The kitchen's yellowwood table groaned beneath a cornucopia of cold cuts, patés, pastries, salads and a selection of cottage loaves. Sophie flashed him a worried look, remembering, he was sure, their charcuterie scant hours before. In the event she acquitted herself well and after the meal they waddled like over-stuffed ducks back to the lounge.

"How was the sailing, Sophie?' his mother poured their tea.

'Beyond belief. I can't tell you how much I enjoyed it. Pieter is the consummate teacher. I think I learned more from him this weekend than I could have otherwise in a lifetime.'

'She's too modest, Ma... and a natural. Put me to shame. Ask her however how she fared as shark bait.'

His mother arched her brows. 'What craziness has he been exposing you to. Aboard Rusty's *Scumbucket*, I suppose.'

'*Chumbucket*' he corrected.

'Whatever.' His mother dismissed the interruption with a toss of the head.

Sophie regaled her with the entire incident from start to finish. It was amusing for him to watch them both slide into 'drama' mode. Sophie hamming it unashamedly, his mother lapping it up with 'oohs' and 'aahs'. He smiled to himself. Sophie may be a hard-nosed reporter but she wasn't above a bit of theatre.

'That's terrifying,' his mother still seemed shocked.

'Well that's the funny thing,' Sophie's tone lowered as if she was speaking in a cathedral, 'I can't recall being frightened at any time — I got completely absorbed — the effortless grace of those creatures. They hardly flex a muscle yet glide through the water as if propelled by a hidden force; the pinnacle of nature equipping her creatures' for their role. In their environment I was a slug. A clumsy intruder. I felt I didn't belong: their dominance was palpable and here was I indulging my thrill-seeking need whilst they were about the serious business of hunting at the top of the food chain. I realised If I came to harm in that cage, it was down to me. Who could put the blame on them? Almost as soon as the thought registered, he came headlong for the cage smashing into it, in the next instant there with me. It was as if I communicated my thought to him — the Universe testing me. It was uncanny.'

His mother turned quietly to Piet looking as if she'd undergone an epiphany. 'I think you may have met your alter-ego, Pieter.'

Sophie and Piet looked at one another. Once again a spiritual ripple touched them. Others were seeing things in them they hadn't put to words.

The rest of the afternoon slid away in convivial camaraderie. Too soon, it was time to get Sophie to the airport. They took their leave. His mother extracted a promise from Sophie not to be a stranger at Verewig.

As they drove away down the farm road, Sophie sat for a considerable time without saying anything.

He glanced sideways. 'Penny for them.'

'Not what I expected at all,' she said simply.

'That's interesting. What did you expect then?'

'More flint perhaps. A hard edge. Something hewed out of the mountains like the estate itself. Highly efficient and functional but maybe a bit distant emotionally.'

'Ooh... begins to sound too close to home for comfort.' he shifted a little in his seat. 'Am I like that?'

She regarded him candidly. 'Yes, it's you. And don't get your knickers in a knot. It's a massive turn on for me. Of course, I love your softer side too — prevents you morphing to macho-man with nothing to offer a woman.'

'Wow, I hadn't thought I'd come under scrutiny to that degree.'

'And passed muster with flying colours.' She chuckled giving his leg a reassuring squeeze.

'So I'm boxed, filed away, indexed. Big relief.' He blew out his cheeks theatrically. 'And how did the folks fare? If you weren't looking at the Flintstones who were you seeing?'

'Two of the warmest and most genuine people I've ever met. And remember I meet plenty in my line of work. Most don't bear a second look. Your parents are different. They haven't lost the simple joy of just being: truly alive in the moment, enjoying those around them. The material trappings haven't corrupted them. That's rare. And quite clearly they're still very much in love. Despite being together for... how many years?'

'Over fifty now.' What Sophie had seen was somehow humbling.

'You're very fortunate, Pieter.'

He reflected quietly — realised he truly was. Fortunate to have the legacy of his parents. Now the bounty of this woman sitting beside him. He stole a look as he drove. She still put him in mind of a sleek on-guard feline — all senses honed. Fully at one with every part of her environment. He did indeed have a lot to be thankful for.

They hit the approach-road just before the airport. He offered to park, see her off properly. She would have none of it. Formal goodbyes were sad creatures she told him — she had no intention of spawning one. He drove the incline to the drop-off-and-go. She took his face in her hands, kissed him quickly, and was gone.

CHAPTER 34

THE QUARRY

Back at Colin Farrell's home in Gauteng on one of his many planning visits, he at last felt at ease among the committee members.

The same team was present. With one addition. Nkosi Mabalane. Although out of uniform in a formal business suit, he was a current serving member of the South African Defence Force. At the rank of Lieutenant General a very high ranking serving member.

He boasted an impressive pedigree. Product of Sandhurst, Britains elite army training academy, he saw service with the British army in Afghanistan, completed a tour to Ireland before returning to South Africa where he joined the local force at the rank of Commandant. A principled man, he worked his way to the top on merit. Every inch the professional soldier, bitterly disillusioned with the havoc the politicians were wreaking in his country. However, he wasn't sitting bemoaning the fact. Nkosi was heavily invested in the Endeavour, fully committed to righting these wrongs. A pivotal figure in all they hoped to achieve. At previous meetings his name arose many times, but the pressure of his duties kept him away so Piet never had the privilege of meeting him.

Introducing them, Colonel Stander got the meeting underway.

'I'm sure I don't have to remind you gentleman of the ever-deteriorating situation in the country, the spate of violence and unrest now surfacing.'

A murmur of assent from around the table.

'As you all know it has prompted us to accelerate preparations. That's not ideal because we are still down on numbers — close enough though. It falls to us now to circle a date on the calendar.' He turned to the man immediately to his left. 'Archie, would you give us a sitrep on troop strength?'

Archie pushed his glasses higher up the bridge of his nose. 'As Ronnie says we are a little shy of where we hoped to be. It means operationally our larger units will be below optimum. Current force is a little over seventeen hundred as we sit. We've shut down recruiting in order to fine-tune the men — final training begun. We've some two hundred men at the farm right now; plan is to roll those camps until the entire force is battle-ready.'

'And how does the programme look? Are we on schedule?' the Colonel sat sentinel over his lieutenants.

'Slightly behind. The men are physically well prepared; all good news. Weapons training has lagged marginally. The hiccup — our loss aboard the Antonov. Happily we've been able to adjust intakes at the farm. I'm pleased to report we're almost on target again. The Chinese kalashnikovs required a small modification to the firing pin — improved their reliability enormously. Compliments in his absence to Fergie and his machine shop.' He glanced back at the Colonel, a question forming. 'Lot of personnel movement to and from the farm right now. Are we still comfortable we're unobserved there?'

'The media spin we put out on Pieter's SAEEI appointment seems to have worked well. Government nor Nuclatom are showing interest in him now. Thanks in absentia this time to Sophie Birman. We're watching for any signs indicating interest in the farm, but none we can see. Nuclatom however remains an enigma. We know of course, they were responsible for bringing down Fotakis' aircraft. Why they have drawn back is something of a mystery. We speculate they believe they've pulled our teeth; consider we're a spent force. We would be well-advised not to drop our guard where Nuclatom is concerned. So, to answer your question Archie, it appears for the moment as if the farm is secure.'

The Colonel glanced around the table.

'Also safe to say, SAEEI continues to be seen as a bumbling Dad's Army. If Nuclatom believes SAEEI were the agency behind the weapons procurement, it's understandable they've lost interest in Pieter. Probably think he's thrown his lot in with buffoons.' He faced him. 'No disrespect, Pieter. Anything to add?'

'Nothing, Sir. Except to confirm I'm not under surveillance. That's gone away. I agree however Nuclatom would be foolish to ignore SAEEI altogether. We've shown intent. I'm wondering if it might not be the time to take the fight to them? Cut off the head of the snake.'

'Eliminate Ivashchenkov you mean?'

'He's shown himself to be ruthless, the driving force. Without him in the mix, I doubt we'd have attracted the interest we have.'

Nkosi Mabalane came into the discussion for the first time. 'Removing him would attract a lot of media attention. Security around prominent foreign nationals constitutes a very sensitive area. We've seen it in South America and Asia. If he was eliminated it would drag the international spotlight onto South Africa.'

'He is a big wheel,' Colin Farrell sounded as if he knew the subject. 'There's no doubt his death would cause a stir.'

The Colonel agreed, 'I'm not sure it would be a good thing at this time, Pieter. We could end up fixing one problem and creating an even bigger one.'

'If I could come in?' Carl brought some simple logic. 'Let's keep a watching brief for the time being, leave our options open. If Nuclatom starts to give us major headaches, that may be the time to reconsider?'

Good advice. They were right; Piet had gotten ahead of himself. The less attention they called down on themselves this late in the day, the better. They moved on.

'How are things with the army, Nkosi, the demeanour of the enlisted man?' Colonel Stander hoped they would win hearts-and-minds in this fertile pasture now that civil unrest proliferated in the general population.

'Much murmuring as I've reported, rank and file expressing anti-Zuma sentiment more openly now. The number is growing. But culturally the African way, is to honour 'the big man' — show respect and reverence. The president has earned the right, become the ultimate chief, in some way deserving of the spoils of office. Never forget his roots go way back in the armed struggle. That in itself secures respect. On the other hand, these men are not stupid. They begin to see he takes the bread out of their families' mouths. So if he were prosecuted through due process, it would be one thing. Open revolt a bit trickier.'

'Which leaves us with the statistical conundrum. Where we can expect support and where not?'

'It's a mixed bag. We will get buy-in in certain areas. For the military at large, there is widespread apathy. Some fiercely pro-Zuma factions of course, like the veterans, but these will be isolated. We know where to expect that. So, all in all, I don't see spirited resistance. After we've secured the strategic targets, the way we address and inform the nation will be key. We must paint a picture of the ruling elite caught with their hands firmly in the cash register.'

Piet could almost feel the mechanism, a country growing increasingly disillusioned, winding tighter like a watch-spring.

'Your speech will hit the right note — our analysts and speechwriters will see to that. If we achieve a broad-based buy-in from the word go, we put ourselves in a very strong position with the international community.' The Colonel was positive.

Nkosi had two roles to fill in the transitional period. Military chief as well as interim president — powerful portfolios. His first task an address to the nation — the one they discussed. That would go out over national TV and radio. Securing those channels in order to be able to effect this, one of their prime objectives.

'The media channels are non negotiable.' Nkosi seemed to have read Piet's thoughts. 'Without control there the enemy has the ability to broadcast propaganda adversarial to our cause.'

'Agreed. We'll have those buttoned-down from the get-go.' They all knew it needed to be the case if success was to be achieved.

'Television and radio are fairly straightforward,' Carl broke the hiatus, 'social-media is where we're going to have to watch our step.'

'The IT boys have it under control,' the Colonel sounded confident. 'Firewalls barring access to major platforms will be in place as soon as we take control. Google, Instagram and Twitter for instance. We'll have those all buttoned-down quickly.'

Nkosi frowned. 'Could that not be seen as repressive? Perhaps a negative in terms of the way we are trying to present?'

'Will only be for a very short time. Just until we have everything bedded-down, under control,' the Colonel clearly had been involved in strategy meetings around this topic, 'then it all opens up again. By such time we'll be keeping an eye on IP addresses we've identified as troublesome.'

'There are those who are going to be shouting 'foul',' Archie wasn't the cautious type but could be relied upon to raise thorny issues.

'Such as Julius Malema,' Piet ventured.

'Certainly him.'

'Don't forget, gentlemen, he is also dodging prosecution for financial crimes. He's going to find himself in the spotlight in short order. The legal boys have a very solid case against him. He will be before a judge very quickly. And his travel document seized.'

'I suppose with the media lockdown in place, he's going to find it impossible to rouse the rabble. Might be able to get some sort of a voice via the international media though,' Colin raised a valid concern.

'Not a lot we can do about that. The press is what it is. We have to show the world we represent the will of the people. They know things have gone terribly wrong in South Africa. We must be seen to be cleaning our house. Miss Birman confirms the image we present is pivotal. Excessive bloodshed seen as negative, indicator of a repressive regime, antithesis of what we stand for. If we can get away with a low headcount, she believes it will go a long way to sending the right message. Hopefully ensure a kinder treatment from the media.'

'There will be hotheads here at home running around trying to make political capital out of the situation. Should we consider a roundup? Especially of those already facing criminal charges?' Piet thought this approach to the known firebrands a sound strategy.

'We're looking at that carefully. Our brains-trust are assessing both sides of the coin. A public relations exercise is a bit of a balancing act. Heavy hand or a free society right upfront? Frankly, it's a bit beyond my ken.'

'However, gentlemen, we've strayed a little from the agenda,' he favoured them all with an inclusive smile. 'I'd like to get back to something I do know a little about. Operations. And in particular Pieter's mission.'

His mission — to command a unit tasked with the capture of the state president himself. A heady undertaking, the emphasis on capture and not elimination. It was felt they could gain favourable propaganda this way. A delicate mission critical to the whole Endeavour. A lot depended upon its success. If it went awry, it spelled trouble — a lot of people would find themselves behind bars — or worse.

To achieve this goal they initially considered storming parliament buildings in Cape Town. The date earmarked, 23rd November. This would fall during the year's last parliamentary term when the president gave his National Council of Provinces address. The problem was, the locale demanded they field a large force. It didn't get much more public. Add to that the fact there would be a large contingent of the crack police-presidential-protection unit in play, and they felt, upon final analysis, the risk of it degenerating into a bloodbath was too great. The plan was dropped.

In its place, an attack on the president's *Nkandla* residence in northern Kwa Zulu province became their operational plan. Used to conduct some of the low-profile public engagements, as well as being the Presidents traditional home, their plan was to mount the raid when one of these engagements was in progress. A softer option all round. The protection detail would be smaller. They could field airborne and ground forces for the action — no challenges to get firearms into restricted areas. The rural location also meant less public exposure, less bloodshed.

The residence did not present in the mould of classical presidential palace. It was a sprawling compound styled on traditional Zulu lines. A collection of thatched structures sat atop a grassy knoll inside a state-of-the-art security fence. For the Endeavour the big advantage was its siting in a remote location.

Zuma started life from humble herd-boy beginnings in the same compound eventually securing the highest office in the land. Once ensconced, he improved the property going overboard with upgrades and additions. The expenditure attracted much criticism, coming in as it did at a hefty two-hundred-and-forty million out of public coffers. Zuma sycophants claimed the spend was both legitimate as well as necessary. The state after all, had an obligation to adequately protect its leader. Security became the smokescreen, the cover-up under which the expenditure got shrouded. An Olympic swimming pool became a 'fire pool', necessary because municipally reticulated water was deemed inadequate and the thatched structures were located in a region notorious for lightning strikes. A lavish pleasure-dome became a 'reception room' to accommodate dignitaries awaiting their audience. A ranch-style cattle kraal proved more difficult to sugarcoat. The final straw however, was a hen house befitting of royal chickens. It could be argued the public was justified in querying how their tax rand was being spent.

This then was their target.

Piet took the Colonel's prompt. 'Everything's on schedule, Sir. We're set to begin final field exercises the week after next. Provided of course Leonard has no hiccups?' They awaited supply of their aircraft from the logistics man.

'All running to programme from my side, Pieter. We've secured a Cessna Caravan from a Roodepoort skydiving outfit — chartered for a three-week stint. They believe we're off to Namibia training for a skydiving boogey over in the States, even pleaded to have a couple of their members join our group,' he chuckled at the recollection. 'Our pilot will collect the aircraft next week, fly it to Fergie's place. Fergie by the way, has done wonders scraping a more-than-passable runway and throwing up a bush hangar for us. From the farm — after the sky-diving training schedule, she'll fly to Eshowe in readiness for the op.'

Panel vans for the ground crew to be moved to the sugar estate in the next days. They're at the farm already decked out in their commercial livery; borehole contractor, satellite dish installation van and a telecoms service unit. The

337

borehole vehicle will tow a compact drilling rig. Under covers, an army tarpaulin in this case, will be your artillery piece.'

The sugarcane estate Leonard made reference to belonged to Pierre Robillard, Kwa Zulu's SAEEI regional representative. A former Mauritian national, he brought his sugarcane husbandry skills to South Africa thirty years previously, his success meteoric: a naturalised South African fiercely committed to the cause.

'We're getting close, gentlemen.' The Colonel eased back in his chair. 'I'd like a report from each of you by this time next week: by which stage we'll have intel on Zuma's movements — planned meetings at *Nkandla*. The following week all being well, a date can be set.' He looked around the room. 'Are there any questions?'

Nkosi half raised a hand. 'Communications on the day. Is there any danger of us losing that ability? It would be a problem if we did.'

'If I could answer, Nkosi?' This was Colin Farrell's baby. 'All commanders will be issued with dual sim-card cell phones — a belt and braces precaution. If we lose comms on one network, we will have a backup on the other.' He explained that a shutdown was highly unlikely even if they were discovered on a network. Service providers in the country didn't have the built-in architecture enjoyed in, say, the United States. But if for any reason they did lose comms, they would simply switch to the other provider. Everyone seemed happy with the arrangement. He went on. 'Our ops room will be overarching watchdog on all phones. They'll be hearing a blow-by-blow account so will be right on top of things at all times.'

'So if I'm understanding this correctly,' Carl worried the detail, 'there's no danger of a blanket blackout such as happened in America post 911?'

'None whatever; as I say, our service providers don't have the levels of sophistication the National Security Agency was able to call on.'

'Comforting,' the Colonel seemed to sum up the feeling around the table. 'And please remember, gentlemen, stay with our protocols. We don't want to advertise what we are about.' The meeting broke up.

CHAPTER 35

FAME

After the meeting Piet jumped on the Gautrain link to Sandton. The high-speed commuter rail was a pleasure compared to the slow crawl of traffic they flashed past. Even so, darkness lowered her cloak as Piet exited the station heading for the nearby Michelangelo hotel — a glitzy iconic tower attracting the rich and famous who visit Johannesburg. It wasn't his sort of place but Sophie chose it as a convenient rallying point to collect him from. After a quick drink, they were going to her apartment where she insisted she was cooking for him.

He dropped on to a stool in the Il Ritrovo bar. Lofted ceilings, dripping chandeliers, plush furnishings, underscored his sense of alienation. He ordered a single malt which turned out to carry a price commensurate with a prime fillet at a good restaurant. He had Fergie to blame for his recently acquired taste in expensive scotch. He thought wryly, however, the frugal Scot might have something to say about the price.

Sipping the drink, he reflected on the meeting he'd just come from — lots to think about.

They were getting close. Push-button time hovered somewhere just below the horizon; the gravity of his responsibility weighed heavily. Abducting Jacob Zuma was no light matter. It would take all their resourcefulness to pull it off. Failure wasn't an option. Mentally he worried every detail of the operation probing for any oversight. It was a comfort to have both Rusty and George on the team. He knew how they thought, how they reacted in combat, how dedicated they were. A massive bonus for the operation. Final training was scheduled at the farm ten days hence.

George would be team-leader of the airborne unit. He had his colours as a Springbok skydiver with thousands of jumps to his credit, so was the natural choice. His twelve-man team would jump at high altitude from the Cessna Caravan, deploying only when close to the ground to minimise the chance of both detection and of drift. It meant only the final two or three hundred metres under a canopy. The HALO (high altitude low opening) technique called for nerves of steel. They would be drilling exhaustively as a team on the farm until George was happy with pinpoint accuracy.

Rusty would be Piet's lieutenant in the ground crew. The air-drop and surface attack were to be coordinated to achieve a maximum element of surprise. They would be confronting two units of the president's protection detail — regular army, responsible for the security at the property, and the Police Presidential Protection unit, tasked with guarding the president's person. The latter would be hunkered in close to him, posing the final cordon of defence they would need to knock down to take him. To gain admission to the crack unit a member had to swear an oath to sacrifice his own life in the line of duty should it become necessary. They would be the greatest challenge.

His cell vibrated. A text from Sophie. *Leaving the parking. Meet you in the foyer.* He told the barman he'd be a couple of minutes, not to remove his drink on pain of death. He laughed good-naturedly, said he'd protect it with his life and continued to polish his glassware.

Sophie hadn't been to the building before — wasn't about to miss the opportunity of giving it the once over. She dragged him along, poking her nose into all the amenities as they made their way back to the bar. Finally settled, a gin and tonic in hand she regaled him with her day's activity.

As she finished she checked her watch. 'Not to be rude my love, but I want to catch the news on TV. Would you mind if we drank up and got on our way?'

'At these prices, it'd be a welcome relief,' he joked.

He settled the bill, leaving a tip he hoped wouldn't cause the barkeep to shatter his glasses. They arrived at Sophie's

Bryanston apartment in the adjoining suburb in no time. The flat was one of four above neighbourhood convenience shops. She scooted for the bathroom as soon as inside.

'There's a bottle of Sauvignon Blanc in the 'fridge, glasses in the cabinet,' she disappeared in a flurry.

He busied himself and took the drinks to the coffee table. His first visit to Sophie's place; he indulged his curiosity. A home is said to reflect the personality of the occupant. In Sophie's case he could well believe it. Colours were neutral, a primary splash lifting the mood here and there. Very Sophie — reflected in the way she dressed. Two architectural line drawings took pride of place on the walls. A classic cathedral; an accentuated perspective of an English village high-street. Simple but compelling. Very Sophie again. Opposite the sofa a flat-screen TV dominated one wall. The ever-present window-on-the-world to showcase breaking news? An obvious must for a journalist.

She returned plopping onto the sofa beside him and fiddled with the remote, the TV flickering to life.

'Something airing from Phoenix, I'm guessing,' he passed her drink and clinked glasses.

'Oh yes indeedee,' she gloated, regarding him smugly. 'You are such a clever man. Wait to see how clever your lady is.' She snuggled into him like a puppy.

The newscaster ran through the main features. Piet contained his curiosity.

'Coming next,' Sophie curled her legs further underneath her.

'One of our associate reporters can consider herself lucky to escape with her life. A great white shark burst into the cage she was diving in during a recent attack in the Western Cape.' The footage shot aboard Rusty's boat started to run; a sweep to the bows where the name *Chumbucket* showed prominently. A marketing technique on all of Rusty's videos. It resulted in a high level of knock-on business for him.

Next to Piet, Sophie scoffed indignantly. 'Associate reporter indeed.' She wasn't above a little professional hubris.

The clip continued. Rusty's cameraman was good. Even the substantially edited TV version lost nothing of the high drama. An initial sequence captured a dark shadow moving into shot below the surface. The camera panned tracking it; already an air of menace intensifying as the animal veered abruptly, torpedoing towards camera. A split-second later the image wavered as the beast hit home. The footage swung to the diver entry hatch. A crew member seen frantically wrenching it open. The water in the cage boiled as the trapped fish panicked. Frantic cries from Rusty's crew sounded indistinctly on the soundtrack. The next instant a few frames as Piet leapt into the cage and then the screen filled with footage of monstrous jaws, a trickle of blood seeping past fearsome teeth. It was impressive stuff. The

shark got out to the top of the cage thrashed convulsively —
and a moment later was gone. Final frames showed Sophie
climbing from the cage, an arm assisting from the water
below. The shot of the arm — Piet's television début.

'Impressive, Miss Birman. Now you're a movie star.'

'More than you know, Mr Rossouw. I posted the clip to
YouTube. It's on its way to going viral. I'm going to be raking
in the cash.'

How right she was. Within weeks the clip received
millions of views across the globe. It made big money. But it
would also attract deadly interest from a local party in their
back yard. The kind of attention Piet could well have done
without.

CHAPTER 36

A BOOKING FOR *CHUMBUCKET*

Ivashchenkov sat in his weekly briefing session with his security chief. Tense and not in the best of humour. Competition had re-emerged in the nuclear space.

The Americans had taken heart from Nuclatom's recent mauling at the hands of the South African judicial system, redoubled their efforts to curry favour at the top. They were engaged in a campaign to win over government officials from a weakening Nuclatom position. The anticipated power station projects were up for grabs again. All the players knew the game. Fawning to black politicians part of it. Throwing money around, distributing bribes, hoping some of it would stick. Praying for favour when the time came. Never a guarantee. For a gambler it would be a high-risk bet: the corporations were all gamblers. It was also cloak and dagger stuff. Bribes needed to be conjured from somewhere, irregular expenditure on the balance sheet accounted for. Research and Development budgets were a favourite clotheshorse. An enquiring shareholder could stagger round in this labyrinth and never find the way out. Such was the face of business in Africa — you needed to be in to win. And rewards were mega-buck.

'I don't like way Westinghouse is back in game. They lobby everywhere.' Ivashchenkov picked at his teeth with more than called-for vigour, removing morsels of *kasha* porridge. He pushed his bowl away across the kitchen counter irritably.

The security chief battled to prevent the rumbling of his stomach. He looked disconsolately towards the empty bowl. He loved *kasha* but knew his boss well enough. In all the years with him, he had never once been invited to share a meal. An occasional coffee, or a glass of beer the extent to which his employer's largesse ran. He shook the thought from his mind.

'We work on it. New energy minister is on our side...'

Ivashchenkov gave him a withering look.

'Idiot. I know this. Zuma can still get occasional thing right.'

The minister in question, David Mahlobo was Zuma's third appointee to the portfolio that year. His two predecessors, both women, failed to push the nuclear programme prompting their removal.

'Get to Westinghouse targets before builds to power block. Zuma weakens — puppet on fist losing power — God knows how long will remain. Throw more money than

American bastards at these people. Get ally's before they do. French nor Americans must be allowed to build position. Even if comes change of president, Nuclatom must be go-to nuclear solution.'

The man licked his lips nervously. '*Da,* we will regain position. We make progress at Koeberg.' Koeberg was the country's only nuclear power station. 'Plant Engineer is working with us. Westinghouse is supplier of new instrumentation technology. Their way to get favour with Nuclear Energy Corporation. Our man will ensure they get problems during testing phase.'

'How much bribe we pay Koeberg engineer?' Ivashchenkov remained sour when considering payment to individuals he felt were undeserving.

'Is reasonable in circumstances — cost of small family car for wife. Says for dropping kids off at school.'

'Let me have copy of management accounts to see what we throw at these monkeys.' He glared a warning at his man. 'Work dirty tricks stuff — more we can frustrate Americans, better for us. Poor reputation at NECSA will not help cause when comes to shoot-out for contracts.'

The man nodded.

'What happens with Frenchies?' The French-led nuclear consortium also chased the contracts.

'Travelling down country track in troika — stuck in rut.' the man dismissed their French opponents with disdain.

'Will not pay for people to help them from rut. You know how is.'

Ivashchenkov scoffed. '*Da.* Gallic pride big as nose on face. French always best, French do not need to buy favour. Would lose nose before pulling out cheque-book.'

'For us, no threat I think.'

'Keep eyes open anyhow. Low budget. Is longer pull ahead than first thought.'

'You think Zuma has trouble?'

Ivashchenkov pulled the corners of his mouth down distastefully. 'Is Africa. Never know what can happen. But understand this; his position weakens — strong wolves stir round him. Maybe can survive — maybe will fall. We prepare for both. I want Nuclatom number-one contender no matter who leads country.'

'Understood. We will dig for more Westinghouse moles.'

'Anything more?'

'No, is all.' The man rose to his feet, ready to leave, when a thought struck him. 'You watch television last night?'

Ivashchenkov looked bored. 'I should have?'

'Might have found amusing — your favourite lady reporter almost eaten by fish.' The man told his boss about the broadcast. 'Is on YouTube too — take a look.' He fished out his cellphone, found the clip then ran it holding the phone so both could view the footage. Unedited it ran longer than the TV version. Near the end, an individual leapt into the water in a heroic rescue bid.

'Stop.' Ivashchenkov stabbed at the screen. 'Go back.'

The man looked uncertain, dragged the slider back.

'From there,' Ivashchenkov pointed.

The footage ran until the rescuer came into shot.

'Freeze.' Ivashchenkov was riveted to the image. 'Zoom to face.'

The image pixelated as the man took the magnification too deep. He came out again and stopped. 'My God, is Rossouw,' he gasped.

'*Da*. Is Rossouw.'

'Should have seen before.' The security man knew he'd blooped.

'Is what I pay you for.'

'Not expected. What is connection to reporter?'

'Big money question — is what we need to find out. Run piece again.'

'There, see writing — name of boat. Go back, freeze. *Chumbucket*,' he murmured stabbing a finger. 'Check for website. Get phone number, make booking. Urgent.'

The security man was having difficulty keeping up. 'Booking? We go shark diving? For how many I book?' He was racking his brain trying to second guess his boss.

'Book whole boat. Corporate function. Say is team-building exercise.'

'What name to use? Not company name?'

'Yes. Must use Nuclatom. Has to be. Otherwise how can attract prey? Make sure as well they know I will be in party.'

'Will blow budget sure as hell. Whole boat will not be cheap. What you hoping to achieve, boss?'

Ivashchenkov waved a hand dismissively. 'To hell with budget. If I read right, will be lump of cheese mouse cannot resist.'

'A trap to lure Rossouw?' He was beginning to catch on.

Ivashchenkov scoffed. 'Can see wages I pay are not waste of money after all. Yes, is trap for Rossouw; make sure best men available.' A smile played at the corners of his mouth. 'And put tail on Sophie Birman. Good to chase pussy as well as trap mouse. I want to know where lives, times of comings, goings — everything. I think pussy and mouse run together.'

CHAPTER 37

CAT AND MOUSE

'You're not going to believe this,' Rusty's voice sounded incredulous on the line, 'I've got a big fish coming onto the boat, and I don't mean out of the deep blue.'

'Jacob Zuma,' Piet ventured, entering the spirit of things.

'On the right track. Dmitri Ivashchenkov.'

He had climbed from the main saloon to *Magus*' cockpit, cellphone reception being much improved up there. He almost dropped the phone over the transom.

'Ivashchenkov? You can't be serious.'

'Better yet. They want to book the whole boat for an entire day. That'll cost them plenty.'

His mind raced. 'Did he call you personally?'

'No. One of his staff. Said the booking was for a team-building getaway.'

'What did you tell them?'

'Said I'd need to check the bookings register — get back to him.'

He was thinking hard. 'How are those bookings, Rusty?'

'Chock-a-block. It's our busy time.'

Mind still churning. 'I need to think this through.'

'What's his game do you reckon?' Rusty asked.

'Right now I have no idea. Give me an hour, I'll call you back.'

His head spun. Their final desert training exercise began in eight days. A crucial part of their planning, vital preparation for the big day. Was it possible Ivashchenkov had found out Rusty was involved? Was this a show of force to let Rusty know he was blown? Did it place Rusty in any immediate danger? None of it seemed to make sense — Piet dismissed it immediately. How did Ivashchenkov even know about Rusty? And Rusty's boat for that matter? Pete had made sure they weren't followed at sea when Sophie and he sailed to Gansbaai for their diving day. Even scrutinised the wharves as they went aboard Rusty's boat.

Then it hit him like a steam hammer. Sophie's video on YouTube. Was it possible he somehow was identifiable on the video? And if so had Ivashchenkov picked it up? Needing better resolution than his cell would provide, he went below to the laptop, exited the weather application he'd left open. He got onto Google, tapped in keywords and found Sophie's post still ranking high on the search criteria he entered. He gave it time to load, skipped the ad and watched it play out.

Towards the end he paid particular attention to the sequence where he could be seen leaping from side-field into the water. It was only a few frames, but there nonetheless. He froze the video mid-jump. His face was turned half towards the camera. He zoomed in. Sure enough, there it was. He would be easy to identify. Even someone only having seen him a few times would have no difficulty recognising him. Ivashchenkov's outfit had had far more opportunity. They'd kept him under close surveillance for weeks at a time. It wasn't Rusty, Ivashchenkov was on to. It was Piet himself. And of course, he would put two and two together, know Sophie and he had become an item. That didn't sit well. Had he unwittingly exposed her to real danger?

He kicked it about for another half hour then called Rusty back.

'Did they specifically use the name Nuclatom when making the booking?'

'Right upfront.' Rusty was emphatic, 'In fact I'm sure they didn't want me to forget the name.'

'They didn't, Rusty. Trust me old friend, they will already have run a profile on you, know we served together, know you would call me as soon as you got their enquiry.' He paused to let that sink in. 'Did they say how big their party would be?'

'They didn't. Were at great pains however, to let me know their CEO would be heading the contingent, even spelt his name out for me.'

'They're pulling draw-stings to bring us together, Rusty. Let's not forget, they brought down an aircraft to further their ends.' His mind worked hard. 'Find out how many in their party. These are very dangerous people.'

'So are we,' Rusty was not a human being to be cowed. 'Would you like me to confirm the booking? Don't forget we've got our training stint just ahead. It's going to have to be before then.'

'Can you shuffle your bookings, tell them the only slot you've got is in a couple of days time. Say it opened up due to a last-minute cancellation?'

'Sure thing. I see where you're going. Force their hand, catch them off-balance a tad. Could give us an edge. Get them to move quicker than they'd planned.'

'We can hope for that.'

'Consider it done. I'll move the bookings around.'

'And Rusty...'

'Yes?'

'Pull at least half a dozen of our guys together including George. I'll get Fergie to send ordnance down to you with a driver. I want us to be well prepared if the party gets rough.'

CHAPTER 38

DEADLY ENCOUNTER

'Be very careful, Pieter. These people are ruthless.' Colonel Stander pushed his cup away. The Truth coffee shop in Cape Town's Buitenkamp Street is a quirky place. A steampunk world of pipes and old metal carefully preserving the industrial feel in the makeover. It is always busy, hectically noisy. A good place for discussing sensitive issues without the risk of being overheard.

'I'm very much on my toes with these people, Sir; organised a bunch of our top guys for the event. Plus we'll have a small cache of arms stowed below deck. If they bring a firefight, we'll be ready.'

'It's still a mystery to me why they are baiting us this way. I can't imagine they plan to eliminate you in such a public setting.'

'Agreed, can't be — ample opportunity to take me out whilst they tailed me. No, there's something else. Whatever it is, we'll be prepared for it.'

'I don't like it, Pieter. They were almost our nemesis once before. I'll rest a lot easier once this event is behind us.'

'Me too, Sir. I'm beginning to feel like a Jonah. First, the police interrogation brought about by my stupid curiosity the night of the fire. Now another slip allowing vacation footage to expose me yet again. Nuclatom and its goons are back in play largely because of me.'

'I don't want you harbouring those thoughts. Keep your mind positive. Stay focussed, concentrate on gathering useful intel from the event. If we can discover their game plan, not get drawn to precipitate action, then we've made useful progress. We're too close now to let Ivashchenkov and his people derail us. You'll need to exercise extreme restraint. Certainly can't afford a firefight, no matter what they are up to. Short of defending your life, play it very conservatively, Pieter.'

'I will, Sir.'

'And keep me updated as soon as you're off the boat — once they're on their way again.'

The following day, near Gordons Bay fifty kilometres east of Cape Town, their team rendezvoused at the Caltex garage on the N2 highway — six travelling aboard two vehicles — a two-hour drive to Rusty's home port. Rusty had stood his regular crew down so the stand-ins could fill their positions for the one day. They would arrive ahead of the Nuclatom party — enough time to be schooled so they could pass as regular deck-hands. Piet didn't think the Nuclatom party would rumble. Even if they did, once Piet's team were aboard, it hardly mattered.

'Are we gonna get a crack at these jokers?' George bristled as they set off.

'Nothing I'd like better old friend, but I'm under orders to exercise extreme caution. Unless we come under direct attack, we're to behave ourselves.'

'Pity. I'm getting hyped with all the training — beginning to feel just like the old days.'

'You'll get your chance. When you're plummeting towards the target at a hundred-and-fifty kilometres an hour, your weapons container hanging below you, adrenaline is going to pump.'

'For the record, try two-hundred kph. And those canisters will be strapped to us until the canopies deploy, only then we'll cut away.'

'Stand corrected, old mate.' Georges province. 'How many of the guys have jumped with full kit?'

'One, and you're sitting next to him. Don't worry, the guys are all top drawer under a 'chute. They'll have no trouble handling the kit.'

'You sure?' At it again. George didn't need Piet babysitting him.

'Piece of cake. Trust me, a couple of weeks from now once my guys are done with the training, they'll be every bit as good as any parabat vet.'

'Apologies, George. I know it's all under control. Can't stop myself from being an old granny so close to D-day.'

'Forget it, Piet. Field commanders job. I know how it stacks.'

Piet slid him a sideways glance. With his stockinged feet on the dash, hunched deep in the seat, he looked as if he hadn't a care in the world. He counted his blessings to have men like George in the force.

They drove without talking for a while, oblivious to the spectacular coastal scenery sliding by.

'I've been giving friend Ivashchenkov some thought,' George took up the conversation again. 'What if he's working with government even closer than we think?' He ran a hand over his baldness. 'What if they're using him as clever bait on a boat known to be operated by a friend of yours — sure to know you'll come running? Ivashchenkov knows already you're into something. What if this is a trap orchestrated with government backing to lure you in — eliminate you easily? How do we know troops won't be deployed to the area?'

'You're in good company, George; the brains-trust considered the same scenario. They still believe Ivashchenkov is operating independently.' He slowed for goats crossing the road. 'Their reasoning — Zuma's position is shakier than ever. They think he's got his hands full just trying to survive politically. Ivashchenkov is aware of it. We don't believe Ivashchenkov would risk exposing the fact there is subversive activity afoot — could bring the whole house of cards down; ring the death knell for his aspirations. And Ivashchenkov's hand is weakening too. He doesn't have time on his side. Nobody in the know believes the ANC will back Zuma for another term. Ivashchenkov has to try to push his deal whilst his pony is still running.'

'Don't trust political analysts. Even our own. They're like financial forecasters. Half the time they're wrong. I'd hate us to be walking unprepared into a well-set trap.'

Piet laughed. 'Which is why you'll notice a nondescript van parked on the side of the road as we leave Hermanus on the last stretch to Gansbaai. There'll also be another stationed the other side of town. Observation posts on the approach roads. Been monitoring traffic flows. Any military convoy we'd know about it.'

George punched him on the arm with some vigour. 'Lieutenant Rossouw strikes again. I should have known you'd have it sorted.'

'You know the game. Out-guess the enemy — be prepared.'

But George, also a strategist, hadn't finished yet. 'What about a deployment by air?'

'Covered. We've got eyes and ears in Cape Town airport's air-traffic control. Any military flight over our theatre of operation, we'd know about it too.'

'Now I can relax.' He pushed the seat-back down, hunkered lower. 'A ride on Rusty's tub whilst those Nuclatom clowns get it off in a lobster pot peering at hungry beasties? Sounds like good fun.' He began to hum tunelessly.

They arrived, spent the rest of the day getting drilled by Rusty. He took them through every aspect of the boat's diving gear. By day's end, everyone knew their role, could perform it seamlessly. Finally Rusty walked them through the boat as if he were a tour guide. He pointed out the concealed location of every weapon brought aboard. In the event of a confrontation, they would be a formidable force.

Just before nine the following day Ivashchenkov's party arrived in a self-drive Toyota mini-bus. Up on the flying bridge where he would have the con to take them out to sea, Piet watched their guests move onto the boat. Under a peak cap pulled down tightly on his forehead, and behind reflective sunglasses, he hoped he'd achieve anonymity. They weren't going to make it easy for their adversaries.

When Rusty had learned of the strength of the Nuclatom contingent once they'd booked, Piet decided to match it numerically. Now he gave the visitors the once-over. Ex-military heavies to a man if he wasn't missing the mark. From where he sat he could see Ivashchenkov giving the

361

boat and crew careful scrutiny. Good strategy, it showed some forethought. The visitors drifted off to various parts of the boat whilst Piet's team were busy casting off. Ivashchenkov looked up and caught Piet steadily observing him, gave a smile, a half-wave. Difficult to determine if polite acknowledgement, or was he letting Piet know he had him marked?

In any event for the next few minutes, Piet hadn't time to worry about it, his hands full easing *Chumbucket* off the wharf, getting her out into the channel. As they cleared the harbour, she began to feel the seaway. He gunned the throttles and she surged forward like an eager colt. Down on the deck the Nuclatom people were donning wet suits and diving gear, Rusty moving amongst them giving instruction.

Using GPS coordinates they surged into the dive location and he throttled back. The boat rolled to the swell, one of the guys deploying the anchor. He applied reverse power to snub it in. Their passengers were keen, milling around the crew as they lowered the cage into the water and secured it. Ivashchenkov was right there, seemingly as absorbed as his staff.

Chumbucket swung to the current, bringing her head into wind. No mistaking the fact a nearby seal colony was upwind, the pungent smell of their habitation carried powerfully on the breeze. This population was what attracted the great whites, seal meat by far their preferred diet.

Piet's guys made a final check of the cage lashings; all set to go. Absent now, only the sharks. Three of their crew started chumming; one pouring burley of fish oil, off-cuts and blood, another casting tuna portions on lines and slowly trawling them back to the boat. Within minutes the first of the big fish materialised. Two juveniles less than three-metres circled teasing the baits. The Russians chatted excitedly in their mother tongue, ribbing one another as they climbed into the cage. The lid closed behind them. Piet checked the two remaining on deck. Sentries for sure — Ivashchenkov was nobody's fool.

Rusty climbed to the bridge. 'Fish in a barrel. Tempting isn't it?'

'More than you know.' Both remembered these men were guilty of cold-blooded murder of Fotakis' crew and the loss of his aircraft, not to mention their equipment. 'Picked up anything of significance yet?'

'Conversing in their own tongue. Seem quite relaxed. If I didn't know better I'd say we had a normal tourist group aboard, same sense of anticipation, same excitement as all my regular clients.' Rusty's eyes never left the water. Before Piet spotted it, he raised a finger pointing. 'First mature adult.'

Piet screwed his eyes against the glare peering where Rusty indicated. For a moment he could see nothing. Then a darkening of the water as a ghostly shape glided by. Initially, the animal showed as much caution as its smaller companions but built confidence with each pass, inching ever closer to the baits.

'Newcomer,' Rusty was in his element busy at what he did best, 'you can always tell by the amount of caution he's exercising. A regular to this location would have been in for a snatch by now. This one won't be alone either.'

No sooner said, than three additional shapes ghosted in showing restraint like their companion.

'These are the whites you have to be careful of,' Rusty warmed to his topic. 'Almost for sure, new to this area. Undoubtedly their first experience around a baiting boat.'

'Dangerous?'

'Unpredictable. I know it gets said about all sharks. With these fella's it's particularly pertinent. They're getting all sorts of feed-back to confuse their brains. The amount of burley in the water should expose a large injured prey. They're not finding that. Just a bulky hull, patently uninjured, a cage full of more healthy food hanging off it. Add to that pieces of fish-meat repeatedly smacking the surface and not acting like floundering prey. They don't know what's going on, but can't resist their sense organs drawing them to the scent like iron filings to a magnet.'

'How visible will they be to the guys in the cage?'

'They'll be slipping in and out of the murk. Now you see me, now you don't. Not the best performers for a cage-dive operator. The regulars are much better value.'

'Do you think they'll move in closer?'

'Hard to say. Sometimes they do, sometimes they stay at a distance the whole day until they get tired of it. Then they go off looking for real food somewhere else.'

'So a bit frustrating for your punters?'

'More than a bit. They want close encounter stuff. Gets the adrenalin flowing.'

'What'll you do if the sharks don't get lured in?'

'Give the chumming a rest, have the guys take lunch then start again. Might attract different fish at a second attempt. If not, weigh anchor, move to another spot.'

They watched the sharks for the better part of an hour but the animals remained elusive. Rusty called a halt, the guys in the cage came up. Last out of the water was Ivashchenkov. He pulled his face mask off and looked straight at Piet.

'Care to join for lunch, Mr Rossouw?' he invited.

So now he knew. He'd had him sussed from the beginning. What was his game? Only one way to find out.

'Why not?' Piet called back, 'I'll get the guys to set a table for us up here.'

Ten minutes later he was seated on one of the upper-deck benches still wearing his wetsuit unzipped to the waist. Piet sat across from him, a fold-out table between them set with salads and cold seafood. They regarded each other warily. A mutual air of distrust merged with something darker. Not outright hostility — perhaps the electricity of conflict as yet unpacked.

Ivashchenkov made the first move. 'How does it go with new SAEEI appointment?'

Straight in. 'It's challenging. New ground to cover, not enough hours in the day.' He knew it to be banal and so did Ivashchenkov. But they fenced. These the opening feints.

'Still time for second occupation.' He gestured expansively taking in the boat, the ocean, the sky. First touch to Ivashchenkov.

'More a hobby — I'm fascinated by ruthless predators.'

He smiled, giving Piet a mock salute. 'Touché.'

Piet returned the smile.

'And for my part, am fascinated by leopards with ability to change spots — ocean gypsy to head of security organisation. Is quantum shift.'

Time for another thrust. 'Hardly compares to the leap from corporate mogul to saboteur.' Piet watched him carefully. Would he rise to the bait — admit it?

Ivashchenkov's smile flickered. Something arctic, frozen, shuttered to his eyes. 'You can recall our Greek friend Icarus

— flew too close to sun. Wax holding feathers melted on wings Daedalus made for him. Icarus fell to death. His crime? Was not impure heart. Heart was noble — helping father escape. Downfall? Not listening to father's advice, knowing better. Do not go close to sun father said, heat will melt wax holding feathers. Father knew limitations of equipment. Pride was Icarus' sin. Not listening to fathers advice. Knowing better. Cost his life.'

Was this as close to a confession as it would get? Or a mythical warning for Piet to stay out of his way? Either way, it didn't sit well. He decided to confront the issue head on. What had he to lose?

'Bringing down an aircraft with total disregard for lives aboard doesn't fit your Icarus analogy. Those men didn't have the fine distinction of choice Icarus had. Someone else took the decision for them.'

He regarded Piet with a poker face. 'Aircraft you say? Sorry, you have me at disadvantage.'

Clearly he wasn't going to step into an open admission. Piet decided he would start another skirmish.

'It seems your nuclear aspirations in South Africa may have to be put on the back burner for a while — now the courts have overturned your deal with Zuma.'

He didn't miss a beat. 'Temporary setback only. Africa is very fluid business environment. Will be back on course very quickly. Especially with new Energy Minister in place.'

'That could all change in a heartbeat,' Piet tried for a nerve, 'if Zuma gets unseated it could put a whole new spin on the way nuclear get's viewed here.'

Maybe he'd found that nerve. Ivashchenkov blinked once uncertainly, collected himself just as quickly. 'Mr Zuma is of secondary importance to our vision. Nuclear energy for power generation is correct path for this country. Has right footprint, is sustainable, has lowest running costs.' He didn't sound convincing.

'And the highest capital cost by orders of magnitude — attractive bait to cast at crooked politicians — brings all the big predatory fish into the swim.'

He gave his mirthless smile once again. 'So you are anti-nuclear, Mr Rossouw?'

'No, I'm anti-feeding-frenzy, when just a few people stand to make billions at the cost of a nation's welfare.'

'Spoken like true patriot.' He applauded theatrically. 'But please remember, without big inflows of capital from international investors behind cutting edge technology,' he made the magicians disappearing 'poof' gesture, 'no harbours, no bridges, no airports, no highways, even — no electricity. Nuclatom is technology investor. Africa would be dark continent without us.'

The primitive side of his picture was much too close for comfort to the way Piet earlier envisaged the continent without colonialism — the argument Fergie had shot down. His turn to falter.

'All well and good,' he regained his composure, 'progress within budgetary targets is one thing but progress at any cost is a recipe for meltdown. I'm sure you've read John Perkins *Confessions of An Economic Hitman*? The international corporates you speak of — he chronicles them — are only concerned with one thing. Their balance sheets. They'll buy politicians and under-budget capital projects to clinch deals. Much later when the fly is in the web, project costs run rampant. They milk the cow dry. All this to dupe unsophisticated and unsuspecting governments. Or worse still, governments who don't give a damn as long as they're getting their slice going direct to foreign bank accounts. To hell with national debt which keeps growing cripplingly to shackle future generations. The taxpayer ends up servicing interest for the dirty money, the country gets poorer.'

'A noble speech. But Perkins writes of American interests. You may notice Nuclatom is not American. We do not operate this way.' He was getting uncomfortable and looked down at the activity on the foredeck. 'But I see they are starting to chum again. Time for second dive. I want to touch noses with big fish.'

Piet watched him climb down the ladder. As well as being a corporate mogul, he wondered if the man was an adrenalin junkie getting his thrills laying his life on the line.

He looked at the lunch table. Ivashchenkov hadn't touched a morsel — come to think of it, neither had he. Perhaps he had more in common with the Russian than he cared to admit.

The crew kept at the chumming, it wasn't long before the great whites were back. 'It's the same gam as before. The newcomers.' Rusty was confident as he joined Piet on the flying bridge. 'Still skittish. Not sure we're going to lure them in close enough to give our punters a thrill today. Maybe time to move to a new spot,' he cast a skipper's eye over the water. 'What did our nuclear mogul have to say over lunch? Plenty by the looks of what got eaten.'

'A smart operator. Speaks in riddles as if he wants you to wrestle for the hidden meaning. One minute you think you've got an admission, the next you realise he's left you with nothing.'

'You're talking about Fotakis' aircraft?'

'I am. I baited him — certain he took it. He's responsible for the sabotage of that plane, I'm sure of that now. But he's much too smart to come right out and admit it.'

'Tricky piece of work then.'

'Deadly. A viper.'

'Any clearer idea of why we're here today?'

'None whatsoever.'

'Well I'm sure it will shake out by the end of the day.' He looked over the rail, shouting down to George. 'Tell the guys we'll do better if we up-sticks — try another location.'

Ivashchenkov was just climbing from the cage after his second dive. Piet watched George walk to him and have the conversation. Presently both looked up at the bridge, George shaking his head — a no go. He broke away to go topside.

'The guy's got a screw loose,' George issued the comment sotto voce as he joined Rusty and Piet. 'Wants to go out of the cage, approach these buggers in open water,' he swept an arm out over the rail.

Rusty looked down at the deck below. 'You serious?'

'That's not the half of it.' George looked as if he was about to blaspheme in front of a preacher. 'I have to invite Piet to join him — I told him no ways you would.' He looked at Piet a little uncertainly. 'Said I should let you know, if you want to find out how Icarus fell from the heavens, you'd go along. He thought you'd agree then.'

'Who the hell is Icarus?' Rusty wasn't much for mythology.

'A character in Greek folklore,' Piet's mind busied itself with angles Ivashchenkov might be trying for, 'fell to his death when he flew too close to the sun.'

'What's that got to do with us?' George's frustration started to show.

'I'll explain it to you guys later.' he turned to Rusty. 'Do you have open water gear aboard, Rusty?'

'This is a dive boat, Piet. We've got everything for any dive. Surely you're not going to let him bait you? With those new whites out there there's no telling what may happen.'

'What have you got in the way of deterrent in the event of an attack?'

'From the whites you mean?'

'From the whites. I'll take my chances with Ivashchenkov.'

'Best I can do is a bang stick.'

This was a makeshift baton with a 12 gauge cartridge at the business end. The idea was as a last resort you could forcefully jab at the shark, detonate the device driving a chunk of metal into its body. Piet had never met anyone who had used one or even heard any other diver talk about somebody who had. For him the baton was largely the stuff of urban legend, not a tried and tested defence against the ultimate predator. Still, better than no defence.

'Okay. It'll have to do. Is Ivashchenkov up to this sort of diving?'

'Apparently so, 'George recalled their conversation. 'As I kitted him out, he told me he once commanded a unit in the Ukrainian *Spetsnaz*. Went to great lengths to make sure I knew they were the planet's best combat-diving force.'

'Russian special-forces marine commandos — they do have a reputation,' Piet said.

'Are you sure you want to do this?' Rusty was the go-to when it came to the marine environment.

'I'm very sure I don't want to do it, brother. But if it's a way into the heads of these people, I'm compelled. Don't worry I'll be fine. Get the gear ready, Rusty.'

Half an hour later under a sky rapidly clouding, they sat at the transom of the boat ready to go. Ivashchenkov insisted the crew keep chumming so the great whites would stay in the area. Circling at a distance three out of the four large newcomers, the ones that concerned Rusty, were still in evidence.

The boat took on the air you'd expect to find at a traffic accident, both camps subdued: a phalanx regarding the divers sombrely. Piet pulled on his face-mask, gave a slight nod to Rusty; then back-rolled into the water. Ivashchenkov followed a half-second behind. He kicked his fins a couple of times heading down then half rolled giving Piet the all okay sign. He took station out to Ivashchenkov's side and a little way back. The bottom was about twelve metres below, just within range of their visibility. They purged buoyancy on the way down levelling out just off the ocean floor. Piet peered overhead. The hull of *Chumbucket* rippled battleship-grey against the overcast. It wouldn't be easy to pick out if conditions deteriorated. He took stock of their surroundings. They were abreast a three-metre ledge disappearing into the gloom and undercut from wave action in an earlier millennium when ocean levels were much lower. Close by, a distinctive slab of the overhang jutted out from the rest of the shelf, a child pulling a tongue. Piet committed it to memory taking a compass bearing to the boat. Next, he checked on Ivashchenkov who was watching him with rapt attention missing nothing, his breathing clearly controlled and efficient, bubble clusters rising to the surface like Indian smoke signals. A man capable of that kind of control so quickly given large predators close at hand, was a rare individual indeed. Even experienced divers used to close contact with sharks took time to adjust — inescapable stimulation excites the autonomic system, pumps adrenalin to the bloodstream accelerating breathing and motor-actions. Virtually impossible to control, it takes time to settle. Piet tempered his earlier assessment. Ivashchenkov was no adrenalin junkie either: if you weren't pumping the stuff your body couldn't get stimulated by it. Not a normal human being then — possessed of attributes no mortal should have. He gestured for Piet to follow and kicked off along the face of the ledge. Piet checked the diving knife strapped to one calf, the bang-stick on the other and fell in behind him.

They rounded a curve where the current became more pronounced. Ivashchenkov reached out grabbing a handhold. Piet followed suit. Out of nowhere, a ghostly shape slid along the rock shelf coming from the other direction. Observing sharks safely from the platform of a boat is one thing, being in their environment with them is another matter entirely. From both viewpoints, admiration comes easily for their magnificently evolved form, effortless propulsion. But sub-surface you realise you now face, in his environment, the planet's most efficient predator. You present to him as a food source. It is a vastly different dynamic.

He was gone in the blink of an eye, the murk swallowing him completely. Piet became acutely aware of this sense of alienation, the old wound itched irritatingly. He looked at Ivashchenkov who gave the okay sign, eyes radiating the unmistakable glint of pure thrill. It certainly wasn't fear.

Slightly apprehensive but keyed nonetheless Piet knew his senses had amplified. They transcended the steady-state — an invigorating natural-high from the endorphins. Exhaust air rattling through his regulator morphed to heavy-metal music inside his head; beads of moisture in his face-mask swelled to miniature goldfish bowls, each a hologram of the vista beyond. The old scar now shot way through itchy and felt as if it were being etched with a tattooist's needle. If he was hyped, the gloom beyond seemed to descend to a lower vibrational state, menacing, foreboding.

Ivashchenkov waved his hand to get Piet's attention, pointed. At the limit of their vision two of the massive predators weaved in and out of sight as if taunting them.

Their behaviour, so far non-aggressive, wasn't neutral either. No doubt the divers had become the focus of their attention. Piet checked his gauge. Still well over half an hour of air remaining so, no issue there. As they watched one of the animals turned, suddenly coming straight for them. He veered abruptly to end his charge and disappeared along the reef. This was a test run Piet knew for sure. Ivashchenkov turned to face him. There was something approaching ecstasy showing in his eyes. Piet gave the hand sign indicating the need for vigilance, swept an arm out towards the deep, the reef at their backs. No sooner done than all three whites, their demeanour altered, materialised again. Weaving like revellers around a maypole their agitation palpable now, they almost certainly readied for an attack. Piet knew it wouldn't be long before they ran at them.

That thought, no sooner birthed, proved to be right on the mark. One of them hunched his body like a weight-lifter pumping muscle and came at them with incredible acceleration. Instinctively Piet reached for the bang-stick. Long before he could unsheathe it, they were buffeted by the turbulent wake his scythe-like caudal fin beat in the water right next to them. Ivashchenkov looked at Piet with the eyes of a schoolboy viewing a girlie magazine for the first time. It was astonishment not fear. Piet now had the baton out praying he wouldn't be the guinea pig needing to test its efficacy.

He peered again into the gloom. The sharks were gone. He didn't like it. Predators this size didn't test their prey then slink away unless they encountered aggressive defensive action. the divers had displayed none of that. The hunters were stalking them. They may not know where the pack were, but with their incredible sense organs, the fish would have them pinpointed to within a centimetre. Not a level playing field.

He gestured to Ivashchenkov to move close into the ledge, only metres away. Having it right against their backs would limit potential attack quadrants significantly. The light failing, visibility deteriorated in step. Conditions tilting the playing field further. He tapped Ivashchenkov on the shoulder indicating they should go back the way they came. He seemed reluctant, but finally nodded and they finned off, keeping a keen awareness of the ocean out on their flank.

They hadn't gone far when they were taken completely unawares as one of the predators came out of nowhere hugging the rock-wall and riding the ridge from the opposite direction. They were as tight to it — was the animal trying to lever them away from its protective face? The same hunched muscular aggression rippled his bulk. Things were getting serious. Piet had the bang-stick ready, but in a repeat of the initial charge, at the last moment the great white broke away leaving them buffeted in the same welter of turbulence. The ultimate test was coming. A survival situation in which they were seriously out-gunned.

In the continuously failing light they scanned around, second-guessing where the next charge would come from. Adopting a back-to-back formation they held station for what seemed an eternity. No sign of an aggressor. Cautiously they moved off, Piet taking the lead.

Every metre towards the boat was a metre well-made; progress slow but whittling the distance down, raising expectations. Their attackers were eerily absent when Piet got a tug on his fin. He almost shot out of his wet-suit. It was Ivashchenkov stopping him to point into the murk. Right at the edge of Piet's vision, barely more than smudges on glassware, he could see the sharks. Their movements were frenetic. Hungry dogs agitating around the feeding bowl. Impossible now to be certain of their number — more than the four of the original gam for certain. A climax was building — gut wrenching to know they were the focus of it. Right then the sanctuary of the boat seemed very far off.

Ivashchenkov gestured to the lower part of the reef alongside them. The undercut they'd noticed earlier stretched in a few feet. His idea was sound. It would give them another dimension of protection. He finned down and disappeared. Piet followed.

Light was even more subdued in there. They felt their way gingerly along, progress slow; a worthwhile trade for the added security. They felt safe for the moment. They would still have to face danger when they left it, Piet knew. No escaping that — there was open water to cross to get to the boat. He began peering ahead for the tell-tale projection, willing it to show against the grey of the ocean. Ahead Ivashchenkov finned slowly, deliberately — a shifting shadow in the semi-dark.

A sudden surge from behind squeezed Piet along the undercut like a pea down a pea-shooter. For a millisecond his brain convinced him it was an ocean current pulsing down the feature. Then he knew with certainty what it was. Events from there ratcheted by in jerky steps. He turned all too slowly and much too late. The monster was right on him. His field of vision was filled by a massive maw wider than his shoulders, the frightening mouth studded with razor-sharp triangles — white spearheads even in the half-light. A reflex saved him. He thrust out the baton prodding for any sort of a hit. He felt contact, not sure where, but no detonation. Enough aggression however to deflect the animal. But his momentum had knocked the bang stick from Piet's grasp, rolled him sideways slamming him into the roof of the undercut with a metallic clang. A searing pain shot through his chest. Face-mask and mouthpiece were gone.

Events stuttered by. He came to rest on the sandy bottom — a rabbit savaged by a terrier. The turbulence stilled. He got himself to a sitting position, still thinking clearly enough to have his back pressed defensively against the rear of the channel. One of his oxygen tank anchor straps wafted out in front of him like a frond of seaweed: the tank hung lopsidedly at his hip. Under the roof of the overhang his mouthpiece gurgled its precious gas away at the end of its umbilicus; the need to fill his lungs now a screaming imperative. He fumbled for the feeder line, dragging the mouthpiece down and sucked hungrily. Back in business. The face-mask was still gone leaving his vision little more than a gradation of grey. He peered both ways along the gulley as far as visibility would allow. Not far. No sign of Ivashchenkov.

Recovering his senses, he wondered if Ivashchenkov had come under attack himself when the man simply materialised. A fuzzy wraith thrusting something into his hand. His face-mask. He wrestled it on and purged it. Ivashchenkov regarded him from close to. Even in the gloom Piet saw him unsheathe his knife. Did he want him to see what was coming? Was his end to be at Ivashchenkov's hand and not the sharks? Instinct kicked weakly, he fumbled ineffectively for his knife. Ivashchenkov held up a restraining hand, moving closer. His blade flashed inches from Piet's face as he began to saw in the crook of his neck. He could feel vibrations passing through the wetsuit. Finally he drew his hand back waving a large flap of neoprene in front of Piet.

His vision dimmed further, delayed shock he thought but the truth soon became apparent. An opaque foggy cloud issued from him. For the first time understanding dawned — he was bleeding and bleeding freely. Searing pain came with the realisation. He looked down to where the wet-suit gaped at his chest. A burst balloon. Across his pectoral muscle a butchers handiwork presented — three large cleavages gaping and oozing freely. His head throbbed — an insistent bass drum.

Ivashchenkov folded the neoprene flap he'd cut away into a makeshift pressure-pad, signing for Piet to hold it over the wound as a wraith-like shape slid past outside their recess. The blood would be exciting them to fever pitch, drawing them in. Suitably cued, a second followed, hugging the bottom and rolling an obsidian eye at them. Food inside a shallow cave. Or would that become grave? Ivashchenkov busied himself with Piet's tank, jury-rigging it behind him so he could at least fin with it strapped awkwardly across his back. Not comfortable but a chance to be moving again.

Moving towards what, Piet didn't care to think about. He couldn't see them making *Chumbucket*. Getting torn to pieces a far more likely and discomforting scenario. Ivashchenkov drew his attention motioning for him to stay put. He finned off along the trench hugging the bottom. It wasn't long before he was back nodding enthusiastically and holding the bang-stick. Piet wished he could feel the same elation. He had little faith in the device. Token only for what awaited them. Ivashchenkov gave a thumbs up, cocking his head enquiringly. Piet nodded — good to go. Ivashchenkov took the lead. Piet was all too aware that sharks detected blood in dilutions as low as one part per million. His body pumped it out like a ruptured oil tanker. They would have them pinpointed every inch of the way. The sanctuary of the boat was a prospect as remote as a distant star.

Visibility remained poor. From within their gloomy burrow Piet thought they'd missed the promontory, their marker. That would turn oxygen-supply into another enemy — flush them into open water whether they liked it or not. Long odds lengthened to impossible.

And all the time Piet kept an eye open for their aggressors, once again conspicuous by their absence. A large wounded quarry in the water should be driving them crazy. They were out there somewhere he knew. Waiting.

They'd swum quite a way. On the point of attracting Ivashchenkov's attention and telling him they should turn around, that they'd overshot — the rock-ledge promontory, like the prow of a ship, ghosted into view. He grabbed Ivashchenkov, indicated both the feature and his compass. He caught on immediately as they positioned themselves under the overhang. For the first time Piet spotted apprehension flicker to Ivashchenkov's eyes; perhaps because he was dragging along an invitation to dinner; a bloodied morsel — chum to these predatory fish eager to feed. He could see Ivashchenkov was as reluctant to break cover as he was but both knew they needed to go. Time worked against them. The air in Piet's demand valve had begun to drag. He pulled harder now to get the last of his oxygen and prayed the dregs would be enough.

No sign of their predators. Far from comforting, in fact darkly ominous. Where were they and what were they doing? The ocean within their diminished field of vision remained eerily empty. They were out there somewhere: perhaps less intimidating to have them visual. Every second, tension ratcheted higher. Sure to come soon. Piet took a compass bearing towards where the boat would be. They set off finning slowly in side-by-side tandem — strokes deliberate in a futile attempt to remain unobserved — their blood spoor would be blaring like a bull-horn. Piet kept throwing anxious glances over his shoulder, a cloudy trail stretched behind them. As obvious to the sense organs of those hunting them as a jet contrail to an aircraft spotter.

Then without warning they were there, confident in their superiority. The embodiment of menace, they came fast and as a pack. Big trouble. The lead fish hurtled at them with deadly intent. In the last instant he veered off. Another in his wake then two more right behind. No break away this time. Piet prepared himself for impact, his knife a puny toothpick against a palisade of ragged spears. The fish hit like a runaway automobile. He lunged feebly with the knife. At the same time a dull explosion reverberated in his ears, a percussion wave shaking him like a bell. The pain in his ears was sharp and excruciating. He was unsure what had happened until the shark rolled away shaking its head violently in its death throes. Under the snout a jagged hole trailed blood. Piet looked at Ivashchenkov holding the bang-stick aloft — a flag-waver at a carnival, his arched eyebrows expressing disbelief.

Out in the murk the injured animal continued to thrash frantically. His fellows started to show a marked interest in him. Already in killing mode, one lunged in to attack. The gam erupted to a feeding frenzy, the ocean billowing in a cloud of blood. Time and again they slammed into the hapless animal tearing slabs of meet from what was already little more than a twitching carcass.

They finned away unnoticed. Helping hands soon pulled them over *Chumbucket's* transom into the well of the boat.

'Nasty wound there brother,' Rusty leaned in over Piet, 'and I'm guessing you guys didn't have the luxury of decompressing on your way up.' He shouted over his shoulder. 'George get a couple of fresh tanks on deck. Let's get these guys sucking some oxygen.'

CHAPTER 39

PROPOSITION

Heading back to shore, Ivashchenkov held court, his team around him at the stern seats. A babble of Russian, the occasional burst of laughter. Without doubt the boss's recent adventure was the topic of animated conversation.

When George climbed to the bridge, Piet had almost exhausted the tank of oxygen for his makeshift decompression. George brought with him the tank Piet had dived with.

'Reckon you've got the canister to thank for not lining a fish's belly right now, Piet,' he exhibited the tank. A number of score marks etched deep in the aluminium, tell-tales of what might have been.

'Not my time, brother,' Piet slapped him on the shoulder and received a stab of pain for his indiscretion.

He knew George was picturing the incident, getting shivers down his spine. He was all but fearless in every area save one — he had a full-blown phobia when it came to sharks. In his mind they were the stuff of nightmares. He wouldn't even swim on a beach where there was a possibility of one being within twenty kilometres.

'Wasn't Ivan's time either,' he gestured towards Ivashchenkov, 'felt you might have left him out there with his marine cousins.'

'Shoe happened to be on the other foot,' Piet thought how easy it would have been for Ivashchenkov to leave him at the mercy of the gam. 'But for him, I doubt I'd be sitting here.'

'Fair enough,' George acknowledged the act of chivalry with a shrug, 'bitter pill to swallow though, if you'll forgive the feeding-orifice pun. He still ranks as a deadly enemy — *lekker* to have let nature take him out of the equation.'

'Not meant to be, George. And make no mistake if we come against him in the field he will still be the enemy, shown no quarter.'

'Have to admit, he seems the genuine hard man, forgive the metal analogy, screw loose, balls of steel.' George could always be relied upon to find humour in most things.

Piet laughed. 'You don't know how close to the mark you are.'

'Oops, speak of the devil.' Ivashchenkov was halfway ascending from the lower deck. 'I'll leave you gents in peace.' George retrieved Piet's dive tank and was gone.

'All patched up from little brush in ocean?' he dropped onto the bench opposite Piet.

'Pretty much,' he glanced down at the field dressing Rusty'd applied. 'Not my idea of a fun-day out though. You on the other hand seem to enjoy this sort of thing.'

He laughed roundly. 'We Russians are little crazy. I think is due to many generations of vodka drinkers: mad antecedents.' He regarded Piet thoughtfully. 'But you also could be Russian — fit picture: namesake in history — famous Tsar. Big man, also would not walk from challenge.'

'Not the sort of comparison I want to be remembered for. Your challenge went against my better judgement. An invitation you knew I wouldn't refuse. Very nearly cost me dearly. My thanks by the way, for getting me back to the boat.'

He shrugged his shoulders dismissively. 'Is pleasure.'

Piet studied him for a moment. "But now it's time to call in my bet. You offered enlightenment on Greek mythology if I went along for the ride.'

'Aah, yes.' He tilted his head back, eyed Piet cooly beneath hooded lids. 'Our friend Icarus — perhaps others like him...'

Piet waited.

'You want to know why Russian aircraft, crewed by Russians, carrying Russian weapons, fell from sky?' This was dangerous territory. For Ivashchenkov at least.

'Something like that,' Piet wondered if he'd get into the meat of it, or leave him hanging like before.

'Off record of course?'

'No-one to listen, I'm not carrying a wire. Totally off the record.'

He seemed to be weighing the way he should deliver the information. 'If I said aircraft engaged on mission which, if successful goes against interests of mother Russia, I suspect would find too patriotic… how you say… hard to swallow?'

'I would.'

'True anyway. But needs more explanation. If I say was directly against interests of corporation I serve?'

'In what way?' Piet acted dumb.

'Come.' His eyes took on the flint-like quality reminding Piet of the predators they'd just escaped. 'Cargo of illegal arms on way to South Africa, manifest showing farm machinery. Even *muzhik* would recognise revolution in making. Nuclatom has big investment in South Africa. Ambitions for much business. Lot of money spent already. Mr Zuma supports our efforts. The one unseated if coup happens. Intervention protected our interests.'

'There were innocent crew on that aircraft.'

'Sadly countrymen of mine. But innocent you think?' he paused, 'of what? Of involvement in act of treason? I would say for sure not innocent. In many parts of world this activity carries death penalty.'

'As it did in this instance. Under the justice system of Nuclatom not under state law.'

He shrugged again. 'And, South African Emergency Evacuation Initiative — would not also deal out death to those getting in way?'

This was getting far too close to home. Piet changed tack. 'Why would you want me on this boat today? You clearly know enough about me and my friends to understand the minute I learned you were to be aboard, I would be here.'

'Yes. Was done to draw you in.'

'For what purpose? Not to attract a dive partner I'm sure.'

He laughed. 'No, not dive partner but dive was fun anyway. I give thanks for being partner.' A serious look stole onto his face again. 'Can be direct?'

Piet nodded.

'Is clear SAEEI is thinly disguised revolutionary organisation. We have done homework. At best you are rag-tag of farmers, of zealots. But am impressed you got to arms supplier. I doubt your organisation has ability to overthrow government. More so now teeth have been lost — not like shark.' He fixed Piet with a hard stare. 'Difficult now to attack anything.'

Bonanza! No knowledge of the replacement weapons. Or the existence of the farm.

'So I ask again. Why am I here?'

'I will do all in power to make sure Mr Zuma's time as president runs full term.'

'You still think you can push your deal through whilst he's in the driving seat? Despite the court's decision?'

'You are well informed I see. We will get deal. Nuclatom is influential corporation.'

'Still doesn't tell me why I'm here.'

He rubbed a hand over his chin. 'You waste your talents at SAEEI. Can do much better. I like to offer job. Nuclatom operates in more than forty countries. Some places security is major concern. Could use resourceful man like you. And of course,' a wry smile crept onto his face, 'when working for me, could not be working against.'

To say it was the last thing Piet had expected would be asinine. It floored him. He had run all sorts of scenarios in his head over the last few days. This was as far removed from all of them as it could get.

'I'm not much good running sabotage operations,' Piet managed after he'd collected himself.

'We do not do sabotage as you call it. It not something you would need to worry about. You... what is English term... sell yourself short. Can do better than security firm, or band of revolutionary farmers, or whatever is. Nuclatom is big corporate — not saboteurs.'

'What would you call it?' Piet shot back.

'Act of war. Protecting sovereign rights.'

He let that pass. 'I'm flattered by your offer. However I don't think I'd be an easy fit in your organisation. In any event I've only just stepped into my new role. I'm not looking for a career move right now.'

He held up a restraining hand. 'Do not say 'no' until have time to think. Salary would be generous, paid to off-shore bank. Hard currency not Mickey Mouse rand. Lot of travel, nice girls, report only to me.'

He smiled thinly, got to his feet and turned on his heel. 'Consider carefully. Is big opportunity.' He clambered back down the ladder.

Piet just sat and stared after him.

CHAPTER 40

POLITICAL WOBBLE

He had Sophie on the phone. They never discussed issues she understood to be sensitive, but quite often chatted politics in general, things affecting their beleaguered country.

'Did you hear there's been another call for a vote of no confidence in our esteemed president?' she was all business.

'The eighth since he took office, isn't it?'

'Social media says eight, but it's actually only six. He's been bulletproof in the political arena. That's changing slowly my sources tell me, opposition mounting within the party. I don't know how much more of this he can withstand.'

'Depends on how many ministerial appointments he's prepared to trade,' Piet scoffed.

'Party big wigs believe he's almost out of control. He's openly taunting his detractors. The executive is concerned he's damaging the very fabric of the party. They've called for this vote by secret ballot. That's a first.'

'Interesting. A secret vote would mean no recriminations possible by him. Can't knock the detractors out of the game unless you know who they are. How do you see it going down?'

'Going to be a close call. Could go either way.'

'Spoken like a true diplomat,' he chided. 'Tell you what, I'll wager a bottle of single malt that he survives.'

'You're getting too used to winning expensive scotch from your wagers,' she taunted, clearly remembering the one he'd won from Fergie.

'Meaning you're in or out?'

'I'll take your bet, Mr Rossouw. Even if it's only to gloat when you have to pay.'

Did she know something he didn't? She was after all a journalist at the top of her game. Information was her stock in trade. Was she setting him up?

'Why am I getting a distinct impression you're not telling me everything?'

She laughed. 'Who's getting cold feet now?'

'Not me. Bet's on.'

Piet could picture a certain Russian gentleman who would be very displeased if Zuma lost the vote. He also wondered, not for the first time, what it would mean for the Endeavour. Would they still go ahead, mount the overthrow attempt even if another hand took the helm? Under new leadership would there be an attempt to rid the country of corruption, break the stranglehold choking it?

In the event he didn't have to concern himself with the last scenario. Jacob Zuma survived, one-hundred-and-seventy-seven voted for the motion, not enough to topple him. A close thing however, one-hundred-and-ninety-eight parliamentarians voted against, with nine abstentions. By a narrow margin Sophie would have to cough up her bottle of Glenmorangie.

CHAPTER 41

DEBRIEF

'He did what?' The Colonel exclaimed.

'He offered me a job, Sir.'

'My God. I hope you didn't take it?' This was as close as it ever got to humour with The Colonel.

Piet laughed. 'I somehow don't think my life expectancy would be so good if I found myself in the Nuclatom stable. Ivashchenkov was at great pains to tell me they were involved in many countries, security was a big issue. If their track record here is anything to go by, I can only imagine it would involve a lot of illegal activity.'

'I could almost guarantee that. There were murmurings they were directly responsible for the death in Algeria two years ago of the regional manager of their French rival, Areva. You also may recall three Russian journalists got killed in the Democratic Republic of Congo several months ago. Intel has it they were on the payroll of Nuclatom, the hit a reprisal. Volatile people to be around.'

'You'd think they'd come under censure from their own government for such activities.'

Colonel Stander scoffed. 'Not a bit of it. Putin has big aspirations in Africa. Russian corporates doing business here get the nod from him. You can rest assured, strategies get discussed corporately at the Kremlin; the cold war now fought in staterooms, in boardrooms. Same objective, different methodology.'

'And I believed the big threat on the continent was China.'

'Make no mistake there's a scramble for Africa. China gets the publicity but Russia is doing a creditable job establishing large spheres of interest. The continent won't look anything like it does now in thirty or forty years.' He smiled ruefully. 'I'm glad I won't be here to witness it. But anyway let's get back to the business at hand. You've spent time with Ivashchenkov now. What sort of man is he?'

Piet wanted to present this the right way. He had downplayed to the Colonel the actual shark attack, the wound he carried from it. It served no useful purpose to focus there. Instead, he considered the other pieces of information that he'd picked up.

'Something of an enigma. Doesn't have stock-standard emotions I'd say. Show's no fear when it would be healthy to do so. I would guess he doesn't have a normal autonomic response system like the rest of us. In the water going out to meet our sharks for instance, he was calm, collected. Clearly not pumping an overload of adrenalin. More at ease than me.'

The Colonel shifted uneasily in his chair, the observation regarding cerebral mechanisms stirring a memory which had often haunted him over the years; a conversation with a certain psychologist some thirty years resonated. A word insinuated itself ad nauseam. *Alexithymia*. The burden of having given the order for the medical record to be expunged — to keep the patient, Lieutenant Rossouw, ignorant of his condition, weighed heavily. Now his soldier described a disturbingly similar condition in a serious antagonist. Could Ivashchenkov be another Pieter Rossouw he wondered? An adversary whom nature had sculpted with a mal-adaption separating him from his kind? A super human. The Colonel shrugged the thought aside, suppressing the guilt for the umpteenth time.

'You believe he doesn't have intel on our activities, Pieter? Something which could derail us?'

"I'd say it was a given, Sir. When he came clean with the fact he'd been responsible for bringing Fotakis' aircraft down, he was forthright, stated unequivocally he considered us a spent force. He has no idea we've re-armed.'

'Good to hear. Ironic isn't it? The government we are trying to unseat turns out to be a secondary foe. Biggest threat — a corporation with a commercial agenda.'

It was as if the remark stirred the fates. Days later Piet found himself once again in the cross-hairs of that very same government.

CHAPTER 42

FARM ATTACK

A week remained before he left for the Karoo, the final training stint. After completion they would be ticking off the calendar to D-day, nervy times for him. He constantly checked off all the things he would be directly responsible for, worried the Colonel over detail beyond his ambit. His commander must have tired of the constant haranguing — if so he didn't show it. Finally, there was nothing left Piet could check upon that hadn't been gone over innumerable times. He needed to chill, a weekend at the estate with his parents seemed to be the ideal vehicle.

He arrived mid-afternoon Friday, tagged along with his father as he went about his usual routine. It was the last payday before the end of the month, his father's custom at this time to meet with the workforce around a *braaivleis* in the old receiving shed.

They entered the building — the aroma of lamb roasting over open coals was mouthwatering. Farmhands were in a party mood, enjoying the occasion. Cool drinks from a big ice-filled tin bath complemented the meat. There was no alcohol. His father, no puritan, did not encourage it. It had been a curse among the coloured population working the Cape wine-lands for as long as anyone could remember. Alcoholism a sad legacy from early days of viniculture when the labour force was part-paid with *papsaks* of wine. It had destroyed families and bred lawlessness. Notorious Cape gang-culture burgeoned massively as a consequence distorting the coloured sub-culture. Not a bright star in the firmament of white agriculture. His father imposed the rule strenuously.

He greeted workers remembered fondly from his days on the farm. Here there was no gulf between employer and employee, mutual respect the glue. It nurtured a solid partnership. One he grew up in. Instantly at ease, it felt as if he had never been away.

They spent a pleasant hour or so before strolling back to the house.

'How are things shaping these days?' His father was talking of his role in the Endeavour.

'Over-worrying the detail of late,' he confessed.

'Only natural. Are you ready?'

He thought of the recent encounter with the shark, the stiffness in his shoulder. He hadn't shared the incident with either of his parents — or Sophie. No mileage in that.

'I'm ready,' It was all he could say. 'How much does Ma know?'

'Only that it'll happen soon; you'll be involved in the field somehow. Much like me, she's not privy to detail.'

He wasn't fishing. 'How's she taking it all?'

'She's concerned for your safety, your wellbeing, just like any mother. But she understands what's at stake. She's a stoic. She'll be fine.'

He was right. She'd be anguishing he knew, but wouldn't show it.

'And what about Sophie?' His father knew him well enough to know he'd shield her too.

'Much the same as Ma. We don't talk about it other than in generalities. As a journalist I think it burns her — knowing there's a major story under her nose she can't harvest. But she respects the need for absolute secrecy.'

'She's a good girl, you'd do well to remember it.' From under knit brows he fixed his son with that fatherly look as old as time itself.

He laughed. 'You needn't worry. When this is all over, I'm going to ask her to marry me.'

He gave Piet a high five as they climbed the porch steps.

They spent a pleasant evening reminiscing old times, avoided straying to the future. Family history could be picked over, enjoyed like tasty morsels. Tomorrow and beyond, dangerous, uncertain, uncharted territory — no signposts to show the way.

He went to bed early. Back in his old room a sense of time dislocation engulfed him, released the tension briefly. Soon asleep, he awoke later with a start. Something had disturbed him. He listened intently in the darkness. For a while there was nothing, then a barely audible murmur. The TV turned low in his parent's room he thought at first. He felt for his cellphone on the bedside table. Just after two-thirty in the morning. Certainly not the TV then. He kept the light off, alarm bells starting to ring. Getting out of bed, he groped for his underwear and eased the door open. A faint glow crept under his parent's door throwing a pale oblong on the passage carpet. He padded down there knowing something was amiss.

He pressed his ear to the door, muted male voices mumbling from within — none his father's. A suppressed snicker, the sound of drawers sliding, then the words '*ipisi yekaka*'. He had a working knowledge of several African languages. This was Xhosa slang for 'piece of shit'. Intruders were in his parent's room! His stomach tightened, implications hammering home. He needed to act fast, no time to arm himself. He grabbed the door handle and burst in. His folk's bedroom lighting had a dimmer switch; turned low, illumination was subdued. But bright enough to expose the havoc already wreaked in the room — clothing scattered everywhere, emptied drawers haphazardly flung to the floor, sheets wrenched from the bed. His mother's inert form, clad only in nightdress, lay sprawled at the bedside. His father too lay prone, an ominous bloodstain seeping from his head. Neither stirred.

Two black guys were busy looting, the one closest heavily muscled, head shaved. Piet went for him in a maniacal charge. The man grabbed a vicious panga from atop the dresser he was ransacking as Piet barrelled into him. They hit the floor in a welter of splintered wood as the discarded drawers took the impact. The flat of the blade glanced ineffectually off his back as it struck home. They grappled, each trying for a hold to immobilise the other. A third individual rushed out of the en-suite dressing room brandishing a pistol and looking menacing. A shot rang out. His aim was off. Piet managed a leg-lock around the big guy rolling him on top, effectively denying the gunman another shot. His injured shoulder sent a bolt of pain right through him as he locked aggressively onto his opponent's throat, choking his air supply. Panic galvanised his movements. Piet held on. If either of the others leapt into the fray he was finished.

His captive dropped his hands, fumbling desperately for the panga lying nearby. It was all Piet needed. He came off his throat cupping his skull with one hand, getting an opposing lock on his chin with the other. Summoning all his strength, he wrenched viciously completing the scissor movement. Piet felt the cartilage go as the man's cervical vertebrae parted — the sound of a whipcrack. Instantly he became a dead weight on top of Piet: the action frightened the others. They turned on their heels rushing for the French doors. He rolled the dead man off him and gave chase scooping up the panga as he went. He raced through the doors and out into the night, no thought for the gun which might be trained on him.

He felt zero emotion, everything etched to crystal clarity. A duty to perform. With disdain these men had broken into his parent's home, left them injured, possibly dead. Retribution was his to exact. He would right the affront. As he ran, a muzzle-flash blazed ahead of him, two shots ringing out. He ducked instinctively running straight at the source. Shrouded in the darkness, the man loosed off another shot, at close range now. The bullet buzzed angrily past Piet's head. Maintaining impetus, he lashed out with the panga. His shoulder jarred agonisingly as the heavy blade struck home. A chilling scream tore the night air, like metal scraping over stone, the echo bouncing back off the nearby foothills. Piet dropped to a crouch waiting for the muzzle flash to fade from his retinas. Footsteps slapped over the grass as his quarry staggered off desperate for escape. Piet let him go, his focus returning to his parents. Seconds might be crucial. He hurried back.

Both were alive. His mother's pulse elevated but regular, her breathing shallow, hair matted with blood at the temple where she'd been struck. The orbital plane above her right eye was badly swollen starting to discolour. He cleared a place on the carpet, propped a pillow under her head and made her as comfortable as he could.

His father was in much worse shape. He had suffered a heavy blow to the top of his head. It still oozed blood freely, his breathing laboured, shallow and raspy. On the floor nearby lay a vicious looking knobkerry. When Piet prised his eyelids back, one pupil presented normally — the other severely dilated. Not an encouraging sign. A marker ordinarily for structural brain damage. He rushed into the bathroom, found an emergency medical kit in the cabinet. A few minutes later he had a makeshift dressing on his father's head stemming the worst of the bleeding. His breathing was a concern, irregular, faltering. Piet rushed to his room, dialled the emergency number on his cell. Within half an hour the paramedics were there, the police five minutes after.

His father was stabilised, then loaded into the ambulance. His mother, semi-conscious by this time, was still out of it. He gave her lots of encouragement as she was handed aboard the vehicle to join his father. He'd packed a few things in an overnight bag whilst the paramedics were busy with them and pushed it in after her.

He watched the taillights, the spinning emergency beacon diminish, finally dropping out of sight in the folds of the farm. He looked to the heavens. A pre-dawn rose-pink suffused the horizon as the lid of night began to lift. Half an hour from now the sun would burst through. He wished his day was starting differently. A tap at his elbow brought him back. He followed the constable to the house, got instructed to take a seat in the lounge. The inspector would interview him soon.

Restless, he began to fidget, finally drifting to the main bedroom. The police photographer shifted his tripod around the room still busying himself with capturing everything for the record — shots from every angle of the man Piet had earlier dispatched. Crude outlines traced in black chalk on the carpet were a disturbing reminder of where his parents had lain — a practice reserved normally for homicides. He prayed silently it wouldn't prove the case here.

Later he gave a verbal account for the second time to the black inspector. The man added notes when he got to the place where Piet recounted how he'd pursued the men outside. He stopped him then, dispatching his constables to the lawns now daylight had arrived. Back ten minutes later they carried gory news. A severed hand found on the grass. It was evident his arc-in-the-dark proved far more effective than he could have hoped for. He felt no remorse. The man got what was coming, paid a price for his transgression.

'Follow the blood spoor,' the inspector barked, sending them back out. He gave Piet a measured look. He recognised it instantly. Antipathy for a white who'd perpetrated a hostile act on those from 'the previously disadvantaged'. In the inspector's lingua franca, anyone from his ethnicity. No matter the justification. Fortunately he represented a small minority these days. Uncomfortable for Piet to confront it so close to home and in a ranking policeman tasked with investigating serious crime. The fact Piet had killed one of 'his', grievously injured another, was an indictment against him. Had the officer been sitting in the home of a wealthy individual of his own race, Piet had little doubt his demeanour would be quite different. He exercised the good sense to keep his mouth shut.

He was finishing his statement as the constables returned. They parlayed with the inspector out of earshot.

After the exchange he came back and a note of recrimination had worked its way into his voice. 'It would seem you are responsible for taking two lives today,' A hint of menace. He returned to the file, added a note. Later Piet learned that the constables had followed the spoor and found Piet's victim slumped against a tree three hundred metres from the house where he'd bled out. There was no trace of the gun.

The inspector's mood turned sour. 'Until we have statements from your parents, you are required to stay here.

Investigations will continue. Do not disturb the crime scene before we advise. A constable will remain until then.'

Piet informed him he had no immediate plans to go anywhere. He had plenty to take care of.

One of the things was to ring the Colonel and advise him of what had happened. The Colonel was at once alarmed, concerned for Piet's parent's wellbeing. Also worried a double homicide might foreshadow serious complications for him. Piet reassured him he would be alright. In a guarded manner the Colonel asked if he thought Ivashchenkov could be involved. Piet told him he didn't believe so, considered it an opportunistic crime, another in the flood of farm attacks all too common in the country those days. He offered help; Piet reassured him he would be alright, and make contact should he need assistance.

He didn't anticipate it then, but in the event, things worsened rapidly. The police returned early the following morning — same team.

'I would like you to come to the station,' the inspector gave no indication why he wanted this.

'For what purpose?' Piet was immediately on guard.

'To assist us with our enquiries,' he responded by rote.

'Am I being charged with a crime?'

'Not at this time.'

He didn't like that implication at all.

'How long will it take,' he tried to get a handle on matters.

'It might be advisable to pack a bag.'

He liked that even less.

'If you're going to charge me, you can do it now.'

'That is not necessary. A matter of going through your statement, asking a few more questions.'

'We could do that here.'

He could see the policeman was becoming irritated. 'There are other police personnel to involve. Forensics for instance.' He furrowed his brow letting his annoyance show. 'Unless of course you would like me to charge you now with obstruction of justice?'

'That won't be necessary.' If he was in a hole, he didn't want to dig it any deeper. 'Give me five minutes.'

The inspector nodded to one of the constables as Piet set off down the passage. The man fell in behind and waited outside the bedroom as Piet went in. He quickly threw a couple of things into a holdall. The last items were the two cellphones sitting on the bedside table; one he used for general traffic, the other for sensitive calls to persons such as the Colonel. He quickly tapped a message into the latter, Being taken to CT central police station. *Concerned. Dumping phone.* He pressed the send button dropping the phone into his pocket. He came out, told the constable he needed to use the bathroom. The man waited outside as Piet went in. He relieved himself then flushed the system, lifting the cistern lid and carefully dropping the phone into the noisily filling tank. Out in under a minute, he went with the constable to the lounge, bag in hand.

'What about the security of the house?' It didn't seem of much concern to the inspector.

'A constable will be on duty twenty-four hours.' His tone was further confirmation he didn't care either way.

'I need to go by the bottling plant, give the foreman instructions.' Piet wasn't going to be rushed before he'd had time to organise things.

Twelve hours later still found Piet at Cape Town central after a gruelling day of interrogation. Taken grindingly through his statement many times he was asked variants of the same questions a hundred times. From the police point of view a simple housebreaking had turned to a double homicide. From Piet's, he had merely exercised his civil rights defending his life against intruders. They weren't happy. He'd killed two of 'theirs'. Had the homicides been avoidable? Could he not have run the intruders off without resorting to such extreme violence? Where did he learn the neck-breaking technique? When they heard he had soldiered as a special forces operative during the apartheid era, matters darkened further. He didn't like the way things were going at all.

Told he would be held in custody until the interrogation was complete, he spent a miserable night in an overcrowded holding-cell populated by society's less desirable element. Normally a situation pregnant with malice: the same cells carried a chequered history of vicious male rape, even murder. News however percolated. He wore the mantle of double killer. A dangerous individual. The inmates gave him a wide berth.

Ten o'clock next morning a constable came through calling his name. He had a visitor. Taken to the same interview room where he'd spent much of the preceding day, he found a waiting Simon Zondo.

'Am I glad to see you, Simon,' he beamed, giving him a heartfelt bear hug.

The lawyer looked exhausted. Piet found out later that he'd taken a call from Colonel Stander very late the previous night. He hadn't bothered going to bed, worked on some papers, then drove to the airport to catch the redeye to Cape Town.

'Sorry for the delay getting here, Pieter, senior council had me in chambers 'till late yesterday. Took the first available.'

Piet waved the apology aside. 'You're a sight for sore eyes.'

'How are your parents faring?' Simon knew it would be a priority with him.

'I wish I could tell you. I was made to surrender my cellphone with other personals when I got hauled in here.'

'Do you know which hospital they're at?'

He gave him the name. Simon found the number online and dialled it. Five minutes later he'd finished the call.

'Your mother is doing fine. She's awake, fully compos mentis. They're keeping her under observation but all being well, she'll go home later today.'

'That's a relief. And my father?'

'Not so good, I'm afraid. He underwent emergency surgery yesterday to relieve cranial pressure caused by a depressed skull fracture. He's in ICU now. It's touch-and-go, Pieter.'

'Will you stay on top of it for me?'

'Be happy to. Hope it won't be necessary. We'll see if we can't spring you out of here today. Unfortunately, I have to be back in Johannesburg with counsel again tomorrow — more pre-trial work.'

'Understood. I'm more grateful you were able to get here than you can know. Tell me where I stand in this mess? Surely they can't hang anything on me for defending myself, my parent's home, against armed violent criminals?'

'I wish it were that easy. Nowadays the law allows for a reasonable degree of physical intervention to repulse intruders. The defender is only permitted to use ultimate force when there is a direct threat on his life.'

'One of the guys had a pistol — loosed off shots at me.'

'Which is where our problems begin. They haven't managed to find the weapon.'

'Can't they put dogs on that?'

'Normally yes. It rained heavily last night. Any scent apparently would have been washed away.'

'It never rains but it pours.' Piet hadn't intended the pun but smiled wryly as he realised he'd made it. 'What about the bullets then?' He thought of the shot that had been discharged in the house. It had to be somewhere — unless it had flown outside through the open doors.

'Unlikely they will find them. They could be anywhere, a preliminary search yielded nothing.'

'So all they've got for the moment is my word there was a gun?'

'I'm afraid so. And there's more bad news.'

Piet looked at him questioningly.

'The fact you pursued the assailants outside doesn't work for us either. Defence is turned immediately to attack. What's known as over-zealous self-defence. As a result of same, a homicide occurred.'

'I think you're telling me I could be facing murder charges?'

'Manslaughter at least.'

'That's not good.'

'No, it's not. But we're not rendered helpless either. They cannot hold you for more than forty-eight hours without bringing charges.'

'Well, won't they charge me then?'

'I doubt it. I don't believe they have a strong enough case to take it to the public prosecutor right now. I've requested forensics to test the severed hand for traces of propellant. They hadn't thought of that apparently.'

'So what's our strategy, Simon?'

'I'm going to demand your release. They may want you to report to the police station every couple of days. Not the end of the world until I can get into the meat of the thing, prepare a defence should they charge you.'

'Reporting's going to be very difficult.' Piet gave him a meaningful look. 'I've got a very important appointment looming which is going to take me away from Cape Town.'

He cottoned on straight away. 'Aah, yes. Quite. So the point becomes moot anyway. Well, we won't concern ourselves overmuch with that aspect then. I'm going to press for your release, point out to them at this juncture they don't have grounds to bring you before a judge on anything that will stick. I'll threaten a frontal assault from the full might of Archer Zondo should they be foolish enough to bring charges now. They know the firm, its reputation well enough. I think it will do the trick.'

Simon was good to his word. Two hours later his personal possessions were returned, then he got driven back to Verewig in a police vehicle. Crime tape closed off his parent's bedroom as forensics hadn't finished in there. He grabbed his car keys, jumped into the Land Cruiser, and made for the hospital.

CHAPTER 43

FINAL TRAINING

He left a day late for the Karoo.

His mother was back at the house, a hired nurse staying there until she was fully over the trauma. The estate foreman ran things in his father's, in his absence. His mother was still beside herself with worry over her husband. He remained in a coma in the IC unit, his condition still described as critical. Piet visited every day but felt utterly useless sitting at the bedside just looking at the iconic figure, swathed in bandages and unconscious, tubes disappearing into him.

'Pull through Pa,' he urged holding his hand on the day of his last visit. 'I have to go now to fight that war you recruited me for. Duty calls.' He smiled down at him. 'I'll be back rest assured.' He squeezed his hand one last time and left to get on the road.

On arrival at the farm Fergie expressed his concern as well as good wishes. Piet wasn't bunking with him in the farmhouse this time, electing to be billeted in barracks with his team. He dumped his bag on a military spring, took a look around. No fancy trimmings. Army 101.

'Where are the guys?' He could see no sign of anyone.

'Out on a 10k run,' Fergie seemed particularly up-beat. 'Care to take a quick tour of inspection?'

'For sure. I've been fretting like an old grandma. It'll help to see the guys fine-tuning.'

'I think you'll be impressed. Everybody's keyed to a high pitch, fitness levels exceptional considering we're essentially a territorial force.'

'Lead on McDuff.' He was already striding off chatting over his shoulder.

'I'll have you know, the McDuffs are a rival clan of the Fergusons. Never beaten us in a skirmish, but no disgrace to the Scottish nation.' Good to be in Fergie's company again.

They did a whistle-stop tour of the farm taking in the shooting range, the drill square, casting an eye over some field exercises playing out.

'How many guys here right now, Fergie?' he asked.

'A smidgin under three hundred. Last intake before D-day. The boys are ready. I wouldn't like to be on the receiving end.'

'What about the airborne outfit?'

'Been here a few days. George is pushing them hard. Jumping even in the afternoon when the north-wester generally starts to push through. Can get quite strong as the day advances. He says he's after pin-point accuracy, even in a blow. Quite the taskmaster.'

Piet smiled inwardly. George might be the clown in civvy street, but once he adopted his military persona, he was the consummate professional. He wouldn't settle for anything but the best from his crew.

As they got back to the barracks Rusty came sprinting towards them, vest and boxer shorts sweat-soaked, chest heaving and marginally ahead of the rest of the squad,. He pushed the button on the big watch at his wrist. The men taunted one another grouping around Rusty. Four black guys in the team. Good to see the close-knit camaraderie.

'Not bad,' Rusty managed between breaths, 'thirty-nine minutes, forty-eight seconds — said we'd crack forty.'

Piet greeted the lads, then took Rusty to one side. 'They know about the break-in at my folk's — the homicides?'

'Not a thing. Had them focused on training — no time to be thinking about anything else.'

'All good, Rusty.' Piet told him he'd had the racial card waved under his nose by the police inspector. 'He didn't like the fact the victims were two of 'his'. I don't want that sort of niggle penetrating here.'

Rusty looked over to where the squad were milling around, steam rising from their sweat-streaked bodies. 'They're a good bunch. None of that crap here, so don't worry.' He changed the subject. 'How's the Old Man doing?'

'On life support, still in a coma.'

'Shitty news. And your Ma?'

'Doing well. No real damage aside from the psychological.'

'Which just leaves you. How you doing?'

'Getting there. Probably be the tail-ender, but I'll be on your run tomorrow.'

'Shoulder good for it?'

'Has to be Rusty. Has to be.'

He gave Piet a look of appraisal. Both knew neither could ever be frustrated by something like the injury Piet carried.

They finished the day with a session of target practice on the range. Activity was frenetic as squads rolled through the facility one after another. Nitrocellulose hung thick in the air, the whole interior swathed in a blue haze. Afterwards their squad hit the showers then headed for the canteen.

'Hey, fellas any chance of an autograph?' George sauntered up as they walked in. He looked buffed and relaxed.

They bantered around a bit. Piet went through the same update regarding his parent's condition.

'Your Old Man's as tough as an old bull elephant,' George's conviction was the real thing, 'he'll pull through. Trust uncle George.'

Piet smiled and nodded. 'Thanks, George. How's it going with the team?'

'Lanyards on weapons canisters, a bit short. We can't run out the landing without getting floored like Victor Matfield's tackling from behind. Fergie has them in the workshop being extended as we speak. We'll give them a whirl tomorrow. Should be alright.'

'And the jolt in flight as you cut them away?'

'Like the bully at school tugging your pants down. But the harnesses can take it. All good there.'

'Accuracy. How's that?'

'Getting there. Not satisfied yet, still got time in hand to get it right. Whole squad has to be on the ground grouped within the space of a rugby field — regardless of jump conditions.'

'I'll stick my nose into the drop zone for a look-see tomorrow.'

'Do that. Afternoon's preferable — conditions getting a bit marginal then. Boys can get that right, we're good to go.'

The whole intake drilled hard for the remaining days of the camp. On the last, the entire force crammed into the canteen. You couldn't have squeezed a watermelon in there with a crow-bar. The Colonel was at the farm to give a final address to the men. The heat was oppressive — nobody complained. An excited buzz, an air of expectancy permeated the room. Everyone knew what approached; the last of war games had played out, beyond here the real thing. The Colonel managed somehow to work his way from the back through a chequerboard of black and white. A ripple of applause followed him to the front. As he mounted the makeshift rostrum, the clapping swelled to a thunderous roar. He looked out over the men clearly touched by the energy in the room. These were his troops, men who would strive to right the serious wrongs in their country. Men prepared to lay down their lives pursuing that cause. He took a moment to compose himself, smiled, raised a hand to quiet the tumult. It gradually died to absolute silence.

'Gentlemen,' he started, a trace of emotion catching in his throat, 'I'm inordinately proud of each and every one of you in this hall today.' He let his gaze rove over them. 'History books are written because of the grit of brave men such as you. But for you and those like you, the world would be a grimmer place. The desire for a just society is the glue bringing us here today, the glue uniting us against the inequity and greed insidiously ravaging our country. We do not see the democracy promised. Only self-enrichment of the few at the expense of many. A bloated oligarchy feeding off corruption. We have a chance to put that right, to root it out wherever we find it. To rebuild a South Africa blessed with its God-given riches, proud of the resources in its people. A country that can rightfully take its place amongst the leading nations on this planet. Operationally you have been given scant detail. I ask your indulgence for that. Many of you have previous military experience and will appreciate the need for our secrecy. An informed enemy could have halted us in our endeavour. We would not be here in this hall today. A force stillborn. So thank you for your understanding, for your discipline. Our security has proven phenomenal — and that because each of you has taken your role seriously. I am able to disclose more today. To show you the picture you strive for. We will pave the way for true democracy through a multi-party political system where nepotism will not be tolerated. We promise you a government without cronyism. A streamlined judicial system with teeth, unafraid to act — and act decisively against any who would seek to destabilise it. Your courts of justice will indeed be courts of justice, not merely courts of law skewed to serve personal agendas. Rest assured, where misdeeds are exposed among the present incumbents they will be brought to book. Those people will serve prison terms for their malfeasance.'

You men will be the agency for bringing change to your country. Your tax rand in the new South Africa will be expended where it rightfully should be in the fabric of civil society — not misappropriated by opportunists at the top.' He gave pause to let his words take hold. 'Nelson Mandela put forward a great vision for our land. A vision where all men would be equal. Where black white and brown would stand side by side bringing their contribution. A society where equality is genuinely protected by a strong constitution. A land of real opportunity. Madiba called it The Rainbow Nation. He did not live to see his dream realised. It was stolen from us all. God willing we will prevail to bring it back, bring it to fruition.' He raised his hand high in the air. 'Gentlemen, I give you The Rainbow Revolution.' The hall erupted to a deafening crescendo.

CHAPTER 44

D DAY

Sophie grabbed his face between her hands, kissed him hungrily. The stream of fellow travellers parted to pass around them. This was OR Tambo airport's busy time. It seemed half the nation was on the move going somewhere through Johannesburg.

'You take care you big oaf,' a frown creased her brow that she couldn't keep from it.

He'd stolen the last weekend to be with her before heading off for the big event.

'That's a promise.' He meant it. This woman meant the world to him now. 'I'll be fine — back before you know it.'

'You'd better be,' she stole one last kiss, 'otherwise I'm coming looking for you. And that's a promise too.'

Time to go. He looked at her longingly, hefted his bag from between his feet, tore himself away. Soon absorbed in the throng he cast one backward glance, but she was gone.

It's a quick flight to Durban's King Shaka airport. In under two hours he climbed into the rental car alongside

Rusty. In the back seat George grinned at him like a Cheshire cat.

'You've got lipstick on your mouth.'

Piet scrubbed furiously. George burst out laughing. 'Just testing brother.'

Piet gave him a zap sign which got him laughing harder.

'How's the accommodation?' he knew they had been billeted in farm buildings on the Robillard sugar estate: their hidey hole where thirty combatants could be effectively kept out of the public eye. Piet had no idea how basic the facility would be.

'All good,' Rusty put the flasher on and pulled onto the highway heading north. 'They've got us in one of the barns. Pierre's told the workforce we're a skydiving team from up-country here to practice in coastal conditions.'

'Yeah, we're aiming for a twenty-four way formation,' George winked, 'wouldn't that be nice in sunny Kwa Zulu Natal?'

'You'd need a bigger plane than the one we've got,' Piet trusted that aircraft capacity was way beyond the ken of Pierre's workforce.

Rusty glanced at him. 'What's the latest on the Old Man, Piet?'

'They're got him in an induced coma. They'll hold it for a while, reasoning that whilst his body is at rest it can only assist the healing. Might be days, could be longer, but they're more optimistic now than they were. They've got the swelling off the brain, a response to the drug therapy, so that's a good sign. He's on blood-thinning medication too. The biggest risk now is a clot.'

'He'll be good. Tough old bird,' George remained doggedly optimistic.

'And your mother?' Rusty asked.

'About fully recovered I'm happy to say.'

They passed the small town of Eshowe, drove another ten minutes before Rusty slowed for a farm road and pulled onto it.

'Hold on to your hat, Piet, a bit rough from here on in. Legacy of fully laden sugar trucks, Pierre tells us.'

They bucked and bounced over a seriously rutted track pulling up ten minutes later in front of their accommodation. Piet walked in and greeted everyone: both teams in high spirits, soldiers before a battle. Two or three of George's guys sat on their bunks tinkering with rigs. Some of his team, rifles stripped, were busy cleaning them. Only two days to go. The weighty wait. Always felt longer than it was — fiddling with kit the classical retreat for a soldier killing time. The enemy would come next.

He reported to the Colonel via cell later that evening. Everything proceeding smoothly: units were soon to be placed on alert all over the country in a state of readiness. Those hours would tick away even more slowly. Finally in the last phase, he would start to call-in to the ops room on a two-hourly cycle. The countdown. Other units would do the same from everywhere. If anything went wrong a halt would be called, the problem fixed. Reset. Start again.

They bunked down late, a palpable restlessness infusing the guys, latrine visits frequent, whispered conversations, muffled chuckles the voice of the night. A pre-combat unit takes on a life of its own.

A long night, but finally, dawn arrived with guys heading for the showers — temporary facilities Pierre had rigged at the rear of the shed — two hundred litre drums straddling fire pits delivering piping hot water to all but tail-enders.

A field kitchen was on tap with a chef to run it for them — a happy Mozambican never without a grin on his face, who turned out to be a creditable cook. They feasted on a farm breakfast of bacon and egg and horse mushrooms grown on the farm. The excellence of the food kept the mood high-key. Piet couldn't have hoped for more to maintain team spirit.

Their host had considered their needs carefully. He knew soldiers who awaited the call to arms had time on their hands. Time to be whittled away free of thoughts of the coming conflict. Pierre's solution — a volleyball court on a patch of bare sand roughed out close to their billet. The guys got into it with gusto.

'Bit different from the old days, hey?' Rusty came alongside as Piet watched a game in progress.

'You can say that again. Do you remember lying in ambush for days at a time stinking like skunks because we couldn't risk the smell of soap carrying on the air?'

'The genesis of my expensive toiletry idiosyncrasies, thank you. These days if it isn't Givenchy you can take it away.'

Piet laughed. 'Rank to swank eh?'

'Hard to believe we fought like that.'

'Isn't it though? Won't matter how we smell tomorrow. We'll be coming in like a whirlwind. Nobody will even get a whiff of us.'

'As long as the weather holds,' Rusty nursed the same concern they all did. 'Looks a tad unsettled a little further north according to my weather app.'

They monitored four different applications. Bad weather could shut them down, had all sorts of consequences. Not the least of which would be the question of how long Zuma would stay at the *Nkandla* compound if they needed to reset. They knew for sure he was there now, knew for certain he would be there tomorrow, after that, it became a lottery.

'They're saying this system is likely to remain fairly static. Maybe a slow drift southwards. We should be alright,' Piet tried to infuse a confident note to his voice.

'When do you make the call?'

'We're going to be able to can it, all the way to last check-in. That's two hours before zero hour. No turnaround after that. Too much in train all over the country by that time. No matter what, it's a 'go' at that point.'

'Let's hope the Universe is with us on the weather then. It's a no go for George's team if it's pissing down. Those canopies don't fly as dishcloths.'

'Don't remind me.'

'Still push the button without them?'

He'd laboured long and hard over that question, but there was only one answer.

'Have to, Rusty. At a push we could use his gang on the ground. Once they're in the air however they're lost to us. If they don't jump then, they miss the fight. We'll be on our own. A smaller force could mean a lot of collateral damage. Plus we lose all the advantage the airdrop gives us — diminishes our chances significantly.'

Obvious that Rusty had teased the question too. He remained silent for a while. 'That's where it's different to Angola. There you went when the General's called it. Regardless. At least this time we get to call it ourselves.' He brightened visibly. 'Architects of our own destiny.'

True. But the lives of his men were the coin Piet traded in. Family in the closest sense of the word — a huge burden. It weighed heavily.

The next day dawned — a different air hung over the camp. Gone the banter, no volleyball. A gravitas now ruled. Men determined and directional went about their chores, upbeat still, but when they grinned at each other more face muscles were at work. D day had arrived.

Piet made a scheduled phone-call to the ops centre. Everything proceeding to plan. Two more check-ins to go during the countdown — then he would make the final call. The weather remained a concern. The front bothering them shifted further inland, seeming to diminish the risk, but another was filling in off the ocean. Worryingly it tracked further southwards than its predecessor. If it continued to develop it would become a factor. Piet could feel the knots in his stomach. Let it not rain on their parade he prayed to himself.

He got the guys to move the vehicles from their temporary garaging. Unlikely looking chariots to carry them to battle — just as it should be. They needed to be undercover until the very last moment. He would ride upfront in the telecoms van, four others including Rusty, with him. The borehole contractor vehicle next in line towing a trailer would carry Weynand, their artilleryman, with his crew; the small field piece hidden under its tarpaulin. The remainder of the force would bring up the rear in the TV-dish installation van.

George approached whilst they were busy making ready stowing arms to the vehicles. 'Got a call just now. Pilot's at the field. Bit early I know, but we're gonna be off.' They gave each other a shoulder bump.

'Every fifteen minutes from here,' he told George. This was the pre-arranged call-in schedule to keep Piet informed of George's position whilst on the ground. Once they were airborne he would switch to VHF and call in on the radio at will.

'Roger that, Lieut.' He never let adversity drag him down. 'Looks like the weather may play ball after all.' He grinned clownishly. 'I'll give you a visual sitrep once in the air.'

They both knew if it turned ugly it would be too late. The same spectre resurfaced. If the weather shut George's team down they were on their own — half the attack force out of the game. They would have their work cut out then. His stomach gave him no respite. They stood little real chance of success without paratroop support.

He did a final tour of inspection, mentally ticking off everything. Nothing left to do — finally ready. George got to the aerodrome, called it in. Now he remained on standby for Piet's instruction to get airborne. That call he would make only when their convoy was well on its way.

Piet worried his watch. Three minutes forty seconds to go — to the point of no return. Not long but it would seem an eternity. He flicked to the weather app on his cell. The system looked unchanged but then he'd flicked to it so often, he doubted he would detect subtle changes. Had it moved closer towards their target? He could no longer be objective. Would they be alright? He prayed so — please let it be okay. Back to check the wristwatch. Under two minutes.

'All aboard guys,' they all showed the level of outward composure a soldier develops in preparation for action. Piet waited until less than thirty seconds remained, keyed the cell for the ops room in Johannesburg. The Colonel took the call personally.

'It's a go, Sir,' It seemed too simple a statement to initiate a war.

CHAPTER 45

LAUNCH

They kept to their schedule towards *Nkandla*. The convoy would split when twenty minutes out, regroup close to the target: individual vehicles being less noticeable than a string. The longer they could project the workaday image the better.

The road carried little traffic. Piet checked the weather app again — with serious misgiving, sure now he could see change. A creep further south — towards them. He radioed George and gave the call for him to get airborne. Visually the sky further north darkened. Deepening his concern. A bank of cumulus now plainly visible, grew spectacularly as these clouds do. Air currents inside them would dictate the point at which they became unstable, changed to storm cells releasing huge volumes of rain which gave them the appendage *nimbus*. Piet ground his teeth willing for it not to happen — not yet. As Rusty had so aptly stated earlier, parachutes don't work in the rain.

Whatever happened, too late now for the ground crew to stand down. The Endeavour was rolling all over the country. Piet's troop however, might be going it alone with no paratroop support. It was a daunting prospect — one he preferred not to dwell upon.

He made contact with the vehicles following, they slackened pace to achieve separation. The convoy de-materialised. He checked the time again. Their ETA to target was now seventeen minutes. George called from the aircraft. They were banking in a shallow spiral climbing to altitude.

'How does the weather look from up there?' he asked.

'We have the system visual,' George's voice crackled back, the static distorting. 'Heavy at the base — holding for the moment.'

Darkening cloud base was not encouraging. Sure indication of rain to come. He didn't like it one little bit.

'Don't worry,' George prepared to sign off, 'it's not going to shut us down.'

He knew George. Short of guaranteed suicide, he would go.

'Eight kilometres,' Rusty studied a topographic map spread out on his knee, his face a mask of neutrality.

Piet kept going to his watch, split-second timing the essence, worrying the detail again but this was something they couldn't afford to get wrong. The minutes ticked agonisingly by — George would call again any second. Piet fiddled with the handset nervously, dreading bad news. Outside the vehicle the first wisps of cloud insinuated themselves into a lowering sky. Further north a brooding cloud phalanx marched inexorably in their direction. Strung tighter than a violin string, he started as George's call came through.

'Go, George.'

'At altitude. Circling co-ordinates. Three-eighths cloud cover.'

That meant more than half the sky was open beneath them. They might yet scrape through.

'What's your take?' Piet's voice was a half octave higher than where it should be.

'We're a go as long as it holds. On stand-by awaiting your finals.'

God bless you, George. At altitude the aircraft would be throttled back, circling, awaiting the call to action. The intensity inside that vibrating fuselage would be electric: each combatant witnessing close-at-hand a killer storm flexing its muscles. Add to it the tension of impending combat, nerves would be stretched to the limit. He thanked God for men like those. There would be no hesitation when told to go. They would peel from the aircraft a cohesive entity, all thoughts of personal safety out the door with them.

What George hadn't told him, something he learned of later, was that the aircraft was being tossed about alarmingly as violent thermals kicked off the edge of the storm.

'ETA five minutes,' Rusty's voice flat and toneless. Piet had his fingers crossed they would yet beat the storm.

They crested a gentle rise. Opening before them the panorama they awaited. A stubby knoll crowned by the *Nkandla* compound, squatted over a shallow basin. The presidential complex — the lions den.

'Target,' Rusty breathed, looking up from the map. He pointed to an earthen berm sloping alongside the road eighty metres outside the perimeter fence. 'Launchpad.'

They pulled off the road. The mound ran at shoulder height. In its lee, save for the vehicle's rooftop, they would be all but invisible from within the compound.

A couple of minutes went by as they waited for the other vehicles to convoy. The borehole truck climbed the bank braking on top. Two of their black squad-members in day-glow vests, jumped out to unhitch the trailer. Hopefully they would pass as contractors for the short time they needed to get set.

They watched as the guys hammered anchors into the ground — arrestors against the recoil of the artillery piece. So far so good. Not many folks about, those that were, paying them no heed. That would all change very soon. Piet spotted two guards patrolling inside the fence-line, pausing to have a chat. A blue wisp carried on the breeze — taking a smoke break. All good. It meant they were relaxed, expecting nothing. Their crew worked steadily, within minutes the field piece was firmly in place still concealed under the tarpaulin.

Set up, getting close. He keyed the mic on the radio to alert the airborne unit. 'George for Piet.'

'Reading you four out of five, Lieut,' George's disembodied voice crackled back almost instantly.

'Stand by.'

'Roger. Standing by.'

Weynand their gunner with his number-two, lugged an ammo box to the field piece. The weather looked about ready to let go. Piet glanced nervously northward. The sky there was now magenta, deep purple folds down on the horizon like a puckered velvet cushion. As he looked, a brilliant release of energy stamped itself right across the heavens — the stark imprint of a skeletal tree. Too late already? Had they lost the race, the airborne side of their operation negated? Not a happy prospect.

'Come on guys,' Piet urged under his breath. The only positive of the approaching storm, the locals were gone to the shelter of their huts. Themselves the only ones abroad. Weynand turned, gave the thumbs up. Stage set. A revolution in the wings.

'George, George. It's a go. Go.Go.Go.' Piet yelled into the handset. He wondered if he shouted to a stillborn. A troop unable to give birth to its mission. On the ground, they were without choice. They had to go. Piet activated the stopwatch at his wrist.

'Roger that. We - are - a - go.' Georges broken syllables stuttered back. Piet's surge of relief, a wave almost of ecstasy. He pictured George slapping his guys out of the open doorway as they peeled away from the aircraft.

He didn't envy them. From five thousand feet the storm would be visible as a maelstrom of nature unleashing her power, their drop zone right in her path. There would be little margin for error as they hurtled pell-mell into a darkening world, white-hot lightning, a near neighbour. A mission for only the bravest of the brave. Silently he saluted them as the sweep hand of his timepiece inched around the dial eating seconds. From this point coordination was key. Meticulous planning and exhaustive training would finally be put to the test. Airborne and ground commandos were required to hit the complex simultaneously producing a saturation attack. The alarm and confusion created would straight away put the enemy on the back foot; with their small force, a vital element. Get it right, they wouldn't know where to turn, gunfire coming at them from every direction. A confused enemy is already halfway down the road to defeat.

Counting down the seconds Piet gave the order to debuss. They grouped under cover of the vehicles. Up on the rise the artillery team waited.

The sweep hand arced on … thirty-five…thirty-four… thirty-three…thirty-two…thirty-one… 'Fire!' Piet yelled, as it brushed the six-o-clock position.

The detonation was powerful even to ears covered by pressed palms. The artillery piece recoiled, still moving as the team had the next shell in the breach. A second shot boomed instantly. In no time they laid down three rounds; thirty millimetre high-explosive shells packed to detonate at impact. They sprinted at the fence, the explosions echoing back from the foothills, difficult to separate from rolling thunder. They leapt through a ragged hole big enough for the passage of a small truck, a shallow crater smoking beneath it.

They knew the layout of the compound backwards — hours poring over satellite images had imprinted it in all of them.

Over the first thirty metres they encountered no resistance. Then an early salvo sounded as the perimeter guards opened up. The shots went harmlessly overhead. Aiming high, sure sign of inexperience. They returned fire, professionals battle trained. There was no contest. The enemy was out of the equation in seconds. Now they raced the slope. Half way to the residence Rusty's guys broke away for the barracks and the job of taking out that stronghold. The rest of them pushed hard making for the main residence — the place they expected to unearth their quarry. They crested the rise as a heavy exchange opened behind them. Rusty's platoon had engaged.

Piet hand-signed the guys to a wider formation as they came to the house. This far in they were sure to meet resistance. Next moment the roof thatch exploded with the force of a grenade. Piet flung himself defensively to the ground flashing a glance as he rolled — just in time to see a canopy disappear into the hole. One of their paratroopers had punched through. Bullseye whether intentional or not. Surviving the impact was another matter altogether.

Right then the door of the house burst open, two burly individuals automatics blazing, hurled themselves into the fray. It was a foolhardy move. Out in the open they stood no chance against automatic rifles, were cut down like scythed corn.

'There'll be more,' he motioned two of their team out to the flanks. 'Cover the back.' The rest of them made the doorway and Piet flung himself full length inside, rolling for cover. The tactic proved a lifesaver. Deadly rounds splintered the doorframe where he'd passed a millisecond earlier. No inexperience here. The cover of a heavy Chesterfield where Piet had come to rest, offered scant protection from sustained 9mm fire. He readied himself for another dash.

The confrontation intensified outside. Sounds of heavy engagement carried even above the rumble of rolling thunder. Persistent lightening flashes were a constant now — harbingers of the racing storm. Piet prayed Rusty's small force weren't taking casualties. How had George's team fared? He readied himself to break cover when more gunshots reverberated from deep in the house. A sigh of relief. The parabats were busy. A salvo rang out close at hand. Behind blazing weapons two of his squad flashed through the doorway, barrelling in beside him.

More reason to depart the Chesterfield. 'Follow my lead,' he shouted, breaking away and sweeping ahead with a burst of fire where he thought the enemy to be.

The fire wasn't returned. Against the far wall he'd found his mark. A grisly spectacle lay there in a rapidly pooling slick of blood, his jaw wiped away by Piet's shots. A pulpy mess lay underneath him, an arm still twitching as they steeplechased the body.

Searing lightning suddenly illuminated the half-light of the room followed by thunder reverberating into the hills and attenuating with distance — a disagreeable grumbling. The storm arrived with a vengeance unleashing its fury in a torrent of rain that hammered the thatch with the intensity of a waterfall. The afternoon light toned to an oily mauve dragging the shadows with it. They probed their way further in.

Piet felt as if he'd walked this place a hundred times, knew every corridor, every turn from the layouts they'd studied. Not a corner unknown to him. Or so he thought.

They penetrated to the core of the building — a collection of reception suites: beyond lay the formal chambers where the big man hosted visiting dignitaries. They picked their way past two more downed defenders, testimony of the roof-crashing colleague somewhere ahead of them.

Lightning came almost continuously now. He peered guardedly around a corner. Shattered ceiling boards hung in disarray almost to the floor, webbing harness a telling pendant hanging in the void. Their paratrooper's point of entry. From the intensity of the resistance they were encountering, it meant he would have been under fire the instant he crashed through. No small testament to his military skills that he'd prevailed.

They pushed deeper, the rain by this time, settled to an insistent tattoo. Above it the sharper note of small-arms fire — Rusty's engagement playing out at the barracks.

They felt their way with extreme caution, no way of knowing the strength of the Police Protection Unit. Underrating them would be serious folly. That much they knew. Piet eased his head around another corner. A hail of bullets tore plaster from the wall as if to underscore the point. He wiped alabaster from his eyes and pressed his body hard into the protection of the wall.

Across from his position, leopard-crawling stealthily, several of the team inched forward. He waited for them to sign the 'in position' then stuck his weapon around the corner loosing off a short burst. Answering fire came immediately, muzzle flashes all his guys were waiting for. A deadly barrage took out three protectors concealed behind a heavy overturned table and a sofa pressed to service as a barricade. He risked a peek round the corner. No fire. Clear so far.

As they pressed in, signs of more defensive action became apparent in the adjoining room. Several bodies littered the floor.

'Firebird,' a voice came out of the shadows. Their call sign to identify each other in close combat situations.

He knew the voice, gave the response. 'Burning bright.' George came purposefully into the room.

'Am I glad to see you jokers,' he had his face blacked like the rest of them, 'thought for a while you'd stopped for a sandwich on the road. Wondered if we might have to do this on our own.'

Piet scoffed, welcomed the banter. 'Don't you ever knock at doors?' He pictured George's harness hanging through the roof.

'You saw the grand entrance? Always did like to gatecrash.'

'How many of your guys engaged?' Piet asked, getting serious again.

'All but three. Worked through the back as planned. Taggert bought it,' he gestured towards a camouflaged form outside the room. 'Took a couple with him though.' His voice thick, a loss never easy to take.

'Other casualties, George?'

'Two didn't make it into the LZ. This bitch of a storm got them — tried to muscle us all. We were right next to the cloud-wall on the way down, the thermals hectic. Those guys got sucked in. I had a close call, deployed and passed through a veil of rain. Chute went soft, tickets I thought. Falling like a stone by then — chose the softest landing I could see.'

Three lost. All bad news. Piet detailed a couple of the guys to move Taggert's body into an adjoining room where there wasn't so much blood and gore.

He turned to George. 'You must have drawn fire from the start?'

'Started popping off at me the second I dropped in. Luckily, I had the 9mm out anticipating trouble. Proper shoot out at the OK corral.'

'The rest of the unit — where are they now?'

'Doing a sweep from our end of the building. Couple of the guys guarding the entry point.'

'Same at the back. I've got a couple of guys out there. Any sign of our target?'

'Our sentries got sight of him once; tried ducking out with a couple of his protection unit. Quick burst sent them scurrying back.'

'Still in the house then?'

'As far as we can tell.'

'Where then?' Piet wracked his brain for a location they could have gone to earth in.

'Firebird.' Another call from out of the gloom.

'Burning bright,' George and he responded simultaneously.

Four more of the ground-squad, headed by TJ the platoon leader, came in.

'Sitrep please guys?'

'All clear in the east wing after a bit of a skirmish. Two bandits down.'

'Police protection guys, TJ?' He wondered how many would be in the contingent.

'Civilians, heavily armed. Put up a hell of a fight. Brace yourself for a shock.'

'Okay. Let me have it.'

'Guys were on Rusty's boat the day of the shark dive,' — TJ one of their team aboard that day.

445

'You can't be serious,' Piet gaped. 'Ivashchenkov's goons?'

'The very same.'

'You're certain?'

'No doubt about it.'

'What the hell were they doing here?' A rhetorical question.

'Probably babysitting the boss,' George answered anyway.

But it presented an interesting possibility. Was the Nuclatom chief there right now? Why else would he have his heavies there? But if so where? And, where was Zuma?

'Okay, guys, we need to run them to ground. Any suggestions?'

TJ came in again. 'Where we took out the Russians, there's a concrete stairwell going down to a basement. Could be a wine cellar, except there's a heavy steel door. Wine cellars have steel doors?'

'None I'm aware of,' Piet knew all the ones he'd seen rarely had a door at all. 'No basement shown on the architectural plans either. You think the guys you took out were protecting that basement?'

'Could be. They sure as hell showed spirited resistance.'

'A bunker I'm thinking,' George put into words what they were all thinking. 'Anyone want to take a bet we'll find our rabbit down the hole?'

'Let's go take a look.' Piet formed the men up. 'Don't let your guard down fellas. Something tells me this fight is far from over.'

They got to the east wing. Piet took a look at the downed Russians. TJ was right. Both were on Rusty's boat the day Nuclatom had hired it.

He went to the top of the stairwell, the steps beyond deep in shadow. They had completed a sweep so he thought it safe to flick a light on. He fumbled at the wall locating the switch. The broad stairs spiralled out of sight. Following the steps down, dull yellow light radiated from head-high wall lamps. It jarred that the whole structure was cast in off-shutter concrete — no attempt at decorative finishes. A stark contrast to the luxury above. He hefted his weapon, beckoning for a couple of the guys to follow him down. They descended cautiously, finally confronted by the heavy steel door. Nothing felt right.

He glanced toward the ceiling. In the corner a perspex sphere looked over them myopically.

His brow furrowed. 'What's a CCTV camera doing here?'

Then it struck him like a thunderbolt. 'Hit the deck,' he screamed, flinging himself down and dragging the man at his shoulder with him.

None too soon. An ear-splitting roar boomed in the confined space as thousands of steel balls, garden-pea size, pinged of the unyielding surfaces. Claymores. Vicious anti-personnel mines. On their feet they would have been cut to shreds. Mercifully damage was minimal. Dropping below the kill zone, their worst injury a gashed forehead to one of the men crashing into a stair edge on his way down.

George picked his way down over a bed of spent metal, slick as an ice sheet. 'Very unfriendly, Lieut' he made light of it but Piet was sure he'd already run the picture of how different the outcome might have been.

'Downright hostile.' Piet turned to the heavy metal door, walk-in safe type. 'You got it right when you guessed bunker, brother. Time to fight fire with fire. Get Weynand's team to drag the artillery piece in here. Our quarry's on the other side of that door. Let's winkle him out.'

'On it. Gonna take a while in this deluge.'

It still hammered down, lightning torturing the sky without rest. 'Better post someone at the fence whilst you're about it. We're going to be here a while — I don't want any surprises from outside.'

Forty minutes later all was set. In the spiralling stairwell, the gun sat as far back from the door as they could manage, still retaining line of sight. Weynand's team could be credited with a job well done wedging the piece into the stairs. He'd also rigged a remote system to release the firing mechanism; a nylon cord snaked over the stairs, crossed the stairhead and passed around the leg of a heavy table dragged into position so the leg could serve as a crude pulley. The cord's end was out to the side of the room, as far from the opening of the stairwell as they could get. That aperture would in itself be like an oversize canon muzzle as the explosive shell impacted. Getting caught directly in its path a certain ticket to the grave.

'Ready when you are,' Weynand called out. Only he had the luxury of ear protectors, everyone else, hands clamped tightly over ears.

Piet gave the countdown, dropped his arm.

Like the blast of a furnace, the stairwell gushed a great gout of orange flame, a mushroom of smoke: the noise indescribable. Piet's ears rang like a doorbell. They let the worst of the smoke dissipate then under torchlight, picked their way carefully down the stairs.

There was absolute chaos. Their field piece, wrenched from its carriage, lay twisted almost beyond recognition on the lower landing. Large chunks of concrete were scattered about where the blast chiselled them from stair-risers. Piet regarded the bunker door with grim satisfaction. Lower hinge blown away, the heavy metal slab hung precariously from the top. It left an opening they could squeeze through.

Piet glanced over his shoulder. George and three team members stood by. 'Single file behind me guys, keep the spacing generous, no telling what other surprises there may be.'

He waited as they shuffled into position. 'Keep your wits about you,' he threaded his way around the tortured metal of the door. Pitch black. Underfoot bare concrete suddenly gave way to rich carpeting. He played the cone of his torch over pastel surfaces as he inched forward. A room opened up. Killing the torch he stood stock-still. Nothing stirred. Light danced behind him as George followed along the passage. He killed his beam and eased alongside.

'No sign?' His voice was a whisper in Piet's ear.

'Nothing,'

'Would have had a go at us if they were here.' Piet could hear him checking his ammunition clip.

"Agreed. Let's find a light switch, see what we've got.'

A large room sumptuously furnished like those above.

'Nice pad,' George moved past the furnishings trailing a hand over the back of a designer couch. 'I could slum it in a place like this.'

Piet crossed to a door, opening it with caution. A motion sensor activated a ceiling light, an extractor fan humming to life. The aroma of expensive coffee hung faintly in the air. The doorway he stood in appeared the only entry to the room. No escape route there. He moved back into the lounge, George coming out of a side room.

'Bedroom. Just the one way in and out,' he'd anticipated Piet's question.

One last door, he moved to it. A well-appointed bathroom. Again single access.

'We missing something?' he asked George.

'Has to be another access,' he looked as confounded as Piet, 'no-one builds a bunker with a single entrance. That's a tomb.'

'Agreed. Concealed so let's see if we can dig it out. You take the bedroom. I'll start with the kitchen.' Their other two guys joined and Piet tasked them to organise a search outside the house; he was beginning to think they'd got something wrong.

He opened every cupboard, tapped every panel but found nothing. George fared no better in the bedroom. He took the lounge next, shifting furniture, lifting rugs, rapping for voids with the stock of his rifle.

Piet moved to the bathroom. It seemed the least likely place to conceal an underground passage, an escape portal. But there had to be one somewhere.

He almost missed it. In the shower enclosure, an ornate soap dish fixed on the back wall caught his attention. There was no soap tablet in the dish. It looked as if it had never cradled one. He was turning to leave when some instinct tugged him back. He stepped into the shower, took hold of the tail of the gilded mermaid holding aloft her seashell and gave it a tug. The whole thing felt like one of the doors on Fergie's armoured cars. A hidden mechanism ratcheted audibly, the tiled wall swinging heavily towards him. Very clever. Piet dragged the panel wider and peered inside. A narrow passageway stretched away to darkness.

'Got it, George,' he shouted over his shoulder. He came into the room and they exchanged smug smiles.

'Let's hope our rabbit hasn't bounded too far from his burrow,' he chirped.

'It's narrow in there; not much room,' he peered into the opening, little wider than a mans shoulders.

'That's for sure.' The tunnel would only permit passage for a single person. 'No point in us going one behind the other,' George tapped the surface. 'You go, I'll head outside see if I can find the other end. If Rusty's got the barracks locked down, maybe he can spare some help.'

He left as Piet stepped into the passage.

CHAPTER 46

DOWN A HOLE

The passage, rough-hewn, made no attempt at cosmetic finishing, sides and roof bagged with a cement slurry, the type used on swimming pools. In places, the skin crumbled away at pressure points, timbers knocked in to lend support. It was a squeeze getting past these. He'd never been comfortable underground. Now the image of a catacomb worked its way into his brain. He drove it out. The thought of hundreds of tons of earth suspended above his head just the other side of the pupa-like tube wouldn't help.

He applied himself to fathoming the strategy of the quarry he hopefully pursued. Unlikely Zuma would be alone. An accompaniment of members of his presidential protection unit seemed likely. Hardened and ruthless men. He would need to be vigilant. Where did this tunnel lead? With the residence compromised what would they do? Distance themselves from it he felt sure. That meant a vehicle. His guys had the garage complex under guard, autos there inaccessible. Would they then try for a vehicle somewhere outside? That seemed more probable.

Presently the tunnel floor began to incline upwards. Faintly he could hear the sound of rushing water, intensifying as he got closer. The ground underfoot started to cloy with a layer of mud. He picked his way through, his boots sucking at each step. He flicked the torch on, the ground underfoot had been churned by someone before him. More than one person by the looks of things. He wasn't chasing a red herring after all.

An air current brushed his face, somewhere close by must be an opening. That gave him a lift. Suddenly the end of the tunnel opened ahead. He picked his way towards it gingerly, the sound of rushing water all about him. A massive four metre stormwater pipe dropped ten metres to a river of raging stormwater. At several levels side transits fed huge volumes of run-off.

He slanted the beam up, illuminating missile-like raindrops driving through an open manhole. He killed the torch, allowed his eyes to re-adjust. Ascending from where he stood, steel hoops set in the concrete led to the manhole. He swung out, started climbing, reaching the top and out into the night in seconds.

The storm still raged and he was soaked in an instant. Thunder rolled in the nearby hills and lightning lit the landscape as it flashed and stuttered. A particularly powerful surge charged the air with electricity you could feel as he got his bearings. The main residence stood off two hundred metres. He was close to the elaborate chicken coop, a two-storey brick structure with external steps for egg collection. Sitting on one of the lower treads, dissolving rapidly in the downpour, lay a wad of orange clay such as he had just trudged through. His quarry had gone to ground.

He eased the safety on his weapon and moved to the bottom of the stairs. Little chance of detection in the roar of the rain, but he was taking no chances. He worked halfway up the timber treads until level with the threshold and the gloom beyond. The ammonia smell from the chicken urine made his eyes water. The occasional clucking of a fussing hen could still be heard above the downpour — otherwise all was quiet. Now a dilemma presented. He would have to enter but crossing the threshold posed his greatest danger. Creating a diversion was an option. Risky, but he could think of nothing better.

Carefully removing a spare magazine from his webbing he weighed it experimentally in his hand and climbed two more risers staying visually out of the opening. Getting into position, he hefted the missile into the coop to where he judged the birds to be roosting. The magazine clattered along the floor and pandemonium erupted. Chickens took to the air frantically screaming their terror and scattering everywhere.

He hit the floor in the midst of the confusion, rolling defensively to crash into the lower perches reducing them to matchwood. More birds were put to flight screaming. The air was a confusion of feathered bodies and thrashing wings. Impossible to locate anybody in such chaos. But whoever was in there would now know they had company.

He lay perfectly still, his weapon cradled against his body, finger on the trigger. Birds alighted on him then leapt away again. He waited. Eventually things calmed down. The birds were still agitated but not frenzied. He continued to wait. Finally reward came. A boot scraped on the floor nearby, someone grunted with the effort of adjusting their position. Mentally he fixed the position in his mind, waited some more. Straining, he could vaguely detect laboured breathing. Someone with an asthmatic condition was working hard at not betraying their position.

No other foreign sounds, just the fussing of the birds. He was certain his fellow occupant was Jacob Zuma and almost as sure he was alone. Time to take a chance. He slid the torch into his hand pointing in the direction he'd fixed and pushed the slider. The beam pierced the blackness. In its path, denied their roosts, a press of chickens huddled on the floor. An avian eye, glowing as if backlit, occasionally reflected his torchlight. Beyond the birds lay the dishevelled form of Jacob Zuma curled to a foetal blob. Wisps of vapour rose from his drenched and ruined suit. Even in the torchlight his pallor was grey. He looked anything but happy. Piet clambered to his feet issuing the statement he had so often run in his head.

'Mr. President, exercising my powers of citizen arrest, I am taking you into custody to face charges of serious crimes against the state.'

He tried to bluster, stammered a response. 'Who are you and … and… what is your purpose? This is a treasonable act.'

'The game is up, Mr President. If you'll forgive the idiom, the chickens have come home to roost. I'm taking you in.'

'I think not, Mr Rossouw. Put down weapon, turn slowly.' He froze. A pencil beam blinked on, blinding as it found his eyes. He recognised the voice at once. Dmitri Ivashchenkov had the drop on him. He was guilty of a terrible operational blunder.

'Again you impress me. Is not small achievement to take presidential compound. I salute you. But is all over. You lose.'

His mind raced. 'You think so? As we speak my men have the compound locked down. There's no way out.'

He gave a throaty chuckle. 'We are in chicken house, your people do not stop us. I too have men outside — busy coming. Nuclatom has resource. We go to King Chaka airport — jet is there to fly to O R Tambo. Police unit will meet Mr Zuma and escort back to state residence in Pretoria.'

'I wouldn't bet on that. We're not an isolated force here. This is a national initiative.'

Piet couldn't see his eyes at the other side of the beam. There was a significant pause before he responded.

'Will not create problem either way. You fail — Mr Zuma wins. You win — we offer Mr Zuma political asylum in Russia. Continue fight another day. Nuclatom operational in both outcomes.'

'Possibly. But not run by Dmitri Ivashchenkov. You will be facing murder charges for the death of the crew aboard the Antonov.'

He laughed.

'And right now you are left with the thorny problem of me.'

'Aah, yes. How do you say? Fly in ointment.'

Piet said nothing, trying to scheme a way out of his predicament. He couldn't expect the cavalry to come rushing in. A chicken coop wasn't the first place they'd think of searching for him. When they worked it out it would be too late. It left him in a pickle.

'So we have dilemma, I believe you say. Cannot leave free like chickens here. Too dangerous.'

'Why can't you just shoot him right now?' Zuma shuffled behind them. 'He is busy in an act of treason. There would be no recriminations.'

Ivashchenkov chortled. 'We share history, Mr President. Perhaps you do not understand. Have faced death together. That way we are brothers.'

Piet tried to digest this latest to see if it gave him any sort of an edge.

'Cannot shoot brother like dog. But does not solve problem. Mr Rossouw comes with us for time being. I decide fate on way to airport.' He waggled the beam at Piet. 'Now sit with chickens — we wait.'

They didn't have long. Presently a soft tapping sounded on the stairs — an uttering in Russian.

Ivashchenkov responded. Piet saw a shadow duck into the henhouse. A brief conversation followed.

'We go now.' Ivashchenkov energised his torch.

Piet got to his feet encouraged by some spirited prodding from the pistol of Ivashchenkov's goon. He led, Piet followed. Last out, moving stiffly, was Zuma. They formed up and moved off, the rain still lashing mercilessly. Passing by the stormwater feature, Ivashchenkov called a halt. He sent his man over to it. Piet heard a metallic scrape then the distinct clang of the lid dropping into place.

'In case Rossouw's army come down tunnel. Leave no easy trail.' The sarcasm was heavy.

They moved off again and arrived at the perimeter fence — well away from the breach Piet's artillery had blasted — he could see no way past. Then the ground in front of him swallowed the security man.

Ivashchenkov waved his pistol. 'Follow.'

He did, stepping down a short flight of steps to another concrete culvert, this one rectangular — the type seen under many national roads. Except here was no public thoroughfare. A very private escape route in times of crisis, serving a paranoid president. They sloshed through ankle-deep water past a heavy concrete panel hung off industrial hinges. A castor at its outer edge was axle deep in the muddy water, the rail on which it must ride totally submerged. The barrier would be impassable when locked. *This wasn't on the plans either,* Piet mused, as they left it behind.

Out into the rain again. A double-cab Ford liberally bespattered with mud waited on a rough track.

'Nothing better at short notice,' Ivashchenkov made a mock apology. 'Rental company in this part of country have limited choice.'

He got bundled into the front seat, Zuma and Ivashchenkov climbing in the back. The security man drove. They slipped and slid their way out of there travelling rough terrain. Eventually the same urban road appeared that Piet's convoy had driven down a short while before. The intervening hours seemed like an eternity. So close to nailing their objective; now he was a prisoner at gunpoint, the quarry being whisked away from them. He would find a way to fulfil his mission or die in the attempt.

Ivashchenkov's cell buzzed. A lengthy call during which he said little. Finally he dropped the phone back in his pocket.

'Seems your people become nuisance,' he was rattled. 'O R Tambo is closed to traffic. No matter, we fly to Lanseria.'

'It's going to get much worse. Believe me.'

'Regrettably, will have to dispose of you after all. A pity, there are many qualities to admire.'

By this time they were well along the highway getting close to Durban's international airport. Ivashchenkov said something to his driver; the vehicle started to slow. Piet sensed they looked for somewhere to pull off where he could be dealt with, his body thrown into the bush. He had to make his move now.

He glanced at the driver — who shot a frenzied look back realising something was coming. Piet didn't disappoint, lunging for his throat with both hands. A gunshot sounded from the rear of the cab, a searing pain shooting across his lower back. Everything happened in a split second from there. The driver lost control of the Ford which spun several times on the slick surface. They glanced a lighting standard on the hard shoulder which raked along the passenger side;

it tore the passenger door open explosively. No strap to hold him, he fell into the void, the concrete rushing to meet him. The last image he remembered was of the driver wrestling the steering wheel and somehow raising a booted foot to help him on his way.

CHAPTER 47

TOUCH AND GO

He found himself back in the tunnel connecting the residence to the stormwater system. This time he had company. A solitary black rat padded along in front of him. He could hear the patter as his feet hit the hard-packed earth. It was a muted sound but carried quite distinctly. Presently a companion scurried past him joining his friend upfront. The sound of their footfalls amplified. Next instant there were three — the sound growing all the time. It built to a mind-numbing roar. He peered over his shoulder checking for the source.

The tunnel heaved with a river of the creatures, a furry wall studded with eyes bright as glowing diodes. They seemed desperate to catch him. His stomach lurched. He increased pace. Out in front there were now perhaps ten of them. The horde bringing up the rear threatened to engulf him. He shot another nervous glance over his shoulder. They were right there. He increased pace, his heart starting to hammer. Mercifully the ground began to trend upwards. He knew he approached the discharge port. He reached it and launched himself out into the void. All around him thousands of furry bodies followed, cascading to the dark waters below. He struck with force and blacked out.

***

He came to to find himself hiding under thorn scrub. Sparse foliage, less than ideal to offer adequate cover — all there was. But he had been smart, compensating for the dearth with layers of chicken feathers stuck all over his fatigues and beret: waiting patiently for the approach of the enemy, confident his subterfuge would keep him from detection. A movement stirred the bush fifty metres distant. He took a bead, easing finger pressure steadily onto the trigger. A fully uniformed soldier broke cover and strode purposefully towards him.

'Don't be silly, Pieter. You look like a bloody chicken. The enemy will spot you in a jiffy.' It was the Colonel in full dress uniform.

'With respect, Sir, it's part of the plan. They'll be here to collect the eggs soon, won't know what hit them.'

'Good thinking, Lieutenant. Command should have thought of that. Great to have you aboard. It's this sort of strategy makes you invaluable to the cause.'

***

Ivashchenkov lifted his eyelid none too gently with a thumb tip and shone a pen-light directly into his eye, painfully bright, it blotted out all peripheral vision.

'Well that's a good sign,' he remarked to someone Piet couldn't see. 'I want you to monitor him every two hours. With the cranial trauma he's suffered he's not out of the woods by a long shot yet. It could go either way.'

Good to have the Russian batting on his team.

***

He came out of a deep sleep, Sophie stroking his hair gently.

'Good morning, sailor. Did you have a good night's rest? There's coffee at the bedside.' She fussed around him a little more. 'How was the mission?'

'Couldn't have gone better. We got Zuma — all his cronies. And guess what? The guy who escaped the night they attacked my folk's place was there too, wearing my grandfathers gold fob-watch like a medal.'

'What did you do?'

'Took it from him, twisted his neck for his troubles.'

***

He could see the hull of *Chumbucket* undulating in the ripples at the surface: returning from a lengthy dive rising slowly, careful to decompress on the ascent. But not this slowly. His spent air bubble clusters remained frozen in the water in front of his face mask; each one a microcosm of the image at the surface. A thousand George and Rusty's peered over the transom grinning inanely. He tried to respond by kicking his fins to get there faster. It made no difference. He was set in this treacle like a fly encased in amber.

Totally frustrated, he wanted to get his prize to the surface to show it off to his brothers. He looked down. Below him, line astern, were three adult great-white sharks threaded on a nylon cord that he'd pressed into service as a makeshift leash.

***

He peered skyward to the masthead light atop *Magus'* twelve-metre mast cursing himself roundly. The fault had given notice weeks earlier, an electrical short he omitted to fix. Now it flickered intermittently, annoying the hell out of him. It wouldn't wait any longer. Scaling the lofty spar was a daunting task without the comfort of a bosun's chair, a companion to winch you aloft. He had the luxury of neither, would have to scale it the old fashioned way. Hand over hand. A job for the young and fit, neither qualification he could claim, but the responsibility couldn't be shirked further.

He tossed a couple of tools, together with a replacement globe, into a sailmakers pouch shinning the first couple of metres without much effort. Working higher it got tougher. Two-thirds of the way up his muscles threatened to lock in protest. He couldn't do it. Too old for this sort of caper. All-engulfing fatigue washed over him. Desperately tired, he looked towards the troublesome light. No longer flickering but glowing steadily. As he watched it began to intensify, gradually morphing to the eye of a vortex of brilliance. He would not have to struggle further to fix it. It was fixing itself bringing with it the most wonderful warmth the likes of which he had never experienced. He suddenly felt completely at peace.

Until he remembered Sophie. She would see in an instant it was his responsibility to fix the light — no one else's. There would be recrimination if he allowed an outside agency to do his work, no matter how tempting it might seem. He struggled free of the cloying aura finding his feet once again firmly planted on deck. Overhead the lamp flickered once more. His head ached abominably, a dull band of pain creased his lower back.

***

'Mr Rossouw, Mr Rossouw.' A voice bounced in his head.

'Time to wake Mr Rossouw.' he became aware of a gentle slapping on the back of his hand, struggled to raise his eyelids. The light wasn't harsh. Even so, he blinked defensively as it painfully probed into his head.

'Would you like me to dim the lights a little?'

He thought he managed a nod. The nurse straightened, the starch in her uniform crackling electrically as she went to fix the lights.

He tried to ask for a drink but his voice wouldn't come. His mouth worked stickily, like a hinge in syrup. He gave up, closed his eyes again.

'Doctor will be here in half an hour.' She scratched a note on the pad and returned the clipboard to the foot of the bed. He must have fallen asleep immediately, because the next thing he became aware of was an Indian gentleman taking his pulse, peering into his eye behind the same pencil-beam he remembered from before.

'I'm Dr Khan, your attending surgeon, Mr Rossouw. You must be wondering where you are?' He stopped Piet as he made a feeble attempt to respond.

'Don't exert yourself at this point. Rest is much more important. Let me give you the information.' He continued with his ministrations, shone the torch in Piet's other eye.

'This is the ICU at Milpark hospital Johannesburg. You've been unconscious for five days suffering extreme head trauma plus a bullet wound in the lower back, considerable damage to your T10 vertebrae, trauma to the spinal cord. Fortunately only bruising or you may have been confined to a wheelchair permanently. We've inserted a plate to repair the bone damage. You have also dodged the bullet, if you'll excuse the pun, in escaping permanent brain damage. We did cranial surgery repairing a fracture, easing pressure on the brain.'

He contemplated Piet quietly. 'You are a very fortunate man. Either of those traumas could have killed you. It seems the Universe isn't calling you home just yet. What you need above all else now is complete rest. We will be sedating you for a while. Your powers of recovery seem as robust as your will to live. Continue to make progress at this pace, we can look at visitors in five or six days. Meanwhile, as I say, complete rest.'

He did make steady progress. The 'no visitors' ban got lifted after a week, amended to limited visitation for close family. Technically it excluded Sophie, but she was obviously top of his list; they would have to sedate him for a further week to exclude her. Currently out of town on an assignment, she would visit as soon as she flew in that night. His father was still in hospital, also making steady progress, so unable to come. His mother was due to fly in with George and Rusty two days hence.

So his first visitor was the Colonel. As always he delighted in seeing him, especially as he was now officially off the critical list.

'Pieter, my boy, you have no idea how it gladdens my heart to see you awake and on the road to recovery.' He took Piet's hand in both his squeezing it affectionately. 'You've had us all extremely worried.'

'Sorry for that, Sir. Can't seem to stay out of the wars.' He smiled sheepishly.

'Well, you've gone a long way in helping to win this one. How much do you know?'

'Very little. There's not much penetrates the deep recesses of the trauma unit. I think they have a policy of choking news from the outside to protect us broken puppies.'

'In which case, let's treat this as your de-brief.' He pulled a chair to the bedside, dropped into it.

'Let's start with your journey here. That started at the side of the highway near Durban's King Chaka airport. You were more dead than alive I might add. Our chaps occupying the airport found you when they went to the highway to erect a control barrier and divert traffic. You were airlifted by chopper to Durban central hospital. Right behind the last flight out of King Chaka before we closed it down. An executive jet bound for Lanseria.'

'It wouldn't have been a Gulf Stream would it?'

'Actually, yes. But how on earth could you possibly have known that?'

'I'm pretty sure I know who's. But, carry on, Sir, I'm interrupting.'

'Sounds like you're already ahead of me. We slipped up badly letting that last flight creep out of King Chaka. Zuma and Ivashchenkov were aboard — but I can see you already know that.'

'It was the Nuclatom jet. Ivashchenkov couldn't resist bragging about it when he let me know he was going to make good Zuma's escape.'

'And they may have gotten clean away had it not been for an incredible intervention. But more of that presently. Let's get back to you for the moment.'

'So, as I say, you'd gone into ICU at Durban central — by this time we were directing your journey from the Ops room in Johannesburg. Durban didn't have the right equipment — we took the decision to casevac you to Milpark. You were stabilised and whisked here. They have all the bells and whistles Everything. Robotics, the finest trauma unit in the country, the best surgeons. Got inside your cranium using non-invasive surgery. In the event it looks like we made the right decision.'

'What happened to Zuma, to Ivashchenkov?'

'Very nearly slipped under the radar, as I mentioned. We didn't know then of their whereabouts. Or the fact you'd even located Zuma. We knew from George you were somewhere in hot pursuit. But no more.'

'Hot pursuit turning to capture. Not very glorious I regret.'

He brushed that aside with a dismissive wave. 'So, to continue, we'd no idea they were bound for Lanseria. Which meant we weren't even looking.'

'What happened?'

'The fates were with us. We may have dropped the ball but someone else knew Ivashchenkov was inbound.'

'His French rivals, Areva? After the death of their regional manager in Algeria, they certainly had an axe to grind.'

'Much closer to home.' He beamed, excited to share the snippet. 'Would you believe, Kosmo Fotakis?'

Piet's reaction was explosive. 'Kosmo Fotakis?'

'Yes. It seems he has friends in the tower at Lanseria, being paid to alert him of movements of the Nuclatom jet. Fotakis was onto them. With some of his own heavies, he was there to meet the plane when it arrived from Durban. They seized both Zuma and Ivashchenkov. Then forced the pilot to taxi the aircraft to the service apron at the rear of the field. There they torched it. Sixty million dollars up in smoke. By this time our people were arriving, Fotakis had the nous to hold onto Zuma. He could see something was happening on the ground. The police detail on their way to meet Zuma ran into our troops on the way to the field. We engaged, neutralising them.'

'Good old Kosmo,' he chuckled. 'How did we wrestle Zuma away from him?'

'We didn't have to. As soon as he could see we controlled the airfield he handed Zuma over without demur. However, he refused to hand Ivashchenkov over. According to the commander on the ground, he said something strange. 'Icarus was one of ours.'

Piet smiled. Icarus had been a Greek. And so was Kosmo Fotakis. Ivashchenkov must have given him the same homily as he gave Piet in trying to justify the downing of the Antonov, he reasoned.

'Where is Zuma being held?'

'Leeuwkop prison. Out there between Johannesburg and Pretoria. He's already come before a judge, a trial date set.'

'And Ivashchenkov?'

'Disappeared without trace. Fotakis claims the man overcame him, escaping. No witnesses so we can't be sure.'

'Ivashchenkov is a slippery customer — it's possible.'

The Colonel just shrugged noncommittally.

'And the Endeavour? How successful were we?'

'Beyond our wildest expectations. The military side of things was over in a little more than twenty-four hours.'

'How serious was the headcount?'

'Well below what we anticipated. Thanks in part to Nkosi. He is amazing, rallying the people to the cause through his TV appearances, his radio broadcasts: being openly compared to Botswana's Seretse Khama as one of Africa's true democrats. Bodes well for the future.'

Piet had a hundred other questions he wanted to fire at the Colonel but the nurse came into the room at that point.

'I'm sorry, Sir, but I have to ask you to leave now. Mr Rossouw needs rest.'

'Yes of course, nurse.' He scraped the chair back, turned to Piet. 'I'm only flying back to Cape Town at the weekend so I'll be back before then. There's lot's more, as I'm sure you can imagine.'

He patted the sheets, turned on his heel and was gone. Piet fell asleep almost immediately.

He awoke, the ICU lights dimmed for the night, the nurse at his beside fussing with his hair. A little too familiarly he thought. Except it wasn't the nurse.

'Hello, sailor,' she whispered next to his ear, brushing a kiss across his lips. 'I know you'll have lots of questions, but I've been cautioned by the nurse not to overtax you. I just had to see you. I'll come by early tomorrow, we can catch up properly.'

'Just one question for tonight then.'

'What's that?'

'Will you marry me?'

Epilogue

The days following seemed to drag interminably. Unable as yet to walk left Piet bed-ridden; more than a little frustrating. His renowned patience for waiting out events seemed to have evaporated to the ether. His nagging headache wouldn't leave and pulsed in waves, despite medication. Accompanying the headache came a vague sense of dislocation.

Still being urged to rest and sedated much of the time, a bare minimum of visitors was permitted. Then only for limited periods. The state of his health still raised concern, he wasn't allowed much latitude.

There remained little else to focus on save for the mission itself. For him, there was still a loose end. Ivashchenkov. Had Fotakis quietly despatched him at the airport, disposing of the body, or was the man still at large? As soon as he got out of the hospital he resolved to find out. He would visit Fotakis, get it out of him one way or another. His job wasn't over until Ivashchenkov was dealt with.

And if still alive, likely he felt the same way about Piet. He had, after all, been a key player in bringing down his aspirations in South Africa — the Russian would want to settle the score. The more he thought about it the more he became convinced Ivashchenkov still lived. He recalled his survival skills during their dive together — the shark attack. Wily as he was, Fotakis would be no match. Piet would need to be on his guard.

He began to watch the hospital staff carefully. Second guessing the Russian. In his shoes, Piet would certainly have the hospital infiltrated with an assassin.

That opened a field of suspects. His dressings were changed every five days. Due a change today, the nurse arrived with all the apparel, a male orderly in attendance. Piet hadn't seen him before. Late twenties, well built. From his accent, clearly not a native South African. As they rolled him onto his stomach he asked the man's name.

'Zbigniew Kowalski. My friends call me Spiggy.'

Eastern European. Polish if he wasn't mistaken. Could this be Ivashchenkov's man? It seemed highly likely.

Piet dropped a couple of teasers letting him know he knew — would be watching his every move. He couldn't see the other's face as he lay face down but verbally the orderly failed to react.

They rolled him back over. 'All done, Sir,' he beamed trying to lull Piet into a false sense of security he had no doubt. 'See you next time.'

Piet watched him go. He'd left the metal kidney dish sitting atop the trolley straddling the bed. In it lay the scalpel used to cut away his dressings. He stretched forward, palmed the instrument and hid it under the covers.

The headaches went on unabated. He started wondering if perhaps they were slowly poisoning him. After all, Ivashchenkov now had a man in the hospital. Better to stop taking the meds. Piet took to hiding them away each day. The headaches persisted.

Colonel Stander was in town and dropped by early in the day. Piet voiced his concerns to him about Ivashchenkov wanting to eliminate him, told him about the orderly planted in the hospital. His revelation seemed to unsettle the Colonel. He scrutinised Piet with concern. He didn't seem as convinced as Piet. Piet told him yet again, the fallen Phoenix would rise from the ashes.

The Colonel promised an open mind — would make further investigations. His concern turned then to Piet's headaches, and the need to bring in a specialist to get to the bottom of them. Piet welcomed that. They were now unrelenting — would drive him insane if he couldn't get surcease.

In due course, he underwent a series of sessions with a psychiatrist. They covered everything from childhood, through his army career, his ocean wandering, the attack on his parents, the recent military adventure. He wanted access to the old army records from Piet's hospitalisation thirty years earlier, especially the X-rays. Piet told him the Colonel could help him with that.

The following day Piet began to wonder at all this inquisition. What bearing could events from thirty years ago have on headaches he suffered today? Unless, of course, there was a conspiracy afoot. Had Ivashchenkov gotten to the new doctor with the intent of building a case — have him declared insane? If they could institutionalise him, it would be an effective way of shutting him down. The more he thought about it, the more sense it made.

Colonel Stander was back the following day. He looked haggard and distracted as he came to the bedside to greet Piet, there to chat with the psychiatrist. They had only just exchanged greetings when the man arrived giving a welcoming hello. They exchanged pleasantries, then he took the Colonel off to the nurse's station nearby.

'He's got us all very worried, Doctor.'

'With good cause, Colonel. He's displaying some very psychotic behaviour.'

'You mean this fixation with the Russian, Ivashchenkov?'

'Primarily, yes. We see evidence of post traumatic stress, but there is also something else at work here.'

The old warhorse suddenly looked his age, remembering the *Alexithymia* diagnosis he was responsible for burying all those years ago.

'He told me a few days ago, he suspected a ward orderly to be a plant from Ivashchenkov, intent on eliminating him.'

The medical man raised an eyebrow. 'That's significant. A night nurse dug these out of a slit alongside the piping of his mattress.' He reached into a drawer pulling out a box holding the scalpel and a bunch of pills.

A shadow of real fear ghosted over the Colonel's face. 'Do you think he's capable of trying something serious?'

'Until right now, I'd hoped not. Now I'm not so sure. There is a possibility he may have to be institutionalised.'

The phone rang and the doctor picked up.

The Colonel glanced through the glass wall separating the nurses station from the ward. Piet caught his attention, made horns with index and little finger, pointing them back at his eyes then indicating the doctor on the other side of the old man. Bushcraft silently telling a colleague you had eyes on the enemy.

The Colonel shook his head almost imperceptibly, then buried it in his hands, his shoulders shaking.

THE END

GLOSSARY OF TERMS

Abbrev.	Description
Alexithymia	The inability to recognise or describe one's own emotions
Alter ego	A person's secondary or alternative personality
ANC	African National Congress. At the time of writing the ruling political party in South Africa
Apartheid	The policy of separate development of the races in South Africa pre democracy in 1994
Balamut	Russian for troublemaker
Boeremag	'Farmer Force'. A white supremacist group active in 2002
Boet	Brother (Translation from Afrikaans)
BEE	Black Economic Empowerment. A racially selective programme not available to whites launched by the South African government to redress the inequalities of Apartheid
Braaivleis	Barbecue (Translation from Afrikaans)
Casevac	Military term for the emergency patient evacuation of casualties from a combat zone

Abbrev.	Description
CCMA	The Commission for Conciliation Mediation and Arbitration. An independent organisation dealing with disputes when an agreement cannot be reached between an employer and an employee or trade union.
Compos mentis	Latin. In full control of one's mind
Contretemps	Fr. A minor dispute or disagreement.
Davos	Small town in Switzerland and the seat of the World Economic Forum
DA	Democratic Alliance. At the time of writing the main political opposition party in South Africa
Deja vu	Fr. 'Already seen'. A feeling of already having experienced or lived the current situation
EFF	Economic Freedom Fighters. At the time of writing a minor and far left political opposition party in South Africa
Eskom	Electricity Supply Commission of South Africa. The national power utility
Gam	A collection of sharks
Highveldt	The plateau above 1500m in South Africa
Intel	Abbreviated term for 'intelligence' used in the military
Kak	Shit (Afrikaans slang)

Abbrev.	Description
Kameez	A long tunic worn by people of South Asian cultures
Kasha	A type of Russian grain porridge
Knobkerry	A fighting club whittled from a branch or root of a tree to leave a bulbous mass at one end. Common in east and southern Africa
Koeksisters	A traditional Afrikaner confectionery made of fried dough infused in syrup or honey (Translation from Afrikaans)
Kop	The head (Translation from Afrikaans)
LZ	Paratroopers abbreviation for landing zone
Lekker	A sweetmeat often used informally to indicate something good (Translation from Afrikaans)
Meisie	Girl (Translation from Afrikaans)
Moolah	Slang meaning money
Muzhik	A Russian peasant
Nada	Slang meaning 'nothing' (From the Latin 'nata' meaning small, insignificant)
NECSA	Nuclear Energy Corporation of South Africa
Nek	Neck (Translation from Afrikaans) Often used in South Africa to describe a minor pass in mountainous terrain

Abbrev.	Description
Nogal	Sufficient, somewhat (Translation from Afrikaans)
Ouens	Slang meaning blokes, mates, men.etc. (Translation from Afrikaans)
Ou	Abbreviation of Ouens
Ou swaer	Old friend (Translation from Afrikaans)
Panga	A broad bladed axe-like blade used as a weapon and an agricultural tool. A machete.
PPU	Presidential Protection Unit. An arm of the South African Police Service responsible for guarding the President and other high office bearers
'Recce'	Abbreviation for the South African Defence Force Special Forces Reconnaissance unit
SAEEI	South African Emergency Evacuation Initiative
SVR	Sluzhba Vneshney Razvedki. Russia's external intelligence agency
Seun	Son (Translation from Afrikaans)
Sitrep	Informal abbreviation for 'situation report' often used by the military
SOE	State Owned Enterprise

Abbrev.	Description
SWAPO	South West Africa Peoples Organisation. Opposition party fighting in the civil war in Angola in the mid 1980's
Tekkie	South African slang for a tennis shoe
Terra firma	Dry land as opposed to the sea
Troika	Russian vehicle pulled by a team of three horses abreast
Verkrampte	Conservative (Translation from Afrikaans)
Verligte	Liberal (Translation from Afrikaans)
Verewig	Forever' (Translation from Afrikaans) The Rossouw Cape wine estate
WEF	The World Economic Forum is the International Organisation for Public-Private Cooperation. The Forum engages the foremost political, business and other leaders of society to shape global, regional and industry agendas.
Zhizn' ebet meya	Russian slang 'life is fucking me'

ABOUT THE AUTHOR

Driven by the urge for adventure, Michael left England as a young man astride a bicycle. He eventually arrived in what was then Rhodesia and lived there for twelve years spending time in the bush-war as a volunteer in the Rhodesian Air Force. Disillusioned with the way the country headed, he returned to England and purchased a small yacht setting off again this time heading for New Zealand and Australia where he spent a year in each country. However, Africa was in his blood and he moved to South Africa to settle. He has a wife, two married daughters and writes full time.